Ailinn's hands tremb[led]
before the silver war[rior] [she]
looked openly into his eyes. . . .

But as their gazes entwined, Thora jostled her, causing
Ailinn to lose her hold on one tray. It flipped upward,
sending a shower of berries into the warrior's lap and
splattering cream across Thora's nose, mouth, and chest.
The bowls and tray clattered to the floor followed by an
enraged screech from Thora. Impulsively, the Norsewoman drew back and directed a blow at Ailinn.

Lightning swift the silver warrior bolted to his feet,
blocking Thora's attack with one hand while sweeping
Ailinn behind him with the other. Hakon, likewise,
bounded to his feet and drew on his sword. But before the
steel left its scabbard, the white Dane's blade flashed
before him.

The Dane continued to secure Ailinn against himself,
his long fingers pressed against the curve of her spine.
Only after Hakon had resheathed his blade did Lyting
relax. He began to turn and their bodies parted. Cool air
rushed between them.

Yet, when the Dane's eyes sought hers, Ailinn felt a
liquid warmth spread through her, heating her all over
again. . . .

Also by Anita Gordon

THE VALIANT HEART

THE DEFIANT HEART

ANITA GORDON

BERKLEY BOOKS, NEW YORK

THE DEFIANT HEART

A Berkley Book / published by arrangement with
the author

PRINTING HISTORY
Berkley edition / July 1993

ISBN: 0-425-13825-9

A BERKLEY BOOK ® TM 757,375
Berkley Books are published by The Berkley Publishing Group,
200 Madison Avenue, New York, New York 10016.
The name "BERKLEY" and the "B" logo
are trademarks belonging to Berkley Publishing Corporation.

PRINTED IN THE UNITED STATES OF AMERICA

10 9 8 7 6 5 4 3 2 1

DEDICATION

For my children, Kimberly, Scott, and Christopher. You've always been the precious lights of my life. And for the newest "sparkles" in our family, little grandson, Sean, grandbaby, Beau, and our personable son-in-law, Dave.

AUTHOR'S APPRECIATION

Very special thanks to Jim Shellem for his nautical expertise and advice, not only in editing the pertinent scenes, but as the "architect" of the sea battle.

Also, warm and special thanks to my parents, Jim and Betty Barbour for the "care and feeding of the muse" while she was laboring in the face of her deadline.

And last, but not least, heartfelt thanks to my marvelous editor, Melinda Metz, whose support, guidance, and confidence saw this project to fruition.

Note on pronunciation: Once again, I have used Icelandic (Íslensk) which preserves the language of the ninth-century Norsemen. The character "ð" is pronounced like the th-sound in "the"; and "þ" is pronounced like the th-sound in "thin."

PART 1

A furore Normannorum libera nos, Domine.

"From the fury of the Norsemen deliver us, O Lord!"

Prologue

The North Sea, 915 A.D.

The mighty fleet of *drakken* swept north, carving the fogbound sea. Swift and silent they coursed, triumphant high-prowed dragonships, their hulls heavy with plunder—serpents in the mists.

Onward they plowed through trackless ocean and sunless haze, bearing their precious cargo—ivory, gold, and womanly flesh—far from the Isle of Eire, far to where gelid shores and hoarfrost lairs brinked the earth.

A horn brayed long and deep, sending chills to crawl over Ailinn as the lead vessel signaled its companions through the curtain of gray. The others quickly took up the call and repeated the blast from stern to stern till the waters vibrated with the sound of trumpeting beasts.

Ailinn drew the mist-sodden blanket about young Lia and hugged her close. "Shush, love. Rest now," she soothed.

Lia shuddered several times beneath Ailinn's arms, but her cries quieted to a broken sniffle.

Heavyhearted, Ailinn laid her cheek against her step-cousin's small, dark head and closed her eyes. She breathed the dank sea air and listened to the muffled sobs of the women about her. Listened to the rhythmic drub of a wooden rod as a Norseman smote his buckler over and over, pacing the oarsmen's strokes.

"May God remember us in our hour of need," Ailinn prayed softly over Lia. "May God protect . . ."

Ailinn swallowed her words against the knot of anger that rose in her breast. For a countless time this day she shuttered her heart against the pain, against the horrors that burned in her soul.

Where was the Almighty in those desperate moments before dawn? Why didst God hold back his hand when the blood-thirsting devils descended upon Clonmel? Why?

She squeezed her lashes against the fresh flow of tears. Still, they trickled paths over her cheeks. Instinctively Ailinn rocked Lia in her arms, a gentle, comforting motion.

Cold. She was so cold. And so very tired. 'Twas a chill and a weariness that only one who had passed through the darkness of death and the shadows of Hell could know. If there remained one shred of gratitude she could lift heavenward, 'twas that Fianna, her mother, and Lorcan, her stepfather, did not live to see Munster ripped wide by Danish blades. Would that God had seen her to her own grave with them and spared her this agony.

Ailinn thrust aside her self-pity. Her heart ached for her stepcousins. Lia and Deira had witnessed their parents lying in a pool of blood, their father with his head crushed and their mother savaged. Rhiannon had shrieked wildly for her father, the overking. He was a dauntless, hard-bitten warrior. Still, there was no sight of him when they were dragged from the compound with the other women.

Sweet Jesu, the sight of it!—everything hacked to pieces. In their contempt the Norsemen hewed down every object and beast that misfortuned to occupy the walled yard. All about lay the wreckage of implements, furniture, and crockery. Huts were torched and pens smashed down. Blooded hounds cluttered the yard. Everywhere there was death. Ailinn saw those she had known from her youth lying vacant-eyed, their lives poured out on Eire's sweet earth. Many more were beyond recognition.

The preparations for the bridal feast, so joyfully made the day before, lay in ruin. Sprays of hawthorn, decorating the doors and walls of buildings, shriveled with heat as flames devoured the structures and those who had fallen within.

Longships—dozens upon dozens—awaited, blackening the

River Suir. Ailinn was boarded with the others and shackled to the thick mast. As the ships slid away, she watched the billowing smoke climb the skies over Clonmel.

Ailinn shivered as she tasted the salt of her tears. A breeze stirred and teased a strand of auburn hair across her face. Dragging it down, she squinted her eyes open to seek Deira and Rhiannon. Instead, her gaze met with the hard, flinty stare of the man called Hakon.

She stiffened with revulsion and loathing. God willing, she would kill the cur with her own hand given the chance. 'Twas he who had slain their maid, Bergette, and violated Deira and Rhiannon before her very eyes.

Ailinn averted her face and stared gloomily into the mist. Fresh currents of guilt surged through her. 'Twas, in part, her own actions that provoked the Norseman to lay hold of her stepcousins and defile them so savagely. Even now as she glanced to them, Rhiannon clawed her with eyes sharp as talons, then gave Ailinn her back as she slipped a comforting arm about Deira.

Pain lanced through Ailinn and wrung her heart. She grieved for them both and for all the women who suffered the dark lusts of the Northmen. None escaped, not even young Lia. None, save herself alone.

Her eyes drew to the ship's graying chieftain, a massive, grizzled warrior—Skallagrim, she heard the others name him. 'Twas he who claimed possession of her despite Hakon's heated protests. Whatever his intent, Skallagrim neither pleasured himself upon her nor allowed his men sport of her.

Ailinn felt the weight of Hakon's steady, piercing gaze. A chill curled along her spine. She feared he yet purposed to have her.

In that first, horrifying moment, when the Norsemen burst through the chamber door, her eyes had beheld Hakon's crimsoned blade flashing. Flashing its terrible downward stroke as he severed Bergette's life. Ailinn screamed at the butchery, drawing Hakon's attention upon herself. In a heartbeat he leapt for her, yet she fought him with a frenzied strength as pure, unholy terror erupted through her every nerve. The fine bride's veil and crown of hyacinth ripped from her hair beneath his hands as she wrenched free and fled for the door. In the next breath she slammed into the hardened chest of a huge, brutish Northman who reeked of smoke, sweat, and death.

Ailinn's blood ran cold as Skallagrim held her in his iron grip and ran a gauging eye over her. Hakon argued hotly with her captor whilst their comrades began to push into the small room and lay hold of the young women there. Though Ailinn understood naught of their twisted tongue, Hakon plainly deemed her his prize and demanded her back.

But Skallagrim refused to release her, using his authority to end the matter. 'Twas then in the heat of his anger that Hakon seized Deira and ravaged her. He next laid hold to Rhiannon. The heathens abused the other maidens as well, swiftly, brutally, shouting their coarse pleasure. Several flaunted the stained gowns of the virgins they sullied, pleased with the spoils of conquest.

At that, Skallagrim studied Ailinn a long, considering moment. He marked the bridal array that adorned her—the unblemished gown, the remnants of bruised blossoms that yet clung in her hair. A light came into his flat eyes and his craggy, bearded face spread with a grin as though he had found some great treasure. With Ailinn secure in his grip, he hauled her from the building and down to the River Suir.

Lia tensed against Ailinn, netting her back to the moment. She looked up to see Hakon unfold to his full height. He stepped forward with sure footage on the forging deck.

Ailinn's heart thudded against her ribs as his gaze prowled over them. She tightened her grip on Lia, but he only rumbled a sound deep in his throat, then moved past to the rear of the ship, where he replaced the man at the steering board.

Ailinn vented her breath. Gently she fingered back a tangle of hair from Lia's pale cheek.

"*As pas de peur, ma chère cousine. Reposes-toi,*" Ailinn becalmed, unmindful she had slipped into Frankish.

She, Lia, and Deira learnt the tongue at their nurse's knee and exercised it most often to share a confidence or voice their griefs. Now the familiar words rushed forth, consoling in some wise—old friends, intimate and dear.

Lia quieted once more as Ailinn soothed her fingers through the girl's sable tresses. What wouldst come of them, she brooded—Lia, Deira, Rhiannon, the maidens of Clonmel, herself? Were the remainder of their days foredoomed to enslavement and submission amongst the heathens? And Skallagrim—what plans did he hold for her? Surely, he spared her apurpose. Though she loathed to concede it, for the moment her safety lay with the rugged chieftain. But her kinswomen and friends she was powerless to aid.

Dispirited, Ailinn began to sing softly, lulling Lia with an old strain that was tinged with a sadness peculiar to Gaelic melodies. Her crystalline voice carried along the ship's length and drifted out over the deep waters. The men fell silent. Even the oar-pacer muted his strokes.

Tears ached in Ailinn's throat, but her voice never faltered. Once anew, she thanked Heaven above that her mother and stepfather did not live to suffer this day or witness her fate. She embraced their memory and held them dear. For the briefest of moments she recalled her mother as she lay dying, her husband's and daughter's hands clasped within her own thin strength.

"Hold fast, my dearest Ailinn," Fianna heartened. "Sometimes the darkness holds the light."

Ailinn staved the memories before their keen edge pared too close. Lifting her gaze, she beheld her new masters. They wore the blood of her people.

Raw, mordant anger churned Ailinn's soul. What small light remained in her life after Fianna's and Lorcan's deaths today went out altogether. In the darkness that engulfed her world, she knew only a scalding hatred for all Norsemen. Her body they might use and break, but in her heart she vowed ever to remain defiant.

As the ships sliced the waters for distant shores, Ailinn ended her song. "I am sorry, Mother. Night hast fallen and I cannot see beyond. There be none to aid me or bring forth the hope of dawn."

Chapter 1

Hedeby, Danmark

A bright smile slashed Lyting's sun-coppered features as he leapt from the prow of the *Sea Falcon* to the wharf's solid planking. 'Twas good to be in Hedeby once more.

As he secured the ship to one of the stout bollards, he scanned the bustling quayside with its colorful mix of humanity.

Já, 'twas good, he avowed warmly, his pulse quickening to the pace that thrummed along the dock and on through the town. This voyage wouldst be his last for many a year to come—a final excursion before his return to Normandy. Then wouldst he set forth for Corbie and begin studies under the Benedictines, bound by holy rule.

Mayhaps, in time, he wouldst yet return to these shores.

With a staunch yank he finished lashing the lines and slanted his gaze back to the sleek ship. Lyting's grin widened. His sister-in-law, Brienne, and her friend, Aleth, gaped from their perch. The scene before them, he imagined, was wholly unlike any they ere witnessed in their native Francia.

Hedeby. Gateway of Danmark. Mistress of trade and crossroad of the North. The town nested in a ring of heavy defense works on the Schlei fjord which cleft deep across the narrow foot of the Jutland peninsula. Traffic intersected her boundaries east from the Baltic and west from the North Sea. Along the military road, Hærvejen, goods flowed north and south.

Lyting looked on with amusement as Brienne nudged Aleth, pointing out a man who ambled the pier in wide, baggy pants gathered below his knees. Aleth, in turn, gasped at the necklace one woman wore, an extravagant piece crowded with large rock crystals, set in silver mountings.

The planks shuddered beneath Lyting as his brother, Rurik, jumped to the wharf beside him. An instant later Aleth's husband, Ketil, appeared above them shouldering a narrow wooden ramp.

Lyting tossed a spiritous glance from one to the other as he helped brace down the thick board. "Best secure the keys to your coffers. Methinks your wives look ready to spend last year's gain."

Ketil guffawed in his flaming red beard, his broken features crinkling. "And what better enjoyment than for a man to squander a bit of coin on his lady? 'Twill be most happily rewarded in the end." He winked, then leaned forward to cast Lyting a purposeful nod. "Mind, 'twould do you well to find a warm and lovesome maid and bind yourself there. Far better than the cold stone walls you seek," he said, dispensing his all-too-frequent advice.

Rurik chuckled deep and rich as Ketil withdrew. "Marriage agrees with our friend. Who would have thought that such a wisp of a girl as Aleth could tame that bear?"

Lyting shared the laugh, his smile lingering as his golden brother mounted the plank to rejoin his wife in the ship. Rurik dropped a kiss to Brienne's lips, then a second to the small, dark head asleep at her breast. Aleth moved to Rurik's side just then, bearing a second child, identical to the first, and gave the mite over to his father.

A certain pride swelled through Lyting as he looked on the Baron and Baronne de Valsemé as they stood with their young heirs and gazed townward. Norse and Frank, they tarried, content in each other's presence. *Nei*, Norman, Lyting amended, melded by heart and blood.

Danish by birth, Lyting and his brothers had grown to manhood in Jutland's north on the inlets and broads of the Limfjord. Their father, Gruel Atli, warred for a decade in Francia alongside their famed uncle, Rollo, and the Norsemen of the Seine.

Nearly four years past, the Frankish king, Charles, came to

terms with Rollo, granting him both fiefdom and title and creating for him a coveted place within the ranks of Frankish aristocracy as Duke of Normandy. For their part, Rollo and his men agreed to defend Charles's realm and take the waters of Holy Baptism.

In his stead, Rollo awarded Atli for his loyalty with the barony of Valsemé, the former holding of Richard Beaumanoir, Brienne's father. Atli did not long enjoy the fruits of his warring. Scarcely did Lyting arrive from Limfjord and Rurik return from his travels in the East than their father died. With his last words Atli conferred the barony and his untouched bride—Brienne—to Rurik's keeping.

Yet, 'twas a position swift challenged. Jealousies and treacheries ran deep within the barony. The blood of the brothers spilt upon the blade—so much, near lost.

Near lost. Lyting touched the faint scar that lined his cheek, his crystal blue gaze drifting to Brienne.

"By the Mass!" Ketil's oath ruptured his thoughts. "Didst you bring your full worth?" He grunted as he hoisted a small, iron-clad chest from the cargo hold onto the deck's planking. " 'Tis a rock, Lyting."

Lyting shook free the old specters and crossed over the ramp. "There be little need for coin or goods where I am destined," he tossed easily, smiling. "And I have brought my wealth apurpose."

"Destined indeed," Ketil rumbled, poised to argue the point. But when Lyting forbore him a glance, Ketil harnessed his tongue.

His lips twitched beneath the curling blaze that shrubbed his face. "Say you, 'apurpose'?" Ketil notched a brow at Lyting, then bent to retrieve a second trunk from storage. "Mayhaps you shall yet restore my confidence and lavish the treasure on some fair damsel."

"Have heart, Ketil," Rurik called back as he turned Brienne down the ramp. " 'Tis burdensome enough that Brother Bernard watches henlike over Lyting, sparing his virtue all earthly temptation. But ever eager you be to thrust every unpledged maid onto his path."

Barely surpressed laughter rippled through the baron's crew and men-at-arms who labored to make fast the *Sea Falcon*, preparing to haul her ashore.

"And well he should have heeded my advice on the day I wed Aleth," Ketil persisted. "There be no want of maidens in Normandy who would welcome him to their arms *and* beds. 'Twould be little surprise should Hedeby's daughters prove as ardent."

Lyting shook his head good-naturedly and began to interrupt Ketil's discourse, but his friend gave him no pause.

"That snow-bright hair of yours tempts the women as honey doth flies." Ketil gestured to the exceptional white mane that spilled past Lyting's shoulders. "I held hope 'twas to that end that you avoided my lady's shears of late. Forsooth, you look as fierce as any of our battle-hungry kindred gone *i viking*. Women admire men of courage and steel," he asserted with a stout nod of his head. "Especially the lustrous maids of Danmark."

"Oh, Ketil." Aleth wagged her head, a soft smile etching her features. "Grant Lyting a measure of peace and do come along."

Aleth turned to Rurik as he remounted the plank and accepted his outstretched hand. Leaning upon his strength, she allowed him to assist her ashore.

Eager to follow his diminutive wife, Ketil caught up several bundles from the hold and motioned for Lyting to aid him with the solid chest that stood betwixt them. Together, the men took up the weight and crossed the deck.

"Be not disheartened, friend," Lyting cheered as they descended. With a shrug of hard-muscled shoulder, he repositioned the small coffer of riches so that it rode more securely against the curve of his neck. "This be for no silken-thighed temptress but for one of true metal and a voice that fair rings to the heavens. 'Tis the Bell of Saint Anskar I seek."

"Bell? What need you of a bell?" Ketil's brows hoisted apart.

"Have you heard naught of blessed Saint Anskar?" Lyting beamed him a glance as they gained the wharf. "He didst establish a church at Hedeby this century past and furnished it with a fine bell. When Anskar died, so did his mission. 'Tis said the church yet stands, boasting its bell. 'Tis my intent to make fair purchase of the piece for Valsemé's own church. Again, there be little use for coin when I enter the cloistered walls of Corbie."

"Corbie. Bell. Bah! 'Tis no bell you need, but a flesh-and-blood woman. A flesh-and-blood woman who will help you *ring* your blessed bell of Saint Anskar!"

Ahead of them, Rurik and Brienne broke into gales of laughter. Their twins looked on them in wonder, then, caught up in the merriment, joined with peals of unrestrained delight.

The small party of Normans threaded their way through the crowds and carts that choked the waterfront. Arabs in long, fluid robes strolled the docks, some stopping to haggle slave prices with Rus traders who offered sturdy young Slavs. Frisians, garbed in striped tunics and possessing long wilting mustaches, bartered fine Rhenish glassware from straw-packed barrels.

Lyting and Ketil exchanged glances to see how prominently the merchants of Sverige figured amongst the Danes this season. Hedeby changed masters with regularity these days, Lyting acknowledged soberly, a bedeviled state spawned years past when the Swedish king, Olaf, seized control of the market-town. Thenceforth, Hedeby had passed back and forth, betwixt Swede and Dane, in an endless power struggle to control the bounty that trafficked her borders.

For all that, Hedeby prospered and life proceeded largely undisturbed. Though it might rub his Dane's pride, 'twas the Swedes who had fortified her with defense works. And likewise, through them, that the most exotic of goods flowed— luxuries from Byzantium, the Bulgar Khaganates, and the Caliphates of Baghdad.

Ketil gave a snort, drawing Lyting's attention to one Swede who dangled a bauble before a shapely Danish maid. She trilled a small laugh as he folded the trinket into her palm. But at the same moment her gaze fell on Lyting and her lips fell open. The Swede twisted round to follow the maid's interest. Icily he flicked an impatient glare over Lyting, then turned back, shifting his stance to block the maid's view.

Lyting caught the flash of white teeth cutting a swathe through Ketil's beard.

"*Nei*, friend. Not a word," he warned but was hard put to temper the grin from his own face.

From above, a horn sounded, long and deep, drawing Lyting's eye to the earthen rampart that rose over Hedeby and to the watchtowers atop it. Again, the horn blazoned, rich and full-bodied, signaling ships arrived from the sea.

The oddest of presentiments rippled along Lyting's spine as he turned to view the palisaded harbor.

"Let us hope they be not more Sverige-men," Ketil gruffed.

Lyting watched as the first warship slipped through the sea gate, lying low to the waterline, its serpent's prow gleaming.

Keen of sight, he marked the boisterous celebration on-board. The sea warriors axed open casks, ladling up horns full of ale and hailing those ashore before they swilled the contents. As the oars dipped the waters, the men took turns stepping out upon the shafts and "dancing" over them along the length of the ship. Their comrades cheered them on, then roared with laughter when they lost their balance and splashed into the Schlei.

Those who accomplished the deed rewarded themselves with more drink and gladdened themselves further, pillaging lips and fondling breasts of the female captives chained at the mast.

"*Nei*, friend. Not Sverige-men." Lyting steeled at the sight. "They be our own kinsmen, fresh from a raid."

Shackled together by ankle cuffs and chains, their wrists tethered, the maids of Eire shuffled along the timbered street in a single column.

Ailinn strained to sight Deira and Lia where they walked ahead, separated by a dozen or more women. She could not glimpse them. Rhiannon, unhappily, trod directly behind, her tongue no less sharp for her trials.

"Why should these Norsemen favor *you* above the rest?" she hissed past Ailinn's shoulder. "Every wretched day since our taking have I struggled on that, choked on that. And though I be ill to think on it further, 'tis plain. Their greed for gold outweighs the lusts of their loins."

"Hush, Rhiannon." Ailinn cautioned in a tight half-whisper. "They keep watch of us. Hold your tongue lest you would see us flogged."

"Flogged? Not *you*," Rhiannon bit out. "Not *you* who they spare of their appetites and suffer no hardship. *You*, who they cloak warm in wool whilst the others of us near freeze upon the open sea. Have you not guessed it?" Rhiannon baited, her voice satin with confidence. "They think you to be me—

daughter of Mór, princess of the Eóganachts and Domnal's bride. They see a hearty ransom in that."

Ailinn ground her teeth, incredulous at Rhiannon's assumption.

"How should they know aught of us? These be black-shielded Danes who fell upon Eire like wolves out of the North, not the Norwegians who infest our fair isle. Didst you imagine them to have stopped and questioned their Norse kindred before entering the Suir to determine who was who amongst the Irish? The Norwegians be their foe as much as any. I have heard it in your father's hall."

" 'Tis as I say, I tell you," Rhiannon contested. "They chose to attack the compound of a *ruri ri* thinking to find great wealth there."

Rhiannon jabbed at the back of Ailinn's arm. "They didst not know we two exchanged places that morn. They found us in my chamber, didst they not? And there be you, wearing *my* wedding mantle, *my* gown, a garland in your hair."

"Enough, Rhiannon!" Ailinn's temples throbbed as she scourged the dark memories from mind's eye. "Even should you have the right of it, who would give ransom now? Who amongst our menfolk survived the terrible slaughter that soaked the dawn? How can any of us know?"

"Mór lives!" Rhiannon declared fiercely. "And these Norse devils will not treat you so finely once they learn the truth. *Ní hea*." A gloat coated her voice beneath the words. "Not when they find that their prize captive lacks one drop of Eóganacht blood, royal or otherwise. That she springs only from the Corcu Loígda—the conquered Érainn—footstool of the Eóganachts for centuries past."

Ailinn's anger screamed through her veins. "I am sure you will hasten to apprise them and better your condition as swift as you can accomplish it."

A contented, deep-throated sound reached her from behind, but Rhiannon abstained from comment. Ailinn envisioned the cat who savored its cream. And the one about to swallow its prey.

As they left the quayside to enter the town's forest of reed-thatched dwellings, Rhiannon's silence continued to stab at her back, sharp as any two-edged blade.

* * *

Lyting hefted the iron caldron into place, suspending it on hook and chain over the room's central stone-lined hearth. He glanced across the *skali*, the *hus*'s fine main hall, and grinned. Brienne and Aleth yet lingered at the door, ogling the vibrant spectacle of Hedeby's streets.

Rurik emerged from a back storeroom just then, dusting the dirt from his hands. He glanced to where little Richard and Kylan trotted merrily along the *langpallar*, the raised side-floors that lined the *skali*'s walls. A smile warmed his features as he joined Lyting.

" 'Tis a fine lodgement. The lads seem happy enough, and methinks the ladies will be comfortable here for the span of our stay."

Lyting chuckled. "If they don't burst with wanting to explore the merchant's booths and craftsmen's quarters."

Rurik's gaze traveled to the women, and he shared the jest. With a gleam to his eyes he stepped toward the sleeping-platforms. The twins giggled with delight when he held out his arms for them. One after the other they launched themselves at their father's chest. Catching them up, Rurik held them high in the crook of his arms and jostled them gamesomely, like two little wheat sacks.

"What say you men?" He winked conspiratorily at Lyting as he addressed his sons. "We be finished here atime—our trunks stored and everything put to rights. Shall we check on the *Sea Falcon* and see whether Ketil and the others have secured her ashore? 'Twould not surprise me if the crew should need your help to set their camp and raise their tents."

Brienne and Aleth came away from the portal as Rurik addressed Lyting, though he spoke for them to hear.

"We still need provision the *hus* if only for tonight. Mayhaps you would be of a mind to escort the ladies about the town. I would do so myself, but with warships in port, I prefer to see to the *Sea Falcon* personally."

Lyting nodded. "Best we double the watch tonight. I'll tent with the men and see it done." Lyting graced Brienne and Aleth with a generous smile. "Meantime, perchance, my ladies would accompany me, and we shall discover what pleasantries Hedeby offers this season."

Amidst high spirits and joyous articulations, the women hurried to gather their cloaks from the wall pegs.

"Be mindful to return with some food for the kettle and oil for our lamps," Rurik chided, then dropped his voice to an undertone as he skimmed a look to Lyting.

"If there be aught the ladies especially favor, secure it with coin when they are not mindful and bid the merchant hold it. Ketil and I will settle with him later."

Lyting's eyes sparkled as they departed the *hus*. He turned back and set the key to the lock. " 'Twould seem I shall spend this journey laboring to empty both our coffers."

"Ah, but mayhaps you shall find your bell," Brienne offered brightly.

Lyting straightened to find three widening grins. By their expressions, they clearly held Ketil's advisements in mind. He began to lift a finger and forestall the all-too-predictable comment when Richard began to bounce in his father's arm.

"I help you ring it, Uncle," he chirped.

"I ring it," Kylan joined gleefully.

Lyting squeezed the bridge of his nose between thumb and forefinger and shook his head in mock dismay. His shoulders vibrated with silent laughter. The Lord's Cross, he discovered ever anew, must be borne in many ways.

Lyting's bootfall sounded bluntly on the wooded walk as he guided the ladies along the fresh-water rivulet that flowed through the heart of Hedeby.

Houses lined the street cramped one upon another—yards neatly fenced, rooftops nearly touching, attendant sheds and workshops to the back. Rapturous aromas of fresh-baked bread, hearty stews, and grilled fish wafted from open doors to swamp their senses.

For a brief time they wandered. Lyting pointed out curiosities and directed them to tented stalls where visiting merchants spread exotic wares—rare spices and rich brocades, ropes of seal hide and walrus ivory. Brienne took special interest in a belt fashioned with metal plaques from Persia, thinking to gift Rurik. Aleth looked at gaming pieces for Ketil.

Where the lane abutted the main north-south thoroughfare, they turned left and crossed the rivulet. Diverting once more, they entered the craftsmen's quarters. Brienne and Aleth examined the potter's bowls, watched the jeweler cut and polish his amber, then lingered over the weaver's array of *hlað*—colorfully patterned ribbons.

Lyting watched with enjoyment as the women chattered back and forth, excited as two fresh-cheeked maids attending their first fair. While they made their choices, he moved to the horn-carver's display, hoping to find something fitting for each of them. Something small, thoughtfully chosen. Something by which they might remember their sojourn here. Remember him. In years to come. Long after he departed Valsemé.

Lyting lifted a handsome, fine-toothed comb and wondered why so cheerful a task should drag at the heart of his soul.

"Red deer." A voice disrupted his thoughts. "They be carved from the antlers of red deer."

Lyting found a whiskery little man sitting off to the side, whittling an indiscernible object.

"Each be fitted with its own case. There be needles, spindles, knife handles, and spoons there to satisfy any maid. And should you be in need of a fine wool cloak for your heart's lady, I have several in trade."

Lyting threw up a hand to halt the man before he attempted to sell him the stool and table as well.

"Two comb sets will do." He reached for the pouch at his hip, glancing over to the weaver's shed at the same moment.

The women were gone.

Lyting's heart jolted from his chest as he broke into a run and spanned the distance between the comb-maker's and weaver's stands.

"The Frankish noblewomen, where be they?" he demanded sharply, jarring to a halt, every muscle battle-tense.

The weaver clutched the roll of linen to his chest and fell back a pace at the storm on Lyting's face. With a quick, trembly gesture he pointed toward the end of the row of workshops where it opened to the streetside.

Lyting caught sight of Brienne's flowing veil and mantle and bound the length to reach them. Stuffing his heart back into his chest, he halted aside them, but before he could utter a word, his heart jammed against his ribs again as he beheld the women's stricken faces.

He followed their gaze to where a group of the sea raiders led their shackled prizes along the wood-paved lane. Females all, the captives scuffed slowly over the planks, dragging the chains that bound their ankles and bit their flesh. Some sobbed softly while others moved their lips in prayer.

"Oh, Lyting, Lyting." Brienne gripped his arm, her voice aching with compassion.

Lyting knew that both Rurik and Ketil had taken pains to forewarn their wives that Hedeby was a major slave market. Still, to witness the wretched plight of these women was more than either could bear.

Brienne's grip tightened, bringing his eyes to meet hers—great violet orbs, filled with her heart.

"Oh, Lyting. Cannot we help just *one*?"

A faint memory whispered, cautioning that the last time Brienne so pleaded for his aid, and in similar tone, it very near cost him his life. But even as he hearkened that dim warning, his gaze fell upon an auburned-haired beauty, her face the gift of angels, her form exquisitely modeled and all too traceable in her clinging gown. She held herself proudly, defiant, a fierce courage upon her brow.

Unbidden, his feet carried him forward.

"These dogs will rue the day they laid hand to a daughter of Mór." Rhiannon chafed Ailinn's ear as they moved along the walk. "I shall gain my freedom, heed my words. And once ransomed, I shall exact my vengeance. 'Twill then be Norsemen who empty their lifeblood upon stout Celtic blades."

Ailinn's patience neared its end. Rhiannon embroidered retribution with every step she took, envisaging and savoring a conquest that could never exist beyond the scope of her own imaginings. Did Rhiannon's venom so blind her? Naught would ever be the same, even should she return to Eire's green shores.

Bone weary and nerves rubbed raw, Ailinn resolved to set the matter to her stepcousin straight forth. Bluntness was all Rhiannon truly understood. 'Twas unhealthy to nurture disillusions, if not starkly dangerous. They need come to grips with the reality of their plight if ever they hoped to survive it.

"These Danes should have taken more care," Rhiannon continued. "Domnal will one day rule from the Rock of Cashel and command the armies of Munster. He shall avenge me, his bride, and prove himself the Northmen's bane."

Ailinn could tolerate no more. "Rhiannon, take the sunbeam from your eye. You have been sullied at the hands of the Northmen. Domnal will no longer want you."

Rhiannon fell deathly silent. But a breath of a moment later, pain knifed across Ailinn's ankle as she felt her fetters hard yanked from behind, her step short-chained.

Ailinn spilled forward, barely breaking the fall with tethered hands as the ground rushed up to meet her. Palms, elbows, and thighs burned as she landed facedown with a distinct "whoof," the air forced out of her. She shook her head, raising upright slightly, and found herself staring at two booted feet.

Ailinn began to push away, but a warm hand closed about her upper arm while a second encompassed her opposite hand in sure, solid strength. Tiny tremors chased through her, one trailing quickly upon another, as she felt herself drawn upward.

The boots passed from view, and her eyes encountered iron-forged legs encased in snug fitting breeches—long legs, appearing momentarily to be without end.

But as she rose farther, they disappeared beneath a fine cloth tunic—this, sword-belted over abdomen and hip. Her gaze traveled higher, skimming the trim line of body past the cinctured waist to a steely expanse of chest and shoulder.

Ailinn's breath grew shallow. Her hand burned within her captor's hold. Uptilting her chin, she swept her gaze over the tanned column of neck, square cut of jaw, then upward the final distance to behold crystal blue eyes and hair . . . hair as bright as day.

Ailinn wavered, her bone gone to liquid, and sought to regain her footage. The man's hand slipped at once from her arm to the small of her back to steady her. In so doing he pressed her closer and held her a scarce whisper apart.

She dared look on him again, tracing the clean lines of his face, so strikingly handsome. The man possessed a leonine quality, dangerously male and not to be underestimated. Yet it was his eyes, more beautiful than most, that held her captive. They penetrated the depths of her, as if to strip her bare to the core and lay open her heart.

A blur of movement obtruded upon her edge of vision, wakening Ailinn to Hakon's approach. Beyond his shoulder she espied Skallagrim watching, close-faced.

Without word the man released her. He ran a long gaze over her, then grazed her eyes with an intense, unreadable look. Drawing forth his coin pouch, he turned to Hakon.

Ailinn's pulse raced. The man intended to purchase her! In an instant, the dreamlike haze that enveloped her dissipated and reality clattered hard down upon her once more. She darted her gaze all about her, collecting the images to heart—knots of townspeople lining the lane, coarsely assessing them; her kinswomen herded like animals, manacled and abused; and their captors, the murderous pagans who had ravened Munster and enslaved them.

Like a storm on the horizon her fury gathered, swift and terrible. She brought her eyes to the man who purposed to buy her and saw him for the first time for what he truly was—a heathenous Dane, fierce and untamed. His incredible snowfall of hair spilled to mid-chest with barbarous effect. Upon his cheek he bore a scar, token of a violent past.

Ailinn castigated herself for every heated tremor he stirred to life within her. He was no different from the rest. And here he stood, brazenly offering coin for her. To what purpose, if not to fill his bed with her and abuse her there?

As the man turned to face her, a tempest of emotion ruptured within Ailinn. The horrors and outrages of the past week rushed forth and overwhelmed her. She met his eyes with icy contempt. Then, in the full gale of her fury, she spat on him.

Lyting fell back a pace, stunned by the maid's vehemence. She sliced him with a look of unveiled loathing, as though he alone were responsible for the misfortune of her people.

Slowly he wiped the moisture from his cheek, locking his eyes with hers—large, brown eyes, dark about the rims but golden in their centers, warmed with honey. Rich auburn hair tumbled in disarray about a heart-shaped face, the features delicate, refined, the skin flawless as cream beneath the smudges.

Lord in His mercy, but she was a magnificent creature. All the more ravishing in the high grip of her anger. Lyting braced himself against the fire that swept through his veins. Her spirit was unbroken, and that pleased him immensely.

"What price do you set on this woman?" Lyting angled a glance to the sea raider who stood right of him.

" 'Twould appear she does not wish *you* for her master." The man's mouth dragged upward, the words more barb than jest.

Lyting sharpened his focus on the seaman, caring naught for his tone.

The man burned with brash confidence, legs spread apart and arms crossed chest level. He bore no great height but looked hard as stone. His hair shone dully of tarnished gold, and a month's worth of growth covered his jaw.

"I wouldst have her nonetheless." Lyting weighted his words evenly.

The man gauged him with darkening eyes for one brief but deliberate moment. He then broke away his gaze and took an unhurried step toward the maid. He cupped her chin, but she wrenched from his touch, recoiling. He merely chuckled and brushed his fingertips along her neck.

A burr climbed Lyting's back. The man reminded him all too well of another. Another whose name was no longer spoken within the barony. Their physical aspects were markedly different, yet the two were of a kind. Predators.

"This one is not for purchase," the man breathed, a hard glitter to his eyes. "But there be others to choose from."

"None other will do," Lyting clipped.

The sea raider narrowed his gaze, wolflike. "Then you need be content without her. She is not mine to sell, and her owner holds plans for her." Something obscure flickered in his eyes. "Be assured, she shall be well used."

Ailinn started when Hakon crouched to unlock her ankle chains. Rising again, he grasped her by the arm and hauled her from the line. As he led her away, she cast back a frantic, searching glance for her stepcousins. Instead, she met the dazzling intensity of the white Dane's gaze.

Skallagrim joined Hakon just then, and she found herself pulled farther along the network of streets. As they entered a side lane, she braved one last look back. Instantly she espied the towering Dane as he left the walk to join two women.

Ailinn's ire flared. The man possessed a female for each arm, yet his base cravings drove him to acquire another!

The image of the tall Dane and the women continued to nip at her, vex her. Their elegant dress suggested they be wives of status. Certainly not slaves. The Norse were polygamous devils, she had once been told, who enjoyed as many wives as they could maintain and kept even more female slaves beneath their roofs. Yet, 'twas appalling that the man should openly seek her purchase within his wives' view.

A sudden realization lurched through Ailinn. The women's garments were wholly unlike those of other townswomen she had seen. Rather, the gowns of these women were much like her old nursemaid's, Bergette's, only far richer. Upon their heads they wore the distinctive flowing veil of the Franks—the *couvre chef*.

Ailinn pondered this, mystified, when she was brought to a sudden halt. Looking up, she found herself before a small house, stave-built with vertical planking. The carcass of an entire oxen was upraised on posts above the portal, sacrificial offering to the exactions of the Nordic gods.

Ailinn gaped up at the poor beast, aghast at the practice.

Before her, the door drew open.

As Ailinn lowered her gaze, the breath sealed in her throat. A brutish-looking woman, thick and raw-boned, filled the entrance, scowling down at her.

Chapter 2

The bell of Saint Anskar. Lyting slipped the pouch from his belt and weighted it in his hand as he gazed on the hallowed piece.

After returning Brienne and Aleth to their lodgings, he had set out about town, restless, knotted up, with a sharp need to stretch himself.

Enwrapped in thought, the cheer sapped from his day, he ranged the full breadth and reach of Hedeby. With a sharp jolt he stayed himself as he quested yet another doorway, another yard, for a glimpse of auburn hair.

The beauty eclipsed his every conscious step—scorn-filled eyes, emblazoning her memory to heart.

Wresting himself from that vision, he set himself to a more purposeful task—locating Anskar's church. His inquiries led him here, eastward, to the harbor end of town.

Beneath the shadow of the earthenworks stood the modest structure that once served the saintly archbishop. A sorry thing that it should serve the populace of Hedeby nowadays as a fish *hus*. He only hoped the owner would be agreeable to parting with its bell and wondered ruefully if 'twas currently employed to signal the arrival of the day's fresh catch.

Lyting hefted the pouch once more in his palm and started forward. An outburst of laughter from the direction of the docks brought him round. Six of the *drakken*-warriors made their way toward him along the walk.

In their midst strode a bull of a man whom Lyting recognized from earlier that day when he sought to purchase the maid. Broad of feature and build, he bore himself with a decided, self-assured gait. His teeth gapped beneath a passing smile, and braids plaited the iron-gray hair at temple and jaw.

"Ho!" a voice called out from the troop.

Lyting cut a glance over them. Again the voice bellowed in greeting. This time a man stepped apart and waved an arm wide, his features lost beneath a dense growth of beard, its dusky brown shade at odds with his coppery ravel of hair.

Lyting looked about himself to see if there be someone near who might be the object of the man's enthusiasm. But in the next instance the man abandoned his comrades and hastened directly toward him, a wide grin brightening his face.

"Lyting!" The raider grasped his arm in friendship and clapped a hand robustly to his shoulder. "I thought you to be in Francia wielding sword and might for your uncle, the duke."

Lyting swept a gaze over the disturbingly familiar features, then likewise broke into a broad grin.

"Stefnir? I didst not recognize you beneath that thatch."

"Been *i viking* the month long." Stefnir rasped the beard with his knuckles. "You wilt recall how lean be the spoils in the service of our king and how spare the women." He winked a smile. "I set off to fill my coffers and enjoy some wenching this spring."

Remembering his comrades, Stefnir turned and motioned them on.

The grayed warrior buckled his gaze on Lyting as he advanced and the distance narrowed betwixt them. Lyting met the silent measure of those eyes. Muscles lightly reined, he held his stance, absorbing the tremor of boards beneath his feet as they shivered with the men's heavy, booted passage. Without utterance the raiders continued on.

"Your leader?" Lyting nodded after the older man, careful to conceal his sharp interest.

"Skallagrim? He commands the *drakkar Wind Raven*. I joined under his sail. These few . . ." Stefnir gestured to the dragonships anchored within the palisade. "These be but a small portion of a great fleet that voyaged under Harald

Split-Brow. We fell upon the Saxons and Irish whilst they still licked their wounds from the late autumn raid."

Stefnir clamped open hands to the sides of his belted waist in obvious satisfaction. "The main body of *drakken* returns north with Harald. Skallagrim and some of the others had more pressing needs and diverted to Hedeby. But what of you? How fares your father and his new domain?"

A tiny muscle twinged the corner of Lyting's eye. "He died shortly after my arrival three years past."

A shaft of surprise widened Stefnir's eyes, then passed. "Gruel Atli was a fierce and courageous warrior. Though his absence be sore felt, 'tis comfort and glory that his sword now sings in the halls of Valhalla."

Lyting reserved comment as to where, in truth, his father's spirit might dwell, and whether 'twas Valkyries or Angels who saw him there. He deemed it best to not decry the old gods too hastily with an epostulation of the cross and risk affronting Stefnir. If his old friend indeed served beneath Skallagrim's command, there be information he wouldst glean of the raid on the Celtic Isle and of the beautiful captive who so haunted him.

"My elder brother, Rurik, now holds fief and title and rules as Baron de Valsemé," he revealed simply.

A smile crept over Stefnir's lips and trailed up to his eyes. "I imagine that set ill with Hastein."

"*Já*. That it did." Lyting shut his mind to his half-brother and all the black, fetid memories. "But his obsessions no longer afflict us."

Dispelling the shadows with a sound mental shake, Lyting delivered a friendly clout to Stefnir's arm.

"What say you we find ourselves some skins of wine and joints of meat? I wouldst hear of your adventures across the sea."

"And I, the maids of Francia." Stefnir's face split wide with a grin.

A brief time later Lyting and Stefnir sat before a vendor's stall over beakers of ale and steaming bowls of venison stew.

"Last year's raid brought the Irish to their knees," Stefnir said around a jawful of meat. "This year Harald wished to break their spine."

Lyting held intent on each word, restraining the questions he would ask while Stefnir quaffed down the contents of his cup and sleeved the wetness from his mouth.

"At first sight of the dragon-prow, these Irish hide their treasures away. Harald came away with few spoils last autumn, thought he scented a hoard beneath his feet. They be a clever lot, the Irish, but Harald be shrewder. He took as captives some of their soldiers—Munstermen—and kept them alive long enough to learn the location of their *souterrains*—ancient underground caves."

Lyting girt his patience as Stefnir attended to the last of his stew and called for more ale. But a moment later Stefnir rewarded his forbearance.

"We swept down upon them like a sky full of hawks—swift, without warning, before the first rift of dawn. Harald marked the monastery and surrounding grounds for himself. The chiefs closest to him blanketed the area as well, claiming all the choice sites. This maddened Skallagrim, that they should seize the church coffers solely unto themselves, for those be the far richest to plunder in any Christian land.

"But Skallagrim is an artful fox. He was amongst those who loosened the Munstermen's tongues and recalled that one spoke of 'overkings' who dwelt upon the Suir. We sailed inland atime, leading a fair division of the fleet which was likewise displeasured by Harald's wiles. Soon enough we came upon a compound, boasting many buildings, ablaze with torchlight and decorated for feasting. Before the first chink of light punctured the night, we fell on them, undeclared."

Stefnir stayed his tale while the vendor's round wife refilled his beaker. She then topped off Lyting's, which, like his bowl, stood scarcely touched. A frown puckered her brow as she withdrew and padded back to the stall, Stefnir's eyes following the sway of her hips.

"And how fared the raid?" Impatience scrubbed through Lyting, keen to have a full recounting, yet knowing when he did, he would ill like the taste of it.

" 'Twas not the sort of victory I sought." Stefnir stirred from his distraction. "Not one a warrior boasts of, or a skald deigns worthy to set to verse. 'Tis no honor to slay men befogged in their cups." He took a swill of ale, then cocked a brow at Lyting and smiled afresh.

" 'Twould seem the Irish enjoy their drink as much as we.

'Twas a wedding feast we interrupted, though, in truth, the event had yet to take place. We discovered the bride and her handmaids yet in her bower. Odin didst smile on me that I should be among the first to sample that fair, virginal gathering."

Lyting came forward on the stool, gripping his cup so hard he risked to break it. But Stefnir continued without notice, tossing a hand to the air.

"Whatever be their customs, their men began their celebrations aforehand, making light of our work. I'll give you this . . ." He held Lyting's gaze. "The 'overking'—whoever he was—purposed to impress his guests with his importance and power, and displayed a great portion of his wealth in the hall. That, too, eased our task."

"But what of the bride?" Lyting brought his cup down solidly on the table, sloshing its contents. "What of the maidens trapped in the bridal chamber?"

Stefnir stilled his beaker midair, casting Lyting a curious, heedful look.

"Didst one possess dark red hair, the color of an autumn wood afire in its crown? A maiden of rare beauty," Lyting pressed.

"Já," Stefnir acknowledged slowly, pensively, then pulled on a long draught of ale.

"I didst seek to purchase such a maid this day, from one of the raiders who drove their fettered captives through streets. He appeared to know your chieftain, Skallagrim."

Stefnir spewed his mouthful of ale, missing Lyting and the table, but sprayed a cat that dozed nearby. He then sat choking a full minute, pounding his chest while the feline shook itself indignantly and swished away, tail flicking high in the air.

"You?" Stefnir uttered in astonishment. Slapping his thigh, he threw back his head and bellowed with laughter. " 'Twas you who sought to purchase Skallagrim's prize slave, while the rest of us were near deprived of our vitals for merely looking upon her overlong?"

He wiped the tears from his eyes. "I heard the tale that someone, not of the fleet, sought to possess her. You be fortunate to still carry something of use betwixt your legs. Curse that I should be bridled aboard the Wind Raven with watch at the time and missed the sport. Tell me in truth. Didst you lock horns with Hakon over the doe?"

"Hakon." Lyting tested the name and found it to resonate unpleasantly with that of his dead half-brother. Ill portent or coincidence? he wondered, then tucked the thought to memory. "What be his tie to Skallagrim? And what of the maid?"

Stefnir rose, a smile stretching his beard. "My friend, you have set your desires upon the bride, herself. And should you be intent on that quest, you will need defy both a dragon and a demon. But, come. Let us walk atime, and I will tell you aught I know."

After pitching a small coin to the vendor's wife, they proceeded along the rivulet, westward through town.

"Skallagrim and Hakon quarreled bitterly over the girl. Hakon gained the chamber before the rest and, if believed, first seized her. When I entered, Skallagrim had her in his grasp. From their argument I garner she slipped from Hakon's hold only to be snared by Skallagrim. In the end Hakon yielded. Skallagrim not only commands the crew of the *Wind Raven*, he is Hakon's uncle as well."

Lyting lifted a brow at this. "Hakon said Skallagrim intends to use the maid to some end."

"Ah, the pity of it, too." Stefnir sighed. "We capture a nymph of such marvelous beauty that she stirs a man's most lust-filled dreams but to gaze on her. Yet, we be forbidden to sample that sweet nectar. Wouldst you believe, Skallagrim preserves her virtue to gift her to another, not even a Norseman?"

Lyting halted in his footsteps. "Skallagrim does not pleasure himself upon her?" he voiced in amazement. "She be unravished? A virgin?"

"Skallagrim assumes so. He could not verify that detail with his crew so eager to aid him. Her attendants proved virgins, and the preparations within the compound were so elaborate 'twas probably to be her first joining."

Lyting rubbed a hand across his jaw, envisioning the Irish maid—the delicate contours of her face; the slim, straight nose; and full, enticing mouth. He blinked away the image and picked up his pace once more.

"'Tis singularly odd that Skallagrim did not have her himself. Be the man a eunuch?"

Stefnir laughed. "*Nei*. But mayhaps no better fortuned. Rumors abound that he was unmanned a few years back. Some say he near be taken with a fever and left impotent. Others claim he put aside a lover who thereupon revealed herself to be a witch and put him under a curse. When his member stirs, 'tis said it becomes a great gnarled root, twisting this way and that so he cannot engage in the act or is too painful."

Stefnir shrugged. "Wherever lies the truth, there be one thing for certain. Skallagrim does not take his women openly on raids as do the others. At times he keeps a woman in his tent. Let us hope he enjoys some success. 'Tis a wretched thing to befall a man."

Lyting nodded absently, his thoughts running far ahead. "What need has Skallagrim of a virgin if he cannot make use of her himself?"

"Silk. He means to use her to gain concessions in Byzantium's silk trade."

For a second time Lyting stopped abruptly midstep and rounded on his old comrade.

"On Odin's beard, 'tis truth," Stefnir swore. "I sat about the fires with Skallagrim one night while he was in one of his more agreeable moods and drink had eased his tongue. He claimed she be more valuable to him than gold. But only if he can deliver her to the East undefiled."

Stefnir gestured that they divert along a side lane. Lyting easily matched pace, though his mind was set to spinning.

"Like myself," Stefnir continued, "Skallagrim voyaged on this raid for quick plunder—to enrich himself as he might before setting sail for Miklagárd, the 'Great City' of Byzantium—Contantinople. As he tells it, he hunts Arctic furs in the winter months and trades in Byzantium during the summer. His sister, Thora, maintains a *hus* there in Hedeby. 'Tis his anchorage, so to speak." Stefnir directed Lyting right on a northward walk.

"It might surprise you, but Skallagrim is a man of far-sightedness. For years he has courted Byzantium's officials and labored to see the silk trade opened to Western markets. The Byzantines impose many restrictions and tariffs and allow precious little of the stuff to pass out of their walled city.

"Evidently, Skallagrim neared an arrangement last summer. He woos a high court official, a thoroughly—and advantage-ously—corrupt man who holds sway with the minister of trade.

He possesses a reputation for generosity to those he befriends. And those who gift him well.

"Among other diversions, the man collects beautiful concubines from all over the Empire and beyond. But he accepts only virgins, not wanting to acquire them disease-ridden and possibly pregnant. 'Tis my belief he harbors some personal fetish to be the first to broach those fair portals himself." Stefnir snorted.

Lyting envisaged the beauty trapped within the Byzantine's exotic web as he employed his methods to break and subdue her. Bile rose in Lyting's throat.

"Anyway, when Skallagrim ensnared the Irish beauty, arrayed in her bridal raiment, he saw her usefulness and felt he had gained better spoils than even Harald Split-Brow in the end. He intends to sail with her at week's end for Byzantium."

Lyting's thoughts churned with his rising emotions as Stefnir came to a halt. On a brief glance Lyting realized they stood before the slave *hus*.

"Mere talk of this woman doth whet my appetite," Stefnir declared. "What say you we entertain ourselves with a few Irish wenches?"

Lyting suddenly felt as though he observed his old friend from a great distance. He recognized that, had Skallagrim openly shared his captive, she would find no rest to her days for the ceaseless demands of men like Stefnir.

"*Nei.*" He concealed his disgust. "There be matters I need attend for now."

"Well, perhaps we can enjoy a bladder of wine before I leave to rejoin the king's fleet," Stefnir called cheerfully as he started for the portal. "You have yet to tell me of the maids of Francia."

Pausing, he put one hand to the door's framework and glanced back. "One caution, friend. Should you harbor thoughts to gain the maid, watch Hakon. I believe he means to have her, regardless of his uncle's plans."

Lyting nodded gravely, then took his leave. As earlier, he walked atime, his thoughts chasing round and round as he wrestled with what he deemed a most unreasonable urge to protect the maid. He reminded himself that she belonged to Skallagrim. Reminded himself that he purposed to set his path for Corbie upon his return to Normandy.

He remained unappeased, a storm of unrest gathering in his soul.

Be it God's design or Devil's temptation that his path should cross with this woman's? Soul and flesh, ever the struggle. Deep within, he sensed 'twould be an age before he regained his heart's peace.

Climbing to the top of the earthenworks, he surprised the watchman. After an exchange of greetings, he remained and faced seaward, tracing the ribbon of the Schlei to where it disappeared into the distance.

Thoughtfully he scanned the masts of the *drakken* moored within the harbor.

Turning slowly round, Lyting drifted his gaze over the crowded rooftops of Hedeby. Somewhere beneath their thatched crowns dwelt the maid of his enchantment.

Ailinn thrashed within the grip of the two Norsewomen as they strove to force her onto her back upon one of the two room's raised side-floors.

'Twas only a matter of moments before they would fell her to their purposes, Ailinn knew. There be no escape. Only brief victory, vanished in a blink-of-eye. The sow she'd first encountered before the portal now grappled for her ankles, intent on snatching her from her feet. But they would not have her so easily. They would taste her mettle and know the fires that forge the Irish.

Ailinn twisted and kicked free of the sow, her feet slapping down atop the platform. The other two women stepped up, onto the planking, dragging her with them.

A dark blade of fear rode Ailinn as she strained against them. Did they aim to harm her? Prepare her for some grim Nordic ritual? Sacrifice her to the gods? Her thoughts strayed to the poor ox outside the door.

Summoning her strength, Ailinn threw her weight to one side, propelling herself and her unwanted companions off balance. As one, they crashed into the loom that stood braced at the end of the flooring. The piece tottered, one of its uprights dropping off the edge of the settle, then keeled sideways and clattered to the floor.

Ailinn grimaced as the Norsewomen wrenched her arms,

one seizing a fistful of auburn tresses and jerking her head backward.

The sow stumped forward, drawing back her hand, wide and open-palmed. Ailinn braced herself for the blow. Just as the hand began to fall, Skallagrim roared from his chair.

Thora. The sow had a name. Ailinn gasped for breath. Like Hakon, the woman yielded to the chieftain's will.

Slowly Skallagrim rose to his feet, pegging Ailinn with his eyes. He started forward with purposeful steps.

The women eased their hold a fraction, then slammed Ailinn flat against the wall where the loom had been and held her there. Ailinn stiffled her cry as pain fractured the back of her head and splintered down her spine.

Skallagrim's shadow fell across her. For a moment he stood, breathing down upon her. For all her worth, Ailinn could not still the tremors in her legs.

A wave of terror crested through her as Skallagrim unsheathed the knife at his waist. Firelight glinted along its honed edge as he brought the steel within view. Turning the blade, he pressed its cold shaft against her throat.

Ailinn swallowed beneath the thirsting metal as his meaty fist moved to the top of her gown. With a swift, stout yank he rent the fabric from her breast. Ailinn squeezed her eyes shut, the tear of cloth filling her ears as he stripped away its full length.

Cool air rushed over her bared flesh. She sought to distance herself, mind and soul, from her vile plight, but Skallagrim jolted her back. Dropping the shorn gown in a heap at her feet, he seized upon the remnants yet trapped at her back. They joined the rest in a puddle as he pulled her from the wall and lowered the blade to rest between her breasts.

Fear stalked through Ailinn. She forced her eyes to meet his, craving to slice him through with her contempt, yet knowing she did no more than amuse him for she could not win past her panic.

Skallagrim regarded her stolidly, his eyes unstirred in their depths. Closing his hand over hers, he isolated one finger and applied precise and calculated pressure to the joint.

Pain cleaved through Ailinn's hand and ripped along her arm. Her knees doubled beneath her, and she dropped to the flooring.

Instantly the women pushed her onto her back and held her by neck, arms, and shoulders. The sow, Thora, forced her legs apart and held them as Skallagrim knelt before her. Ailinn stiffened as hands touched her. She steeled herself for the coming pain, then sickened before the promise of a torturous death. She was a weak-kneed creature after all, she decided, closing her eyes. May Saint Pádraig and the Heavenly Host conduct her swiftly to her reward.

No pain followed. Only the grunt of the sow. Ailinn peered through her lashes. The woman nodded her affirmation at something while Skallagrim likewise indicated his approval. At that they released her legs, and she found herself hauled upright and set to her feet.

Ailinn stood before Skallagrim, her cheeks glowing hot. She sought to cover herself with her hands, neither shred of cloth nor scrap of modesty left to her. He roved an eye over her, smiling within his beard. Once more he growled his approval, then moved apart. Taking a small caldron from over the fires, he added its contents to an oaken tub that stood toward the opposite end of the room.

Incredulous, Ailinn allowed herself to be led forward without further struggle and watched as Thora sprinkled petals and herbs over the inviting waters. They meant to bathe her!

Rapidly she pieced together bits and fragments of the past days. Skallagrim did not appear intent on ravishing her himself and withheld her from his men. Nor would he allow the woman, Thora, to strike her. But why? She was but a slave now. Be there some reason he did not wish her marred?

And what of their crude examination of her? Her cheeks flamed anew. Didst they inspect the proof of her maidenhood? Praise God that she yet be chaste. What would have befallen her had the evidence no longer been intact? What would befall her now that it was?

One of the blond giants prodded her from behind and gestured that she step into the tub. Ailinn complied, knowing herself to be in dire need of a thorough scrubbing.

The next moment she reconsidered, wincing at the heat of the water. Immediately the women surrounded her. Scooping up handfuls of soft soap from bowls, they lathered her from head to toe, none too gently, then doused her with bucketfuls of clean water and repeated the process.

Ailinn spluttered beneath the second downpour. Parting the
sopping hair from her face, she discovered Hakon leaning
against the open door. Before she could cross her hands over
her breasts, an expanse of cloth snapped open in front of her,
blocking the view. Ailinn looked up to find Skallagrim
outstretching a great square of linen. He did not trust Hakon,
either, she decided as she rose on shaky legs and stepped into
the folds.

Skallagrim left her to the women's ministrations as he
proceeded to the portal and set Hakon to some task outside the
building. While Skallagrim yet turned from them, the two
Norse "guardswomen" dried Ailinn roughly, whispering and
tittering amongst themselves as they yanked her hair and
pinched her flesh.

Skallagrim caught the last of this and drove them from the
house at full bellow. He then harangued Thora at length,
pointing to Ailinn, then to the door, and betimes, the rafters
and floor. Ailinn understood naught of it yet dared not move.
She stood clutching the linen about her till Skallagrim ceased
his rantings and, at last, motioned that she wait upon the settle.

Thora notched her chin, her ire fermenting as she crossed to
the back of the room. Withdrawing a shapeless tunic from a
chest that stood there, she returned and thrust it in Ailinn's
face.

Fish eyes, Ailinn bethought as she slipped the garment over
her head beneath Thora's cold and glassy stare. But when the
cloth's harsh texture sent a rash up her throat and provoked her
to scratching, Skallagrim ordered her remove it and set to
searching through his own sea chest.

Ailinn's heart strained as he brought forth objects that once
graced Mór's hall. Finding a garment, he withdrew it and bore
it to her, a soft-green gown—her stepaunt's, Murieann's. A
fresh shaft of pain pierced Ailinn's heart and continued on to
her soul.

Tears welled as she drew on the gown. Murieann was slight
in build like her youngest daughter, Lia, though Deira be taller.
Was. Ailinn shivered as she tugged down the fabric and fretted
anew for her stepcousins. The hems fell far short of ankle and
wrist.

Skallagrim returned to the sea chest and brought forth a
braided silken cordage to girdle the dress. This, too, she

recognized as Murieann's. As he started toward her, Thora caught at his sleeve, desiring the cincture for herself. But Skallagrim shrugged her off with a growl and bore the piece to Ailinn. When he turned round, Thora stood over his sea chest, unfolding the bridal mantle.

Ailinn clutched the girdle to her breast as Skallagrim howled at Thora and tromped back across the room. But Thora found her voice and matched him for volume. Like a badger with its catch, she clung to the elegant cloak and would not leave go.

On they bickered while, soundlessly, Hakon entered the house and took up a place on the settle opposite Ailinn. Half-reclining, he listened amusedly to the squabble while he drifted his gaze over Ailinn. She shivered beneath his hungry perusal as he grazed the curves beneath her gown and lingered over her bare legs.

Ailinn diverted her attention back to the warring couple and to the bridal mantle. Rhiannon's mantle.

What if Rhiannon be right? The thought harrowed. What if the Norsemen believed her to be a valuable hostage of royal lineage? And what would come of her when they discovered that she was only a poor relation of a vanquished tribe—Ailinn of the Érainn?

Still, 'twas like fitting together shards of broken pottery. 'Twas hard to match the edges. Pieces were lacking and she could scarce make sense of those she held. If the heathens thought to gain ransom, why then their concern that she be a virgin? An unravished bride would be worth more than one spoiled, undeniably. Yet, her instincts told her more lay behind Skallagrim's interest in her virtue.

Ailinn massaged her forehead. She understood little of men's dealings—their barterings for power and wealth . . . and hostages. Rhiannon understood. 'Twas why she first cast her net for Domnal of the Raithlind Eóganachts, certain that he would be next to rule the Rock of Cashel. 'Twas why they exchanged places that fateful morn. . . .

Her thoughts spiraled back to that grim morning, only 'twas not grim at its outset, but rather a day of high cheer and merriment—Rhiannon's wedding day.

Ailinn, Deira, and Lia, and all the other maids who attended the bride awoke before dawn, restless in their sleep, having captured fair little of it.

They rose, giddy for the day to come when Mór would make the traditional "bridal ride" with Rhiannon, and Domnal would appear with the Raithlind and abduct her. Afterward, all would return to the compound to fulfill the ceremonies and feast away the remainder of the day and night.

Lia had laughed so gaily, Ailinn recalled, and proposed they slip out of the compound to roll in the morning dew for good luck. Good luck, Ailinn thought bitterly. Before they could even dress fully, they heard the clash in the courtyard.

"Bran!" Rhiannon screamed. "The Dalcassian! He has come to seize me. He vowed as much."

Rhiannon wrung her hands, eyes darting from wall to wall as though she looked for a weapon to seize upon. Then a thought sparked to life in her eyes.

"Help me, Cousin," Rhiannon pleaded, gripping Ailinn. "Bran must not find me. His manhood was sore offended when I chose Domnal over him and rejected his offer of marriage. But he doth not seek me this day to soothe his bruised pride alone. 'Tis insult he issues—and challenge—to Raithlind and Caisil and all Eóganachts alike."

Ailinn tried to pull from Rhiannon's hold, heedful of her blurring of falsehoods and truths, and wary of her reference to herself as *cousin*—a relationship Rhiannon loathed to acknowledge lest she have desperate need of Ailinn for some self-serving end.

"Bran knows that, in time to come, Domnal wilt claim the throne of Cashel," Rhiannon continued, undeterred. "Long have the kings of Munster sprung from our line, and Domnal be favored to succeed. The Dalcassian views him as his foremost rival, for he covets the crown himself."

The din mounted in the hall.

Ailinn winced as Rhiannon's nails stabbed into her.

"Bran must not succeed. 'Tis *me* he wants, to strike at Domnal. *Please*, Ailinn," Rhiannon's voice rose an urgent note. "Take my gown, my mantle. He knows not my face. Let him think you to be me, and go with him. When he discovers his error, 'twill be too late. I shall get word to Domnal at once, I promise. He camps nearby awaiting the 'bridal-ride.'"

Steel rang on steel without.

Alarm filled Rhiannon's eyes. "Quickly, Ailinn. 'Twill be

strife for all Munster and a warring of tribes shouldst Bran succeed and spoil Domnal's bride."

Ailinn snatched free of Rhainnon's grip, her temper flaring. "Yet you would see him spoil me? 'Twas your own sharp tongue that brings Bran down on us now—not challenge to Domnal—and well you know it. Far more than male pride and injured manhood drives Bran. Rather, 'tis the grave insults you hurled at his people when he offered for your hand. Still, you would preserve yourself at my ruination that you might sit in queenly splendor at Cashel."

"What?" Rhiannon shrieked. "Would you have seen me accept Bran to my marriage bed? Taint the blood of the Caisil with that of a baseborn Dalcassian forevermore?"

"Baseborn, Rhiannon? Bran be a Dalcassian prince."

"There be but one kind of Dalcassian," Rhiannon sneered. "Swine, not fit to tend me in my chambers."

Ailinn took a swift step forward, causing Rhiannon to fall back a pace.

"And 'twas the very fullness of those sentiments that so inflamed Bran and now brings him beating down upon our door. Do not deny it. I was present when you vented your spleen to the Dalcassian envoy and rejected their prince's proposal. Did you think Bran would countenance such insult and swallow it meekly? Now we *all* suffer the blight of your words, Rhiannon. I bear no wish to hazard defilement because of them."

"But you need help me." Rhiannon clutched at Ailinn.

"I shall take your place, Rhiannon," Deira offered quietly and came forth to stand before them.

Rhiannon whirled round, eyes flashing. Though three years younger, Deira nearly matched her for height. "Mayhaps so!" Her voice filled with renewed hope.

"*Ní hea*, Deira," Ailinn protested, her stomach clenching tight at the thought.

"'Tis all right, Ailinn," Deira comforted. "Domnal will come for me. But Rhiannon be right. The Dalcassian must not seize her, or so much more bloodshed will follow. 'Tis best for all that I go with Bran. He'll not harm me once he realizes his mistake."

Ailinn held no such confidence. As ever, Deira placed others before herself. But this time, overtrustful and uncom-

prehending of the full of the situation, she put herself at risk.
That, Ailinn could not abide, though Rhiannon appeared eager
for her to do so.

Ailinn looked on while Rhiannon set out her jewels and
spread her wedding gown. White. It struck Ailinn as singularly
odd that, where most brides chose bright-colored gowns,
Rhiannon should insist upon white as though to attest to her
purity. Ailinn held her own opinions on that matter. Mayhaps,
what Rhiannon truly feared was what Bran would discover of
her. Or how he might use that knowledge.

Bran. What had she heard of him? A brave and fierce
warrior? Prudent and fair? She had seen him once, a solid-built
man with fiery curls covering head and chin, favorable enough
to look upon. Shouldst she go with him, feigning to be the
bride, 'twas likely he'd be angry when he discovered the ruse.
But should he decide to keep her . . .

Ailinn watched Rhiannon unfold the shimmering bridal
mantle, a heavy brocade of white woven with emerald green
and shot through with threads of gold.

Mayhaps, 'twould not be so terrible a thing, she pondered.
In the next moon's turning she would be eighteen. At times
Ailinn wondered if her uncle ever intended to find her a
husband. But though she loved her stepfamily, and Deira and
Lia as sisters, she held no true place amongst the Eóganachts.

'Twould be great chance, to go with Bran, she deemed.
Perchance, he would take her to wife to right his offense—if
there be one. Or perchance, he would keep her as his
concubine or mistress. 'Twas allowable under Brehon law,
though not a station she desired. Yet, if he "ruined" her, she
reasoned, 'twas probable he would keep her at his side in some
wise to amend his wrong. She might still find more acceptance
amongst the Dalcassian under Bran's banner than ever she had
amongst the Eóganachts.

As Ailinn looked to see Deira take the gown from Rhiannon,
she realized that naught truly mattered save her stepcousin. She
could not allow Deira to risk herself.

"I will take your place, Rhiannon." Ailinn swept the snowy
dress from Deira's hands with gritty determination.

Shouts heightened on the other side of the door. Blades
clashed and scraped.

Hurriedly Ailinn slipped into the gown. A flurry of hands

attended her, the maids white-faced for all they heard. The rich mantle weighed heavily upon her shoulders as the attendants secured it in place with gleaming silver brooches.

Rhiannon directed that Ailinn's auburn tresses be drawn back and hidden beneath the cloud of veil, lest Bran know her own to be raven. Lia quickly fashioned a crown of wild hyacinth from sprigs waiting in the crocks and set it upon Ailinn's head.

"*Non. Non. Ma chère*, Ailinn," Bergette implored, breaking her silence. "'Tis evil, I feel in my bones. You must not go with him."

Ailinn looked on her Frankish nursemaid, surprised she had forgotten her till now. Before she could reply, a man screamed out in pain, and she heard his bulk clump against the other side of the door.

Icy ripples of fear purled through her. This was more than simple abduction. Bran would not strike Mór's compound and slay the wedding guests to wreak vengeance for Rhiannon's insults.

A great blow fell upon the door, so hard the boards shuddered. Several more blows followed, accompanied by the cracking and splintering of wood. Bergette rushed forth to interpose herself betwixt Ailinn and the portal, her arms outstretched in a protective gesture.

Ailinn braced herself, her nails biting into her palms. She prepared to confront the flame-haired Dalcassian, but when the door burst open, 'twas not Bran who entered in. . . .

Ailinn withdrew from her reverie, her gaze traveling to Hakon. He watched her, fires banked in his eyes.

Fresh pricklings of fear combed through her. She averted her eyes to find Skallagrim folding the bridal mantle back into the sea chest. Just as Ailinn became aware of the room's uncommon silence, Thora's bulk moved before her and blocked her view.

Face dark with anger, Thora yanked the silken cordage of Murieann's girdle from Ailinn's grasp. She lumbered back across the room with the prize, then on a sudden, inspired thought, retrieved a leather strap from the side floor and flung it at Ailinn's feet.

Ailinn recovered the strip, realizing Thora intended she

should belt her gown with the piece, then recognizing the strap to be the tether that had bound her wrists.

Mayhaps, 'twas a more fitting girdle than the braided silk, she reasoned with a twinge of despondency. She was a slave now. A slave with an uncertain future. But, then, what future ever be certain?

The hours dragged slowly as the day aged to evening. Skallagrim saw that Thora set Ailinn no task that might cause her injury or mar her with bruises. Thora took unkindly to his interference but, in the end, busied Ailinn with simple chores— setting the loom to rights, twisting thread, tending the hearth fires, and replenishing the men's cups.

Ailinn felt Hakon's burning gaze outline her every movement. She grew discomfited beneath his interests and breathed relief when at last he departed.

Meanwhile, Skallagrim sat in his carved chair without remark as he shaped a portion of bone into a gaming piece. 'Twas not until he rose that Ailinn spied the battle-ax resting against the chair's side.

Skallagrim moved to the end of the room, where a frame bed sat upon the elevated flooring. When he beckoned she join him, Ailinn's heart rose to her throat.

Warily she crossed the hall. But as she reached the platform, Skallagrim tossed several fur robes to the floor, then bid her step up onto the planking. Slipping an iron ring about her ankle, he chained her to the foot of his bed.

Long afterward, Ailinn lay awake in the dark while Thora snored softly upon her pallet and Skallagrim rattled out long, deep breaths. Embers glowed red within the hearth, partially illuminating the room.

Ailinn fixed her gaze upon the gable end of the hall, to the triangular opening just beneath the slope of the roof. There she could view a sprinkling of stars.

In all Creation, didst God know she be here? Didst He heed her prayers or abandon her amongst the pagans?

Her thoughts went to Thora. The Norsewoman would ride her hard, if allowed, deeming her no more than a common slave to be exploited and abused at will.

Hakon, too, would clearly use—and abuse—her, but in other, unpleasant ways. He was a black-hearted heathen, and only Skallagrim stood betwixt him and his desires.

Yet, 'twas the chieftain's own designs that preyed most heavily upon her mind. What cold and bitter fate didst he cast for her? What faceless destiny waited on the morrow?

Inexplicably her thoughts turned to the white-haired Dane, as ever they had this day. She regretted not her insult to him, she told herself, for he was a godless Norseman like the rest. Yet, she could not help but wonder whether her life would have been better had he succeeded in purchasing her and she lay this night beneath his roof.

An accompanying thought startled Ailinn, and she turned into the furs and closed her eyes against the vivid image it formed. Warm currents rushed through her. Still, the vision lingered, bringing heat to her cheeks.

If the man sought to acquire her, then surely he intentioned that she lay beneath more than his roof. . . .

Lyting drew deeper into the shadows as voices erupted nearby, two noisy revelers fracturing the late-night silence with their song.

Swathed in a great, gray cloak, Lyting tugged the hood downward. Even on a moonless night his bright mane marked him. Tonight the moon hung like a fat crescent in the sky, and he held no wish to be discovered.

He remained in the darkness of the narrow side lane as the merrymakers passed into view—two Danish seamen with a maid betwixt them. Angry shouts discharged from a neigboring *hus*, and someone hurled a bucket from the door of another.

Lyting stepped to the edge of the passage as the trio continued on, then returned his interest across the wooded lane to the *hus* of Thora Kolsdóttir.

It had been a fairly simple matter to locate the *hus*. He had arrived in time to observe Hakon enter the dwelling and to overhear the voices raised within. Presumably, 'twas Skallagrim and Thora who matched volume for volume, though he could discern little of their argument.

He had waited, palm resting on sword hilt, unsure why he had come or what action he might take if need arose. Soon the *hus* quieted. Still, he waited.

Once, the door opened and a dour-looking woman stepped forth to pitch a bucketful of water into the yard. 'Twas then that he glimpsed the maid's slender figure as she moved near the portal—garbed in green now, her rich auburn hair spilling past her hips. An instantaneous flash of heat had jolted through him, taking him by surprise.

Lyting girt himself, even now, against the directness of that response, so immediate, instinctive, elemental—all spurred by the mere sight of the Irish beauty.

Mayhaps he should have sought to free another, a small voice pricked from a remote corner of his mind. This one lay beyond his grasp. Yet, had he emptied his coffers and found sufficient coin to deliver every captive borne from Ireland, he knew in his soul that he still would be here tonight.

In time Hakon emerged from the *hus* and departed in the direction of the docks. Lyting eased his vigil, resolving to stay atime longer, until he need leave to take up his watch of the *Sea Falcon*. There, at the harbor, he would have clear view of the *Wind Raven* as well.

Sleep he could not seek before dawn's breaking. But he held certain that when he finally gained his rest, his dreams—like the thoughts that weighed on him these many long hours—would be inescapably entangled with masses of auburn hair.

Chapter 3

Ailinn trailed Thora along the street, clutching a bundle of soiled linens to her hip. Ankle cuffs and chains hampered her steps.

Thora scowled back at Ailinn's lagging pace with mounting impatience. Grasping a handful of hair at the side of Ailinn's head, she forced her on at a quickened pace.

Ailinn boiled as Thora released her a short distance later, her scalp yet screaming its protest. She blinked away the moisture that had sprung to her eyes. The Norsewoman wielded her authority with obvious enjoyment. But Ailinn refused to add one crumb to her pleasure. Whatever Thora wrought upon her, she vowed she would not cry out, nor plead, nor allow one tear to fall. Masking all emotion from her face, she fixed her gaze past Thora's broad back and struggled on beneath her burdens.

Increasingly Ailinn grew aware of the marked interest her passage stirred. Men turned from their tasks to appraise her from beneath arched brows and partially lowered lids, their gazes bold, assessing, edged with a certain hunger. By contrast, the women glared, sharp-eyed and tight-lipped.

Ill caring for the attention she drew, Ailinn shifted her eyes to the weathered boards beneath her feet and proceeded along the course in Thora's shadow.

In short time they reached the harbor. Thora led Ailinn along the wharf to the farmost end. Here, the planking ceased and the shore stretched a fair distance to the palisaded seawall.

Numerous tents occupied a large, open tract of land that lay between the selvage of water and the border of town. Ships, likewise, populated the expanse, having been grounded ashore. The largest vessels remained moored at pilings mid-harbor or tied at the piers. Ailinn sighted Skallagrim's dragonship, its monster head grinning. Her stomach twisted into a hard, icy knot.

Gruffly Thora directed that she kneel with her bundle upon a little projection that jutted off the quay. Handing Ailinn a paddle board and small, wooden tub filled with soap, Thora motioned that she commence with the washing. Thora then stepped several paces apart to join a clutch of townswomen gathered there. Proudly she lifted aside the bright panel of cloth that covered the front of her chemise and displayed Murieann's girdle.

Ailinn simmered as she thrust a tunic into the water and swished it about. She derived a small measure of perverse satisfaction seeing that the cord barely met about Thora's thick waist. It had hung at length on Murieann's slender form.

Ailinn turned back to her task, chiding herself for such an unchristian and mean-spirited thought. Yet, 'twas not the thought itself that disturbed her so much as her pleasuring in it. In truth, she felt no charity toward the Norsewoman, nor any of her kind. Only a rocky barrenness of heart.

Overhead, gulls cried out against the clear-blue vault of sky as they stretched their wings to the warmth of the sun. Along the wharf seamen mended nets and loaded waiting craft while merchants vended their goods.

Ailinn scrubbed at a stubborn spot, then doused the linen once more and sat back on her heels. Brushing away a wisp of hair from her eyes, she squinted against the brightness of the day and envied the birds their freedom.

Joyous squeals of children erupted nearby, drawing Ailinn's eye. She caught a vivid patch of color as it swept up into the air—a small boy in naught but a red tunic, being hoisted high above a man's head. The sprite's waggling legs and squirming bulk obstructed her view of the man. The child laughed gleefully and tossed back his dark headful of curls as his captor apparently nuzzled his stomach.

The man began to lower the child and Ailinn next found herself gazing fully upon the white-haired Dane. In a heartbeat

his crystal blue eyes met with hers, but not before she realized
that he stood in the shallows before her stripped bare to his
loincloth!

Ailinn gasped, letting go the linen from her fingers. Quickly
she tore away her gaze and snatched the garment back up from
the water. She felt shivery and breathless and jolted to her very
core.

Ailinn scrubbed at the tunic vigorously, heat flaming her
cheeks. The vision of sculpted muscles, expansive shoulders,
and hard, sinewed legs continued to burn in her mind's eye.

Several minutes passed before she found the courage to look
toward him again. To her relief, he was absorbed in play with
the child—children—she corrected as she discovered a second
little boy, clad in blue, a twin to the first.

The Dane caught the babe up beneath the arms. Stepping
deeper into the water, he swung the child round in a wide
circle, lifting and dipping the boy in one continuous, wavelike
motion.

Ailinn watched, momentarily transfixed by the warm, fa-
milial scene playing out before her. It stunned her to see this
caring side of a Norseman. At the same time she found herself
wholly affected by the sheer magnificence of the man.

He moved with power and grace—beautiful, potent, thrill-
ing to behold. The word *leonine* again sprang to mind, as it had
yesterday, when her eyes first touched him. The long lines of
his body appeared supple, resilient, yet well defined. Their
underlying strength had been forged, she imagined, through
years of discipline and rigorous training.

Ailinn gazed on the rich play of muscle through his chest
and arms, then drifted her eyes to his handsome features. She
noted the ease of his smile and the unmistakable affection
contained in his eyes as he looked on the babe and lifted him
heavenward.

Ailinn returned her attention to the garment in her hands and
began to beat it with the small paddle. *His?* she wondered of
the children, noting they bore him little resemblance, what
with their ebony locks and what appeared to be thumb-size
impressions in their little chins. He had none, though she
bethought to have glimpsed dimples in his cheeks.

She wisked a glance to the Dane and back again. Aye,
dimples. Creases, really. Deep ones. In each cheek.

Ailinn reversed the cloth and pounded it soundly.

And his eyes . . . she summoned them to mind. His eyes
were as blue as the lakes of Killarney, though lighter—brilliant
and clear. The children's were indiscernible at this distance,
obviously not the same sparkling shade.

Ailinn rubbed soap into a stain, then stayed her busy hands,
startled that aught about the Dane should be of concern to her.
She turned the cloth over and took up the paddle again.

Of course the man wouldst have children, she reasoned with
herself. Likely he had sired more than these two.

Ailinn stole a sideways glance of his splendid frame.

Many more! Indeed, what woman would turn him from her
bed?

She plunged the garment into the water and sloshed it around.
Withdrawing it, she wrung it hard, then slapped it down on the
growing pile of sodden cloths.

As Ailinn reached for another linen, she felt the heat of his
eyes upon her. Imagination, she reproved and dismissed the
unsettling feeling. Still, the sensation remained.

Slowly she lifted her gaze and immediately lost herself in a
crystal blue sea. Ailinn took a long, difficult swallow, her
mouth and throat suddenly gone dry. Several moments passed,
an eternity, before she could pull away from his intense regard.

She lowered her eyes—a mistake—for they came to rest
upon his flat, tapering waist. Then the narrow strip of cloth
fastened low about his hips. Then his long, hard, marvelously
sculpted legs.

Ailinn felt the thud of her heart, high in her chest, and
listened to it pound in her ears.

The vibrations of the wharf-planking alerted her to Thora's
approach. A moment later the Norsewoman barked out some
displeasure and gave a jarring shove to her back. Ailinn nearly
pitched from the landing, inadvertently toppling a small mound
of Thora's chemises into the water.

Pain seared her scalp as Thora dragged her upright by the
hair. Ailinn saw the Dane start forward, thunder in his face.
But at the same time she glimpsed Thora's hand in her edge of
vision, drawing back to strike.

"*Skallagrim!*" Ailinn hurled the name as though it were a
weapon.

Thora stayed her hand midair and growled beneath her

breath. Releasing Ailinn, she stepped back, lips thinned and nostrils flared. She then jabbed a finger toward the fallen clothes, carping in astringent tones till Ailinn retrieved them from the water.

Satisfied, Thora straightened, smoothed the panels of cloth that overlay her gown front and back, then, casting a glance to the white-haired Dane, returned to her friends.

Anger exploded through Lyting. He started forward when the bearish-looking woman descended upon the maid. Thora Kolsdóttir. He recognized her from yestereven and gained an instant dislike for the woman. A moment later he halted as the maid called out something and Thora's arm went rigid. The woman looked ready to chew iron rivets, but she released her hold on the girl.

Lyting rubbed his hand along his jaw. What couldst the maid have spoken? He watched her pluck the fallen garments from the river. A smile touched his lips, then died as he discovered Thora's eyes upon him. Incredibly, she tried to draw his interest as she strutted toward the cluster of women, giving a slight pitch to her great hips. In truth, the movement produced more joggle than sway. Meanwhile, her companions whispered and tittered amongst themselves as their eyes glanced over him.

Lyting felt nauseated. Then his anger boiled afresh. How long had these women been observing him? Had they seen how his gaze fairly consumed the maid? How their eyes met and wed for that one brief moment? Jealous shrews. Was *that* the cause of this scene? Didst they punish the maid on his account?

His choler rose another degree as the women continued to graze him with covetous eyes. If 'twas a closer look they desired, then they would have it, along with a blistering piece of his mind.

He began to take a forward step, but the children chose that very moment to wrap themselves about his legs.

"Look, Uncle. Ketil." Richard waved toward the wharf.

"Ketil," chimed Kylan.

Lyting bridled his impulses, remembering the lads. He hauled his eyes from the women and sliced a glance along the pier. There, he spied Ketil examining a length of line. Nearby stood Skallagrim—watching, solemn-faced.

Lyting stilled as he and the chieftain regarded each other across the distance. Skallagrim raised his bearded chin, then shifted his gaze to the maid and then to his sister, Thora.

"Up, Uncle." Kylan pulled at Lyting's thigh and hip in an attempt to scramble upward. Richard likewise began to scale his uncle's other leg.

Stifling the fire that yet burned within, Lyting looked down on the round little heads and allowed a partial smile to return. He tossled their ebony locks, then lifted them, one to each hip.

Again, the boys called out and waved at Ketil till they captured his attention. Ketil's teeth gleamed through his haze of beard, and he lifted his hand in acknowledgment.

Lyting nodded a greeting to Ketil as well, his arms occupied with the two lively pups. Still distracted, he deflected his gaze back toward the maiden.

'Twould seem that Skallagrim watched over his prize captive as closely as he, himself, did. Likely, the chieftain was not the sort of man who would welcome interference with that which he held as his own—slave *or* sister.

Lyting stabbed a look back at the women, yet debating whether to confront them with his displeasure. A muscle flexed along his jaw. Teeth clamped tight, he vented a breath. For the moment he would resist the temptation—as long as they left the maid undisturbed.

Já, he resolved, glancing once more toward the auburn-haired beauty. He would remain here for the time, near at hand, and enjoy sporting with young Richard and Kylan.

As his humor flowed slowly back, Lyting sank down into the coolness of the water, drawing the boys with him. Their gasps quickly dissolved to laughter as he squiggled his fingers over their soft bellies and flashed them an openhearted smile.

Ketil watched with gladsome approval at the cheery little scene. 'Twas good to see Lyting relaxing with the mites. He loved children and should have a hall filled with his own. But with his mind set on shutting himself within the sterile walls of Corbie, Rurik and Brienne's children would be the only ones Lyting would ever enjoy.

A shame, Ketil opined as he examined the line of seal-hide for imperfections and tested its strength. The Good Lord saved Lyting from the brink of death, well and true. But that didst not necessarily mean that He spared him apurpose for Corbie.

Lyting thought in that vein, however, and it seemed naught could dissuade him.

Ketil chuckled at Richard's antics and waved again. He caught the twinkle in Lyting's eye as he scooped up the boy and dangled him upside down.

"You sailed with that man?" a roughened voice sounded off to his left.

Ketil turned and took measure of the weathered sea-warrior who stood several arm's lengths away. He possessed as brambly a mane of hair and beard as himself and stood nearly as tall.

"*Já*," Ketil answered with a shadow of caution. "We arrived yestermorn from Normandy."

The man seemed to consider this for a moment, then his eye ranged to Lyting. "Your friend tried to buy a slave of mine." He nodded toward a maid who labored over her wash at the end of the wharf. A maid of exceptional beauty.

Ketil lifted a brow in utter surprise. He had heard of the incident from Aleth and Brienne. But they made no mention that the maid Lyting sought to free was one so fair.

Ketil tugged at his beard, a smile spreading beneath the fiery thicket. 'Twas a good sign. Mayhaps, his badgerings and advisements would bear fruit after all.

Ketil smoothed his mustache and shrugged casually. "I imagine that one draws many an eye."

"*Já*, that she does. But your friend seemed more intent than most." The man looked again to Lyting and considered him with a hard stare. "Normandy, eh? Has your pale-haired friend a name?"

Ketil bent an eye over the sea-warrior, gauging how he should respond. "Lyting Atlison, blood-nephew to Duke Rollo himself and brother to the Baron de Valsemé. We sailed under the baron's banner. And you?"

The man rolled an eye to Ketil. "Skallagrim, master of the *Vind Raven*. I sail under my own banner." Unexpectedly one side of his mouth drew into the semblance of a smile, then faded. His attention returned to Lyting.

"Best advise Atlison to take a long, cold swim. His desire for my slave is obvious, but the maid is not for purchase. He'll have to find another to bed."

"Him?" Ketil fairly choked, though the thought of Lyting "in lust" was wondrously heartening.

Again, a faint knell of caution sounded somewhere in Ketil's brain, and he felt a compelling need to put Skallagrim's concerns to rest. He hoped Lyting would understand the necessity to depict matters as he must to their Odin-worshipping kinsman.

"*Nei*, there be naught to glean in his interest," Ketil avowed. "Those Franks have turned him into a knee-bending Christian. He seeks a monkish life on our return to Normandy. 'Twas not for himself but for the baronne that he sought to acquire the maid. She is a softhearted woman, a Frank."

Skallagrim looked to Ketil skeptically. "Odd that she would choose a slave of such beauty to tempt her husband."

Ketil huffed into his beard. Obviously Skallagrim had not seen the Lady Brienne nor heard the saga of hers and Rurik's joining. Theirs was the sort of love tale which the skalds remembered in verse and celebrated in the halls.

"*Nei*. I didst not mean that the baronne selected the maid. She left the matter of purchase to Lyting. He is after all, a full-blooded son of Danmark. Understandably, he chose the most beautiful."

To Ketil's surprise, Skallagrim cracked a smile.

"I imagine the baron wouldst have been appreciative of that, had he succeeded!" Ketil remained silent as the chieftain cast a suspect eye to Lyting. "He seeks to be a monk, say you? I have heard that the Christian religion can unman a warrior. But he does not look unmanned from here."

"Lyting honors the vows he seeks to embrace, even now," Ketil maintained staunchly but truthfully. "He suffers as any man who denies his body. He finds his relief as you suggest, by taking frequent swims in cold lakes!"

The tension seemed to seep out of Skallagrim's shoulders and limbs. His smile reappeared, then mellowed as he shook his head. "'Tis unfathomable, this priest-class devotion to celibacy that the Christians so revere."

Ketil found no response as his thoughts went to Aleth. To his mind, the fairest and most enjoyable achievement of Divine creation was Woman, and *she* God fashioned expressly for Man.

"At least your friend will enjoy the riches of the church without the need to first plunder them!" Skallagrim grinned.

Ketil gave a brief nod and matched his smile as though to agree. He hoped Lyting would move with care about Skallagrim and the beautiful slavegirl. A misstep could prove fateful.

Ailinn rose to her feet, slipping a last glance to the Dane as she took up the dense weight of wet linens. Their eyes brushed for the barest of moments before she turned and followed Thora back along the wharf.

The vision of the bright-haired warrior continued to play in her mind as she and Thora retraced her earlier steps, turning down one lane, then another. Suddenly they came upon a gathering—mostly Arabs and Northmen—crowded about something of interest. In their midst Ailinn spied the maids of Clonmel, displayed before all as common slaves, proffered for a bit of coin. 'Twas then that her gaze fell on Lia.

"Ní hea!" Ailinn lurched forward a step, her shackles trammeling her footfall. Their eyes found each other's just as Thora cuffed Ailinn alongside the back of her head, where marks would be hidden beneath the hair.

Ailinn bent beneath the blow, clutching the sodden laundry to her side. She tasted the sharp, bitter hatred that filled the chalice of her soul. Hatred for all that was Norse.

Slowly she straightened and cleaved Thora with such a look of vehemence and utter loathing that the Norsewoman drew back a pace.

Ailinn's eyes then sought Lia's once more. Their gazes met and held across an ocean of pain in one last farewell.

As she forced her steps on to follow Thora, Ailinn felt her heart splinter, then burst into a thousand pieces.

Woodenly Ailinn tracked Thora's steps back to the house. As she approached the portal, she observed Hakon within the fenced side yard, his back facing her.

Unclad to the waist, he peered into a small disk of polished metal, nailed to a sapling, and scraped away the growth that covered his jaw. Though Hakon appeared unconcerned with the women's arrival, Ailinn saw that he watched her in his mirror as she moved toward the door and entered the dwelling.

Thora had no sooner set her to a task than Hakon appeared

on the threshold and stepped inside. He paused by the barrel of ale that sat near the entry and took a hollowed gourd from the wall. Ladling up a portion of the golden liquid, he drank it slowly, his eyes passing over her where she knelt by the hearth. Draining the last of the beverage, he returned the dipper to its peg, wiped his mouth, and departed without a word.

Unease settled in Ailinn's bone. She strove to force Hakon from her mind as she coaxed the embers to life. Thora lingered by the door a moment longer, gazing after Hakon's back. Her eyes then drew to Ailinn.

Thora moved to a weathered trunk that sat along the wall. Opening it, she withdrew a stout chain, several arm's lengths in measure, and a heavy lock. Her countenance lightened as she started toward Ailinn.

With a grunt, Thora half-bent, half-squatted to remove the linkage that bound Ailinn's ankles. She then reshackled Ailinn's left leg with the second, much longer piece of chain. Rising, Thora proceeded to wrap the end about the carved, timbered post opposite the hearth and secure it with the lock.

Ailinn remained motionless as Thora sought her mantle and advanced toward the door. On a parting thought, Thora turned back, grabbed up an abandoned distaff bearing a fluffy knob of wool, and returned to Ailinn long enough to thrust it into her hands. She then seized upon a shallow basket—one Ailinn recognized from yestereve as having held the supper's fish—and quit the house. Thora's voice sounded outside as she presumably informed Hakon of her departure.

The moment drew out. Stillness descended upon the house. Silence.

Ailinn sank beside the hearth, alert, observant, her ears strained for the slightest sound. She fingered the wool, then absently began to twist the fibers to begin a thread as she glanced about the empty hall. Abruptly Ailinn stayed her hands and dropped her gaze. Thora had provided her no spindle. The Norsewoman never intended that she should work the wool.

Just then the room darkened as though the sun had escaped behind the clouds and had been momentarily blotted out. Fine hairs raised along the back of Ailinn's neck. Her gaze drew to the door to behold Hakon framed within its portal.

Ailinn ceased to breathe. Hakon's eyes smoldered deep in their sockets, two burning coals, scorching through her. She prayed he had come for naught but the ale and would quickly slake his thirst and be gone. Her hopes withered as Hakon stepped inside and passed the barrel, sparing it no interest.

He came to a halt. Tunic in hand, he wiped the sweat from his bare chest, then threw it to the side-floor. Eyes never leaving her, he continued forward.

Ailinn rose on watery legs as Hakon uttered something in his Nordic tongue and closed the distance.

"I do not understand." Her grip tightened about the distaff, and she edged backward.

Again Hakon spoke, these words different, though as incomprehensible as the first.

"*N'on digná tu.* I do not understand. Leave me be!"

The ankle cuff bit into her flesh as the chain jarred to its end and held fast. Still, she strove to remove herself, straining against the bonds, her leg and the linkage stretched tight.

Hakon bridged the narrow space in an easy stride and clamped iron fingers about her arms. Terror sheared through Ailinn as he hauled her against his rock-hard chest. Frantically she thrashed and pitched within his hold but gained no advantage. A slim hope glimmered—a single word. Yet, as the name of her grizzled protector rose in her throat and reached her lips, it was crushed beneath Hakon's bruising mouth.

Ailinn cried against the assault, her pleas stifled beneath his ravaging kiss. Desperately she angled the distaff and stabbed for his side.

Hakon snarled and wrenched back as the stick caught him low across the waist. Knocking the piece from her hands, he thrust Ailinn to the floor, then dropped to cover her. But she rolled from under him and clambered to gain the side-floor. Hakon aided her efforts as he grasped her about the waist and tossed her up onto fur throws.

Pain tore at Ailinn's leg as the chain jolted against its limits once more. In the skip of a heartbeat Hakon flung himself atop her. Pinning her arms, he pressed her into the pelts. She felt the hard length of his ravenous passion as he ground his hips against her.

Yanking at the folds of her skirt, he bared her leg and swept his roughened hand upward over thigh and hip to capture her buttock. Forcing her against him, Hakon seized her lips in a brutal kiss.

Ailinn writhed beneath him, each breath hard won, the air pressed from her lungs. Just when she feared she might suffocate, he shifted. Grasping the fullness of her breast, he coarsely caressed her. Ardor blazed in his eyes. Impatient, Hakon fisted the gown's neckline and tore it free.

Crippling fear overtook Ailinn as the fabric rent. The sound of it filled her ears, then changed and swelled in volume to an earsplitting roar. Just as cool air touched her breast, Hakon's weight abruptly left her. He catapulted backward by an unseen force, and Ailinn next found herself staring up through open space at the rafters.

Twisting, she caught sight of Skallagrim as he hurled Hakon across the room. Like a great, raging bear he set upon Hakon. Dragging him to his feet, he slogged him in stomach and jaw, then backhanded him across the face.

Hakon hurtled rearward against the side-floor, yelling out as his ribs struck against the edge of board. Mouth and nose bleeding, a cut above his eye, he stirred to gain some advantage.

But Skallagrim's fury stormed unabated. Grabbing an ax down from the wall, he clutched the shaft at each end then started once more for Hakon. As Hakon recovered his footage, Skallagrim caught him straight on with the ax handle. Ramming it across Hakon's throat, he shoved him up against one of the hall's stout posts, nearly lifting him from his feet.

"Cease, Uncle!" Hakon rasped beneath the wood. "Wouldst you kill me for a mere kiss of your slave? I didst but seek a taste of her lips and fill my hand with her breasts."

"You lie," Skallagrim growled in his face.

"*Nei*," Hakon spat with disdain. "I wouldst not spoil that which you so favor to gift the Byzantine. I have not forgotten her usefulness to you."

Skallagrim eyed him with a hard, incisive gaze. "See that you remember." His words resonated. "'Twill be a long journey, Hakon. Take what slavewomen you will to satisfy your lusts for the duration. But be assured, touch this one and I shall personally cut your throat, nephew or not."

At that, Skallagrim released Hakon. Angrily Hakon snatched up his tunic from the side-floor, and with a single glance back to Ailinn, he stalked from the hall.

Ailinn gripped the wreckage of fabric to her breast. Eyes

huge and nerves racked raw, she trembled violently as her grim-faced master approached.

The chieftain looked down on her, marked her ruined dress, the fear in her eyes, and then examined her for bruises. Freeing the chain from the post, he led Ailinn to the back of the hall, where he secured her, as the night before, to the foot of his bed.

As Ailinn huddled upon the pallet, Skallagrim positioned his great chair to face the door, then took up his seat. Placing his ax across his lap, he kept watch, prepared for any who wouldst give challenge or dare to thwart his plans.

Chapter 4

The twins trotted happily along the lane ahead of their uncle, their little mouths puckered around a piece of honeycomb.

As they approached the *hus*, Lyting lengthened his stride to catch up with them, then pushed open the door before sticky little hands could touch it.

Aleth greeted them with a smile and shake of her head as the three entered in, licking their fingers and lips.

"Lyting, how you do spoil the children!" She laughed, catching up a damp cloth and coming forward.

Her smile widened as, one after the other, Richard and Kylan offered up their portions of the waxy comb for her to taste.

"*Merci. Mais non, mes petits.* Though, mayhaps we best tidy you up before you give your *maman* and *papa* a big hug." Aleth canted a glance to Lyting. "You as well." She raised on tiptoe to wipe a trace of honey from his chin.

Lyting chuckled at her motherly attentions and shifted the small crock of golden nectar from beneath his arm.

"For you, my lady. A small token. How would men such as we fare without your tender ministrations?" He winked at the boys.

"You could use a little fussing over," she chided, tugging at one of the long, silvered locks that reached low on Lyting's chest. "When you be of a mind to part with some of this bountiful mane, come to me. I shall see that you have a fine cut."

"Soon, Aleth." He flashed her a smile, the creases deepening in his cheeks. "I confess, I scarce look forward to the tonsure and have been enjoying the full wealth and measure of my hair these months past. But 'tis yours for the shearing when the time comes."

Lyting gave over the jar to Aleth, then glanced toward the door at the rear of the *skali*.

"They are in the yard," Aleth advised as she set the crockery on the side floor. Kneeling to the boys' height, she began wiping Kylan's face. "Be along with you, now." She shooed him blithely. "I'll bring the boys in a moment."

"*þakk*, Aleth."

As Lyting emerged from the building, he beheld Brienne, all grace and loveliness, sitting beneath an ancient silver lime tree. She looked off to the right, her elegant profile silhouetted against the dark luxury of her hair, which flowed freely, as Rurik preferred.

The lime spread out all about her, above and behind, shimmering with pale green foliage. Translucent and heart-shaped, the leaves were richly silvered underneath with fine hairs so that each new breath of air stirred them to glitter and wink with sunlight, the effect spellbinding.

Had it not been for the faint line that traced Brienne's forehead, Lyting would have thought her to be merely preoccupied, lost in pleasant thoughts. But now he saw that her gaze was fixed on Rurik where he stood stone still, gazing out over the fence, a parchment in his hand.

Brienne began to lift a hand toward Rurik and her lips parted softly as though she would speak. But then she hesitated, apparently deciding otherwise, and let her hand fall once more to her lap. As though Rurik sensed her thoughts, he looked toward her and met her eyes. Lyting felt the fine strand of tension spun out betwixt them.

Uncertain of the scene, Lyting cleared his throat. The two turned as one, Brienne smiling with a genuine warmth and gladness to see him, Rurik coming away from the corner of the yard to greet him.

Feeling the moment to be yet awkward, Lyting glanced again to the spectacular tree and attempted to lighten the mood.

"My lady has chosen her time well," he teased gently. "For all its glory, one is not able to long enjoy the shelter of the lime. Soon 'twill begin to drop a sticky dew from its leaves and continue till summer's end—a vexsome trial for even its most devoted admirer."

"Mayhaps 'twould be worth enduring." Brienne tilted her face upward and lovingly scanned the luminous canopy.

Just then Rurik came to stand aside her, propping his foot upon the bench where she sat. Brienne immediately laid her hand to his knee, her violet eyes coupling with his.

"My dear husband holds that the lime is much like a beautiful woman, difficult to possess and not without her trials. Each ordeal, says he, is a testing of a man's true mettle—his steadfastness and determination. A testing of his very heart and soul."

Lyting swept his gaze to the tree, all expression deserting his face. Golden-brown eyes and deep auburn hair shimmered before his mind's eye as one with the leaves. He blinked away the vision and suddenly 'came aware that his heart had begun to race and his blood to pound through his veins.

The boisterous invasion of children broke the spell. Giggling and squealing, the twins scurried across the yard and into the arms of their parents. Lyting stepped apart and rubbed a hand across his eyes. When he glanced back, he met Brienne's silent, questioning gaze, her head tilted to one side.

Kylan quickly reclaimed his mother's attention, placing small hands to her cheeks and turning her face to his. Rurik, meanwhile, had plucked up young Richard and perched him on a hip. Irrepressible, the babe tugged to be higher and would not be satisfied till he could wrap his arms about his father's neck.

Rurik chuckled. Giving over the parchment to Lyting, he disengaged his young heir and resettled him against his chest. At once Richard began to pat at his father's chin.

Lyting's gaze dropped to the cockled vellum as it curled in on itself. It bore precise, heavily inked characters. He recognized them to be Greek.

One fine brow rose a fraction. A message from the East? Byzantium? It had been years since Rurik served there, a member of the emperor's elite Varangian Guard.

He skimmed the parchment once again. What nature of missive didst the scroll contain? he wondered. Surely it held importance to have been transmitted from such a great distance and after so many years of silence. Its content obviously troubled his brother.

Lyting cut a glance to Rurik and found him watching. With a brief nod Rurik indicated he should examine the document more closely, then turned to walk about the yard with Brienne and the children.

Unscrolling the piece, Lyting studied the rows of neat, compact lettering. At first glance the script appeared as thwarting as the Roman system of writing. He had begun instruction in both forms—Greek and Latin—under the tutelage of Brother Bernard in preparation for Corbie.

His grasp for the Greek, though rudimentary, far exceeded his capacity for the latter. But then Greek was already familiar to him. He had studied it years past when he readied to join Rurik and the Varangians in the East. To that end his brother had dispatched a Byzantine scholar to Limfjord to instruct him personally in the language and strict codes of court etiquette. But Lyting never reached the golden city, for Norwegian Harald struck Denmark and ravaged Jutland's western coast. Abandoning the prospect of a bright future with the Guard, he took up sword and shield to defend his homeland. Sailing with the Danish fleet, he engaged the Norwegians on the North Sea. . . .

Laboriously Lyting's eye moved across the script as he sounded out each letter, each word, groping for the meaning. Someone had died, a Varangian—Askel the Red. The name rang familiar, but Lyting could connect it with no accounting that he might have heard. Other names followed, these also Norse. The parchment was dated five months prior at Dyrrachium, signed by one Stephanites Cerularius. Again, the name held no significance.

"Some ale, Lyting?" Aleth proffered a cup at his elbow.

Lyting pulled his gaze from the text and accepted her offering. "þakk, Aleth." As he drew on the liquid, he caught sight of Kylan yawning hugely in his mother's arms.

"You have fair exhausted these little ones, Lyting," Brienne called out. "They shall need their naps early."

Aleth crossed to disencumber Rurik of little Richard, who was rubbing his eyes. As the women advanced toward the house with the children, Lyting saw Brienne's gaze stray to the parchment. She hugged her son to herself, though her smile remained fastened in place.

"*Merci* for amusing the boys, Lyting." Her words gave no hint that aught disturbed her. "Mayhaps I shall be able to enjoy a little rest myself."

Lyting regarded Brienne as she disappeared into the darkness of the *hus*. Withdrawing his gaze, he rolled the letter closed and tapped it thoughtfully against his palm. With unhurried pace he approached Rurik and extended forth the scroll.

"We sailed for Hedeby earlier than first you intentioned. 'Twas for this, was it not?"

Rurik nodded, a somberness to his eyes as he accepted back the parchment.

Lyting dredged distant memories and long-forgotten conversations from the backwaters of his mind.

"Askel the Red—didst he not serve under your command in Constantinople?"

"*Já.* Askel was one of my finest officers. He, Koll, Leidolf, Thengil, and Vegeir were as my right hand when we quelled the palace uprising and preserved Leo's crown. It earned us the title of the 'Dragons Around the Throne.'"

Lyting recognized the last three names from the scroll.

"I recall the tale, though the details be somewhat clouded now. You foiled a plot to assassinate the emperor, Leo Sophos, and his infant son. 'Twas a rather elaborate conspiracy, was it not? Knotted with complexities, double-dealings, deceits. A 'tangle of vipers,' you called it, 'nesting in every corner.'"

"*Já.* Distinctively 'Byzantine.'" A grim smile etched Rurik's lips. "I never told you the full of it, *broðir*. But mayhaps 'tis well that I do so now, for I know not where this will lead." He looked to the scroll, venting a breath, then met Lyting's gaze.

"I joined the palace guard shortly after Leo's third wife had died, and he had taken Zoë Carbonopsina as his mistress. The Church's Eastern 'Greek' branch is more rigid in matters of marriage than Rome. Even in the event a spouse dies, second marriages are frowned upon and third marriages strictly prohibited. Leo, himself, had reinforced the Church's position years earlier, issuing a special law of his own. But then his first wife died childless, as did his second. When he took a third wife, 'twas an open breach with the Church. But soon she, too, died, leaving Leo without male issue."

Rurik pushed a hand through his golden hair and stepped toward the lime tree.

"A fourth marriage was beyond question. I can tell you that Leo's brother, Alexander, was well pleased that the line of succession should pass to him. But then Zoë conceived. Leo saw to it that she spent her confinement in the palace's 'purple chamber,' where all the empresses officially birthed their children. Zoë presented Leo with a son, and from that time he devoted himself to seeing his heir legitimized.

"After much controversy, the Patriarch agreed to baptize the child in the Hagia Sophia and to christen him Constantine Porphyrogentius, 'born in the purple.' But 'twas a condition that Leo set aside Zoë. Instead, three days after the ceremony, Leo married Zoë and elevated her to the status of Augusta."

Rurik began to pace. "A storm of angry protest arose, fueling the many factions and quarrels that beset Leo from the past. He was even barred from entering the church on Christmas Day and again, twelve days later, on the Feast of the Epiphany. Yet, Leo was intractable. Resolute. He turned to Rome, circumventing the Patriarch's authority, and appealed directly to the Pope—much to the Pontiff's delight. Leo received his dispensation. His marriage was validated. With that accomplished, he forced the Patriarch, Nicholas Mysticus, from his chair and replaced him with another.

"You can imagine the response that wrought." Rurik threw a hand to the air. "The political parties—the Greens and the Blues—the exiled Patriarch, a score of others, each with its own squabble, all clawing for power and profit." He stopped his pacing. "And then there was the emperor's brother, Alexander, an indolent, self-pleasuring creature who had much to lose."

Rurik expelled a long breath, lifting his face heavenward and bracing his hands on his hips. "Mayhaps 'twas best, *broðir*, that you didst not come to Constantinople as we planned. Sharks swarmed about the throne. Death waited in the shadow of the crown."

Rurik fell to a reflective silence.

Lyting bided the moment, digesting all his brother spoke.

"And what of the plot to remove Leo?" he prompted several minutes later.

" 'Twas nearly the emperor's undoing." Rurik paced to the fence, then turned.

"Shall we say, I 'intercepted' secret directives that involved a conspiracy to murder the Imperial family—exclusive of Alexander, that is. The assassins plotted to provoke the Blues and Greens to riot in the Hippodrome whilst the emperor was in attendance. Riots in the Hippodrome are also distinctively 'Byzantine.' "

Rurik's mouth set in a firm line, his features darkening with memory.

"The riots were intended to conceal their treachery. The emperor's assassins would already be positioned in close proximity to his person—presumably trusted, high-ranking members of court to enjoy such privilege of access. We knew not their names. Meanwhile, within the Sacred Imperial Palace, the child and empress were to be slain.

"With this knowledge in hand, I chose five of my most capable officers, and together we laid schemes of our own to snare the conspirators. The emperor proved cooperative, though he insisted he keep his appearance in the Hippodrome and force his opponents' hands openly. Zoë feared for him but refused to leave the imperial grounds for safety, preferring to die in the purple if necessary. The child, we managed to spirit from the palace in Helena's care and kept them both under heavy guard elsewhere in the city."

Lyting's eyes snapped to Rurik's. *Helena*. The noble lady who once held his brother's heart in Byzantium. The cause of Rurik's years of wandering. He had not known that she aided him in preserving Leo's throne and family.

Rurik shifted his stance. "The designated day came. Our Varangians were carefully posted about the palace grounds and throughout the Hippodrome. Another complement guarded the empress in her private residence, the Pantheon. I, myself, and my officers escorted Leo to the imperial box, the *kathisma*, which overlooked the arena from an upper balcony in the Hippodrome. Dignitaries and courtiers awaited us in the royal box. They were our chief concern.

"The mood of the crowd was sullen that day. Early on in the games, an upheavel ruptured below, then spread through the spectators like a rapid fire feeding on dry kindling. During the tumult, the conspirators made their move."

" 'Twas your own blade," Lyting recalled aloud, "that smote the assassins' steel and saved the imperial neck. You shielded the emperor with your body, didst you not?"

"*Já*. I to the fore, whilst Askel guarded both our backs. I felled two of them, Vegeir a third. The trio proved to be patricians of high office, one a member of the Senate. We quickly removed the emperor to safety, but it took hours to quell the broil below. The Blues and Greens had taken over the arena. Scores were arrested and interrogated."

Rurik turned and braced his hands against the fence, slightly crushing the parchment.

"Though the conspiracy lay shattered and most involved, seized, 'twas plain that we had not apprehended the architect of the scheme. Personally, 'twas my belief that he served Alexander, but every trail we followed evaporated before we uncovered its end. He simply faded chameleonlike into the sea of officials and retainers that surrounded the throne.

"Of course, he might not have survived the revolt. Many died in the melee. When I left Constantinople, 'twas with the frustration that, dead or alive, he had eluded my grasp. And, if he had survived, 'twas likely he yet abetted the emperor's degenerate brother."

Lyting watched the muscle flex along Rurik's jaw as he obviously grappled with that frustration once more. Rurik, he knew, would never have left the city had it not been for Helena's death. Shortly after Rurik routed the conspirators, the emperor lavished honors and riches on him and his officers. Leo had intended to elevate Rurik to one of the privileged ranks so that he might reward him further with Helena's hand in marriage. But Helena fell suddenly ill and died within days. After her funeral Rurik left Byzantium and took up the life of trading—a hollow man, until he came to Normandy. . . .

"Since my leave-taking," Rurik broke into Lyting's thoughts, "I have maintained loose ties with the Guard and kept an ear open for news from the East. The year I came to Valsemé, Leo died—a natural death. Alexander usurped the throne with little delay and exiled Zoë to a nunnery. My men kept careful watch to see if any aided him, but Alexander was so intoxicated with his own power 'twould seem he heeded no man's counsel.

Scarcely a year passed when he, too, died. Patriarch Nicholas Mysticus, whom Alexander had recalled, took control as head of the Council of Regency for young Constantine.

"His rule proved as brief as Alexander's, for this year past, another palace revolution occurred, led by Zoë and her generals. Zoë expelled the Patriarch and assumed power in the name of her son. She rules today, bedeviled with many of the old contentions along with new ones she inherited from Alexander and the Patriarch, namely a war with the Bulgarians. Adrianople has already fallen, and now they move on Dyrrachium. Many of our Varangians have joined the Byzantines in the field to repulse the Bulgarians—including Askel."

Rurik paused and reached for the wide silver armband that encircled his left forearm.

"Before departing Constantinople, Askel felt an urgency to send me this."

He drew off the piece and held it forth to Lyting.

Taking the band, Lyting examined it. As he turned it over, his gaze fell to the runes graved on the underside. These he read with relative ease:

> *The spider yet spins in the*
> *palace of the Caesars.*
> *Leidolf, Thengil, Vegeir dead.*

His eyes went immediately to Rurik, then to the parchment. He drew a brow downward as he puzzled the armband and the letter. Something felt amiss. Darkly amiss.

"Does the letter reveal what befell Askel in Dyrrachium? In truth, I could unravel little of it. Who is this Stephanites Cerularius? 'Tis odd that he should write you of Askel, and that he names the others as well."

Rurik opened out the parchment. "He claims to be a friend of Askel's. Evidently he commands a *skutatoi*, an infantry unit, mainly of spearmen. He admired Askel's skill with spears and they struck a friendship. According to Stephanites, Askel confided the information contained in this letter and directed that, should he die, Stephanites was to see it set down and dispatch it to me through the merchants of Hedeby."

Lyting rubbed his hand along his jaw, an obscure thought

nettling at the back of his brain. "And what of Askel's missive?"

"He apprised Stephanites that Thengil and Vegeir died of a sudden and suspicious sickness, 'not unlike Helena.' Leidolf was found murdered in the men's baths. 'Twas Askel's belief that the one we ever sought—the one behind the plot against Leo and his family—had resurfaced and was carefully removing the 'Dragons' from 'around the throne.' There be no telling who this man serves now. Ten-year-old Constantine is the last in the line of the Macedonians. Askel feared that Zoë and her son are again in grave danger."

Lyting's brows drew together. "Yet, if that be so, why didst he leave Constantinople for Dyrrachium? Though there be many Varangians serving in the palace guard, that left only Koll from the original six to try to expose the man."

"I have no solid answer." Rurik shook his head. "It makes little sense unless Askel was on the scent of something."

"Or someone."

"Exactly. Stephanites says 'twas not a Bulgarian's blade that felled Askel. He disappeared from nightwatch. His body was found the next morning in the desert."

"Then Askel *was* tracking someone."

"Or mayhaps followed out of the city."

"Still, there is something I do not understand." Lyting's thoughts congealed at last as that which plagued him came to the fore of his mind. "Askel took pains to send you an incripted message from Constantinople—in runes, secreted on the back of an arm bracelet—as though he knew not whom to trust. Why, then, once in the field, would he detail the entire story—not to a Varangian bound by a code of brotherhood— but to a Byzantine soldier? From what you have told me, you six tasted full well of Byzantine duplicity."

"I have been struggling with that as well," Rurik agreed. "When I remind myself that 'twas Stephanites, not Askel, who authored the letter, it begins to come clear."

Rurik held Lyting's gaze, the blue of his eyes draining to a flinty gray.

" 'Tis my belief the letter is a lure, designed to draw me back to Byzantium, with Helena as the prime bait. It intimates that, like the rest, she, too, was murdered. He who wrote those lines knew full well that I could not bide to leave them rest."

Lyting marked the complexity of emotion that passed through Rurik's face. "Then you think Stephanites is Askel's murderer?"

"I know naught with surety. Much lies in darkness." Rurik brooded for a moment. "One thing. Neither Askel nor Stephanites knew that I had abandoned my life of trading and now rule a barony in Francia with wife and sons. Both sought to reach me through Hedeby, knowing it to be a major crossroad and market center of the North. That proved wise on their parts for the pieces found me easily enough. They came into the keeping of Issac the Jew, an old acquaintance, but he is too feeble to journey south anymore. He sent word with the ships bound for Normandy, and safeguarded the items here."

Lyting nodded, recalling the messenger, one of Issac's kindred. "Have you determined what course you will take?" Lyting handed him back the arm bracelet.

"*Nei.* I need think on this longer. Even if Stephanites proves false, I doubt he is more than an underling for the viper behind all this. I'll examine the band and scroll further and ask about. Most of our Norse merchants traveling the Eastern routes are Sveirge-men, as are the Varangians. Mayhaps I can glean something of value from them. There appears to be an abundance of Sveirge-men here in Hedeby this season."

"Methinks Ketil would agree." A smile touched Lyting's lips, then dimmed. "Do you think to journey to the 'Great City' yourself? To Miklagárd?"

Rurik pressed his eyes closed a moment, then drew a long breath as he straightened and regarded Lyting.

"If one thing distinguishes a Varangian, 'tis his fierce loyalty to the 'throne of the Caesars.' 'Tis a loyalty he carries in his veins till the day his blood flows no more. And yet, for myself, there be new loyalties of equal import. They bind me by oath to duke and king alike, to Normandy and Francia. And there be my people of Valsemé, and, not the least, my family which I am loathe to leave. Still, Zoë and Constantine need be warned, and I wouldst make contact with Koll. The possibility of Helena murdered tears at me, I confess. But as to whether I wilt undertake this journey, I have no answer."

Rurik tucked the parchment inside his tunic and slipped the band onto his arm. "Sorry to burden you, *broðir*, but I thought you need know shouldst anything befall—"

He broke off the grim thought, then affected a smile. "I think I shall envy you your peaceful days at Corbie in some ways."

Brienne came forth from the *hus* just then and started toward him. The blue returned to his eyes, and he broke into an open smile.

"And in other ways I shall not." Rurik's gaze shone down on Brienne as she stepped into his arms.

Lyting watched as Rurik secured Brienne against his side and dropped a kiss to her lips. Rurik continued to hold her as though he did so against the moment he might have to part from her.

Lyting dropped away his gaze, a tide of conflicting emotions sweeping through him. He glanced to the shimmering tree, then back again and caught the last of what Brienne spoke.

"The children are sleeping soundly. Ketil returned and has taken Aleth out. It seems he is anxious to spend more coin on her, but he would not say what has taken his eye this time." She laughed.

"I, too, shall take my leave." Lyting chafed to be moving, the familiar restlessness returned tenfold. "Unless there be some task you need me attend, *broðir*, there are some purchases I wouldst also make."

"Ah, Anskar's bell," Brienne said mindfully. " 'Twill be a fine addition to Valsemé's church."

Lyting's brows lifted with surprise. He had forgotten the bell since his encounter with Stefnir. In truth, 'twas combs he would seek and a very long walk.

"*Já*, the bell," he repeated, wholly distracted. "I'll leave by the side yard so I don't risk waking the babes."

Brienne's violet gaze followed Lyting as he departed. Pensive, she leaned into Rurik's chest and watched Lyting's bright head and broad shoulders disappear down the lane.

"When first I saw Lyting," she reminisced, "he was shrouded in a monk's garb. It did not seem to befit him then, nor does the thought of him wearing it now."

"Be you of a mind with Ketil, *ástin mín*?" Rurik bent to the sensitive spot behind her ear.

"Mayhaps." She tingled at the warmth of his mouth and touch of his tongue. "You are the one least surprised by Lyting's decision to take the cowl."

"I simply hold my peace." Rurik began a slow, downward path, pressing kisses along her neck.

Brienne quavered as shivers of fire showered her throat and shoulder. Reluctantly she resisted the sensations erupting inside her. Leaning back in the circle of Rurik's arms, she gave him an expectant eye.

Rurik drew her against himself once more, undeterred, and brushed his lips against her midnight hair.

"You would have to have known Lyting in his youth and what it was like for him to grow up as youngest to a half brother like . . ." He stopped himself short of voicing Hastein's name aloud.

"How so, love?" Brienne pressed, quivering as the tip of his tongue traced the shell of her ear. "How couldst *that one* have possibly affected Lyting's call to the monastic life?"

Rurik pulled back with a sigh, realizing Brienne would own no ease till she had a fuller explanation. He sent up a small, hope-filled prayer that the twins would nap long and deep, and that the others would find much to occupy themselves for the coming hours. He would yet savor this time alone with his ravishing wife. With temporary resignation he covered her hands with his own.

"Our half brother bedeviled Lyting from infancy, just as he did every other living creature. Have you noticed how ever vigilant Lyting is? How keenly alert? Like the forest animals he so beloves, 'tis fair impossible to steal up on him. Even when he appears asleep, 'tis only a light, surface sort of slumber he keeps. Always with a sword at hand. 'Tis born of the hazards he endured in his youth. The constant threat of our half brother's shadow."

Sadness suffused Brienne's eyes as she envisaged the ordeal of Lyting's childhood. She knew firsthand of Hastein's twist-edness, having witnessed the full magnitude of his barbarity unleashed upon her brother-in-law.

"It must have been horridly difficult for him. But how didst that bear on his resolve to enter Corbie?"

Rurik turned over her hands in his as memories of his own youth glanced through him. He leveled his gaze over the top of her head.

"My brothers were a study in contrast. The one, malicious and spiteful, who derived pleasure in tormenting the most innocent of creatures. The other, profoundly humane and caring, who, despite danger to himself, came ever behind, righting the wrongs, easing the suffering.

"Even as a small lad, Lyting took it upon himself to rectify our half brother's cruelties. Like you with your herbs, love, he was a healer of sorts, tending the injuries of animals he found callously brutalized and left to die—putting them from their misery only when faced with no other choice. That deeply affected him. He deplored the senselessness of it all.

"As he gained in height and strength, he aided those children younger, pitting himself against our half brother with varying results. Not all the scars he bears were gained that night he defended you, *ástin mín*, though most were inflicted by the same one's blade."

Seeing the pain that creased Brienne's features, Rurik drew her against him and stroked her hair.

"Now Lyting wishes to right the ills of Normandy wrought by our kindred. Never was he part to their plunderings in Francia. He arrived shortly after the king concluded his treaty with Rollo. Lyting was swift to embrace Christ's cross from the first. Far quicker than I," he added with a smile.

Brienne tipped her face upward and searched Rurik's face. "Then you think Lyting *should* enter Corbie?"

"I simply trust his judgment."

Brienne's lips parted to speak, but he placed a finger there. "*Ástin mín*, Lyting must follow his own heart's calling."

Brienne gave a smile and small nod of agreement.

"Now, my love"—Rurik's eyes glowed softly—"shall we discuss my brother the day long or avail ourselves of the fine new mattress of eiderdown that awaits us within?"

He trailed kisses over her temple, cheek, and jaw and teased her lips apart. "I wouldst favor a set of daughters to match our sons," he whispered against her mouth, then drew her into a deep, intoxicating kiss.

Brienne melted into Rurik, her passion spiraling to meet his. Vaguely she felt her feet leave the earth and herself lifted high, deliciously weightless in the power of his arms. Without breaking their kiss, Rurik carried her toward the *hus*.

Crossing through the portal, Brienne caught a last glimpse of the silver lime, sparkling and winking on a breeze. As it passed from sight, she wondered hazily where the "heart's calling" would lead her noble brother-in-law.

A fire burned in Lyting's soul. He traveled the streets of Hedeby—north to south, east to west—five times over and five times more. Pace unabating, he drove himself on, a boil of argument.

Mounting the steep ladder to the crown of defense works, he circled the town once, twice, thrice. At last he halted and braced his hands against the low timbered wall.

Below spread that small portion of the world that was Danmark, stretching forth to the grayed rim of the horizon. Lyting focused to the distance. He skimmed the muted line where sky met earth, then allowed his thoughts to slip past and continue on with mind's sight across the heath.

Southward rose the great Danevirke severing Danmark from Frisia and the East Frankish kingdom. Farther to the south and somewhat west lay Francia, his adopted homeland. There he committed himself by sword and by oath, the sum of his days for three years passing contained in a single word—Valsemé. Another name waited there to encompass his future—that of Corbie.

Lyting moved along the battlement to gaze westward. Across a short portage the rivers Rheide, Treene, and Ejder flowed into one another and connected to the North Sea—once his battlefield. Beyond that vast body, lay the land of the Saxons and isle of the Celts. From those fertile shores came the maid of fire and beauty to haunt him with her golden-brown eyes.

On he strode atop the great earthen mound, past the towers and woodworks. He paused to gaze northward, reaching across time and distance with heart's memory to the magnicient blue waterways of the Limfjord and the place of his birth. There was he formed and nurtured. There didst he grow to manhood.

At what age had he realized that Limfjord held not his future? When did he first perceive that his destiny lay apart from her? And yet, Lyting mused, when he sought to journey east, he found himself west. And when he thought to return to the family's holdings in north Jutland, his father bid him south to Normandy. He had not returned since.

At length Lyting came to stand and look eastward. He tarried a while, arrested by the light fracturing the surface of the Schlei as it coursed slowly toward the Baltic. Across that near-tideless sea lay the passage to Byzantium.

Lyting closed his hands to fists. Where bided his destiny now? Where in God's holy truth didst the Almighty intend that he serve?

Guilt rode him. He chastised himself for not having offered at once to sail in his brother's stead for Constantinople. Purposely he held back. Underlying his impulse to aid Rurik was his increasing obsession with the maid of Eire. 'Twas the thought of her that spurred him to voice his willingness to undertake the journey. In verity, the words near tripped from his tongue. But if last night's dreams be counted, his motives were not so high-minded. His first act of the day was spent, not on bent knee in prayer, but in the icy river, quenching the passions kindled in sleep, quelling their obvious effect.

Saints breath! What madness possessed him? The girl belonged to Skallagrim. *Skallagrim*, he emphasized sternly. And the chieftain commanded a *drakkar* of warriors eager to safeguard her from all, including himself.

Didst he imagine to join with the convoy and keep guard of her on the journey east? To what end? To see the maid safely into the arms of the Byzantine? Or, mayhaps, escape with her into the mountains, forests, or grasslands—all crawling with fierce barbarians?

And what of Rurik's missive to the empress Zoë and young Constantine? 'Twould still need be delivered. Still necessary to reach Miklagárd and hazard the reprisal of his choleric kinsmen.

Lyting tossed back his mane of hair and set his face to the heavens.

Mayhaps 'twas all a testing. Brother Bernard warned that the path of the religious be an onerous one, beset with many trials, most especially those of the flesh.

From the first, he resolved he would embrace the devout life only if confident he could honor the requisite vows. He would not live a lie. To that end, he self-imposed his own trials and took up the practice—*nei*, the cross—of celibacy.

"God's mercy," Lyting muttered suddenly aloud, frustration shunting through him. He thought he had mastered his earthly desires. Yet, since arriving in Hedeby, he had spent most of his hours concerned with the girl, either standing watch in alleys or taking long swims. He felt weary, embattled—spirit and flesh warring within.

Lyting closed his eyes, drew a breath, and steadied his thoughts.

Rurik gave no indication that he would ask him to delay his entry into Corbie and voyage east. Certainly, he was the logical choice due to their ties of kinship and his training in the language and court formalities. Still, others were capable of the task. They need only make contact with Koll—if he be yet alive—or the Varangians. Rurik could supply names and directives. There also remained the possibility that his brother would choose to return to the imperial city himself.

Depleted by his hours of roaming and arguing in endless circles with himself, Lyting headed toward the ladder and began to descend. Stefnir came to mind.

If Skallagrim joined the raiders solely for quick plunder, as Stefnir had said, then it stood to reason that few, if any, of the *Wind Raven*'s crew would sail on with the chieftain for Byzantium—only the merchantmen among them, and not all those would be destined for Miklagárd.

Hakon would for a certainty.

Lyting halted as his foot met with solid ground. If Stefnir's words be true, Hakon purposed to defy his uncle and possess the maid for himself.

Lyting steeled, his warrior's blood stirring in the well of his soul.

Corbie, he reasoned, had stood for centuries and would remain for many more. Certainly, 'twould be there the day he sought her door.

But time ran short for the child emperor and his mother. And for the beauteous maid of Eire.

Lyting swept through the portal of the *hus* and into the *skali*, a swirl of cloak and energy.

Ketil and Aleth looked up from where they sat on the side floor, playing a game of draughts. Brienne paused in bathing the children, and Rurik turned where he stood before the hearth. On a small, scarred bench next to him the parchment from Dyrrachium lay open.

Lyting crossed the hall, his bearing charged with power and purpose. Picking up the document, he raised crystal blue eyes and met Rurik's gaze directly.

"On the day you became baron, my *broðir*, I plighted you my sword oath. Faithfully have I served you, and faithfully do I serve you still. I seek no release from my vow, nor shall I till the day I commit myself to Corbie."

He drew a breath and straightened his stance, resolution reflected in the clear blue of his eyes.

"By your leave, I shall sail in your stead. I shall deliver your message to Byzantium."

Lyting closed his hand to a fist and struck it over his heart.

"By *bouche et des mains*," he reaffirmed his sworn vow, "I am your man."

Chapter 5

Ailinn sat quietly upon the fur pelts at the foot of Skallagrim's bed and watched the chieftain as he conversed with one of his men at the portal of the house.

She remembered the man with his coppery hair and brownish beard. Remembered him from the Norsemen's harrowing invasion of the bridal chamber so many weeks ago.

When the man turned and departed, Thora scuffled from her stool by the loom and prodded Skallagrim with questions. At the chieftain's response, she drew her substantial dimensions to full height, paused for the space of a heartbeat, then stirred the hall to motion.

Ailinn fought the urge to shrink back as Thora made an undeviating line toward her, Skallagrim's key in hand, and unshackled her from the bed. At once Thora set her to work, filling extra lamps with oil and wicks and dispersing them about the room.

Trunks were next opened, three in all. Out came brightly embroidered pillows and additional furs to furnish the raised side-floors, then glasswares, carved platters, and drinking horns with silver rims.

Hakon arrived amidst the whirl of activity. He remained just outside the door at first and exchanged words with Skallagrim. Moments later he stepped inside.

Ailinn bristled. 'Twas the first time Hakon had shown himself at the house since his earlier attack on her. She saw that the cut above his eye had scabbed over, its dark crust in contrast to the angry red flesh swelling beneath.

As Hakon's eyes drew to hers, Ailinn diverted her gaze. She held her attention rigidly to her present task—draining crimson berries from their tub of water and transferring them to a large wooden bowl.

Hakon advanced deeper into the hall, moving unavoidably close in the confines of the room. It was all Ailinn could do to brace herself against the sudden assault of emotions—anger, hatred, bitterness, and fear pounding through her. Just as Hakon reached her, Thora motioned him over and directed him to mount a wide strip of tapestry across the end wall. Ailinn silently vented her relief.

Meanwhile, Thora proceeded to replace the panels of cloth that overlay her gown with fresh ones. Likewise, she exchanged the large oval brooches at her shoulders for a more elaborate pair and suspended strings of glass and amber beads between them, bringing a scowl from Skallagrim. But Ailinn observed that the chieftain had changed his tunic as well and now wore a finely wrought neck ring of polished silver about his throat.

Hakon made no such efforts and took up a place on the settle near the open fire pit to drink a cup of ale. Ailinn thought he looked to sit beneath a dark cloud, so grim was his cast.

At Thora's hurried bidding, Ailinn filled bowls with clotted cream and placed them on a tray with the berries. Thora rushed to arrange platters of food, her tongue and temper growing sharp. When Ailinn failed to understand her latest dictate, it brought an angry shout. But Thora restrained her hand as it pulled upward, obviously mindful of Skallagrim and the rewards of his displeasure.

Ailinn kept her gaze from the discolorations along Thora's neck and arms, and dared not draw attention to herself—to the bodice of her gown where Thora's forced handiwork rejoined the jagged tear, or to Murieann's coveted girdle which now lay upon her own hips.

Hostility flashed like heat lightning in the depths of the Norsewoman's eyes as Ailinn continued to stand unmoving. Thora took Ailinn by the arm and propelled her to the far end of the hearth. There, she drove her to her knees and left her cooking oatcakes on the stone slab that spanned the hearth's width.

Ailinn exhaled, thankful for the respite. As she turned the little cakes, she wondered for the first time what had prompted the rapid preparations. But before she could ponder it, Hakon shifted his position into the fringe of her vision. Ailinn tensed. Calmly he drew on his cup, reclining on the very spot where, earlier, he sought to violate her.

A knock sounded upon the door, solid and sure.

Ailinn lifted her gaze as Skallagrim moved toward the portal. Thora ceased her bustlings to quickly brush back her hair. Hakon rose slowly to full height. He fixed his stance, feet spread shoulder-width apart, his weight in his heels. Anticipation layered the air. Ailinn found that she, too, held her breath as Skallagrim drew wide the door.

Her eyes rounded. Upon the threshold stood a magnificent-looking man, golden of hair, impressive in stature, and richly dressed. A man of station and consequence. She whispered a glance over his features. Features that were strongly familiar. . . .

Without pause he stepped apart from the door, exposing a second man to view and allowing him forth.

Ailinn's heart leapt wildly as the Dane with starbright hair filled the portal. His entrance brightened the very room itself, sending the shadows to scurry into every crack and corner that the hall possessed.

Ailinn's mouth went dry as his eyes skimmed to hers—a nearly imperceptible motion that he accomplished in the course of his turn to address Skallagrim. The look might have been viewed as a glance to Hakon or Thora, yet his eyes touched hers for one stolen instant, setting her heart and hope on wing.

Had he come for her? Her thoughts skittered and her pulse livened. Mayhaps God in His Heaven had not forgotten her after all.

Reason cautioned that the man could have come on any number of matters. Cautioned that, even if he did seek her purchase, he was no more than a murderous heathen like those who had seized her—a barbaric Norseman with a sword's sting upon his cheek—no doubt harsh and cold-blooded.

But her heart ceased to listen as she visioned the Dane as she had seen him earlier that day at the river. His affectionate enjoyment of the children and his caring way with them disputed a more violent image.

Ailinn looked to the two men once more. Brothers. They must be brothers, for they favored each other with a powerful resemblance. Both were similar in age, height, and build—warriors, the two of them— one silver, one gold.

Ailinn bridled her thoughts as the men moved toward the hearth with Skallagrim. Conscious of their towering nearness, she gave her attention to the browned cakes and began removing them to a platter.

Above her the introductions and cordialities continued. Thora consumed the men with hungry eyes. She pushed forward of Hakon, smiling and gabbling, eager for Skallagrim to present her. A jarringly girlish laugh escaped her when he did.

Hakon remained lodged in his stance as the chieftain gestured toward him with an open hand and spoke his name in introduction. A pause followed. The golden man acknowledged Hakon with what seemed a spare but formal greeting. The silver warrior made no response.

Ailinn raised her eyes and found the Dane's gaze hardened over Hakon's swollen features. He flicked a glance to Thora, keen to her bruises, then bent his gaze to her, where she knelt at the hearthstone.

Ailinn heated as his eyes traveled over her breast, tracing the entire length of uneven stitches that reached from the neck of her gown nearly to her waist. His gaze turned glacial. In a breath his eyes skimmed over her, questing for marks upon her flesh. Finding none, he shot a look back to Hakon, arrow-swift. The two faced each other without word—Hakon bearing challenges in his posture; the white Dane contemptuous, hard-eyed, piercing Hakon to the marrow with his frigid gaze.

Thora moved off, then returned a moment later with a large cream-colored jar with red markings. She initiated a light chatter as she prepared to present the wine. At the same time she motioned for Ailinn to rise from her place and aid with the drinking horns.

The tension in the air dissipated somewhat. Thora continued to smile and direct a genial flow of words toward her visitors. Yet, when Ailinn met her eyes, she found flames kindled in their depths. 'Twas as though Thora blamed her for drawing the silver warrior's disfavor down upon herself and Hakon.

Taking up two of the ornamented horns, Ailinn waited as Thora filled them with a rich garnet wine. Visibly pleased with the offering, Thora relieved her of one of the vessels and turned to the golden man.

Of the two men he looked to be the older and the one who held title—a lordly figure amongst Norsemen. The lavish gold brooch at his shoulder and gem-studded buckle at his waist spoke of great wealth.

Be they brothers of royal blood, mayhaps?

Her brows flinched downward, for the man's image did not fit this place somehow. She snatched another glimpse. His attire was a mixture of exquisite Nordic jewelry and clothes that were . . . Frankish?

Ailinn blinked. His raiment was much as Bergette once described, both in words and in pictures scratched out upon the earthen floor in her stepuncle's hall. Ailinn pondered this as her eyes slipped over the cross-garters that bound his legs, then drew to the cut of his cloak. The fabric of his tunic could easily be the famed Frisian cloth of the East Franks. Deep blue in color, like that of a midnight sky, the tunic carried a border of gleaming falcons about its hem.

With a sudden flash, Ailinn recalled the two women who had accompanied the white Dane on the previous day when first she encountered him and he sought her purchase. She strove to retrieve the details from memory, but Thora disrupted her thoughts as she grasped the second horn and took it from her hands.

Ailinn's gaze followed the Norsewoman, trailing to the bright-haired Dane while Thora proffered him the wine. His garments were Norse in style, unembellished with simple body-skimming lines. Again, the fabric was superior in weave, the same weave as the brother's.

Unintentionally Ailinn's gaze slipped higher, colliding at once with the Dane's brilliant blue eyes, so intense and penetrating. She gasped at the contact and dropped her gaze to the floor.

Heat swept a crimsoned path over her throat and cheeks. Her heart hammered and her hands shook as she took up the remaining vessels and held them for Thora to fill. To Ailinn's dismay, the wine spilled over the rims.

Thora bit out a string of chastisements on a low, tethered breath. Stern-faced, she wiped the dripping horns, then gave them over to Skallagrim and Hakon. Rounding on Ailinn, she motioned her away.

Ailinn strove to clear her thoughts. She continued to cling to a small reed of hope as she took up the tray of berries and cream at Thora's command. Had the Dane come for her? Should she dare pray that he did?

She scoured her mind for what Bergette once told her of the Norse conquests in Francia. Sorely Ailinn wished now that she had given the tales closer attention. Foremost, she recalled Bergette's fuming protest of the Northmen's treaty with the Frankish king. They now ruled in Francia—*Normanni*, her nursemaid called them—their domain no less than a duchy, their rough-hewn leader no less than a duke.

Bergette had scoffed that barbarians should be granted fief and title. Unlike Eire, where Northmen erected new settlements on Irish soil and installed their own kings, in Francia the Norse were part of the Frankish nobility itself. Despite her nursemaid's sharp opinion, Ailinn thought some wisdom lay in that. Better to yoke Norse prowess to preserve the rightful throne than allow new kingships to take root and war against the old.

Were these men Normanni then? her thoughts came round.

Thora nudged Ailinn to take up the platter of hearth cakes and follow her. This she did, bringing along with it the tray with the berries. Her heart quickened and her senses sharpened. How she longed to flee this place and escape the hands of Thora, Hakon, and the unfathomable chieftain, Skallagrim. Surely, her fate with the silver warrior could be no worse than the one she already faced. Indeed, she believed it would be much improved.

Keenly alert, Ailinn waited with Thora while the men settled themselves. Skallagrim offered his great carved seat to the golden lord, then assumed a smaller chair for himself. The white Dane and Hakon took up places on the raised side-floors, directly opposite each other.

Thora proffered her offering of meats and breads. Disappointingly, it passed untouched, though Hakon motioned for more wine. While the Norsewoman stepped apart to retrieve the jar, Ailinn presented her tray to the golden man.

He spoke with the chieftain, his voice deep and rich. She glanced over him, observant to every detail and aught she might glean. Unexpectedly he lifted his eyes and met hers. Steel blue. They held recognition in their depths. 'Twas as though he knew of her and now compared her to those reports.

Ailinn withdrew her gaze, marking the cleft he bore in his chin. The dark-haired children sprang to mind. They owned like indentations upon their little chins, and their indistinguishable eye color could easily have been the same as his. One of the Frankish women, Ailinn remembered, possessed ebony tresses—the one that was so exceedingly fair.

Ailinn's heart skipped several beats as she turned to serve Skallagrim. Perhaps the woman was this man's wife, not the other's. An effusion of fresh energy washed through her. She sought to scan the golden lord's hand for a ring, but Thora prompted her to serve the others.

Ailinn's breath fell shallow as she moved before the silver warrior and offered him her tray. His eyes reached up to hers and enwrapped her in that clear blue sea. A rush of excitement surged through her, for his gaze held a depth of unspoken words. Certainly he had come for her.

He continued to drink of her with his eyes as he spooned cream and berries onto an oatcake. Pinching up the sides, he took the treat and tasted it. She watched the line of his jaw and his beautifully carved lips as he ate. Again, she met his gaze. His expression revealed naught, though his eyes shined softly upon her.

Thora moved before the white Dane just then and bumped Ailinn aside with one large hip. With a brusque nod of the head, she signaled for Ailinn to remove herself and serve Hakon.

Ailinn gripped the platter and tray tighter. Turning to Hakon, she avoided his eyes but felt his hard stare all the same. He swiped a single cake from the platter and tore it with his back teeth, then downed more wine. Hostility wreathed about him, envenoming the air.

Ailinn began to draw away, but Hakon trapped her wrist. The pressure of his fingers brought her eyes to his as he relieved her platter of another cake. Ailinn fought her revulsion, abhorring his touch. She thought to hear the silver warrior move, but Skallagrim's voice broke over the hall. Hakon released her as the chieftain ordered away the women and their trays.

Skallagrim gulped another mouthful of wine, wiped his mouth with his hand, and eyed the lord of Valsemé.

"My man, Stefnir Hranason, tells me you seek passage to Byzantium, Baron."

"*Satt*. True." Rurik nodded. "Though 'tis my *broðir* who will actually undertake the journey and sail in my stead."

"The monk?" the chieftain blurted, coming forward in his chair.

Lyting's brow skidded upward. He exchanged a swift, sharp glance with Rurik.

"He *is* to join the Christian priest-class, is he not?" A veiled look came into Skallagrim's eyes. "I have it on your friend's word—the great red-haired bear who serves you."

Lyting masked his surprise and rose to his feet. Facing the hoary chieftain, he pulled open the neck of his tunic and exposed a silver cross, gleaming against his chest.

Rurik played the moment, lacing his fingers together as though the chieftain tested his patience. "'Tis a private matter—a mission of gravest importance that requires my brother to delay his entrance into the holy brotherhood. Lyting travels as my personal emissary to the very highest levels of the Imperial court."

Skallagrim elevated a brow, then settled back and sipped his horn, obviously wary, distrustful. "How grave? And how high?"

"None graver. None higher." Rurik held him with an unwavering gaze. "And potentially profitable to those who keep his company."

Skallagrim pared Lyting with a critical gaze. His glance slipped past to where his Irish prize stood behind the hearth, then to Hakon, who glared at the younger Atlison's back—when he wasn't sliding glances to the maid.

Skallagrim's jaw hardened at that, his teeth fusing to rock. He looked again to the girl, then fixed his eyes on the baron's brother. Suspicion perched in his eyes. He did not need another cock in the pen. Despite the silver that Atlison's passage would bring, he would not risk spoiling the girl. Hakon would be enough to manage.

"With respect, Baron, I, myself, am a man of considerable means and significant connections. To my thinking, 'tis your brother who stands to profit by *my* company and the transport I can provide.

"Of course, others can supply that as easily as I." Skallagrim shrugged. "We sail in convoy to Kiev and on to Constantinople. Truth to tell, what with goods and slaves, I am already pressed for space. The *Wind Raven*, of course, is a warship, too large and fragile for the journey. She must be stored in Gotland. I shall take a lighter, clinker-built vessel from there and change that again in Kiev for a small but sturdy Slav boat that can withstand the rapids of the Dnieper. You can appreciate my limitations, Baron." Skallagrim opened his palm to the air. "I could, perhaps, take your brother as far as Gotland."

Lyting watched as Rurik allowed a mingling of impatience and displeasure to cross his face. They had anticipated the chieftain's resistance and concurred that their best approach lay in appealing to the man's pride and greed. Lyting maintained his silent stance as Rurik's hand moved to this throat and drew on a thong that lay hidden beneath his tunic. He produced a small leather pouch. Slipping the strap over his head, Rurik did no more than hold the bag in sight, baiting Skallagrim.

"I know well of trade routes and ships—firsthand," Rurik emphasized tersely. "I also know how many men and goods each type of ship can hold," he dismissed Skallagrim's excuses. "What I seek is a seasoned voyager, one experienced with the particular perils that are inherent in traveling the Dnieper. My message *must* reach Miklagárd and not fall fallow in the hands of nomadic tribesmen or lost to the bottom of the Dnieper."

Rurik gazed at him levely. "Stefnir vows you are such a man for the task. To be plainspoken, I give credence to his word only because Lyting does. Stefnir is known to my brother from the years they fought in the king's service upon the seas, preserving Danmark."

Skallagrim's eyes sheered to Lyting, surprise firing them.

Rurik pressed on. "I can compensate you with more than mere coin. Through my brother, you can gain access to the one above all who can grant the allowances you seek in the silk trade."

Before the chieftain could question how he came by such knowledge of him, Rurik spread open the bag's puckered mouth and plucked an enameled gold case from its confines. Skallagrim's eyes bulged as Rurik opened the box. Inside nestled a lustrous piece of cloth—silk of Imperial purple.

" 'Tis death to the man who secrets silk from Miklagárd!" Skallagrim exclaimed in an astonished breath. "But death most vile to any who would thieve dye-goods of the emperor's purple. How didst—?"

"I neither secreted nor thieved the silk," Rurik declared resolutely.

Extracting a single golden *solidii* from the royal wrappings, he upheld it, exposing the coin's crisp image—a miniature portrait of the Imperial personage.

" 'Twas the gift of Emperor Leo Sophos himself."

Skallagrim thumped back in his chair, clearly amazed. A sudden comprehension rippled through his eyes. He wet his lips. "There be tales that persist of a Varangian named Rurik—one of ours, a Dane, not a Swede—who won fame and riches by his daring and later traveled the Volga—"

"The same," Rurik acknowledged, cutting the chieftain short. Before Skallagrim could make further comment, Rurik dangled before him the prize pearl of temptation.

"If you wouldst know, I send my brother to hold audience with the dowager empress, herself."

"Zoë?" Skallagrim near choked with wonderment.

Ailinn grew restive, unable to comprehend aught of what transpired amongst the men. She continued to pray desperately that the white Dane had come for her.

Skallagrim had appeared guarded, even quarrelsome, at first. She could not see what the tall Dane revealed to him, for his back confronted her like a wall. But the chieftain's entire countenance and manner altered when the lord brought forth an ornamented box which yielded a golden coin and scrap of purple cloth. Mayhaps these men were royals after all.

Her thoughts snapped back as Skallagrim called for more wine. Thora hastened to serve while the chieftain and the golden lord continued to speak, their words falling in agreeable tones. Meanwhile, the silver warrior resumed his place on the side-floor and readjusted his tunic. Hakon's ill temper continued to smolder visibly, darkening his cast.

Thora fawned over her guests, her excitement saturating the air. Ailinn's heart began to pound solidly once again as Thora motioned for her to bring the trays of cakes and berries.

Had the men struck a bargain, then? Forged some agreement and settled their affairs? Would she be free of this detestable place in the coming moments, trading one future for another?

Ailinn's hands trembled as she stepped before the silver warrior and looked openly into his eyes. She must know. Surely she could read something there. But as their gazes entwined, Thora jostled her with a hip, forcing her aside and causing Ailinn to lose her hold on one tray.

It flipped upward, sending a shower of berries into the warrior's lap and a splattering of cream across Thora's nose, mouth, and chest. The bowls and tray clattered noisily to the floor, followed by an enraged screech from Thora. Impulsively the Norsewoman drew back and directed a blow at Ailinn.

Lightning swift, the silver warrior bolted to his feet, blocking Thora's attack with one hand while sweeping Ailinn behind him with the other. Hakon, likewise, bounded to his feet and drew on his sword. But before the steel left its scabbard, the white Dane's blade flashed before him.

Rurik drove from his chair and reached for his hilt, but Skallagrim stayed him.

The chieftain remained seated. Tenting his fingers, he contemplated the scene. His gaze shifted betwixt Lyting and Hakon, then he smiled with satisfaction deep in his beard. Mayhaps Atlison *was* the answer to his needs after all. The baron's brother would bring silver to his coffer, audience with the Byzantine empress, and the perfect counterbalance to his most immediate problem—Hakon.

"Lord Rurik, I believe my ship can carry another after all." He squinted an eye over Lyting for one final estimation. "He returns to confine himself to a monastery, you say?"

"The holy brothers prepare his place even now."

"Christians," Skallagrim grunted, though obviously content with the answer as he drained the ale from his horn.

Lyting and Hakon remained fixed in their stances, steel gleaming in their hands, challenge burning in their eyes.

Ailinn clung to the tall Dane, her breasts pressing into his back. She quaked against him as firelight danced along the blades. For one blood-chilling moment she relived her first encounter with Hakon when he burst into the bridal chamber and reaped death at her feet.

She squeezed her lashes shut against the memory, sinking her fingers deeper into the Dane's garments. Desperately she prayed that he would take her from this place and now.

Skallagrim's voice rolled across the room. She heard Thora move off, then the scraping of Hakon's sword as he returned it with measured slowness to its scabbard.

The Dane continued to secure her against himself, his left arm and hand curved back, his long fingers pressed against the curve of her spine. He waited until Hakon had fully resheathed his blade before he restored his own.

Ailinn felt his weight shift and his arm relax. He began to turn and their bodies parted. Cool air rushed between them. Yet, when the Dane's eyes sought hers, Ailinn felt a liquid warmth spread through her, heating her to her toes.

Skallagrim's voice rumbled loudly, dispelling the sensation. Ailinn glanced to the chieftain. Her heart pitched when he motioned for her to withdraw to the pallet at the back of the hall. Anxious, she looked to the white Dane, seeking some sign—any sign—that she should stay by his side.

His gaze held hers, his expression intense, unreadable. Then his lashes dipped and brushed his cheeks. She thought to hear frustration in the breath he released. He raised his beautiful blue eyes and with a scant nod of his head indicated that she should obey Skallagrim's order.

Ailinn's spirits plunged. Reluctantly she stepped apart, longing for all the world to remain in the stronghold of his shadow, dreading he might leave her here.

She calmed herself as she traversed the room. Mayhaps there yet be matters the men need discuss, arrangements to complete. Thrice had the white Dane appeared in her life—the first and second times by mischance, true, but the third with purpose. She felt an unwavering certainty that his visitation this night affected the course of all of her tomorrows.

Ailinn assumed her place at the foot of Skallagrim's bed and waited, attentive to the men's every gesture and utterance. She held fast to her fragile hopes as the golden lord and Skallagrim rose from their chairs and locked forearms, sealing their bargain. The chieftain turned and clasped the silver warrior's arm as well.

Hope burgeoned as Skallagrim accepted several plump pouches, presumably filled with coin. But could a slave bring such wealth? she wondered, disbelieving any could. The doubt nettled, and her heart tripped a little. Still, she eased toward the edge of the raised side-floor, prepared to spring to her feet and leave at the first signal.

The men conversed a moment longer and drank a final toast from the ornamented horns—all except Hakon, who brooded nearby. Ailinn twisted the fur robe beneath her fingers, then rose to her knees and gripped hold of the bed's carved end post when the three moved toward the door.

Had they forgotten her? Her nails dug into the wood. She fixed her gaze on the brothers where they stood waiting while Skallagrim drew open the door. The grievous truth crushed down upon her as the men began to depart. The silver warrior had not come for her.

Ailinn's heart plummeted, and a gulf of despair overtook her. She watched, disconsolate, as the golden lord passed through the door and the white Dane stepped to the portal.

He hesitated upon the threshold and looked back. Their gazes met and held across the room—brilliant blue and darkening brown. Then he turned and was gone, taking with him his shining presence and her last ray of hope. Ailinn thought her heart would crack.

She sank to the furs, fighting back her welling tears, tasting sharply of her aloneness. The pull at her ankle cuff and the clank of chains roused her from her gloom. She found Skallagrim shackling her to his bed. A chill penetrated her bones. She was truly forsaken—cursed and condemned—to the hands of this brutish man and his murderous kin.

Later, Ailinn lay awake upon the furs while Thora snored on her pallet and Skallagrim tossed in his sleep. Hakon no longer occupied the hall.

Through the opening beneath the eaves, she silently viewed the stars—silvery points of light illuminating a world plunged to darkness.

Ailinn's thoughts drifted to the white Dane. How could she have been so wrong? Yet, he protected her. But then he left her.

A single tear cascaded over her cheek, followed by another and another. Truly, God *had* abandoned her. There would be no escape from Thora, or Hakon, or the inscrutable Skallagrim.

Ailinn could not think on the days that lay before her—however many, however few. She no longer possessed her own life. She was the chieftain's slave. By all that she could garner, he had already set the seal upon her fate.

Bereft of hope, Ailinn looked to the stars in the heavens. Tears glistened on her cheek as she braced herself for the coming dawn.

Lyting lingered a time with Rurik, a short distance from Thora's *hus*.

It had taken a supreme force of will to compel his feet to move and leave the maid within. Such pain cleaved her eyes, imploring that he not abandon her there. Her look lanced straight through his heart and lodged in his soul.

Despite Skallagrim and Hakon, he vowed to win her free and shelter her beneath his protection. When he sailed from Byzantium, 'twould be with the maid of Eire.

"Do you come now, *broðir*?" Rurik asked for a second time.

Lyting dragged his attention from the direction of the *hus* and found Rurik regarding him with an inquisitive gaze.

"*Nei*, I keep watch tonight."

"I thought Audun and Magnus—" Rurik halted midsentence, comprehension breaking in his eyes.

He pressed his lips to a thoughtful line. Reaching inside his tunic, he took hold of the leather pouch and drew it forth, then slipped the strap over his head. Rurik gave the bag with its valued contents over to Lyting.

"It gladdens me to know that matters are in such capable hands." Esteem reflected in his eyes. "*Gott kvöld, broðir.* Good night. I will see you on the morrow."

Rurik smiled and departed, heading back along the walk toward the lodgings where his family awaited.

Lyting placed the thong and pouch around his neck, then stepped to the familiar passageway. On impulse he looked up to the starry heavens and thought of the autumn-fire maid. Then, enfolding himself in his great mantle and covering his bright hair, he melted into the shadows and took up his vigil.

* * *

In the chill of early morning, while the skies yet slumbered overhead, Ailinn hastened to keep pace with Skallagrim along the dark and timbered streets.

She knew this moment would come. Dreaded it. And now its yoke was upon her.

For three days passing she and Thora had prepared provisions for a journey—barrels of salt fish, hard-baked bread, tubs of cheese and berries. They worked long, filling skins with water and casks with ale. Skallagrim brought forth furs, seal hides, and walrus ivory from storage. He sorted, counted, and bundled. Together, he and Hakon removed the goods and foodstuffs from the hall. The time of waiting was at an end.

Ailinn braced herself as the future rushed into the present, and Skallagrim led her to her fate.

The day yawned awake and the skies paled as Ailinn and the chieftain emerged from the last cluster of houses and reached the harbor. Crossing the wharf, they continued on.

A crisp breeze played over Ailinn as she looked up. Her gaze drew to the end of the pier, then turned cold. Directly ahead waited the great serpent ship that had borne her here. The monster-headed prow gleamed with the morning's light, its grin frozen in time by the wood-carver's art.

Ailinn's stomach wrenched to think she must board the ship once more. Where now? she wondered. To what desolate, unconsecrated corner of the world wouldst it deliver her?

She kept close to Skallagrim as they wended their way amid the activity on the dock. Men moved in a continuous flow, to and from the ship, onloading barrels and crates.

Aboard, a clutch of crewmen raised the mast, then slotted and secured it in place. Several dispersed to attach the rigging. Ailinn's steps faltered, for there, fitting a mast line to the bow, stood the Dane with star-bright hair.

Ailinn forgot to breathe, surprise overtaking her and something akin to joy.

She watched as he wiped his brow and moved to affix two more lines to the side of the ship. He looked different. More handsome, if possible, less barbarous. His mane of hair had been trimmed to shoulder length.

Heat climbed her cheeks as he raised his eyes to hers. She

blamed it on the warming rays of the sun but could not explain the explosion of fire within.

Skallagrim prodded her forward, across a narrow, ridged plank and onto the vessel. Conducting her toward the bow, he chained her to the empty shield rack that ran along the outside rail and left her there.

Ailinn waited. Time and again, her attention strayed to the white Dane. She guarded her interest, fearing the chieftain's unpredictable response. Yet impulse warred with wisdom, and try though she did, she could not wholly keep her eyes from the silver warrior.

With the spar set and sail lashed in place, the men lowered the piece, bracing it above the decking on three upright supports, spaced down the center of the ship. With that complete, the chieftain relocated Ailinn to the mast, where he chained her as he had on the previous voyage.

Ailinn shifted to find a comfortable position, the boards hard beneath her, the irons weighing heavily upon her leg. She glanced out over the water, then to the gulls reeling and screaming above. Finally she returned her gaze townward and drew it along the shoreline and dock.

Ailinn stilled as she beheld a group of slavewomen there, being herded toward the ship.

She rose, buttressing herself against the mast as she recognized some amongst them to be maids of Eire, seized in the raid on Clonmel. She bit her lip and studied each one. At the site of Hakon to the rear of the group, her hand flew to her mouth, stiffling a cry. With him he brought Deira and Rhiannon.

An eternity passed before her stepcousins finally boarded, but at last they came within arm's length, and crying out, the three clung to one another with fierce joy. Hakon growled to quiet the women as he shackled them together at the mast.

Ailinn wiped her tears, then gave Rhiannon's arm another squeeze and took Deira's face between her palms.

"Merciful God, I thought never to see you again." She swept a searching glance over the other captives and returned her gaze. "Know you aught of Lia?"

Pain fractured Deira's brow, and the light died in her eyes. Ailinn knew with surety, Lia had been sold. An aching sadness clutched at her heart.

"Was it Arabs who made her purchase?"

"*Ní hea*. 'Twas a great Norse devil," Rhiannon stated with contempt for their kind. "By now he has taken her far from this place."

Ailinn swallowed the lump that rose in her throat and said a brief prayer for gentle Lia.

While the sun still climbed the early morning skies, Skallagrim ordered for the mooring lines to be cast off and the oars set to the water.

The ship glided from the dock—an imposing sight with its high, sweeping lines and the bright-colored shields, now hung along the sides from prow to stern.

As the vessel slid across the harbor, Ailinn looked to the white Dane where he plied his strength to a long, oaken oar. Of a sudden he directed his attention past the crew and ship and back to the quayside. A brilliant smile broke over his face—a startling slash of white across sun-deepened features. Ailinn's heart jarred in its place.

Composing herself with a firm mental shake, she followed his gaze to the wharf. There, a man and woman waved in farewell. Ailinn looked again. 'Twas the golden lord and the Frankish lady. They stood intimately close, their sides pressed together, each holding a dark-haired babe.

The lord trailed off his wave and lowered his hand to the lady's hip. The gesture left no doubt in Ailinn's mind. 'Twas the golden lord who was married to the lady of Francia, not his brother.

But what of the second Frankish woman? She scanned the wharf and piers but did not sight her. Ailinn puzzled that. Surely if she be his wife, she would wish to see him away. Ailinn's brow fluttered upward. Mayhaps the other lady was not bound to the white Dane, either.

She surveyed the wharf a final time, then caught herself. Why should it matter? she admonished. He was a Norseman. For whatever reason God ordained that their lives should continue to cross and intertwine, and regardless that he seemed preferable to any of his kind, she must never forget the blood that flowed in his veins.

As the dragonship slipped through the palisaded gates, Skallagrim commanded that the great, square sail be hoisted and sheeted to the wind. Ailinn tasted the exhilaration that swept through the men, her own mounting as they coursed the wide waterway. She gave herself to the moment—the steady swell and dip of the ship; the stiff, moist breeze buffeting her cheeks and tossing her hair in a fiery dance; the creak of wood and snap of sail; the faint saltiness to the air. Above, sea-swallows followed in their wake, and along the river, beech trees leafed to a pale green, gracing their passage.

Time slipped past unmarked until hours later they gained upon the mouth of the river. A tremor passed through Ailinn as she viewed the vast sea that lay ahead. Beyond its watery domain awaited her unnamed fate.

She took a swallow against the dread that weighted her soul. Ignoring her earlier thoughts, she looked to the silver warrior. He met her gaze at once as though sensing her need. She found strength there and solace. The distance between them diminished, crystal blue eyes encompassing the golden-brown depths of her own.

As their gazes wedded and held fast, the *Wind Raven* passed out of the River Schlei and into the deep-blue waters of the Baltic.

PART II

"In fire, gold is tested."

Chapter 6

The granite cliffs of Gotland rose from the sea. Like ancient guardians, they confronted the *Wind Raven* with high, harsh brows and demanded whether it be friend or foe.

Undaunted, the *Wind Raven* continued on, its supple frame bending and flexing as it rode the rhythms of the sea. Rounding the island's southeastern coast, the vessel skirted the shoals and followed the cliffs northward.

Lyting moved to trim the sail and gain the wind's best advantage, feeling very much at ease upon the waters. He spotted colonies of black guillemots and snowy white gannets nesting high in the crannied walls. The gulls that had followed them since Oland, watching for the ship to drop bait lines, now left their company to reel and dive noisily at the shallows, seeking a more bounteous supper.

Lyting smiled, enjoying this time. Enjoying it, despite the concerns that preyed heavily upon his mind.

He glanced to where the women huddled at the mast. The auburn-haired maid shared her mantle with another, a frail-looking girl with haunted eyes. Another young woman, raven-locked, crowded in close with them.

The three obviously knew one another. Hakon claimed the two and apparently intended to take them the full distance to Miklagárd.

Lyting stroked the new growth of his beard. He need approach Skallagrim about garmenting the women more suitably for the voyage East lest they grow sickly. Retaining one's body heat upon the open waters was ever a problem, and already, the one girl looked to be unwell.

He regretted he could not aid the other women as well, but the *Wind Raven*'s crew would disperse once they landed, most heading north with their slaves to the trade center at Birka on Sverige's mainland. He prayed for God's mercy upon the captives. He could do no more.

Lyting drew into his cloak as the breeze's cool fingers slipped through the weave of his tunic. He would welcome a warm meal and a dry bed this evening. Skallagrim had pushed them hard in the past days, foregoing the customary landfall at night and making the crossing in less than a week. They had eaten their meals cold and navigated the waters in the dark, gauging the depths with weighted lines and following the coast of Sverige, ever to the left, *larboard*, side.

Twice, he had spared the *Wind Raven* from running aground due to the helmsman's misdirections. This gained him a measure of Skallagrim's respect. Lyting hoped 'twould prove beneficial, though he held no wish to repeat such near disasters to improve his standing with the chieftain.

As the day advanced, the longship continued north, skimming the coastal waters till at last it reached the lagoon-harbor of Bogeviken.

Ailinn steeled herself. After days and nights upon the dispassionate sea, she wondered whether she had been brought, at last, to the doorstep of her fate. It cut at her heart, but in the coming moments 'twas likely she would be separated from her stepcousins forevermore.

To her astonishment, the great dragonship slowed and seemingly glided onto shore. Many of the Norsemen leapt from the vessel's sides and into the shallows where they muscled and guided the ship onto the sands. Others, from on shore, abandoned their labors and hastened forth to assist their efforts.

Once they stabilized the ship with timbers and braced a boarding plank in place, the men swarmed back onboard and applied themselves to securing the vessel. The deck became a blur of motion as the oars were taken aboard, the gear stored, and the lines coiled and stowed.

Ailinn lost sight of the white Dane. He had been occupied with the rigging before he moved off toward the stern. Rhiannon distracted her with a complaint, and when she looked back, he was gone.

The chieftain's voice boomed suddenly nearby. Ailinn found him gesturing for the women to be removed and for the sail and mast to be dismantled. Aiding Deira to her feet, she again quested for the white Dane. Again, she could not find him. Would their paths part now also? The thought stabbed at her.

His presence should be of no consequence, her mind argued, reminding for a repeated time that he was a Norseman, the same as the rest. Not at all the same, her heart whispered back and refused to listen further.

The women shambled over the deck in their fetters, the lot of them bound one to another, before and behind, by a length of chain running through the loops attached to their ankle irons. Hakon stepped along the line, prodding those who faltered or slowed.

Deira shrank behind Ailinn as they passed Hakon. Rhiannon, who followed Deira, gave her Norse master a deliberated look, one which held neither fear nor provocation. 'Twas as though Rhiannon measured him behind her sharp eyes, discerning how best to gain some advantage.

Hakon's gaze slid to Ailinn, chilling the blood in her veins. She stiffened and directed her attention toward the plank. When her turn came, she climbed up without delay and cautioned Deira to follow with care.

Ailinn halted, her heart quickening. Below, two men aided the women's descent. One of them she recognized not at all, an inhabitant of this place, perchance. But the other was the silver warrior.

Her blood began to flow again. The knots that had corded her insides now loosened and slipped free only to reach up and tangle themselves about her heart.

She began to make her descent, her footing less sure. As she approached midpoint on the plank, the warrior came forward and opened his hand to her. Ailinn drew a thin shred of breath as she laid her own in his. Their palms joined, flesh to flesh. At once the heat of that contact spread along her arm and flooded her whole being.

She started to pull back, but his grip held her firm and he

drew her down the remaining length of the plank. Releasing her, he attended to Deira, guiding her by the elbow and minding that her footage did not slip. Ailinn watched, unconsciously closing her fingers over her palm, trapping in the warmth and memory of his touch.

Rhiannon slowed, her gaze fixed on the white Dane. She ignored the other man's offer of assistance as her eyes slipped over the handsome warrior, and she turned to his aid.

Provoked by her stepcousin's guile, Ailinn strayed a glance over the cove. She found no bustling town there, only a quiet settlement sprinkled around the harbor. Here and there, enormous slabs of stone loomed, shaped like axheads set on their blades and covered with carvings. Monuments of some nature, guarding the inlet.

Where be this place? Her forehead lined with frustration. One should know better where Destiny abandoned them to finish their days.

Ailinn returned her gaze to find that the women had finished disembarking and that the white Dane had vanished once more. She located him on deck a moment later, where he labored amongst the others, lowering the ship's stout mast.

Skallagrim's robust voice severed her attention. He tarried atop the plank, calling back a final charge, then descended, followed by Hakon. Ailinn's breath stilled as the chieftain trudged toward her, signaling for the slaves to be untrammeled and split apart. She clasped Deira's hand and Rhiannon's as well, her fears realized.

As the chain slipped from her ankle iron, Skallagrim grasped Ailinn by the arm and pulled her from the line. She twisted to see her stepcousins for a final time. To her relief, she saw Hakon take hold of each one and follow behind.

Ailinn thanked the Almighty for this small time of grace, knowing full well 'twould eventually reach its end. Her spirit dipped at that thought, but as she dropped her gaze to the ground, another man joined them. Her eyes widened as she recognized the booted feet. Ailinn looked up to find the silver warrior walking beside her.

Saints forgive her but she nearly smiled. She bit down on her lip, lest one escaped, and swiftly glanced away. Still, her heart swelled, an expansive feeling that she could not restrain. 'Twas as though a candle flamed to life there, warming her within and glowing bright against the gloom of day.

The six progressed around the harbor's edge, coming at last to a small holding. It boasted a sizable longhouse, domestic and work buildings, and a modest shipyard, presently engulfed in noise and activity.

A smile touched Lyting's lips, for there, men shaped the shell of a new ship, building from the keel upward, using naught but hand and eye to guide them. He ran his keen eye along the ship's sweeping lines, recalling the happier moments of his youth. To his mind, the finest passion and achievement of his people, the very essense of the Norsemen's spirit, lay in that of the clinker-built ship.

Just then two men came away from their work, hailing the chieftain and Hakon with visible recognition. One was a younger version of the other, both having reddish-blond hair and thin, high-bridged noses projecting straight off the brow. Lyting quickly found himself entangled in introductions. The older man identified himself as Olaf, the master ship-wright and owner of the holding, and the other, as his eldest son, Rig.

Lyting waited, silent but heedful, as the chieftain spoke with the shipwright and Rig and Hakon renewed an apparent friendship.

Rig sharpened his interest over the captives, and his smile increased. Lyting wondered how far Rig's friendship extended with Hakon, for he appraised the women as though he expected to be offered his choice of them.

"*Komið*. Come," Olaf bid them. "Gytha brews the finest beer on Gotland. What say you, we open a fresh cask?"

As they converged on the great *hus*, two children spilled from the door and into the yard, laughing and squealing—a boy of about six years, chased by a mere breath of a girl, no more than four.

"Eirik! Dalla!" A handsome woman, round with child, emerged from the *hus*, calling after the children. She caught her steps at the sight of the men and came forth at once to greet them.

The keys of authority she wore at her waist proclaimed her to be Olaf's wife. She wore the customary attire of a

Norsewoman, yet she looked to be of different lineage. Saxon, Lyting thought, or mayhaps Breton.

"Gytha!" Olaf beckoned heartily. "Skallagrim and Hakon return to us. They bring with them a lord of Normandy."

Lyting began to correct the shipwright, for he held no lands or titles. But as he met Gytha's clear gray eyes, he found them plumbing the depths of him. Her gaze moved to the Irish beauty beside him, then back again and bound him.

Lyting felt a sudden surge of accountability. Didst she think the maid to be his? That 'twas he who had enslaved her and now pleasured himself on her, sating his days and nights?

"*Velkomin* to Gotland." She only smiled softly. "You must be tired and thirsty from your voyage. *Komið*. The beer is fresh-brewed."

She turned and clapped her hands after the children, instructing them to bring cups from the *hus*, and then led the men and their captives to the brewing shed.

Skallagrim began to speak to Olaf of wintering the *Wind Raven*, though the shipwright appeared more absorbed at the moment with the backview of his wife as she disappeared into the small building.

"You brought the *Wind Raven* ashore at Sven's *naust*?"

"*Gott*. Good," Olaf said distractedly. "All the easier to store her up."

"Take your eyes from your wife's skirts," Skallagrim chided. " 'Twas not what I said, though, indeed, the *drakkar* is secured near Sven's boat shed. She's opened up a seam along her *larboard* bow. Lyting has also found something amiss with the rudder that will require your attention."

Before Lyting could respond, Olaf broke away from the others.

"Gytha! Leave it be!" he cried as she struggled to shift a hip-high cask through the portal of the building. He hastened to put a halt to her efforts, then heaved the barrel, himself, just outside the door. "I'll not be having you harm yourself. There be men here aplenty to do the heavy work."

Gytha began to open her mouth as though to disavow any would assist her, but Olaf stayed her. "You are my *wife*, Gytha. You need but ask. They will all honor you."

Eirik and Dalla returned with boisterous good cheer and stacks of wooden cups. Olaf grinned down at his children, both images of their mother—the boy full of questions, and the girl a mischieveous elfin child whose large, smiling eyes silently paired the star-bright warrior with the autumn-fire maid of Eire.

Obviously content with his portion in life, Olaf pried open the lid to the cask and set it aside. Gytha attended to the beer, ladling the cups full with the children's aid and presenting them to the men. She next saw to the captives with equal care.

"What fault didst you find with the rudder?" Olaf questioned several minutes later. Lyting shifted his gaze to the shipwright.

"The underside of the reinforcing block at the pivot point shows several cracks, some rifted deep and severe enough that I'd not trust the piece for another venture."

The chieftain concurred with a nod. "Best look to it and replace it if you must, Olaf. I've found Atlison, here, to be uncommonly familiar with ships. I'll be surprised if you don't agree with him."

Lyting ignored the darkling look Hakon hurled at him for drawing Skallagrim's favor. "My uncle was a shipwright on the Limfjord. I spent much of my youth training at his side."

Olaf scratched his chin. "Limfjord is as pirate-infested as the waters of Gotland."

"*Satt*. True. But it proved valuable training for my time with the fleet at Nørdby and Søndervig."

"You were at Nørdby and Søndervig? With the king?" Olaf's excitement grew. "The skalds claim those to be amongst the finest and fiercest battles fought in Scandia—the Danish sea tactics, brilliant against the *Norge* men. I shouldst like to hear a full recounting over a bottomless horn of Gytha's beer."

Hakon's face darkened, and Lyting regretted having opened this door. Even Rig hung upon his words. Gratefully, Skallagrim diverted the conversation along a more pressing path.

"As would I, but later friend. We need get word out about the island to any who wouldst sail with us in *felag*, fellowship, for Kiev."

"Consider it done," Olaf agreed. "And I'll see to the rudder's block as well."

"What of the *Sea Goat*? Is she readied for the voyage?"

Olaf shook his head. "A storm caught her off Oland last week, and she took hefty damages. She won't be seaworthy for another month."

Skallagrim frowned. "'Twould be too late to join the convoy. We need reach Kiev by the first of June. Have you other vessels suitable to the rivers?"

"One, but 'tis promised to Bjorn Pálsson. Sven has several of varying sizes, though."

"Good. Let us see to them. I wish to be under way as quickly as possible."

"You will stay with us until you sail, of course," Gytha asserted.

Skallagrim regarded Rig just as the young man's eye wandered to his prize slave. "*Já*, Gytha. But we need not crowd the hall. We'll tent apart of the *hus*."

"As you will, but I shall expect you to take dinner with us," she said firmly, then smiled. "Lyting can share with us his adventures with the king."

Olaf prodded Rig from his musing. "Take the small boat around the cove and help Hakon transport whatever equipment he needs."

Rig dragged a parting gaze over the captives and, acknowledging his father, left with Hakon.

"I will see to your women while you are gone," Gytha offered and beckoned for the women to follow. She halted as the two darker-haired women joined her. Wrinkling her nose, she drew down a disapproving brow over Skallagrim.

"Slaves or no, you could allow them a bath." She drew up her chin and led the women toward the longhouse. "Dalla. Eirik. Come," she called back.

As the men started to depart, Olaf chuckled and rolled an eye to the chieftain. "You should know better than to bring the women round to Gytha like that."

The chieftain's beard expanded with a grin. "I do. Those two are Hakon's. Mine is clean enough."

Lyting gazed after the women, his curiosity grown. "Gytha takes an uncommon interest in the slaves."

"Gytha was a slave herself until a year ago," Skallagrim apprised. "Olaf's slave, though 'twas more in title than in fact where he be concerned."

Lyting's brows parted with surprise, comprehension sifting through him.

"I would have freed her a time ago." Olaf's shoulders rose and fell. "I wished to take Gytha to wife. But a man cannot marry his slave, and in freeing her, I feared she would make use of her new rights to leave me and return to her homeland. So, instead, I gave her reasons to stay—first Eirik, then Dalla."

Lines rayed Olaf's eyes as he smiled deeply. "She has grown to like her life on Gotland, as wife to a shipwright. This new child, she gives me most willingly."

Lyting pondered Olaf's tale as he retraced his steps around the harbor with the chieftain and shipwright. He thought on Gytha's trials, and on how God had brought forth this unassuming man from among those she considered enemy, to deliver her, and love her, and turn her sorrow to joy.

Love. The word caught in his soul and pierced him straight through.

Lyting compelled his thoughts back to the present, ignoring the sting that burned in his heart.

Lyting and Skallagrim admired the broad-beamed *knarr*, a merchant ship of deep draft with half decks fore and aft, the center open to carry cargo and livestock.

The men exchanged corresponding glances. She was a beauty, but her tunnage was too great for portage overland. Upon the rivers they required a fast ship, powered by sail and oar. On land it must be light enough to transport, even with its full cargo still laden aboard. Unfortunately, *knarrs* were more suited to the open seas. They moved on.

"This one is built of oak, twelve strakes high, and will take a crew of ten," informed Sven, a stick of a man, tall and balding.

"How old is she?" Skallagrim left Lyting's side to inspect the vessel's hull more closely.

While the chieftain discussed capacity and speed, Lyting scanned the workyard. He preferred a smaller vessel. One swift that required as few extra crewmen as necessary. No need to compound the difficulties of transporting a ravishing virgin undefiled.

His eyes alighted on a newly finished ship, standing in the yard. There, a man affixed a gilded wind-vane to the prow, topped with a roaring lion. Lyting joined him.

"Has she performed her sea trials yet?" he asked of the

craftsman as he estimated her breadth amidship. She could take a crew of five.

"Tomorrow," the man returned and began to knot bright-colored streamers onto the curved, punctured underside of the vane.

As Skallagrim, Sven, and Olaf trod forward, Lyting gestured to the vessel. "This one would serve us well."

" 'Tis a mite smaller than what I had in mind." Skallagrim scanned her from bow to stern.

"*Já*, but to our advantage. She will be swift as a hawk, able to maneuver and outrun anything larger or heavier."

Skallagrim pursed his lips, then shook his head. "The Baltic pirates be my foremost concern before we reach Kiev. If they set upon us and ensnare us, I'd prefer to have more men and more steel at my disposal to greet them."

Lyting recognized the difference in their paths of thought. Skallagrim had fought his battles primarily on land, whether while *i viking* or making overland portages. He apparently felt more secure in meeting the pirates with the same "stand and fight" mentality and with a complement of men.

But the sea was Lyting's own experience—a great floating battlefield. At times the fleet "stood and fought," the great longships lashed together. But more often survival depended on skill and dexterity with the ships and in making them respond to the tactician's commands. Battle tactics and sea maneuvers, those were the essence of war upon the waters. They reminded Lyting of Ketil's gaming boards.

"Still, I would like to partake in the sea trials on the morrow," Lyting voiced, thinking that he would need speak anon of the matter with Skallagrim.

Sven readily agreed to take him on, and Olaf declared he would join in the trials, also.

As they made their return to the holding, Olaf prodded Lyting to share a tale of Nørdby or Søndervig. Lyting complied, deciding it an opportune moment to describe for his companions the art and strategem of running blockades.

As Lyting, Skallagrim, and Olaf approached the ship-wright's holding, young Eirik propelled himself from the ribbon of shadow that bordered the longhouse and hastened to join his father.

Olaf tousled the lad's hair. "Were you a help to Hakon and your *broðir*? Did you raise the tents?"

"*Já, Faðir*. One. They sent me off after that and took the slavewomen inside with some skins of wine."

Skallagrim's head jerked around. He pinned a hard-eyed look on the boy. Oblivious, the child fell into a skip, kicking up small, gritty sprays of sand with his toes.

"They made some fearsome noises, too, and the sides of the tent started to rumble. I waited to see it would fall down." He toed up more sand. "Rig grunted like a pig! And Hakon groaned and shouted, too. Sounded like something got ahold of them both and wouldn't let go. I thought I should help, but then one woman cried out—a different sort of cry. I think they hurt her."

"By the gods!" Skallagrim swore as he hulked forward. "It best not have been a virgin's cry."

Lyting raced with the others to the far side of the longhouse, his heart catapulting out of place. They arrived in time to see the curtain separate on the front of the wood-framed tent and Rig climb out. Bare to the waist and ruddy with exertion, he tightened the drawstring on his pants, then adjusted the bulge beneath.

Hakon followed, unclad. Snatching up his tunic from just inside the tent, he drew it over his head, then arrested his movements at the sight of the others. He observed the storm on Skallagrim's brow, then let the shirt drop to cover his male boldness.

A smile unfurled across Hakon's lips. Lyting felt a challenge there, contention, presumably over the matter of the maid whom they both claimed. The gleam that shone in Hakon's eyes gave a knife-twist to Lyting's insides. Had Hakon defied his uncle and violated the beauty after all?

Skallagrim pounded forward as though he feared the same. But Hakon stepped aside and yanked back the tent drape to reveal the two dark-haired slaves within—one with angry flashing eyes, her lush breasts exposed to all; the other with her head and torso turned away, clutching her clothes to cover her nakedness as she sniffled softly.

"Ease yourself, Uncle. You bade me bring women to satisfy myself. I did and I have. You'll recall, these are *my* spoils of the Irish raid. Yours is inside the *hus*."

A tinge of resentment clung to his words. Hakon crouched down and idled a finger over the younger girl's back. We'll be along shortly.

Rig grinned and scratched his stomach, prepared to reenter the tent.

"*Now*, Rig." Olaf ordered stiffly. "*Komið* now. While we have the day's light, we work. Hakon, cover up your women before every man in my shipyard abandons his task to take a turn on them."

Olaf heeled off toward the *hus*, Eirik tracking after him. Disgruntled, Rig caught up his crumpled shirt and headed for the workyard.

As Hakon straightened, Skallagrim eyed the equipment that lay stacked and forgotten to the side of the tent, then fixed his nephew with an impatient stare.

"Now that your most basic needs are met, mayhaps you can apply yourself to the concern of our encampment. Atlison can assist your efforts." He gave a blunt nod to Lyting, indicating that he should remain. At that, Skallagrim stalked off, dogging Olaf's path back to the longhouse.

Lyting and Hakon faced each other. The air lay thick betwixt them. Slowly Hakon's mouth curled upward.

"How long has it been since you had a woman, 'monk'?" His tone echoed disdain, then he chuckled. "Take one. The raven-tressed girl there is full of spit and vinegar, but you'll find her a hot piece and willing enough. Now, this one . . ." Hakon pulled the younger girl from the tent and held her before him. She trembled miserably. "This one is the sweeter morsel. Prettier, don't you think?—though frightened as a fawn."

He dragged the veil of hair from her shoulder, baring a smooth, ivory neck, mottled with bruises.

"She'll grow more yielding in time," Hakon breathed as he dropped a kiss beneath her jaw. "They all do, given suitable inducement."

Lyting narrowed his eyes and bridled a thoroughly unchristian but wholly Norse impulse to run Hakon straight through. But that would guarantee him naught but a length of steel through his own belly. Every man on Gotland would uphold Hakon's right to deal with his slaves as he pleased and would avenge him as a matter of personal duty in preserving the Law Code.

Little use would he be to anyone dead. Certainly not to the Irish captives, or the child emperor and his mother. Frustration chafed at his self-restraint. He girt the emotion and chose a divergent course.

"Your fawn is a fragile creature, Hakon. Look at her. She is far from hale. I question whether she can sustain the ordeal of our impending journey. Why not sell her to the shipwright, or leastwise, leave her here until your return?"

"For Gytha to free, or as a gift to Rig?" Hakon barked a laugh. "*Nei*. She'll weather the journey fit enough. Besides, I have a mind to keep her."

He loosed the girl, then motioned for the women to dress and hauled on his own trousers as well. Turning, he lifted a mocking brow at Lyting.

"If you fear for that little one, 'monk,' offer your prayers and sacrifice. But take heed. She is *my* concern. None other's. I might share her around, but I have no intention of releasing her." His eyes glinted as though he wrested a small victory.

Lyting bit down on all that he would say, his jaw hardening to rival all the granite on Gotland. He moved off and took up the necessary boards and poles to frame a second tent.

Internally he boiled. His hands were bound until the convoy reached Constantinople and the court of the emperor. There, he hoped to gain the aid of the Imperials, in gratitude for the message he bore them.

Lyting watched Hakon lead off his captives to the *hus*. Prudence and caution need be his watchwords. If only he could convince Skallagrim to take a smaller ship, there would be fewer men to abuse the slavewomen and less of a threat to the chieftain's unblemished prize.

Lyting labored atime longer, erecting a third tent and staking tall lamp irons into the ground. He then abandoned the site and set off around the cove to retrieve his sea trunk.

He reflected on the captives as he walked, wondering if they had long known one another. Childhood friends? Kinswomen, mayhaps, joined by a bond of blood?

From what he knew, the auburn-haired beauty was the daughter of a wealthy lord, seized on her wedding day. Had it been an arrangement entangling riches and title? Or a love match, perchance? And if her bridegroom had survived the raid, would she run eagerly to his arms once delivered back to her people?

Lyting envisaged the scene, ignoring the leaden feeling in his heart. Instead, he imagined the maid of Eire, overjoyed and aglow with a sun-brilliant smile.

The shadowy bridegroom dissolved from his mind's eye, and he found himself wholly entranced. When Lyting reached the longship atime later, he couldn't recall the journey.

Chapter 7

Ailinn smoothed back the fall of hair from Deira's face and dried her cheek. But tears welled anew and spilled from beneath the girl's sodden lashes. Her shoulders began to shake, and she bit her lip to stiffle an oncoming cry.

"God's mercy, Deira," Rhiannon hissed. "Don't be such a mewling creature."

"Rhiannon! Hold your tongue," Ailinn reproached and enfolded her stepcousin in her arms. "Hasn't there been abuse enough this day? She can bear no more."

Rhiannon's eyes flashed green fire. "If she wouldn't resist them so, they wouldn't hurt her. Do *I* show bruises?"

Rhiannon eased back with her handwork on the raised side-floor where they were chained at the rear of the hall. Contemplating Deira's quivering form, she emitted an exasperated sigh and came forward again.

"You must learn to shut them from your mind, Cousin. Even when their hands are upon you, close the door within and let them be done with it. One man is much like another. The act the same. And it *does* find its end, now, doesn't it?"

Deira burrowed into Ailinn's shoulder.

Rhiannon threw a hand to the air. "You must take hold of your circumstance and reshape it, Deira." She leaned back again and plied the bone needle to the cloth. "Elsewise, you best find a way to hold fast and endure, lest fate consume you and devour you alive."

Deira cast back an utterly horrified look at Rhiannon.

"Saint's breath, Deira." Impatience gusted across Rhiannon's brow. "You truly are a milk-faced kitten. As long as you still draw a breath, you can—"

"Enough, Rhiannon!" Ailinn sliced through her words. "Leave her be and tend to your own fate."

Rhiannon's eyes flared for an instant, then thinned to feline slits.

"I intend to." Her voice rose and fell with a cadence filled with collusion. "But I shall not simply take hold of my fate. I shall bend it to my own will with both hands."

A chill spiraled through Ailinn at the thin smile etched on Rhiannon's face.

"You shall see," Rhiannon promised. "You know that you shall." Her voice dropped to a near whisper. "Prepare yourself, Ailinn of the Érainn. You cannot escape the hungering appetites of these Norse wolves forever."

Ailinn took a small swallow, knowing Rhiannon meant to inform their captors of her own noble identity and see their places changed once again. Ailinn struggled to calm her pulse.

For the moment the shipwright's wife afforded them a small respite, demanding no more of them than simple mending. The men had withdrawn some time ago, and a caldron of stew simmered over the central hearth, its hearty fish-and-vegetable aromas pervading the hall and rousing the appetite. Thinking to alter their conversation to a more useful course, Ailinn openly questioned where they might be.

Deira wiped a tear. "I have been watching where the sun rises and sinks each day, and how the men take their measurements with an instrument they hold in their hands. 'Tis like a small wooden sundial." She smiled faintly, then gathered her brows in thought. "I think we have sailed mostly east and north."

"Good, Deira." Ailinn gave the girl an affectionate squeeze. Her own instincts agreed, but it pleased her that Deira had been so observant.

" 'Tis my guess that we are on a large island," Rhiannon added, surprising the other two. " 'Twas my custom of an evening to sit by the peat fires in my father's hall and listen to the talk of men. They spoke often of the Norse devils and sometimes of their homelands."

She squinted as though into the past, trying to recapture long-faded tales.

"The Norwegians have a harsh, mountainous country with their western coast naked to the seas, and near the full length of their eastern boundary wed to that of the Swedes. To the south of them lie the Danes, but theirs is not a single land. 'Tis comprised of islands except for one arm of land that juts northward from the East Frankish kingdom."

"Then, are we still amongst the Danes?" Deira pressed.

"Mayhaps not. Some islands belong to the Swedes and others rule themselves."

"The men grow their beards," Ailinn remarked, a sudden realization dawning. "If they do not shave them, it could mean we are to continue on to a greater distance still, for the beards provide them warmth upon the waters."

As they considered this, Ailinn envisaged the star-bright Dane and the pale, golden-brown growth that had begun to cover his jaw and upper lip. It matched his lashes and brows and enhanced his masculinity in a most disturbing way. Would he accompany them to their journey's end?

Ailinn abraded herself, banishing the Norse warrior from her thoughts. If anything, Hakon's and the other man's abuse of her stepcousins in the foregoing hour served to heighten her revulsion for men of the North and fuel the fires of hatred she kept alive in her heart.

Deira's soft voice carried her back. "If we sailed eastward, then the coastline we followed to the north was likely that of the Swedes," she reasoned carefully. "But what lies beyond the sea to the east?"

The three exchanged glances, none sure.

Ailinn's spirits contracted, as she thought on the Arabs clogging the street in the slave-market town where she last saw Lia. Did Skallagrim intention dooming her to one of the scorching desert kingdoms of the East? Mayhaps 'twas best Lia was sold to a Norseman after all.

Ailinn steadied her concerns and strayed a glance about the hall, settling it, at last, upon the shipwright's wife where she sat at the loom with her daughter, weaving a decorative braid.

Rhiannon matched Ailinn's gaze. "She's not one of them. What do you think she is?"

"Does it matter?" Ailinn didn't care for Rhiannon's scrutinizing tone. She caught up a childsize tunic from the small stack of clothing and examined the tear in the front.

"It would if she could speak our tongue." Rhiannon chewed her lower lip, studying the woman.

"She's not Irish," Ailinn maintained, experiencing a sudden desire to shield the woman from her stepcousin.

"True." Rhiannon nodded, deep in her thoughts. "I do marvel that she provided us water to refresh ourselves and clean garments, sorely worn as they are."

"She appeared extremely disturbed when the men removed you both from the hall," Ailinn offered as she plied needle and thread to the rip. "When her husband came in, she filled his ear—'twould seem with genuine concern."

"Well, she can give us all the water she likes and stacks of clean, boiled clothes." Rhiannon held her forearm beneath her nose and sniffed several times. "But we will never rid ourselves of the stench of the Norse bulls who mate us."

Deira paled. Blue veins appeared beneath the translucence of her skin.

As Ailinn and Rhiannon attended to their stitching, Deira lifted her arm and smelled along its length. She bent her head to draw a breath of her dress, sniffed her hands and fingertips and, finally, a clump of her hair. She shuddered at Hakon's distinctive odor.

Scent pulsed with memory. Dark memories. Unutterable. Soul-crushing. Their horrors seeped through Deira and pooled in her soul.

Drawing up the cloth of her skirt, Deira rubbed it over her neck and along her collarbone, then reached down to stroke it over her legs and scrub the scent away. . . .

Hakon lounged on the side-floor, looking loathsomely content as Deira filled his cup. He reached out a long finger and ran it idly down her arm. She gasped and jerked back, trembling. Wary, she moved on and stood straining at arm's length to pour the next man's beverage. Hakon chuckled and drew on his beer.

Ailinn's anger crackled live about her as she watched the Norse devil torment her stepcousin. Flashing fire in his direction, she continued spooning honey-sweetened curds into small wooden bowls.

Her hand stilled when Hakon paused deep in his cup, his eyes slashing over the rim. She followed his dissevering look and found at its end the white-haired Dane.

Slowly Hakon lowered the cup, his dislike for the warrior palpable, as was his conceit. Eyes glittering, Hakon seized on a joint of meat from a nearby platter and ripped a mouthful from the bone. He then shifted his position and gave his interest to a conversation nearby.

A chill of foreboding swept through Ailinn, stealing her breath and finding the core of her bones. She forced her attention to the task at hand. With a downward glance she discovered the shipwright's diminutive daughter waiting to receive bowls of thick curds and berries to serve to the men.

The exquisite little girl took it upon herself to lesson Ailinn and pointed to the pudding-like fare.

"*Skyr*," she pronounced.

Ailinn smiled and repeated the word, then topped the *skyr* with small crimsoned berries which the Norse apparently favored. The child pointed once more.

"Lingonberries," she declared distinctly.

Handing the girl two filled bowls, Ailinn crouched down and pointed her own finger to the child, herself.

The girl brightened and said, "Dalla."

With her offerings in hand Dalla padded across the hall, ignoring her half brother, Rig, and Hakon completely, and made a direct path for the silver warrior.

Lyting contemplated letting out his belt a notch, so full was his stomach. Rarely did he indulge himself to such excess, but Gytha's stew proved indescribably delicious, the bread fresh-baked and her beer, truly, the finest he ere tasted. He fantasized of secreting her into the kitchens of Corbie or, possibly, sending monks to Gotland to study under her instruction. His stomach ached dully, reminding of his intemperance.

As Lyting considered his belt once more, he felt the pull of a pair of eyes. Looking up from where he sat on the side-floor, he found the elf child, Dalla—pretty in her brightly paneled dress, with her long silken hair caught up from her face and merrily beribboned.

Dalla scrutinized the contents of both her bowls with utmost care. Choosing the one that appeared the fullest, she bestowed it cheerfully on Lyting.

Lyting's stomach throbbed at the mere sight.

"þakk, little one," he voiced with aching appreciation. He wondered what he might do with it. A puppy would prove a useful companion at the moment.

Dalla remained rooted to the floor, her eyes fixed on him, as she waited for him to sample the treat. Bracing himself, Lyting complied, a small spoonful, excellent. He smiled his approval.

Satisfied, Dalla headed off to deliver the other bowl elsewhere in the hall.

Gazing down at the bowlful of *skyr* and lingonberries, Lyting knew Dalla would soon return, expecting to find it emptied. Without benefit of a puppy to assist him, he let out a sigh and a notch of his belt.

Lyting ate slowly, listening to the talk in the hall. Men continued to arrive as they had over the course of the past hour, seeking out Skallagrim, who they heard sought to sail in *felag* for Kiev in the coming days.

Though the chieftain made plain his intention to make the crossing into the Gulf of Riga, catching the river Dvina to the Dnieper, some urged for the convoy to take the northerly route through the Finnish Gulf.

Naturally, from there, they would follow the river Volkov to Lake Ilmen, where portages could be made either to the Volga, leading east to the Khagnates and Caliphates, or to the Dnieper, flowing south to Kiev and, ultimately, the Black Sea and Byzantium. Thus, the men argued, they could cross the Baltic in greater numbers and separate later at Lake Ilmen for their respective destinations.

But Skallagrim held his ground. In his estimation, passage by way of the Dvina to the Dnieper was the quickest route to Kiev and no more hazardous or difficult than the other. Perchance, he suggested with a sharp eye, what the others truly desired, more than the safety of numbers, was the opportunity to barter their goods at Aldeigjuborg and Holmgarð— important centers on the River Volkov.

Lyting found himself amused, believing the chieftain had pierced the mark. He spooned up the last of the curds and berries from the bowl and listened to Skallagrim state, in unbroachable terms, that he would sail into the Gulf of Riga.

Time was his outstanding concern, the chieftain stressed. He wished to depart with the first convoys out of Kiev destined for Miklagárd. The men would need make their choice—to travel by way of the Dvina or the Volkov. But he reminded that Constantinople was the most fabulous crossroad of the world, its wealth and luxuries beyond imagining. The trade centers of the Rus could be visited upon their return journey—as he, himself, intended to do.

Skallagrim settled back in his chair, his watchful gaze straying to his prize slave, as ever it did. Lyting noted that the chieftain was not alone in this. If only he could convince Skallagrim to sail with a smaller crew. Then they would have naught but those outside the ship to concern them.

A handful of men took their leave of the hall, but most lingered to discuss the Dvina route and estimate how soon they might expect to reach Kiev. They talked further of ships and tunnage and compared the commodities they each brought in trade—notably amber, wax, honey, furs, and slaves.

Many began to throw in their lot with Skallagrim, vowing to bind themselves in *felag*. After one man made his declaration, he boldly appraised the three slavewomen—obviously the chieftain's, for the shipwright owned none.

"You bring few slaves this year, my friend, but these you have here are exceptional. 'Twill be a good voyage. *Já?*" He grinned in wolfish, high spirits, tipping his ale cup toward the tempting prey.

Skallagrim scowled.

"*Já,*" Hakon rejoined when his uncle offered no response.

Dalla chose that moment to retrieve Lyting's bowl. As she disappeared across the room, Lyting glanced to the chieftain once more. He sat like a boulder upon his chair, his expression darkened but his color increased. He prowled his gaze about the hall and took measure of those who would sail with him to Kiev.

Alert to Skallagrim's shifting mood, Lyting remained vigilant. The chieftain kept the auburn-haired maiden near to his side while the other two slavewomen took up the pitchers and refreshed the cups in the hall.

A few men grew boisterous as someone grabbed at the raven-tressed slave. She rewarded him with a lapful of beer to cool his ardor. Except for the recipient, the others found this most entertaining. Even Hakon appeared impressed.

Skallagrim's voice then rose in the hall, drawing their attention. When they looked, he stood from his chair and raised his cup high.

"Let us drink to our fellowship, to the journey before us, and to the adventures that await! There be enough men now pledged to fill six ships. So drink deep of your cups, my friends, and on the morrow, see to your craft and gather your goods and slaves. In two days time we sail for the Dvina and the riches of the East."

The hall took on a festive air, quickening with laughter and the clamor of voices. Skallagrim reseated himself and fell to conversation with Olaf and several other seamen who shared their narrow table. Lyting could only wonder if they discussed the merchant ship that Skallagrim selected earlier at Sven's, and whether he now considered these men for his crew.

Gytha set a large platter of salt herring, cheeses, and fruit before them, then stepped aside for the chieftain's slave to attend to the men's cups.

Skallagrim's gaze brooded over his Irish prize as she poured the drink for those at table. Drawing on his eating knife, he carved a wedge of cheese and ate it slowly from the blade. He then browsed an eye about the hall. More than once he stopped to stare down one man or another who showed immoderate interest in the slave beside him.

Olaf leaned to the chieftain's ear, making some comment above the din. Skallagrim nodded and brought his gaze round, then halted at the sight of his other table companions.

Lyting felt his own choler rise as he watched the men there rake the maid with ruttish looks, their blood warmed by drink and her exceptional beauty.

Skallagrim's face took on a ruddy cast as one man bolted down the contents of his cup, seemingly for no more than an excuse to compel the maid to come to his side and refill it. All the while his eyes moved hotly over her, unaware of the chieftain's jealous possession of her.

Observant, Skallagrim stabbed a chunk of herring with the knife tip and flicked it into his mouth. Not bothering to chew, he swallowed it whole.

" 'Tis fortunate for us all that you have a reputation as being a sharing sort of man, Skallagrim." The man smiled broadly, confidently. "I have seven Saxon slaves, and you are welcome to them all, as often as you wish." His gaze traveled over the Irish beauty. " 'Twill be interesting to see how this one rides on the waves."

He reached for the maid, leaning forward with one arm still resting upon the table and his fingers touching the platter.

Skallagrim's knife plunged through the air, impaling the fruit beside the man's hand with such force that the blade lodged in the wood of the platter.

"You heard wrong," Skallagrim growled. Wresting the knife free, he lifted it, fruit still upon the blade, and gestured with its point toward Lyting and Hakon. Both had come to their feet.

The chieftain smiled soberly, his eyes fixing on Lyting. "We three take a smaller ship this season, one with room for but two more. Those crewmen I have already chosen," he stated flatly. "But if sharing 'tis what concerns you, you will likely find Hakon obliging, leastwise during the times that we camp."

The men left the table in less cheer. As he ate the fruit from his blade, Skallagrim bid Lyting over.

"Make your sea-trial in the morning." Skallagrim's sharp gaze bit into him. "But you best be flat-out certain of the craft's capabilities, Atlison. I have no death wish to perish in the Gulf of Riga."

"Nor do I." Lyting held the chieftain's gaze, his own unfaltering.

Hope swelled in Lyting's chest. He yearned to look to where the maid stood behind the chieftain's chair, but he dared not. By God's might, he would see his quest successfully to its end, his only hope now—that Skallagrim would give him free rein of the ship.

Skallagrim rubbed his bearded jaw. "I must think on who we might take on as crewmen." A sly smile touched his eyes. "But for now, reassure me with another of your tales of Nørdby and Søndervig. The men could use a rousing tale to hearten them for the perils ahead and glean what courage they can." He rolled an eye to Lyting. "You have yet to meet the tribesmen of the Steppe." He gruffed out a laugh and took a swill of beer.

Lyting assumed a place near the hearth on the side-floor, and the hall hushed to hear the tale he would unfold of heroic feats and warrior kings.

Eirik sat at his feet with eyes shining and drank of his every word. Dalla imposed herself sweetly, snuggling beside Lyting and laying her head upon his lap.

Hakon listened from a distance. His mood grew more sullen as he drank. While the Norman enthralled the occupants of the hall with his stories, he moved to where the slavewomen huddled at the far end of the room. Making his choice, he hauled the black-haired girl to her feet and took her from the place.

Deira drew back against Ailinn and began to shake, fearful for Rhiannon, dark memories gnashing.

"Shh," Ailinn comforted, stroking her hair. "Listen to the Dane's voice. How soothing it is. He tells them a tale, no doubt of great deeds—of bravery and glory—like our own people are wont to tell in the halls of Eire. Think on those now."

Ailinn rocked Deira gently and hummed a quiet tune. The warrior's voice faded as she envisoned the sweet meadows of Clonmel where she once ran free as a child. Of a sudden, she came aware of Skallagrim standing over her and of the quiet in the hall. The white Dane had finished with his telling. But why did the others look at her so?

The chieftain gestured to her and then to the hall.

"Ailinn, he wishes for you to sing."

"I didst but hum. Why does he . . . ?"

"He heard you sing before—to Lia upon the sea. Oh, do sing, Cousin." Deira squeezed her hand. "You sing so beautifully, and 'twould cheer me, truly."

"Then, for you, Deira. And for Lia. Here, lay your head to my shoulder." Ailinn smiled. "We shall close our eyes and believe we sit before the peat fires in your father's hall, and that the morrow holds no cares."

The pure, crystal tones of Ailinn's voice floated out over the hall, the strains hauntingly sad and infinitely beautiful.

Lyting settled back with Dalla still upon his lap, wholly arrested, unable to take his eyes from the maid even if he wished. And he did not wish. The melody's lilting airs wreathed through him—ageless and soul-filling. They wrung him out.

As the song ended, Lyting glanced down to find Dalla asleep

on his lap. His heart dilated. Gytha came quietly forward and
gathered up the child, taking her away.

The maid's voice lifted over the hall once again, and Lyting
indulged himself the pleasure of her beauty and the enchantment of her voice as he observed her from afar.

He rested back upon an elbow and allowed his thoughts to
drift. Closing his eyes, the silvery notes bore him up and
carried him on wing. One melody blended into the next. They
shifted of a sudden, altering in character, rhythm, and language.

Lyting plummeted back to the moment as Frankish words—
one after another—spilled distinctly upon his ears. He thrust
upright to the edge of the side-floor, keenly alert. 'Twas a
child's song, one he had heard Brienne sing often to amuse the
twins.

Lyting studied the maid of Eire, wondering how she could
know of it. She finished the melody as quickly as she began it
and reverted again to a lyrical Irish strain.

Thoughtfully he rubbed a forefinger across his lips and back
along his jaw. Had she simply committed the song to memory?
Or might it be possible that she had a knowledge of the
Frankish tongue?

Later, in the depths of the night, when the men had long
since departed the shipwrights' *hus* and found their way to their
beds, Lyting tossed in a fitful sleep, tormented by the dream
that long haunted him.

Swords parried and flashed, his half brother, Hastein,
slashing down on him like a demon in the dark. A woman
screamed. Anxiously Lyting looked for Brienne and found her
cleaved with anguish.

But her features suddenly transformed before him, her
midnight hair firing with the deep reds of autumn. Now 'twas
the maid of Eire who reached out toward him. Tears wet her
cheeks as she cried out his name in warning.

Turning back, Lyting found, not his half brother, but Hakon,
brandishing the sword before him.

Chapter 8

"He is not like the others." Rhiannon's gaze traveled over the long, hard length of the silver warrior.

Ailinn stole a sideways glance of the Dane, acutely aware of his nearness. He stood to the fore of the ship, taking a sun-reading with a small wooden dial of some nature. He held an easy stance, his broad shoulders and well-muscled legs richly outlined by his leather corslet and the trim fit of his trousers. His beard had thickened further, adding to his potent good looks.

Completing his calculations, the Dane moved past the women, his gait steady and even upon the surging deck, his gaze cast out over the expanse of sea, searching the eastern horizon. Rhiannon watched him with close interest.

Ailinn sealed her lips against her annoyance and what impulse goaded her to say. Looking back past the stern post, she focused on the ships that followed in their wake, five in all. They maintained a staggered formation so as not to block one another's wind.

"Ailinn believes the white-haired Dane to be one of the Normans of Francia—a nobleman," Deira replied unexpectedly to Rhiannon's comment.

"Francia." Rhiannon considered the word and the man, dragging a tapered fingertip downward over her throat.

Ailinn's mouth thinned. She wished now that she had held her tongue earlier. Whilst Rhiannon napped, she and Deira had spoken quietly of their captivity in the Norse trading center and of her time at Thora's *hus*.

"The Northmen rule a duchy in Francia that extends to the Channel and the seas." Rhiannon wrapped her arms about her knees and continued to ponder the silver warrior.

"A nobleman you say?" Her brow lined with thought. "Francia is not so great a distance from Eire. Doubtless, these men are adventurers and merchants. They commence their journeys now, for 'tis spring. But they will return homeward when fall nips the air, before winter chokes the rivers with ice. Likely, this Norman also returns to his duchy at the season's end."

Rhiannon continued to stroke a single finger along her throat and contemplate the towering Dane.

Perturbed, Ailinn turned away. 'Twas obvious Rhiannon crafted her designs, contriving how best to gain favor with the man and use him to her ends. Presumably, she would first seek to heighten her value—and her appeal—in his eyes, making known to him her privileged status—an Eóganacht princess—worthy of ransom and of his noble bed, if that be his desire.

Would he desire? The thought rankled.

"He appears to favor you, Ailinn." Deira absently plucked at the nap of her dress. "Ever his eyes are upon you. The others might not see. But I see."

Surprise touched Ailinn's face.

Deira smoothed the fabric of her gown. "The white-haired Dane is the one who tried to make your purchase when first we arrived in the Danish town. Lia and I were chained ahead of you in the line, but we watched all that passed. 'Tis my guess he still wishes to possess you and keep you for his own."

Ailinn's brows whisked high and wide. At the same moment she caught Rhiannon's searing glare in the edge of her vision. She had to bite the inside of her cheek to keep from smiling.

Clearing the tickle that threatened in her throat, Ailinn sobered her expression. "The chieftain does not seem eager to sell me."

"Perchance the Dane will yet influence the chieftain and change his mind," Deira encouraged. "And should he succeed, oh, think on it, Ailinn. 'Twould be as Rhiannon says. In Norman lands you would be so much nearer to Eire. Mayhaps, someday, somehow, you could escape home to Clonmel and be free."

Deira drew up the edge of her gown and began to chafe it against her neck and along her arms. "Of course, there be risk in that as well as advantage. He would likely take you for his concubine. Yet, 'tis far better than so many men wishing to . . ." She retreated into the folds of her mantle and fell silent.

Ailinn's heart cramped for Deira. She reached out and squeezed her stepcousin's hand. Easing back, Deira's words continued to twine through her.

Intimacy with the silver warrior? She glimpsed his commanding figure and found that the promise of that fate held no fear. Instead, it released a river of warmth within her.

As Ailinn brought her eyes from the Dane, she met Deira's gaze. The girl smiled softly, her eyes large and doelike, though sadly wounded in their depths.

"He *is* different from the others. I sense something good in him." Deira lifted Ailinn's hand and put it to her cheek. "Whatever comes, whatever happens to us, I pray he takes you into his keeping and sees you well, and returns with you at his side to Francia."

Emotion welled, congesting Ailinn's chest. Fearful and heartsick for what the morrow might bring, she placed a comforting hand to Deira's head, unobservant of Rhiannon's poisonous glare.

Rhiannon turned away and squinted hard across the unbounded sea. "We'll see who returns to Francia," she grated beneath her breath.

Lyting cupped his hands about his eyes, concentrating his vision on a distant flock of seabirds. The span of sea strained even his sharp vision. 'Twas impossible to identify them with certainty.

He continued to search for a slow-beating cloud of lapwings, or a small bevy of dunlins or plovers. These, or any of the numerous species of shorebirds would signal that they were closing upon the coast of Courland and the Gulf of Riga.

Lyting paced the ship's *larboard* side. He felt the wind on his cheek—a good northwesterly, he knew by experience, having no need to consult the bright threads streaming from the prow's vane, or the ripples on the water purling across the sea.

Except for a brief rain burst yesterday, the convoy had enjoyed bright, sun-filled days, calm waters, and favorable winds. Added to that, their crossing had been uneventful, without menace from sea robbers. By his reckonings of speed, distance, and position, Lyting believed their progress surpassed earlier estimations. He expected they would sight land within the coming hours.

In all likeliness a trap awaited them there.

Restless, Lyting moved to check the rigging.

The *Little Auk*, as Skallagrim called the ship after the little bird of northern waters, had shown herself well in the sea trials, proving light, fleet, and responsive—easily handled by a crew of five.

To that end, Skallagrim had taken on two able seamen, known to him from past ventures. Whatever the chieftain spoke to them concerning the Irish captives, the men had thus far troubled none of them, confining their interests to the slavewomen they brought of their own.

Lyting worked his way back toward Ragnar, the helmsman, who gave him a nod and a smile. Currently they voyaged under full sail power, without need of oars. Due to an alteration of Lyting's device, all but the helmsman could enjoy a small respite. In verity, Ragnar had argued with Orm for that privilege and now sat at the tiller as a child with a toy, controlling the entire ship from where he sat, both by the rudder and, now also, by the sheets—or lines—which Lyting had trimmed astern.

To accomplish this, Lyting had modified the running rigging, leading the lines back through the oar ports and securing them as needed with the ports' wooden plugs. This enabled the helmsman to trim the spar and the lower edge of the sail from his position astern while he tilled the rudder. With the helmsman able to govern the ship alone, it required only one man to hold watch—a decided advantage with so small a crew.

Lyting gazed on the large, square sail. One additional alteration would also prove to advantage, he thought, especially if they were to confront the pirates of Riga.

In the king's dragon fleet, the crews employed various devices to adjust for wind conditions: sometimes long poles to stretch out the lower corners of the sail; at other times iron grips attached along the sail's reinforced bottom edge by which a man could turn the sail by hand and maneuver his craft out of vulnerable situations.

But the *Little Auk* was equipped with neither of these. Lyting's mind explored other possibilities, seeking a way to extend the foot of the sail from the mast to the clew, the outer edge of the sail. As his gaze quested about the deck for a suitable implement, he saw Skallagrim motion Hakon and Orm astern to the *steorboard*, steering board, quarter. They joined Lyting and Ragnar a moment later.

Skallagrim crouched down in their midst and unrolled a hide map, smoothing it upon the deck for all to see.

"The Gulf of Riga," he stated, tracing a finger around its cuplike shape. "The mouth of the Dvina lies here, on her lower end, at the bottom of the goblet."

The chieftain looked up from beneath his shelf of brow. "These lands are inhabited by numerous tribes. We need worry only of the Cours, who control the coastal plain, and of the Semigallians, who hold the plain just south of the Dvina. Our main threat, however, comes not from the Balts but our own kinsmen—the sea wolves of Scandia, who have found a lucrative trade here, bartering the bite of their swords for honest merchants' wares . . . and their slaves."

Lyting's glance skipped to the women chained at the mast.

"Domesnär"—Skallagrim thumped the marking on the map— "Courland's northern tip. 'Tis the most dangerous point we must negotiate in order to gain access into the Gulf. As you can see, the island of Saaremaa obstructs near the entire entrance into the Gulf.

"We will need sail around the southern end of Saaremaa, north of Courland. The shoals of Domesnär will force us up toward the island, bottling us into its neck, here, its most treacherous point." He drew a blunt finger along the hide. "We will need progress in a single line for atime and will be forced to make a 'dogleg' turn as we enter the Gulf, on the leeward side of the island. 'Tis our weakest point. If the pirates attack, they will do so while we are on the crosswind."

Skallagrim shoved to his feet, leaving the map spread upon the deck. " 'Tis my habit to lead in the convoy's largest and best-armed ship. If robbers be waiting, they will seek to ram us with reinforced craft." The chieftain settled an eye on Lyting.

" 'Tis my guess, however, that you bear a different course in mind."

Lyting caught the beam alight in Skallagrim's eyes. He recognized at once that the chieftain sought to taste of a new adventure this season—a rousing confrontation, unlike those he commonly fought. 'Twas the thin edge of danger, a kiss with death and the prospect for glory, that the chieftain craved. A contest upon the seas, likened to those fought by the king's fleet at Nørdby and Søndervig.

Lyting's smile flashed white against his tanned features. "Já. I do have aught in mind."

Seizing the moment, he bent to the map. "We are light, swift, and maneuverable. My preference is to sail the *Little Auk* in first. With her in the lead and the others holding slightly back, the sea robbers will think us easy prey. With luck we can draw several ships off, then this is what we shall effect. . . ."

Skallagrim nodded as Lyting outlined his plan. Hakon and Orm hovered, and Ragnar strained to see. When Lyting finished, the others stood silent, mulling his words.

"We can do that?" Skallagrim asked, amazed.

"On my word," Lyting vowed, his tone confident, filled with an assuredness born of experience.

The chieftain cracked a wide grin. "Then let us make it so. I will till the rudder through the narrows myself. When the moment comes, give your commands."

A cleansing relief poured through Lyting, followed by a rush of pure energy. 'Twas a small victory but key. Vital to their success.

As the men began to disperse, Lyting stepped to check the surplus of oars and line stowed along the *larboard* side. Hakon came to stand beside him and leveled a vacant stare low across the dark, blue waters.

"If your strategies prove wrong in this, 'monk,' I'll feed you to the fish as bait, long before the pirates can board this little bucket."

Lyting turned and pierced him with ice-blue eyes. "If you are capable of following tactical orders, Hakon, I suggest you do so, or stay out of my way. Otherwise, we'll both be examining the Gulf from the bottom up."

Lyting moved off to check more of the seal-hide lines and, finding some to be dry, sloshed them with sheep fat. He then looked to the coals, glowing red in a small iron pot that squatted on a bed of rocks and sand. A covered jar of seal oil waited nearby and, with it, a bundle of kindling.

Lyting went to sit upon his sea trunk, which doubled as a bench, and took up one of the arrows from the bundle there, along with a strip of linen. As he wound the cloth about the arrow's tip, he scanned the deck. All appeared secure. The women had been moved forward of the mast so as not to obstruct his path when he needed to reach it.

As he placed the finished arrow with those already prepared and took up another, he glimpsed the auburn-haired maid. He wondered anew whether she might speak the Frankish tongue. He had found little opportunity to test that possibility. Now he wished he had, for he would forewarn her of what might come.

Lyting placed the second arrow with the others and slipped one of Gytha's twice-baked bread rounds from the leather pouch, propped against his sea chest. Just when he lifted it to his mouth, something flitted past his head. An instant later, on a whir of wings, a little bird perched upon the railing beside him.

A shorebird, its name unknown to him.

"What are you doing so far from your nest, little fellow?" He smiled easily, though his pulse quickened.

The little bird cocked its head, then began to pace.

"Impatient, are you?" Lyting crumbled a pinch of hard-bread atop the rail.

The bird twisted its head and stared at him. It took a series of quick, back-and-forth steps. Stared and stepped. Stared and stepped again. Pecked at a crumb. Called a mellow "chooe-ee" of appreciation and flew away.

Lyting rose, his gaze following its flight to the eastern horizon. He shielded his eyes from the sun's glare off the waters and watched the little bird diminish to a dot. Then he saw it. Faintly. A pale dune ridge, backed by a tall screen of trees, still vague and bluish at this distance.

His breathing deepened and his blood livened as the warrior within steeled. The time of testing had come. If Byzantium's emperor were to keep his throne and the maid her virtue, and if he were to see these women free, then at all costs his plans must succeed this day.

Lyting lifted his face to the heavens and offered a prayer.
Then, drawing on a breath, he sounded the call.

The women grew restive and murmured amongst themselves
as the men hastened about the deck in a fever of excitement.
Chests were flung open, corslets and helmets withdrawn.
Weapons were retrieved from storage—shields and spears laid
out, arrows and bows placed at the ready. Skallagrim took up
a great, twisted horn, and with a series of reverberant blasts,
signaled the ships behind.

Ailinn saw clearly now that the convoy closed upon a
coastline. It appeared to rise up from the waters as they made
their advance. To the right loomed a high, lofty ridge, fronted
with steep banks and crowned with soaring pines. To the left
the land appeared darker, rockier, dominated by the same
stately pines.

From her vantage the sea appeared to arm its way through
the two masses of land, pushing them apart. The mouth of a
river? Could this be the entrance to one of the great waterways
that led to the eastern kingdoms?

She glanced about. The men donned coats of leather, sewn
with protective bone platelets, and readied their axes. Unques-
tionably they prepared for an attack. Ailinn fought down a
wave of panic.

Quickly she sought the white-haired Dane, wishing she
could bridge the chasm of language that lay between them,
wanting desperately to know what dangers waited ahead.

Ailinn's breath caught the instant her eyes touched him. He
stood toward the bow, a princely figure, clad in a corslet of
gleaming chain mail. He turned his bright head and, finding
her eyes upon him, captured her gaze before she could
withdraw it.

The distance faded betwixt them. His crystal blue eyes
shone brilliant now, effused with the intensity of his thoughts.
In that single moment 'twas though he reached across the
chasm that separated them and touched her mind with his.
What language he whispered there, she didst not know, only
that her fears departed.

Again, he turned to gaze landward—his hand resting on his
sword hilt, the sunlight glinting off the ringlets of mail—a
radiant silver warrior.

As they entered the narrows, he took up the helmet that rested at his feet and fitted it to his head. Striding the length of the deck, he assumed his position astern.

A flash of light. The sun, glancing off polished metal. Now a second. From high atop Domesnär's ridge. A third, fourth. Signaling the number of ships in the convoy to a point across the narrows. A point behind the island of Saaremaa. Fifth, sixth. The flashes ceased.

Lyting slowly exhaled. The convoy had been marked. But in so doing, also had the pirates of Riga.

He seated himself on his sea trunk, ready at the oar. In moments they would sail free of the corridor of cliff and pine and be forced, nearly at once by the rocky shoals off *steorboard*, to alter their course and bear up toward the island, windward, losing much of their sail power.

'Twould be a vulnerable position as they filed, singly at first, through the shallows, with the wind slightly aft of the beam. They would need ply their oars mightily then, forging ahead to a point where they could turn downwind again and harness the wind's driving force dead astern.

As they did now.

Lyting raised his eyes to the full swell of sail before the mast. Thankfully, the wind was to advantage this day, allowing the crew to conserve their strength and energies for the time to come.

Behind, the ships continued to course in an alternate pattern, holding to a distance as he had signaled for them to do. Success depended on the *Little Auk* feigning to be easy game—drawing off the sea dogs and breaking the concentration of their numbers.

According to the chieftain, 'twas the robbers' ploy, not to engage the entire convoy, but to mark out their prey and fall upon them like a pack of wolves, seizing only what they could successfully secure and keep within their grasp. Predators, trapping quarry from the herd.

The raiders would expect resistance, but they also relied upon the merchant ships being lightly manned and heavily cumbered with goods. Lyting counted on the robbers underestimating the *Little Auk*'s potential entirely, though he, himself, held every confidence in her capabilities.

Lyting suspended his thoughts as the watery passageway opened upon the Gulf of Riga. Immediately Skallagrim pulled back hard upon the tiller and brought the ship about, northward toward the island. Lyting leaned into the oar in unison with the others, the wind now coming across the *larboard* quarter and its velocity dropping somewhat as they moved in the lee of the land.

Immense quiet hung like a mist over the Gulf, save for the sporadic cries of circling terns or the whistles and "wickas" of sandpipers and godwits calling from ashore. The men continued to ply their strength to the oars, waiting tense and expectant for the first sight of the pirates.

Still, the great quiet loomed.

Steadily the *Little Auk* gained in speed as they traveled windward. Skallagrim guided them close to the southern point of the island which hooked slightly northward, shouldering a partition of pines and creating a blind.

Lyting watched the light sparkle through the stand of trees, winking and glittering in the breaches as the midday sun danced upon the waters behind. He studied the patterns of light and dark. So sharply did he feel the enemies' presence upon his senses, he thought to breathe their foul scent as well.

His gaze locked on a portion of the wood. Movement. Shadows. Gliding behind the screen of trees.

Lyting called out a warning to the others. They laid into the oars with all their might, pulling and pushing as though Fenrir Wolf gnashed at the keel and Hel set the waters afire.

The first of the pirate ships emerged from the palisade of pines, its bow shining of metal. At once it pointed its iron-clad bow ahead of the *Little Auk*'s and began to advance.

Good, Lyting thought. It had taken the bait. 'Twas a matter of course, when posturing one's ship to ram another's, to aim thusly for the opponent's bow. Allowing for distance and "way," the speed, of both ships, the attacking vessel could expect to close upon the other straight on the beam and strike it broadside, midship.

Lyting vowed, however, that this day nothing would be a matter of course.

Before he could scan the size of the oncoming force, a second ship appeared joining the first, directing its fortified bow toward the *Little Auk* with obvious intent.

Lyting strained at the oar, unable to mark what other craft might be issuing forth from the shelter of land, or how great their numbers aboard.

As his muscles knotted and stretched, he imagined the pirates to be grinning wide beneath their whiskers and helmets. The *Little Auk* must appear a small fish, easily swallowed with time to feast on the rest. He hoped they believed that and would continue to follow the *Little Auk* a stretch longer, widening the gap between the other ships of the convoy, purchasing for them a critical space of time.

Despite her size, the *Little Auk* owned significant advantage. Not only did she enjoy a hull lighter than most, but the expanse of her sails measured near the same as those of the larger ships. Comparably, she possessed greater sail power, even in reduced winds such as these.

Now, as if to prove her worth—and in contrast to her namesake—the *Little Auk* surged ahead, skimming the waters fleet as a gull. The pirates pressed after them in fervent pursuit, but as the smaller vessel steadily gained in distance, they slowed, then veered off, having no wish to participate in a stern chase. What first appeared an easy catch was too little a prize to trouble with greatly. Turning back on the merchant ships that lagged behind, they allowed the *Little Auk* to slip away.

Lyting knew a mixture of elation and relief as they achieved their first goal, winning past the pirates through the crosswind leg and now sailing free of the shallows into open waters. A shout of triumph went up onboard.

Lyting's heart drummed, his blood pounding in his veins. Time was precious, the real victory yet to be attained. If the sea dogs believed the *Little Auk* didst but run before the menace of their jaws, 'twas their mistake and one that would cost them.

His energies surging, Lyting secured his oar and bounded to his feet. He shouted for Ragnar to do the same and join him. Hakon and Orm he instructed to remain at their positions.

Grabbing up one of the spare oars and some line, he proceeded to lash one end of the oar to the foot of the mast and the other to the windward clew—the lower, outside corner on the bottom side of the sail—thus rigging a beam to stretch the sail and entrap the wind.

Lyting then ran aft. Taking hold of the sheets, he eased the windward line forward while taking up the slack on the leeward. Simultaneously he called for Skallagrim to come closer to the wind and bring the wind on the beam. As the chieftain complied, the sail snapped full and the ship lurched ahead.

To the pirates, Lyting realized, 'twould appear the *Little Auk* made good her escape, fleeing northeast. But, he held no thought of abandoning the convoy and was far from finished.

As the *Little Auk* skipped across the water, building in velocity, Lyting worked apace. He needed to quickly alter her course and bring her swiftly about. The rudder alone did not command enough force to pivot the ship on his command.

Seizing up another of the surplus oars, Lyting moved to the end of the ship and physically lashed it to the stern post, creating a "sweep-oar," an ancient technology, used through ages past.

With the sweep-oar rigged to augment the rudder, Lyting ordered for Skallagrim to hold his course and for Ragnar to slash the line binding the first oar to the sail's windward clew. He then directed Ragnar to reverse the oar, swinging it over and strapping it to the opposite, *larboard*, clew—the other end still being affixed to the mast.

In combination with Ragnar's actions, Lyting gripped hold of the sweep oar and gave it a massive pull, putting momentum through the turn, swinging the bow away from the wind, and wearing the ship.

The craft "heeled," and the women scrabbled for the high side. At first the maneuver began as a smooth, slow sweep, then accelerated into a fast spin as Lyting brought the wind across the stern.

With the rudder hard over, Skallagrim trimmed the sheets from his position at the helm while Lyting finished bringing the *Little Auk* about, on the opposite beam.

Again, the sail snapped full and the ship shot ahead with high momentum. No auk this, nor gull, either, but a hawk—falcon swift—sweeping down on her prey, marking forward of the pirate's bow.

Ailinn's eyes rounded as the ship sprinted across the waters and closed fast upon the enemy. For all the world it appeared that they would ram the first of the vessels straight on.

Several slavewomen cried out, terrified, and tore at their

hair. Ailinn fought down her own panic and gripped Deira tight.

As the expanse between the ships narrowed briskly, one woman clawed and clambered her way over the others, screaming hysterically. Her terror became Deira's, and Ailinn struggled to hold her stepcousin back.

The woman fought on, heedless that her chains whipped and bruised those about her, determined only to gain the side of the ship. Ailinn feared she would throw herself over the railing. Feared, because one length of chain bound them all.

Impulsively Rhiannon seized the frenzied woman by the hair, yanked her back on her heels, and slapped her down. Ailinn and Rhiannon exchanged glances, and for once Ailinn gave thanks for her stepcousin's steeliness.

Hearts in their throats, Ailinn and Rhiannon watched the distance diminish and braced themselves for the impending collision.

The *Little Auk* raced on the crosswind, bearing southwest, in fierce pursuit of the two pirate ships.

Hakon and Orm labored at the oars. Ragnar hastily dipped the arrows' linen-wrapped tips in seal oil and laid them in readiness on a cover of oxhide. Lyting flamed the coals with bits of kindling, careful not to smoke the fire, lest the pirates be wise to their intent. He then rose apace and resumed his position at the sweep-oar.

Unrelenting, the *Little Auk* drove in for the assault. Ahead, the pirates grew wary and broke off their run on the second of the merchant ships. As they began to bear away, the ship to the fore forced the one to the rear back up toward the island with them and too close to the wind.

The *Little Auk* pressed on, unflinching, without slackening her speed.

The pirates retreated further, hurriedly now, withdrawing landward. But in so doing, they were compelled to bring the wind on their beam, forfeiting half of their momentum nearly at once and with it their maneuverability. Without benefit of Lyting's contrivance to harness the wind, their sails began to luff.

Lyting saw the white expand in the pirates' eyes as the *Little Auk* descended, aiming to ram the foremost ship. At the last moment, he hard muscled the sweep-oar and swerved the ship round to approach the pirate's craft on a parallel course, feinting he would break off their oars.

The women's cries reached his ears, but he shut them out and shouted for Hakon and Orm to trail oars and assist him and Ragnar.

Rapidly the men snatched up their bows, flamed the arrows, and lobbed a volley into the pirates' sail. As Skallagrim brought the *Little Auk* alongside the pirate ship, they discharged another round of the fiery missles and still another and another.

The pirates fell to disorder, some trying to regain "way," others hurriedly bringing forth their own spears, arrows, and bows.

Skallagrim held the *Little Auk*'s course steady, while the crew rained fire into the pirate sail and felled several of the enemy before they could let loose their own deadly shafts.

Then, standing as though in the eye of the storm, Lyting flamed an arrow, notched it in place, and drew the string to his ear. With complete concentration and disciplined calm, he dead-eyed the halyard—the line holding the spar and sail to the mast—and launched the shaft. The arrow blazed across the distance and severed the halyard straight through.

The timbered arm and burning sail clattered downward, collapsing in a fiery heap upon the deck. Flames spread hungrily and with unexpected rapidity, licking high at one end where they fed on a volatile substance—spilled jars of oil, Lyting guessed—setting the wood decking afire.

The *Little Auk* pulled clear of the burning ship and its frantic crew and moved into range of the second ship, positioned ahead and offshore of the first.

Without wasting a moment or motion, Lyting strung another arrow, anchored his aim on one of the trimming sheets that secured the pirate's sail, and shot out the leeward line. The sail flapped uselessly in the wind, and the ship immediately lost all "way." Hakon, Orm, and Ragnar followed with a hail of fiery arrows, lobbing them into the remaining half of the sail and setting it aflame.

With the mast torched overhead, their retreat obstructed by the fiery ship to the fore, and naught but oars to power and maneuver their own vessel, the pirates were left no choice but to make a hasty run cross-channel, toward the shoal waters, and attend to their damages.

Meanwhile, the first three of the merchant ships to have followed the *Little Auk* into the gulf slipped past the tumult and completed the end of the "dogleg"—the crosswind trek. Turning on the down wind, they began to traverse the great expanse of the gulf.

Lyting scanned the waters. The last two vessels of the convoy were beset in the narrows by yet another two pirate ships—the only other ones in sight—the robbers' original strength apparently totaling four.

He quickly adjusted the sheets anew, then joined the others at the oars. Deftly Skallagrim closed in on the first of the two ships.

Seeing their rapid approach and having witnessed the *Little Auk*'s path of destruction, the pirates vacated their attack on the merchant ships and began to seek escape.

Breaking off her assault, the *Little Auk* swung in to assure the vessels were unscathed and to companion them across the waters. Moments later she glided free of the shallows for a second time and turned to catch the downwind dead astern. Her sails filling, she stole across the Gulf of Riga and headed for the mouth of the Dvina.

Lyting stood at the stern and looked back at the burning hulks of the sea robbers.

About him the men spoke exuberantly of their conquest, recounting the details with relish, still exhilarated and flushed with success. The women at the mast appeared pale by contrast, striving to calm their accelerated hearts.

As his own breathing returned to normal, Lyting broke away his gaze and sought the Irish maid. To his surprise, he found her golden-brown eyes fixed upon him.

Just then Skallagrim gave over the tiller to Ragnar, stood and stretched, and came to stand beside Lyting, enormously pleased.

"No longer can we call this ship the *Little Auk*," the chieftain proclaimed in full, spirited tones, claiming the attention of all. "She is far too fierce to bear so gentle a name. Henceforth, she shall be known as the *Little Valkyrie*.

"And you my friend"—he turned and struck a hand to Lyting's back—"you have rightfully earned title this day as *Sjórefurinn*. The 'Sea Fox.'"

Chapter 9

Ailinn remained spellbound, unable to draw her eyes from the silver warrior.

Who *was* this man? her heart demanded. Some legend come to life? Some champion reborn of ages past? Such raw, bold courage. Such mastery and daring. Who *was* this man? This shining lord of the North?

Ailinn's heart continued to thrum in her breast as she compelled her eyes to the wreckage smoldering in the distance, utterly astounded to have survived the tumult.

'Twas Norsemen who had attacked them. Of that, she was sure. They manned distinctive, shallow-draught ships and wore the familiar conical helmets, their beards and locks flowing in pale gold and vibrant red rivulets beneath.

Norse preyed upon Norse. The thought ran through her. Why should that surprise? Ailinn wondered. Did not the Irish prey upon Irish? She ill-liked to allow any comparison, yet 'twas truth. Irish swords had long been raised against their own—long before and with little pause since the Norsemen first plundered their shores.

Ailinn's eyes drew to the star-bright Dane. He confuted all she would believe of his harsh-hewn race. This day he had saved them all, and not one life did he draw. Yet, she held no doubt, put to the moment, he would do what he must.

A vagrant thought came, one that whispered if he bore an interest in her, if he truly desired to possess her, then it mattered little what lot the chieftain cast for her. The silver warrior was a man capable of forging his will into reality.

Ailinn took hold of herself. Idle thoughts, she reproved. But thoughts she could scarce constrain. Would his regard of her change should Rhiannon succeed and convey their true identities? How they had exchanged places scant moments before their capture, and that 'twas Rhiannon, not herself, who was both bride and Eóganacht princess?

Rhiannon little concealed her fascination or hunger for the warrior. Erelong, she would make her move to grasp every advantage.

At length the *Little Valkyrie* approached the far coast, where amber gleamed on white powdery shores and majestic pines reached tall and straight to the heavens, a thousand masts of a vast forested fleet.

The crews of the convoy remained vigilant as they entered the Dvina, watchful for signs of the Baltic tribesmen who might lay in wait for them. Shortly they closed upon what first appeared a small, vacant village, but which proved to be an extensive complex of storage sheds—Norse structures—reminders of their kinsmen's ongoing aggressions in this region.

The day grew warm, but the men forbore their protective corslets and kept bows and blades close to hand. As the merchant ships progressed along the Dvina, the forests thickened further with spruce and pine. Grasses and poa lined the river, brightened with pale blues, purples, and yellows of flowering shrubs. Recent flooding left water glistening in patches on low-lying meadows.

Lyting looked to the sky, bright and clear. The uncommonly hot sun caused him increasing discomfort beneath his chain mail and padded, woolen tunic. Thus far, there had been no sign of tribesmen. 'Twould seem they were occupied otherwise. The river flowed wide and peaceful, and he noted that the others had visibly relaxed. Without further thought Lyting stepped to the barrel of water situated at the bow, grasped hold of his linkage of mail, and hauled it off, over his head.

Ailinn's eyes swept to the silver warrior as his iron-ringed corslet dropped to the decking. Between a breath and a heartbeat, he yanked apart the lacings overlaying his chest and stripped away his tunic. Ailinn swallowed as she viewed him from the side, his superb physique a composite of hard planes and sculpted muscle. Sunlight glanced off the silver chain and ornament he wore about his neck. An amulet, she guessed.

Bending to the barrel beside him, the warrior splashed his face liberally with water, then straightened to full height and laved more over his chest and arms. Ailinn blanched as her gaze riveted on the multitude of scars covering his back—one more alarming than all the rest, a vicious-looking gash, vestige of some gruesome assault.

She stared aghast. What brutality could have befallen him? What grim battle didst he war in to sustain such grievous wounds, all wrought upon his back? A spark of anger flamed in Ailinn. Only a cur would smite another from behind. Considering his numerous scars, an entire pack must have assailed him.

Ailinn skimmed through memory to the day Thora took her to wash clothes at the river—the day she beheld the handsome Dane in no more than a loincloth. She did not recall seeing scars upon his body then. The distance between them had been greater, true, but his back had not been her focus of interest at the time. Rather, 'twas his lighthearted sport with the children that so arrested her.

Questions crowded Ailinn's mind. Undoubtedly, he was a battle-hardened warrior, both upon land and sea. But was he fierce-hearted as well?

He belonged to a fearsome race, she reminded. Conditioned and molded from birth, mentally and physically, according to the customs and precepts of the North. No matter how well he showed himself this day, how valorous before her eyes, within his chest beat the heart of a Norseman.

Norseman. Enemy. The two words traveled through her, oddly dispiriting, yet reluctant to pair. At whatever cost he gained his scars, surely he wrested that victory. Had he not survived to tell of it and win again this day?

A heaviness weighed her spirit as she looked to the tall Dane and the pale slashes branding his back. Somberly she recognized that a man could be devoted to his family and possess a great love of children and still be a killer and barbarian as well. One did not preclude the other.

Her feelings raveled in a hopeless knot at the base of her stomach. She looked to Deira. The girl sat gently rocking herself back and forth, all the while stroking the silken cord of her mother's girdle against her cheek. Ailinn feared she had dealt her stepcousin a disservice in giving the piece over to her. But Deira had fretted so for the cincture, Ailinn cold not deny her.

At first the girdle appeared to comfort her, but now Ailinn feared Deira grew obsessed with it. 'Twas a constant reminder of the horrors they had endured. Silently Ailinn cursed the pagan hands that brought them to this hour.

The silver warrior shifted his stance, and she 'came aware that he turned toward her. Instinctively Ailinn returned her gaze to him, though her last thoughts still grated upon her soul. As she lifted her eyes, sunlight flashed off his amulet.

Ailinn drew a quick breath as she discovered upon his chest no amulet at all, but a shining silver cross.

Startled, she could do no more than stare, a blur of questions and a confusion of thought racing through her. A Christian amongst Norsemen? Was it possible? A rarity if true. Yet earlier, had she not surmised that he and his brother lived in the Christian domains of Francia?

But therein lay the fault of her logic, for 'twas based on his brother's fine Frankish attire and that of the two women who companioned them. Howbeit, the pale-haired Dane wore Norse-styled garments. And though one of the women appeared to be his sister-by-marriage, the other did not so much as attend his leave-taking at the docks. Presumably, she was not his wife. Or lover.

Was he of Normandy or Danmark? Christian or pagan? Frustration rasped at her, harsher than any chain. She pondered the warrior and the gleaming cross upon his chest. Why didst he hazard this voyage? To seek riches in far-flung markets, a merchant and adventurer like the rest?

Hope of his being Christian swiftly dissolved. 'Twas well known that the Norse took a verbal form of Holy Baptism and wore Christ's cross for the sole benefit of being able to barter with Christian merchants and in Christian markets. But the very conduct of their lives made a mockery of their baptismal vows and of Christianity itself. The thought incensed her, for they were naught but pagan deceivers.

Emotion roiled through her. Which was he? True believer or opportunistic trader? Disciple or deceiver? A sudden anger overtook her, to think he could be the latter. Then her choler deserted her just as abruptly as it came, leaving her baffled at the intensity of her reaction and at a loss to understand.

Could it be that she simply disliked the thought of this man making a mockery of anything she held dear or of despoiling the honorable image she held of him?

As the silver warrior moved past her to the back of the ship, Ailinn scoured her heart, fearing what forbidden feelings might hide in secret there.

Iron-gray clouds layered the distant, late-afternoon sky, threatening a downburst. But it wasn't until one of the forward ships signaled it was taking on water from earlier damages that Skallagrim ordered the convoy to put to shore.

Caution prevailed. Scarcely did the crews ground the ships than Lyting and a dozen others leapt down, their axes and shields in hand, and fixed their aim on the forest, scanning for hostile signs. Once the vessels were drawn up, braced, and secured, the crewmen quickly dispersed. Damages were assessed, repairs begun, and cook fires prepared.

Meanwhile, Lyting moved off with a small scouting party and entered the wood.

Rhiannon looked toward the neighboring fire where Ailinn kneaded dough in a wooden trough. One of the Saxon slavewomen assisted her there. Together, they flattened balls of the unleavened dough and spaced them out on the revolving disk of a Norse-style cooking-iron.

Rhiannon lifted her chin. 'Twas only because the Northmen mistook the miserable chit for her own self that they spared Ailinn the labor the other women now suffered—hauling water, gathering kindling, firing the wood with steels and flints.

Internally Rhiannon sneered at Ailinn. She looked forward to exposing the lowborn daughter of the Corcu Loígda—the vanquished tribe of the Érainn—and seeing her put rightfully in her place. 'Twas only a matter of time and the right moment. But a moment she sensed was upon them, as surely as the wind didst blow this eve.

Rhiannon turned back to finish chopping the odorous fish on a scarred, wooden board, then rose and scraped it into the kettle of stew. Resettling herself, she took hold of another strip of dried fish and began to sever it into chunks. At the same time she allowed her gaze to stray about the encampment.

The men off-loaded equipment now—boxes of tools, bags

of tenting supplies, other implements she did not recognize. They were to camp the night, after all. The chieftain gave his orders only after several of his men reemerged from the forest. The white-haired Dane, she observed, remained in absence.

Rhiannon looked with disdain to where the Norsemen erected their tents, framing them front and back with boards that crossed and extended upward above the gabled ends, winglike. Only each "wing" had been carved into a snarling monster head.

No doubt to frighten evil spirits, she scorned as she continued to roam her gaze about the encampment. These Norse sailed with beasts on their ships' prows, atop their tents, and even crowned the headboards to their beds with growling monstrosities. She had seen enough of those whilst lying on her back!

She snorted to see that even now they assembled them for use within their tents. Ever the pagans traveled with their beds—no more than planks and pegs and a rough mattress— ready to assemble, ready to use. Not that the lack of one would hinder their lusts for a heartbeat.

She diverted her gaze, then halted as it drew to Skallagrim's ship. Hakon stood aboard, shifting cargo, pausing now and again to look toward herself and Deira. She knew the look well. He wanted one of them. And when Hakon had a craving to mate, he did not long deny his appetite.

Rhiannon redirected her attention to her task, mind racing. She need not tolerate the heathen's pawing and rutting. Not if he could be enticed to spend himself elsewhere. Her eyes shifted to Deira.

She watched as her cousin stirred the stew with a long-shafted ladle, periodically wiping at her neck and arms with the cloth of her gown as though to remove some imagined filth. 'Twas an unconscious affectation. Pathetic. But one that would serve her well.

Rhiannon stood to her feet and moved to the kettle beside Deira. She wrinkled her nose. "Fish. Eech! It reeks near as much as the men who mount us."

She scraped the pieces of desiccated herring from her chopping board into the broth, satisfied to see Deira's eyes enlarge.

"I scarce can stomach myself anymore," Rhiannon contin- ued. "The pagans befoul us day after day, yet allow us no water to bathe. Truly, with every movement I take I am assaulted anew by their rank odors, layered upon me."

Her eyes narrowed and slid to Deira. "It *does* cling to us, you know—their loathsome scent—trailing about us like a vile mist." Rhiannon made a face and sighed. "And now I must sour myself further with this fish."

Deira's breath slipped from her. Anxious, her eyes skimmed over her hands and garments. She began sniffing them— fingers, dress, hair. Catching up the hem of her mantle, she chafed her throat, then began rubbing her arms.

"Deira. Deira. Calm yourself." Rhiannon stilled her cousin's hands. "You can't scour the smell away like that, goose. Leave some skin. 'Tis water you need and a bit of soap. We haven't the latter, but see here, there is the water that warms by the fires." She gestured to a small, soapstone kettle that sat in the ashes. "Come. 'Tis meant for cleaning the platters and cooking tools, but what say you we spare a little and refresh ourselves?"

Deira darted a glance about, apprehensive, and began to twist the cord of Murieann's girdle that she wore at her hips. "Mayhaps we will anger them, and they will hurt us."

"Don't be a mouse." Rhiannon grew impatient. "The men tend to their ships and do not mind us so closely now. Besides, their only real concern is for their stomachs and that we soon feed them. Here, now." Rhiannon drew Deira down to the ground with her. "We shall both wash. What harm can that bring? First I will assist you, then you can help me."

Quickly Rhiannon dipped a spare cloth in the water, wrung it out, and pressed it to Deira's face. Deira smiled at the soothing warmth and, accepting the cloth, stroked it upward over her chin, nose, cheeks, and forehead, then downward again, along her hairline, and over and beneath her jaw.

Rhiannon swept back Deira's hair, exposing the graceful line of her neck, and encouraged her to continue. From the corner of her eye she glimpsed Hakon watching.

"Doesn't that feel wondrous?" Rhiannon heartened. "Here, let me help you from your mantle."

"But, what if—"

"Deira, if anyone so much as frowns in our direction, I promise, we shall stop. Truly."

Trusting, Deira conceded with a brief nod and removed her mantle, then set aside the precious girdle as well.

Rhiannon worked swiftly to unlace the neck of her gown and open it wide. She cajoled her cousin with pleasant words as she helped to wash further—the base of her throat, collarbone, the curve of her neck, and the beginning of her shoulders. Rhiannon strove to expose as much flesh for Hakon's viewing as possible. 'Twas far from sufficient.

Rhiannon provided her a smile. "Feel better? Now, let's wash your arms."

She folded back Deira's sleeves, revealing long, slender arms which she knew many considered to be lovely, but an asset for which she personally held no envy. Had she not heard that Norsemen possessed a fetish for feminine arms? That they praised their ladies' slim, white arms in verse? The Irish found this very amusing, but to look at Hakon, the reports must have been true.

"There, now. Done. Cover your arms and let us see to your legs. We are almost finished, and 'twill be your turn to help me."

Rhiannon breezed a glance to Hakon, assuring that he still watched them. He did. Most intently.

She began to draw Deira's gown upward—only to the knees at first—mindful to not upset her cousin, but equally mindful to feed the fires of Hakon's desire till the flames licked high. Rhiannon eased the skirt higher still, in such a way that it seemed she only held it out of the way as Deira scrubbed her lower legs.

"Best bathe as much as you can," Rhiannon urged. "No telling when we can indulge ourselves like this again."

She raised the gown high on one side, to Deira's hip, displaying a lean but shapely thigh. Deira began to object and tug it downward. "Wash quickly, if it afrights you, Cousin, but do wash. Wherever the dogs have touched you, surely they have left their smell."

Clearly repulsed by the thought, Deira set the cloth to her leg. Rhiannon slanted a glance to Hakon. He stood motionless, his eyes fixed on Deira, near salivating. Rhiannon smiled inwardly, then yanked the gown downward, covering Deira's leg before she could finish cleansing.

"Mayhaps you are right, Cousin. We shouldn't tempt fate. Here. Refasten your cincture." Rhiannon handed her Murieann's girdle.

Before Deira could retie the belt, a shadow fell over her.

Deira's hands stilled. Slowly she lifted her eyes, only to meet with Hakon's smoldering gaze. Her face twisted with anguish, and she shook her head in dread as he reached down, unlocked her ankle cuff, and dragged her to her feet. Sweeping the cincture from her hands, he scooped her up in his arms and headed for the shrub.

Rhiannon watched Hakon's receding back as he carried Deira a distance and dropped down with her behind a screen of flowering underbrush. A feline smile curved her lips.

Turning, she met with Ailinn's hard-eyed glare.

Rhiannon tossed her head, sending her ebony locks tumbling from her shoulders. Mentally she dismissed Ailinn and took a step toward the kettle. At once pain twinged the underside of her foot as she stepped onto something akin to a root. Moving off it, she discovered the knotted cord of Murieann's girdle. Kicking it aside, she then took hold of the ladle and gave the stew a vigorous stir.

Rhiannon glanced about the camp, avoiding eye contact with Ailinn, and sought the handsome warrior.

'Twas an easy matter to arouse Hakon. But what did it take to arouse the white-haired Dane?

Lyting outstretched his long frame before the crackling fire, leaving one leg bent and bracing himself on an elbow. In his hands he slowly turned the silver arm cuff of Askel the Red and studied the gravings there.

Several men called over from another, nearby fire, hailing him with cups of ale and commending him for his triumph at Riga. Lyting smiled back and nodded his appreciation.

On his return from the forest, after securing the area with the scouting party, he made the expected rounds, joining the ships' crews for a celebratory drink, discussing the tactics he had employed with sweep-oar and movable clew-beam, and quietly accepting their words of praise.

A brief but drenching rain drove them temporarily to shelter, but now they gathered about the fires once more and satisfied their stomachs with fresh roasted game. The aroma of cooked partridge and grouse lingered in sensory contrast to the clean, rain-sweetened air.

Comfortably full and tired to the bone, Lyting was grateful to be relieved of watch this night. Grateful again to find a moment of calm to examine the Varangian's inscription:

The spider yet spins in the
palace of the Caesars.
Leidolf, Thengil, Vegeir dead.

Lyting mulled the words. His gaze then moved from the
runes to two small gravings that had been incised on the
underside of the band as well—one to either side of the cuff's
opening—the *I* and the *omega* of the Byzantines' Cyrillic
alphabet. Rurik and he had discussed them at length, but they
remained a mystery.

As Lyting shifted the band, catching the firelight, he noticed
that the lines of the Cyrillic engravings did not match those of
the runes. The Cyrillic letters looked to have been incised with
a different tool, for the width of the lines were wider, heavier.

Had Askel added these letters in haste, just as he departed
Constantinople? But why use Greek-styled letters when he had
already inscribed the longer message in runes? Symbolic, for a
surety. But of what? Something new that Askel discovered
after making his original engraving?

Mayhaps these letters represented the very thing that prompted
him to leave the city and join the army destined for Dyrrachium.
But, did his interest lay with the army or something in
Dyrrachium? Whatever he uncovered, 'twas important enough
to draw him from the circle of the throne, leaving only
Koll—the last of the "Varangian six," save Rurik—to guard
against the "spider."

Lyting looked again to the two markings. The Cyrillic *I* was
identical to the Greek *iota*, but the *omega* was wholly
different. Instead of being horse-shoe shaped, the Cyrillic
omega looked more like two Latin *G*'s facing each other—
joined at bottom, but not touching at the top. At a quick glance
they appeared to be two little arms, curving upward above an
abbreviated head. Lyting rubbed his eyes, deciding for a
certainty he must be tired to see such things.

For a time he tried to fit words to the characters, but with no
success. Someone's name then? he wondered. Lyting stroked
his thumb beneath his lower lip as he mentally culled the
names his brother had given him.

Continuing to puzzle the inscription, he glanced off to the
right where Skallagrim sat before his tent and mended a line.
To the chieftain's other side, Hakon spoke in low tones with

Ragnar and Orm. The women clustered together on the opposite side of the fire, and he noted that the auburn-haired beauty appeared in a dark mood, provoked by something.

But 'twas the younger of Hakon's slaves that gave him pause—the pale-looking girl with a tangled mass of brown hair. She looked to be in a haze as she rocked herself back and forth, all the while rubbing a green silken cord against her cheek.

Lyting's concern deepened. She was like a dove with a broken wing, fragile, vulnerable. Had her spirit been broken as well?

Frustration bore through him, followed by a welling anger. He felt caged. Barred from helping her in the least of ways, for to do so would bring her naught but greater harm. Hakon had made himself clear. He would give him no excuse to abuse the girl further.

Yet, Lyting resolved, he must do something.

Mayhaps he could arrange something in Kiev. Rurik had provided him names of contacts there, also. One family came to mind in particular, one of a respectably high station. Mayhaps they could make the girl's purchase for him, posing to seek a houseslave and offering Hakon more than he could refuse.

Encouraged, Lyting thought to provide them enough silver to secure her and keep her in Kiev until his return. Against the possibility that he did not return, he would leave additional coin and arrange that she be sent on to Valsemé before winter.

Lyting slipped on the silver arm cuff and raised himself to a sitting position. As he refined his plan, he beheld the raven-tressed slave suddenly stand and snatch the cincture from the younger girl's hands.

"Stop clutching at Murieann's belt!" Rhiannon snapped, heaving the piece as far from them as she could. "She's *dead*, Deira. *Dead*."

"That was needless and cruel," Ailinn rebuked, coming to her feet, fighting the chain that encumbered her ankle. "The belt comforts Deira. 'Tis all she has left of her mother."

"Fool. She cannot hold on to the past any more than she can change it. She must look to the present and take hold of herself. She must look to the portion that now fills her cup and face reality."

"What reality is that Rhiannon? The one our captors force on her? Or the one you do?"

Anger flashed across Rhiannon's features. "What should I expect from a lowly Érainn?" she hissed. "We must each do what we must to preserve ourselves, whatever the cost."

"Even at the expense of your own blood kindred?" Ailinn challenged.

Rhiannon's eyes thinned to slits. "Even that."

"You are contemptible."

"I am strong."

Rhiannon raised her chin imperiously. "I have no intention of enduring a lifetime of abuse or of filling an early grave. I can see to myself. And I *will* survive. I promise you that. But will you? Do you have enough steel in your spine to win against fate?"

"Mayhaps not." Ailinn met her gaze, unflinchingly. "But whatever comes, I will not thrust others in harm's path to save myself."

"Then you are doomed," Rhiannon sneered her satisfaction, her eyes glinting with the fire's light.

"My faith and my hope are in God. His arm is not shortened by our plight."

"Well spoken by the last virgin of Clonmel," Rhiannon hurled with derision. "But what have *you* suffered to speak thusly? What heathen has spread *your* thighs?"

"Look well, Rhiannon," Ailinn grit out. "I wear the same chains as you. I await the same fate as the one you now bear. Do not play the martyr. You do not deserve the crown. Suffer? There is the heart of suffering." She opened her hand toward Deira, then turned back on Rhiannon. "One can only suffer that which touches the heart. But you have shown yourself to have none. Naught beats within the hollow chamber that lays beneath your breast."

"Bitch," Rhiannon seethed. " 'Twas chance that spared you, a deception that protects you still. Many of us will soon be swelling with little pagan bastards. Your own stomach might remain flat but not for long. Not when I . . ."

Torn afresh by Rhiannon's words, Deira gasped and looked with horror at her belly, then grabbed at Ailinn's gown.

"Cease, Rhiannon!" Ailinn exploded. "Shut tight your mouth and *do* take care to not impale yourself upon your tongue."

Rhiannon began to speak again, but Ailinn advanced on her. "By the saints, I'll gag you with my own chains if I must!"

Rhiannon clenched her jaw and reseated herself before the fire. "Doomed," she muttered to herself but so the others might hear. "Might as well be dead."

Great tears spilled over Deira's cheeks. " 'Tis true, 'tis true. They will get us with babes. We be no more than animals to them. Animals to mate." Deira hunched forward and buried her face in her hands.

Ailinn sank instantly to her knees and encircled Deira with her arms. Comforting her, she slipped into Frankish—their "secret" tongue with which they had shared so many privacies in years past, but which now afforded her a way to speak to Deira without Rhiannon's interference.

"*Non, non. Ne pleure pas.* Do not cry. *Viens, permets-moi de te tiens.* Come let me hold you. Sh-h-h-h . . ."

Riveted by the stormy exchange, the men sat motionless, their tongues paused in midsentence and their gestures frozen midair. Like thunder and lightning didst the two women clash—the ebony-tressed slavegirl and the autumn-fire maid.

Now, as their squall abated, the one sat with daggers in her eyes whilst the other consoled the younger girl in a steady flow of words. Words that carried across the fire, distinct and unmistakable.

Lyting came to his feet, his breath trapped in his chest. 'Twas as though a door had been flung open within his hearing, a great barrier removed. He stared at the maid as her voice fell sweet upon his ear, her every pronouncement clearly understood.

" 'Tis Frankish she speaks!" Lyting tossed a side-glance to Skallagrim, then crossed to the other side of the fire.

Lyting dropped to a crouch before the Irish beauty. She sucked a breath and pulled back, enclosing the girl in her arms. Lyting rebuked himself for moving too swiftly. He did not mean to startle or afright her. Never did he wish her to fear him.

"Je ne te nuirai pas. I will not harm you," he avowed in perfectly accented Frankish.

Ailinn's eyes rounded to huge disks and her jaw dropped. She knew that she gaped, but there was no help for it. "You speak Frankish!"

The silver warrior smiled, creases appearing in his cheeks. "I am Lyting Atlison. Ordinarily I speak Frankish each day, for I abide in Francia, in the duchy of Normandy."

Lyting Atlison. At last she had a name to put to him. Oddly, it seemed familiar, as though she should have known it all the while. As though it had long been a part of her. He spoke again, his voice beautiful to her ears, the pitch low and smooth.

" 'Tis my understanding that you were seized in a raid on Ireland. How is it *you* speak Frankish?"

Ailinn searched his look. She hesitated, wondering how much, if anything, she should divulge, then realized it mattered little. Eire lay behind them and to a great distance, and her kinsmen were dead.

"There be those Irish nobles who once fled our beloved land for Francia—a time when the Norsemen relentlessly ravaged our shores."

Ailinn paused for the warrior's reaction, but he remained intent to her every word.

"My stepuncle left with his family at his wife's bidding but later regretted forsaking Eire and returned."

She refrained from adding how Cellach had been scorned by the tribe, and how her stepfather, Lorcan, had given his brother and family a place beneath their own roof. Or how later, after Fianna's and Lorcan's deaths, Cellach had taken her in.

"My stepuncle brought with him a Frankish nursemaid from Francia, for his young daughters. Our families dwelled together for atime." Ailinn's eyes moved accusingly to Hakon. "Bergette was the first to be slain in the women's chamber. She sought to protect me but was felled at my feet by that one's ax."

Lyting envisaged the scene, keen to the pain that underlay her words. It must have been then that Hakon seized her. He recalled Stefnir's words and hated to think of the maid in Hakon's possession. Lyting looked to the two who had been taken with her.

"These be your cousins, then?"

"Stepcousins," she corrected. "Though they themselves be cousins of blood."

"You said your stepuncle had 'daughters.'"

"The other has been sold."

"At Hedeby?"

"What is Hedeby?"

Lyting traced over her elegant features with his gaze, remembering them once besmudged and her eyes fired with defiance.

"The market town of Danmark, where first we met."

Ailinn's eyes widened, but Lyting rose to his feet as Skallagrim joined them, followed by Hakon. The warrior appeared infinitely tall from her perspective. As he spoke with the chieftain, her thoughts reached back to Hedeby and her arrival there—to when he lifted her from the street and held her in his grasp.

"Come. Do not fear." Lyting's hand closed gently about her arm. The image of Hedeby dissolved as the moment blurred from the past to the present. Ailinn found herself gazing up into his incredible blue eyes.

"Come," he repeated, aiding her feet and then Deira. "Skallagrim wishes to know more of you."

The chieftain tugged at his beard and directed several comments to Lyting. Deira eased from Ailinn's side as the warrior turned his attention once more to Ailinn.

"Skallagrim wouldst know what place his men raided, whose hall it was they attacked."

Ailinn's eyes whisked to the chieftain. It incensed her that the heathens should devastate her home, murder her kindred, and not even have a name to put to the place.

Before she could reply, Rhiannon shoved to her feet. Her eyes glowed with a look of triumph and anticipation. The white-haired Dane spoke Frankish. Her moment had come at last, and she readied to reap the victory.

"Tell them," she demanded, grasping Deira by the arm and forcing her forward. "Tell them who I am."

Deira shrank into the cocoon of her mantle, but Rhiannon stabbed her fingers into Deira's arm and compelled her to face the Norsemen.

"Tell them!" Rhiannon growled, giving her a firm shake.

"Leave her be," Ailinn snapped.

"You think I am fool enough to let *you* render my words for their understanding? You'd favor being in my place a time longer, wouldn't you?—wearing the rank of nobility to which you have no claim nor can ever hope to bear. *Ní hea*. Deira will tell them. *Word for word*. But as for you, your time has come."

"What is it your stepcousin says?"

Ailinn felt Lyting lightly touch her arm, but she could not meet his eyes.

"What provokes her so?" he asked again, but Ailinn fixed her gaze on the ground.

"The chieftain is a man short on patience. Do not risk his anger," Lyting cautioned, then added, "If you will answer his questions, I will answer yours."

Ailinn's eyes drew to those of the silver warrior. So many questions were locked in her heart. But would he still wish to answer them once Rhiannon had done with her? Would Skallagrim and Hakon afford him the chance?

Ailinn braced herself, the fated moment upon her.

" 'Twas Clonmel that the Danes attacked. The hall of the *ruri ri*, Mór."

"You're father's hall?"

"*Non*. Rhiannon's."

Hearing Ailinn pronounce her name, Rhiannon released Deira and moved forward as far as her chain would allow. She stood before Skallagrim, her bearing regal. Head held high and straight of spine, she addressed him in Gaelic and, when finished, ordered Deira to translate.

Deira looked to Ailinn and, receiving her reassuring nod, turned to Lyting.

"I am Deira, daughter of Cellach. Rhiannon, my cousin, asks that I give to you her words precisely as she gives them to me. Further, she asks that, as I do so, you translate them for the chieftain, Skallagrim."

Lyting nodded, wary.

Deira waited as Rhiannon began, then transmitted her message as her cousin wished, word for word. Lyting, in turn, rephrased the information for Skallagrim.

"I am the princess of the Casil Eóganachts. Decended from

the kings of Munster. Daughter of the *ruri ri*, Mór. 'Twas Mór's hall that you beset. On *my* wedding day."

Lyting's gaze leapt to the auburn-haired maid.

"*I*, not my stepcousin, was the bride. She and I exchanged places that morn. I was to marry a man of wealth and consequence. A man who would still pay a great sum for my return.

"In the bridal chamber we heard the clamor of swords and arms. We believed 'twas the rival tribe of the Dal Cassis, come to seize *me*, Domnal's bride. We sought to deceive the Dalcassians. My stepcousin dressed in *my* gown, *my* mantle. We veiled her and placed flowers in her hair. I was hidden amongst the other maids. Your men were quick to enter our chamber and despoil our maidens there, including myself.

"But now I make it known to you. 'Tis *I* who am the daughter of the *ruri ri*, the princess and bride. *Not* my stepcousin, whom you cosset. She will bring naught to your coffers. But *I* am worth a very fine ransom."

Rhiannon waited, cutting Ailinn with her eyes.

Lyting finished imparting the message to Skallagrim and found himself struck by the bravery of the autumn-fire maid who had risked herself in the face of danger. And yet, he wondered of her true reasons, for the *princess* impressed him as a coldhearted woman. He doubted Rhiannon would imperil herself, given a similar circumstance.

The chieftain appeared amused with the princess.

Hakon only shrugged a shoulder and crossed his arms. "She might have been the 'bride,' but she was no virgin."

"A fiery one, is she not?" Skallagrim's beard parted with a smile. He directed another question through Lyting.

"The chieftain wouldst know more of the maid. If she is your stepcousin, wouldst she not also bring a ransom?"

Rhiannon smiled, a poisonous smile that took Lyting aback.

"*Ní hea*. She is nothing. Neither be she related by blood nor an Eóganacht. Her mother married my father's brother, well after she was born. She springs from the Corcu Loigda, an ancient tribe of Ireland, defeated and subdued long ago by the Eóganacht."

Derision dripped from Rhiannon's tongue as she made her final pronouncement. "She is Ailinn of the Érainn. Her people were once Druids."

Deira's voice dropped as she translated the last of Rhiannon's words, then added quickly, "Of course, they all be Christians now."

Lyting's gaze traveled to the maid.

Ailinn. Of the Érainn. A name as beautiful as she, herself. One side of his mouth pulled upward into a smile as he tried to imagine her Druid ancestry. The Druids bore an intense love of nature. As did he.

Truly, the maid possessed an enchantment about her. Long had it been his dream—a fanciful illusion—to make love to a woodland nymph or a water sprite. Until now he had never considered that one might exist.

Lyting turned to convey the last of the princess's missive. "Your captive is a most noble and gentle-born maid, Skallagrim, born of a shining and ancient tribe of Ireland—Ailinn of the Érainn."

Rhiannon smiled, casting a look of triumph to Ailinn as she heard the warrior pronounce her stepcousin's name and that of her abhorrent tribe. Rhiannon waited expectantly for Skallagrim's displeasure to fall on Ailinn and for their lots to be recast.

Lyting turned once more to Ailinn, his manner toward her unaltered by the revelations.

"Ailinn." Her name passed pleasingly over his tongue even as he voiced it. "Be there questions you wouldst ask?"

Ailinn glanced about, surprised the chieftain had given no commands concerning her, nor made the least exertion to alter Rhiannon's lot.

"Where do you take us?" The question fell from her lips, though so many poised there.

"You are being taken to the imperial city of Byzantium, Constantinople."

"To what end?" She tried to shield her surprise.

Lyting hesitated. He must guard his words. Skallagrim and Hakon watched. Would that he could give her hope, but whatever he revealed to Ailinn would likely be mirrored in her eyes.

"Skallagrim deigns to gift you to a Byzantine aristocrat in exchange for privileges in the silk trade."

"Gift me? How do you mean? As a slave?"

"As a concubine."

Ailinn took a dry swallow. "But now that will change, will it not? For whatever reason Rhiannon's bridal raiment first halted the chieftain's attack on me, all is revealed. I am not the bride he thought me to be, not a valued princess of a *ruri ri*. Rhiannon shall take my place—"

"Naught has changed, Ailinn." Lyting shook his head, denying her words. "Rhiannon is Hakon's slave, and should he wish to offer her for ransom to the Irish, that he alone will decide. But you belong to Skallagrim. The bridal garments marked you as a virgin. He does not preserve your virtue because you are a princess, but because of your matchless beauty and your virginity, which the Byzantine requires."

Ailinn stared openly at Lyting, astonished by what he spoke. But as Deira rendered his words to Gaelic, Rhiannon grew livid and reeled on Ailinn, shrilling in her native tongue. Lyting blocked her attack, imposing himself.

Skallagrim, too, came forth. Seizing Rhiannon by the arm, he jerked her to his chest. "A torrid one, eh?" He grinned down at her, then looked to Lyting and Hakon. " 'Twould appear the princess feels herself to be wronged in some wise."

"From what I ascertain, she seeks to replace Ailinn in your favor," Lyting commented.

"She's spoiled for the Byzantine, but she does find favor with me," the chieftain proclaimed robustly. "Have you objection, Hakon? I find I harbor a mighty itch in my loins. Mayhaps 'tis a chieftain she needs to bed her, and I a princess to break the 'witch's curse.' "

Rhiannon blanched when Skallagrim squatted to unlock her chains. She stumbled back several steps, then fell full upon her backside. Lying sprawled upon the ground, she upraised her head, only to lock gazes with the chieftain between her parted legs. His grin stretched the wider.

Rhiannon pitched to her stomach and tried to scramble from his reach, but he gripped both her ankles and dragged her back. She swiped clawed fingers at his head, but he only ducked aside, enjoying the game to the full. Heaving Rhiannon upon his shoulder, Skallagrim trudged to his tent, flung back the flap, and disappeared inside with his booty.

The men who had gathered about the fire began to disperse, chuckling at the intermittent screeches and grunts that emitted from the tent. Orm and Ragnar moved off, each choosing a

slave for themselves for the night and offering Hakon the
remaining two.

Hakon looked to Deira, then deciding on the Saxon women,
led them away, leaving Lyting to guard over his and Skallagrim's women.

Ailinn hugged Deira tight. The girl looked distraught and
waxen again. She clutched at the cincture as she listened to the
sounds from the tent. Ailinn made Deira a pillow from her
cloak and urged her to lie before the fire and rest. Disheartened, she sat looking into the night, wondering what would
come of her cousins after she, herself, was given to the
Byzantine.

The fire burned low, the night grew still, and the mating
sounds in the camp finally ceased. While Deira slept, Ailinn
remained steeped in thought, vaguely aware of the movements
in camp and of those who held watch, including Hakon, who
now stood nearby.

Lyting kept his own watch before the fire with Ailinn and
Deira, and now moved to add a fresh log. Kneeling down, he
attended his task, but spoke in low, quiet tones.

"Ailinn. Have faith. I will help you."

For a moment Ailinn thought she had misheard.

"Have faith, Ailinn," he repeated. "I will do all within my
power to see you and your cousins free."

Just then, Rhiannon stumbled half-naked from the chieftain's tent. Skallagrim appeared long enough to hurl out the
remainder of her clothes and motion for Lyting to chain her.
Grousing, Skallagrim jerked the tent flap closed again.

Rhiannon picked herself up and began yanking her gown
over her head. "Disgusting, filthy swine!" She grabbed up her
mantle and scrubbed its fabric against her arms and neck. She
headed toward the fire, muttering, "Freak. *Torc*. Revolting
twisted cock."

Lyting resecured her chains. Humorless and in a fit of
temper, Rhiannon rolled herself into her mantle and, without
further utterance, lay down beside Deira.

Ailinn fixed her gaze on Lyting as he took up his place
across the fire, and thought on his words.

Who was this star-bright Dane? This shining lord of Normandy? And why should he wish to help her?

Chapter 10

Vitholm. Kiev.

The stockaded fortress of Kiev sat high upon the western bluff—the *Starokievskaja Gora*.

Below moved the slate-blue waters of the Dnieper, broad and purposeful, broken intermittently by bars of whitest sand.

Constant timberland had accompanied the convoy since Riga. But now, beneath the lofty eye of Kiev, the extensive forests gave way to an endless plain of shimmering grasses.

The Steppe.

The Steppe, rooted in deep, rich soil—black and loamy.

The Steppe, extending as far as the eye could see.

And Lyting could see far.

Looking out over it, the land sang in his veins.

As the convoy approached the shores at *Vitholm*, Lyting wished he had the luxury of time to climb to the upper city and gaze over the vista. But Skallagrim intended for the convoy to put into port only long enough to secure new Slav ships and transfer their goods. They would then set out immediately for Vitchev, south along the Dnieper, where the main convoy would convene.

Lyting moved astern, to where Skallagrim tilled the rudder.

"Do you wish me to tell the women to prepare themselves for the change to come?"

Skallagrim nodded without word, his interest fixed on the passing shores. More and more the chieftain utilized Lyting to communicate necessities. Still, Lyting took care not to over-step himself or appear avid to do so lest he arouse suspicion.

Ailinn stood at the mast, she, too, captivated by the breathtaking scenery. Near her feet, Deira curled into her mantle and looked to be asleep. Rhiannon sat there also, her forehead creased with thought as she stared into the distance.

Coming to stand before Ailinn, Lyting met her gaze. How those eyes pulled at him. He repressed a deep-seated instinct to reach out to her.

"We have reached the city of Kiev." He inclined his bright head toward the settlement ashore. "We shall dock in the lower city, the Podol, and transfer to other ships. We will then set out for a fortress downstream and camp the night."

"And from there?" Her golden-brown eyes probed deep.

"From there we must pass through or around nine rapids. 'Tis why we need the Slav ships."

Lyting wished to apprise her of how he would seek Deira's purchase and release but decided not to raise her hopes. He longed to arrange for Ailinn's purchase as well, but knew Skallagrim would have none of it. Money could not buy the advantages he hoped to gain in the silk trade.

Feeling the chieftain's eyes on him, he dared linger no longer and stepped off, toward the bow of the ship.

Time would be critical. Skallagrim would expect his assistance at the docks, first in selecting the new ships, then in transferring the cargo. If he were to succeed in his plan, he would need send word to Waldemir in the upper city as soon as they docked. The Slavonic nobleman of Rurik's acquaintance was evidently a man of high importance, for he served the Rus leader, Oleg, at the time Rurik traded here.

Lyting's eyes lighted on Deira. The girl slept often these days. Even when awake, she appeared listless. Lyting felt a sudden restlessness, a need to be on with the day and see his plans through.

The sun still climbed the sky when the ships from Gotland glided into the lively wharves of the Podol.

Ailinn scanned the colorful press of people there, then returned her gaze aboard. Discreetly she centered her interest on Lyting as he assisted with lowering the sail and stowing the oars and lines.

Their duties complete, the men began to climb from the ship. Deira stirred beside Ailinn, claiming her attention momentarily. When Ailinn looked back, Lyting had slipped from sight.

Quickly she sought his shining mane amid the bustle on the dock. Her pulse picked up its pace as he continued to elude her.

A cluster of people began to dissolve, moving off in ones and twos. There, a short distance behind, stood Lyting speaking with a lad of roughly eight years. He pressed something into the boy's hand. The lad heeled round and dashed off along the wharf's worn planks.

Bringing her eyes from the child, Ailinn found Lyting had moved off once more. An instant later she spied him joining Skallagrim and a growing clutch of the convoy's crew members. The chieftain appeared to be issuing instructions. He then gestured to a half dozen men, including Lyting and Hakon, and set off in a direction opposite the boy's.

"Ailinn . . . ?" Deira lifted herself up.

"Sh-h-h, love." Ailinn stroked her shoulder with a comforting hand. " 'Tis all right. We have stopped atime in a place named Kiev. Rest a little longer now. You will need your strength when we make another change of ships."

Ailinn directed her gaze back to the wharf. Finding Lyting, she watched after him until he vanished amidst the throng.

The Podol reminded Lyting somewhat of Hedeby with its wooded lanes and neatly fenced yards, its quarters clogged with craftsmen and artisans. But here the town enclosed a greater tract of land, so that yards were generous, houses larger and set apart, oftimes many-storied.

A vivid mix of people filled the street, Norse and Slavonic, merchants and workmen, clad in a dizzying array of clothes, the plainer ones lost amid the more extravagant: fur-trimmed hats; rich mantles and brocades; snowy linen tunics embellished with vibrant needlework. Women wore neckrings—each representing one thousand silver *dinars* of their spouses' worth, Lyting had been told.

Beneath the high escarpment Skallagrim soon brought them to the cramped workyard of the master shipwright named Ziv.

"Now you shall see for yourself." Skallagrim nodded

toward rows of newly crafted vessels. "Naught be better and none so stalwart to withstand the cataracts of the Dnieper than a good Slav ship."

Just then a squarish man with coarse black hair and two missing front teeth trod forth.

"Ziv!" Skallagrim clasped forearms with the man and greeted him heartily. He then presented the crew, excepting Hakon, who obviously knew Ziv well.

While the chieftain and the shipwright spoke, Lyting's gaze strayed to the fortress atop the plateau. Had the boy located Waldemir? Would the nobleman be willing to meet him?

"Upon your sword, have you ever seen the like?" Skallagrim's voice boomed beside him. "They do not *build* these. They *forge* them—from a solid trunk!" Enthused, the chieftain strode toward the line of ships. Running a hand along the smooth hull of one, he turned and motioned for Ziv to explain the process.

Lyting rubbed a hand over his bearded jaw while Ziv detailed the soaking of the logs and the chipping and burning of their interiors. Normally such conversation would engross him, but in truth, he chafed to be done with the business of the ships and off to seek Waldemir. Equally, he longed to return to Ailinn and keep watch of her.

"Most unusual," Lyting admired one of the ships, circling it. "Somewhat smaller than those in which we arrived."

Ziv's smile faltered.

"And thankfully so," Lyting added quickly. "I, for one, am heartened that the *Little Valkyrie* need not be carried overland. Naturally, we shall need purchase more ships than we brought— about eight in all, I should think. A fine and clever business, Ziv," Lyting chided, a gleam in his eyes.

Ziv's smile lifted back in place, a twinkle appearing in his own eye.

"*Já*. Eight," Skallagrim agreed. He pulled his gaze from Lyting to Ziv and set his mouth with a smile that showed nearly all teeth. "But, having done business so many years, I do not fear to praise Ziv's work. His price is *always* fair."

Lyting repressed his own smile, noting the intimation that underlay the chieftain's tone.

"There." Skallagrim pointed out one of the smaller ships to Lyting. "We shall take that one—you, Hakon, and I—for our goods and slaves." His mind clearly decided, Skallagrim moved off to inspect other vessels.

Relief rushed through Lyting. He had wondered whether the chieftain would consent to his remaining in his company or require him to sail aboard a different ship in the convoy for the remainder of the journey.

It struck him, of a sudden, that Ailinn was not the only one whom Skallagrim kept watch over. While Ailinn might open certain doors to the chieftain with the Byzantine offical, 'twas through himself alone that the chieftain could gain admittance to the Imperial circles. Why had he not considered that earlier? He would need be doubly careful when he slipped away to meet Waldemir.

Lyting felt as restless as a pacing cat. Where was the boy?

One of the men drew him into a discussion, debating the merits of two ships, trying to decide betwixt them. Meanwhile, Skallagrim concluded the details of their transaction with Ziv and arranged for storage of the Gotland ships until their return.

As the chieftain prepared to depart, Lyting looked about once more. His hands clenched in frustration. No sign of the boy.

'Twas time for the crew to begin the arduous task of transferring the cargo. He and Skallagrim's crew would need return for the other ships and bring them round while Ziv and his craftsmen conferred the new ships into the water.

Would the lad wait, should he miss him? Or seek him farther down the dock?

Lyting turned to go as Skallagrim made a final remark to Ziv. From behind, he heard the shipwright's sudden, awed murmur.

"Valsarion."

Lyting paused. The crowd ahead had parted. A nobleman came into view, tall and stern-looking, with dark-gold hair, burnished with the sun's light. He wore a knee-length tunic of green brocade, trimmed in sable, and high leather boots. About his shoulders lay a wide necklace of flat gold links, each perforated with an open, leafy design. Suspended from it was a large medallion.

Valsarion stopped on the planked wharf a short distance away. Slowly he drew gray, crystalline eyes over each of the

Norsemen standing before him, then returned his pale gaze to rest on Lyting.

Lyting met the aristocrat's penetrating stare, unsure of the moment. Before he could dwell on it longer, the boy for whom he waited slipped from behind the nobleman and ran directly toward him.

"The lord Valsarion wishes to speak with you," the child spilled the words out in a breathless rush, his eyes huge, dark disks against his waxen face.

Lyting touched the boy's shoulder reassuringly, aware that all eyes were upon him. Following the lad, he came to stand before the man called Valsarion.

The noble studied him, unsmiling, his eyes cutting deep. Mayhaps 'twas the manner in which he looked over his high cheekbones, his eyes partially shuttered, but Lyting felt as though Valsarion gazed down at him from a chilly height. There was a hardness to the noble's sculpted features. Something unyielding, impenetrable. Even the creases that lined the hollows of his cheeks—running from beneath his cheekbones to the corners of his mouth—appeared etched in granite.

"The boy tells me you seek Waldemir." Valsarion's voice was deep, commanding.

"Já. He is known to my brother. I bear Waldemir and his family a message."

"Waldemir and his family are dead," he said tonelessly.

Lyting started for a moment.

"When didst your brother last see him?"

"It has been at least three years past, perchance more. Waldemir served your prince, Oleg, at the time."

"Oleg also is dead." Valsarion's eyes bore into him. "Igor now rules as Prince of Kiev."

Lyting marked the nobleman's crisp answers, given without explanation, without emotion. He assumed Valsarion served Igor, but deemed it best not to probe too far, lest the friends of Oleg prove to be the enemies of Igor.

"In verity, it has been a long time."

"Indeed." The crystalline eyes continued to study him. "Should you have needs in Kiev, mayhaps I can be of assistance."

Lyting's gaze fell to the medallion, to the creature embossed there—a griffin. Its foreparts were those of an eagle, its back, those of a lion. The griffin glared fiercely—a bloodred ruby for an eye. In its talons it clutched an unblemished pearl.

A chill touched Lyting's soul. He could not leave Deira here. Not with Valsarion.

" 'Tis but a greeting I bear and word of my brother these past years. Waldemir and his family have no need of them now."

"Do I know your brother?" A shaft of interest opened in Valsarion's eyes.

"Waldemir's was the only name my brother mentioned," Lyting returned cautiously, circumspect.

The shaft closed. Once again Valsarion's expression was one of flint. "Much has changed in Kiev since your brother's days here. 'Tis wise to keep that in mind."

Lyting watched Valsarion's departure, his hopes for Deira dimming. A rash and desperate impulse rippled through him simply to seize the Irish captives and flee Kiev. But with the three of them bound in chains, he wouldn't even get away from the wharfs.

Dispirited, his thoughts strayed to the scar beneath his beard, and to those on his back. He must not fail these women, nor the child emperor and his mother. Yet he knew that sometimes one's best efforts were simply not enough.

His thoughts drew to Ailinn. He knew if any harm ever befell her, he would already have drawn his last breath.

Ailinn settled aboard the new, smaller ship, grateful that, while she and her stepcousins each still wore ankle irons, they were no longer linked together by a common chain, nor were they shackled to the mast.

She guessed 'twas, in part, because the goods already packed the space there, owing to the reduced dimensions of the ship. But also, being only three, she, Deira, and Rhiannon could be both easily managed and utilized whenever necessary as movable ballast.

'Twould seem they would sail the remainder of the journey apart from the other women, in the company of Skallagrim, Hakon, and, she presumed, Lyting. He had not said. She did not ask. She feared that his answer would not be the one for which she hoped.

Ailinn whisked her gaze over the wharf and found him

standing there. To her relief, Lyting climbed aboard, stowed
the line, and took up his place at the oar.

Lyting couldn't meet Ailinn's eyes, for his disappointment
bit too deep. Now they must join the main convoy at Vitchev
and from there face the rapids and cataracts of the Dnieper.
Once through, 'twas an easy journey to Constantinople, where,
at last, he would be able to see the women free.

Skallagrim threw off the mooring line and joined them,
bellowing orders for the convoy to embark.

Lyting plied his strength to the oar. Together, he and Ailinn
watched the distance between the ship and the docks of the
Podol widen as Kiev diminished across the waters.

Watch fires burned brightly atop the towers of Vitchev.

Ailinn withdrew her gaze from the wooded hill fortress that
stood sentry high above their encampment on the Dnieper and
looked once more to Lyting.

He sat no more than two arm's lengths apart, cleaning his
sword. They passed the time in companionable silence. Betimes, Lyting would slip a glance to her, and when their eyes
met he would smile softly, then return his attention to the care
of his weapon.

Deira slept nearby, wrapped in a fur pelt. Ailinn thought
Lyting had swayed the chieftain to allow her that, for the night
was chill and Deira looked unwell. Hakon had given Rhiannon
to another earlier, and for the time he held watch. Skallagrim,
too, was absent, making his rounds about the tented settlement
with his drinking horn.

Here, at Vitchev, the great convoy collected from the
various trade routes to sail, as Lyting explained, in "fellowship." She guessed there to be upward to fifty ships already
gathered, filled with merchants, adventurers, their slaves, and
to her surprise, a small number of Norsewomen.

Camp followers, of a sort? she wondered, then decided not.
They appeared to hold wifely status or, at very least, that of
free women who joined their men.

Several snatched devouring glances of Lyting, whispering
and tittering amongst themselves. Ailinn's brow rose a fraction. Dropping her gaze away, she smoothed her gown.

"Norsewomen must be as fearsome as their men. I am

surprised to see that some join the convoy, if the journey be so dangerous."

Lyting looked up, a smile playing over his lips.

"Dangerous enough, but not so great as to keep a Norsewoman from the riches of Miklagárd. I hear tales that Irishwomen are also fearsome, riding into battle, perched behind their men on war-horses."

A smile flirted at the edges of Ailinn's mouth as well. " 'Tis legend really." She looked again to a cluster of women at one cook fire. "And I hear tales that Norsemen take many wives. 'Twould appear that man has three. Is this usual?"

Lyting followed her gaze. At once one of the two younger women there greeted him with her tilting, catlike eyes, communing her interest in him. The other, equally aware of Lyting, lowered her lashes seductively, her invitation clear.

Ailinn cast a glance heavenward, regretting that she had directed his attention to these two prowling felines. But when she looked back, Lyting had already returned to his task, his expression unchanged.

"That is Arnór and his wife Jorunn. The two younger ones are Arnór's daughters. He's taken a fine bit of ribbing, but his women refused to miss the famed markets of Miklagárd this season. There be nothing so dazzling in all the world, I am told."

Lyting smiled fully upon Ailinn, a smile that snatched her breath away—a wide, easy smile, filled with a warmth and mirth that arced the distance and flooded through her.

"In verity, Arnór's family does not travel so far as you might think. They live the year through in Smolensk, a little north of Gnezdovo, where we made portage from the Dvina to the Dnieper."

Ailinn heard little of the last of what he said, her concentration muddled, her pulse still beating apace from the impact of his smile. She looked again to the two sturdy and very blond daughters of Arnór. They looked as if they could more than take care of themselves on such a voyage. They also looked as if they would more than like to take care of Lyting as well! She wondered how Lyting knew so much of their family.

Ailinn discovered Lyting smiling at her as she returned her gaze to his.

"They are friends of Skallagrim," he offered, as though

reading her mind. "One of the daughters evidently had her eye set on Hakon last season."

Ailinn was tempted to add that both daughters appeared to have their eyes set on *him* this season. She bit back the remark and pulled her mantle more closely about her shoulders.

"And do the rich markets also draw you to Byzantium?" she ventured, then feared he might find her overbold.

He smiled in a way that sent warmth spreading through her all over again, like sweet, silken honey.

"I am an emissary for my brother."

"Ah, the man who accompanied you to Thora's. He is a Norman lord, is he not?"

"Rurik is the Baron de Valsemé."

She absorbed this. "Your 'mission' must be important to bring you so far from Normandy."

"*Já.* 'Tis." His crystal-blue eyes melted into hers. "Do you know aught of the duchy, Ailinn?"

"Little. Only that the Norsemen ravaged Francia until the king ceded them lands."

Lyting's hands paused. He could not argue her words. Though neither he nor Rurik ever warred in Francia, he deemed it best not to apprise her that they were both blood nephews to Duke Rollo.

Ailinn continued to gaze at him expectantly, as though to ask if he had taken part in the plundering.

"*Nei*, Ailinn. I harrowed no Franks. In those years you think on, I fought Norge men, keeping them from the shores of Danmark, until after the treaty of Saint-Clair-sur-Epte."

The tenseness went out of Ailinn's shoulders. Norge men. Norwegians. Enmity lay between them and the Danes in Eire, also.

"What more do you know of the duchy?" Lyting asked, his manner familiar, conversational, as though they knew each other well and now sat casually about the evening fires after supper, sharing a pleasant talk.

"Only what Bergette said, that by the terms of the treaty the Norsemen took the waters of Holy Baptism."

"*Satt.* True."

"She also said that many continue to practice their old faith alongside the new. That they embrace Christianity only in so far as it gains them land or advantage."

Lyting tugged at his lower lip as he formed a response, but Ailinn spoke again.

"Bergette further explained how Norse merchants take a form of baptism without water, and that they wear crosses so they might trade with Christians, solely with an eye for profit."

"The merchants you see here be Svear, Ailinn—people of Sverige, not Normandy." Lyting motioned to those moving about the camp. "What Bergette said is largely true—of the Svear and other Norse merchants—though there be those who embrace the faith more earnestly than others."

"Then the Normans wear the cross for land, and the merchants for profit," she commented dryly.

Ailinn's gaze fell to the chain that gleamed about Lyting's neck. Then slowly she raised her eyes to his.

"You also wear the cross."

Lyting saw the conflict in her eyes.

"Rest easy, Ailinn. Christianity has taken firm root in Normandy, and the duke honors the faith by constructing a vast cathedral at Rouen. As for myself . . ."

He hesitated, a part of him wishing to conceal from her his chosen path, another part urging that he place it between them, and at once, lest he lose sight of the future to which he committed himself. Resigning himself to what he deemed he must do, Lyting drew the silver cross from his tunic.

"I, too, embrace Christ's cross and have received the holy waters. If you would know, upon my return to Normandy, I shall enter the Abbey of Corbie and take the cowl."

Ailinn pulled back. "That cannot be so," she returned forcefully, her eyes grown large.

"Ailinn, 'tis truth."

"Ní hea! Non. Why do you tell me this? You are not meant for cloister."

Lyting stared at her a full moment, taken aback by the intensity of her response.

"Ailinn, God calls whom He will."

"Then you must have misheard," she asserted, her tone unbrookable.

"Why does this upset you?"

She looked away. "It does not."

"Why, then? Because I am Norse?"

Norse? The word skipped past her. All she could think on

was an image of a shining silver warrior, defeating the pirates so stunningly upon the waters; and before that, at Thora's, his bounding to her defense, sword in hand, as he protected her from Hakon.

She uptilted her chin, her eyes penetrating into his.

"Tell me you are God's warrior, but do not tell me you are his monk. I have seen you in the eye of battle, seen your mastery upon the sea and your readiness upon the land. Even now you prepare for tomorrow."

Her gaze fell to his sword, shining beside him.

"And what of Hedeby and my arrival there? You sought to purchase me from Skallagrim nearly at once. Do you deny that?"

"I do not deny it." Ailinn's discourse astonished Lyting.

"Why, then, if 'twas not for . . . well, fleshly purposes."

"Fleshly purposes?" His lips began to pull into a smile. Ailinn appeared flurried despite her words, and he happily feasted on the lovely sight of her—her eyes wide and shining, her dark red hair tumbling about her face and shoulders, glinting with gold in the firelight. Saints' breath, but she was beautiful.

"Fleshly purposes," Ailinn repeated, her cheeks burning. "Is it not your wish to take me for your bed?"

Lyting's breath caught in his throat along with his voice. His smile froze upon his lips. Ailinn continued to look on him, the firelight playing over her exquisite features . . . over her softly parted lips. Of a sudden Lyting knew a hunger unparalleled by anything he had ever known or endured.

Já, he wanted her. With his whole being didst he want her. Not as a slave, but willingly, as his lover, his heart-mate. He wanted to spend his passion on her and in her and touch eternity with her through the children they would beget.

Lyting fought to staunch the floodtide of emotions that raged within him and threatened to sweep him away. He had been warned. He knew the dangers—to his soul, to his calling—when he first came on this journey. Now he must confront and overcome his deepest, most elemental desires, lest he be swayed from his path. He had allowed himself too close to the fire, and the fire's name was Ailinn.

Lyting struggled to recover the iron will he normally held

over himself. His sacred call. He must focus himself to that purpose and keep his call before him.

"Upon all that is holy, Ailinn," his voice came roughened, dry. " 'Tis my solemn intent to enter the Abbey of Corbie on my return to Normandy. But first I will seek your release and that of your cousins, and I will see you returned safely to Eire. You have this on my word."

Relief spilled through Lyting as he saw Skallagrim, trudging toward their tents. Desperately he needed to be away, for it tormented him to remain so near the "fire."

He rose unsteadily to his feet, then bent to retrieve his sword. But in so doing, he glanced to Ailinn once more. A mistake. For a bolt of longing passed through him, searing him to the core. He wanted her fiercely.

How would he ever purge himself of the feelings he held for Ailinn? Or was this to be his earthly penance?—that his obsession for her would continue to burn a lifetime within him, long after she returned to Eire, and for all the years he dwelt in prayer within cold cloister walls.

Lyting strode away the moment Skallagrim arrived, his heart and soul aflame, voices clamoring within.

Ailinn stared after him, wholly at a loss and utterly confused. The star-bright Dane. Her silver warrior. Called to a life of holiness and prayer?

She should rejoice that God had claimed the heart of this Norseman and called him to His service. Instead, she felt strangely bereft, robbed in some wise, as though something most precious had just been thieved away.

Chapter 11

"Essupi, 'Gulper,'" Lyting called over to Ailinn, nodding ahead to where the brisk currents began to churn and froth in the rock-strewn waters—the first of the nine rapids.

Lyting leaned into the oars as they began angling toward the banks with the rest of the convoy.

"We will put to ground here." He raised his voice over the sound of the rushing waters, though his gaze remained fixed to the riverbank. "The watch will disembark first, then everyone else, except those who will 'walk' the ships through the waters."

"'Walk' them through?" Ailinn's brow wrinkled.

"*Já.* So that we need not unload the cargo." He could see that she still did not comprehend and he smiled. "You shall see."

His smile faded to a somber line. "Ailinn, tell the others you will be chained together in groups. Should we be attacked and the tribesmen mounted, they cannot easily seize any of you and steal you away."

"And if they are not mounted?" Ailinn called back.

"Then they'll have to kill every man here to have you."

Even as he spoke the words, Lyting knew there were those who would willingly abandon goods and slaves to save themselves. He would not. Stealing a glance to Ailinn, it surprised him to find her gaze engulfing him, concern filling her eyes. Was it naught but dread for the tribesmen that put the look there? Or didst she possibly fear for him?

"Skallagrim has decided to remove your ankle irons," he continued, redirecting his gaze. " 'Tis somewhat rocky ashore. You will still be chained together with wrist cuffs, but your legs will not be cumbered by irons. You will be able to move swifter and more easily, if need be. Use the chains to lash out, should anyone seek to harm you. The chieftain will personally guard you."

The waters grew calmer as they closed on the shore. In the distance, mist rose above the river and the rumbling rapids of Essupi could be heard.

"And you?" Ailinn eyed Lyting's mail shirt. "Will you also guard us ashore?"

" 'Tis my intent, unless Skallagrim directs otherwise."

Lyting fell silent, concentrating on his labors, as he, Skallagrim, and Hakon navigated the back currents and gained upon the land. Helmeting himself, he scanned the sporadic clumps of trees that rose along the banks. The wooded Steppe continued with them along the river and would do so until just past the rapids—a danger, for it offered cover to assailants.

Running the ship aground, they drove the bow into the bank. Immediately Lyting leapt ashore with his companions, and together they dragged the ship partway on shore and tied it to a tree.

Without pause, Lyting retrieved his shield from the ship, drew on his sword, and started forth.

Working apace, Skallagrim off-loaded the women and saw to their chains. Just as he finished and took up his ax, Lyting returned, prepared to conduct the captives along the banks.

"How surefooted be you, Lyting?" Skallagrim scratched deep into his bristly beard and looked back to the ships crowding the shoreline.

"Surefooted enough," Lyting returned, puzzled.

"We will require greater numbers of men to pole through the ships than we will to maintain the watch on land. I prefer you assist Hakon. These nomads usually lie in wait at the worst stretches. I do not anticipate overmuch trouble here, but in that event our force is strong this season. We can afford to utilize more of our men with the ships. 'Twill also gain us quicker passage. Arnór is going to need help also, but first you'll need get off those before you step in the river." Skallagrim motioned to Lyting's garb.

"*Já.*" His voice trailed off as he contemplated the lively currents. He didn't welcome the task of climbing into icy waters.

"Have the Christians burdened you with a mantle of modesty as well as one of celibacy?" Hakon scoffed, misreading Lyting's look. He hauled off his tunic, then sat down to pull off his boots.

Lyting saw now that the men entering the waters were naked.

"That's right, 'monk.' We go in as raw as the day we were born. How else?" He shrugged. "Wouldn't want to get our 'fine' clothes wet—eh?" Hakon's gaze touched Lyting's mail and the cloth of his garments.

Standing, Hakon grinned and thrust his pants to his feet. He then stepped from them, bundled his clothes, and pitched them into the ship. Stretching widely, he strutted a small circle before the women, turned back to the ship, and took several stout staffs from storage.

"Here. We use these." Hakon hefted one to Lyting. "Let's be about it, shall we, 'monk'?"

Lyting caught the stave in one hand, his knuckles whitening about the thickness. He didn't harbor any form of false modesty and was more than aware of the numerous eyes—female eyes—centered upon him, waiting for him to expose himself. Most notably, those of Arnór's daughters and Rhiannon.

A muscle flexed along his jaw, beneath his beard. He prefered to guard Ailinn, but the chieftain's mind was decided and the convoy must not tarry.

Lyting avoided looking to Ailinn as he moved to the ship. Venting a breath, he lay the staff aside, then dragged off his mail shirt, his tunic, and tugged off each of his boots. He stored the items in the ship. His hands next moved to the waist strings that secured his pants. With a sturdy yank he freed them.

Ailinn's heart skittered several beats as Lyting stripped away his trousers and she beheld, fully, his long-limbed, well-muscled physique. She knew she should glance aside but found she couldn't quite drag her eyes away.

He placed his trousers into the ship and began to push the craft back into waters, every muscle of his hard, well-knit body stretching and bunching. Ailinn swallowed around the knot in her throat, wholly aware of the uneveness of her breathing and the pounding beneath her breast. The powerfully built shoulders, the broad back and tapering waist, the firm buttocks, and sinewed legs—everything about him was solid, sculpted and so beautifully proportioned.

Lyting moved deeper into the waters until they rose waist high. Never once did he shudder, Ailinn noted, though she reasoned he must be chilled. He and the other men walked the ships along the edges of the river, plying them with their sturdy poles, testing the beds, and looking for outcroppings of rocks that could damage the hull.

Skallagrim prodded the women forward, giving Ailinn a start. As she picked her way along the bank, the image of Lyting burned in her mind. She knew 'twas a shallow thing to think, but how could such a warrior shut so able a body away in a monastery?

Ailinn felt suddenly drained, sapped of her energies.

Merciful Lord. Was Lyting to do this at every rapid?

Ailinn strayed another glance to the neighboring campfire where Lyting sat with Arnór and his family over the evening's meal.

Jorunn had approached him when first they camped. Afterward, Lyting revealed that she had expressed an interest in learning of Christ and wished that her daughters listen to what he might say as well.

Ailinn gave a delicate snort. Could he be so blind to their designs? She sighed softly. Mayhaps he just could not neglect an opportunity to impart Christ's message.

"*Ailinn,*" Skallagrim pronounced her name slowly in his naturally roughened voice, commanding her attention to him.

He pried loose the lid from a small barrel, set it aside, then reached in and removed the packing of hay. Carefully he withdrew a sizable object wrapped in stiffened leather. After laying it upon the ground, he loosed the bindings and opened the covering.

Ailinn's hand covered her mouth. Within the protective hide lay a gleaming Irish harp, seized from Mór's hall. How long it had been since last she heard the bright strings and, with her own hand, set their notes free to sing upon the airs? Her eyes grew moist as she gazed upon the harp, the soul of Ireland.

Skallagrim held forth the instrument to Ailinn as though, in part, questioning whether she could play it and, in part, enjoining that she take it and do so.

Ailinn accepted the harp into her hands. Lovingly she caressed the lustrous wood and touched the strings. 'Twas a small harp compared to many, its height measuring the length of a man's arm, and its strings numbering thirty.

"Deira, look," Ailinn spoke softly as she laid a hand atop her stepcousin's and stayed her from abrading her neck and arms with the wool of her gown.

Of late, Deira's moods swung from ones of lassitude to ones of extreme agitation. Her worst spells came most often not after Hakon's ravishments, but after Rhiannon's sharp tongue had set her on edge. Ailinn hoped the music would soothe her.

"Look, Deira," she repeated. "A harp. Would you like to hear the songs we so enjoyed in Cellach's hall? Come. Listen. 'Twill hearten you."

Deira let the gown slip from her fingers, but she took up the cord of Murieann's girdle and set it against her cheek. Still distracted, she drew it away and toyed with the ends.

Ailinn spoke firm and confident to her in Frankish. "Soon now, very soon, we shall be to the end of this journey, and, as I have told you, Lyting will gain our freedom in the Great City. He *will*, Deira. Believe that, and listen no more to Rhiannon. Listen, now, only to my harp. And when you be sad, bring forth their melodies to cheer and comfort you. Soon there shall be comfort enough, and we shall be on our way home to Eire."

Ailinn tested the strings, tuning them as needed, then strummed a little run of notes over them and smiled her satisfaction.

Deira edged closer, her mouth tilting pleasantly, her gaze fastened upon the harp in anticipation. Rhiannon regarded Ailinn impassively from where she sat, then returned her attention to Lyting.

Ailinn caressed the strings—plucking, sometimes trilling, them—the notes sounding bright and distinct, bell-like and soul-soothing. Her harp claimed the attention of those around, including Lyting, who paused in what he spoke and turned toward her.

Pleasure spread through Ailinn, and she lifted her voice in the sweetest of songs. As she gave herself to the melody, her gaze drifted to the silver warrior. Their eyes met. Embraced. Crystal blue and golden brown. Within the depths of his eyes, he smiled at her. Warmly. Beautifully. His crystal-blue smile rippled through her—a joyous, singing sensation that kept measure with her song. Lyting rose as she watched, bid the others a parting word, and silently crossed the expanse toward her.

Ailinn felt as though she would melt before the fire as he returned and quietly lowered himself to the ground. He stretched out his full length and reclined, bracing himself up on one arm, his eyes never leaving her.

The chieftain gave no notice, for the music so enwrapped him in its magic. Ailinn continued, unabashedly pleased that Lyting appeared beguiled by her song. The daughters of Arnór did not appear so well pleased, and neither did their mother.

Jorunn came to stand before Skallagrim, just as Ailinn began another sprightly tune. For an instant the woman's pose reminded her of Thora.

Lyting raised himself to a sitting position. His features darkened. As did the chieftain's. Ailinn's fingers stilled upon the strings.

Skallagrim and Jorunn argued back and forth. Finally Skallagrim issued several terse-sounding words in Norse, then stood, gestured to Lyting and then the harp. As he did, Deira shrank away and dragged at her hair, her agitation returning.

Lyting shifted to a kneeling position before Ailinn, his hands braced atop his thighs. He released a long breath.

"I regret that you must cease playing, Ailinn. Jorunn and some of the others fear your music will carry far upon the breeze and alert the tribesmen of our presence here."

Her lips rounded softly. "Oh."

Ailinn gave over the harp to him, then dropped her lashes, feeling the keen bite of disappointment. "*Mais, oui.* The tribesmen. I did not think—"

"Ailinn," his voice gentled. "Skallagrim would not have allowed you the harp if he thought to draw the tribesmen. It seems to me, if Jorunn were truly so concerned, she would have hushed her daughters' shrill laughter earlier. 'Twas enough to stir their dead."

He smiled, sending shivers through Ailinn. Her spirits brightened. He hadn't been deceived by their wiles after all.

His look grew more serious. "The women are but jealous and stir others to complain. Pay them no heed. Yours is the gift of angels and could entrance a man for a lifetime. They fear you and, therefore, deny you your music. But you will sing upon your harp again, I promise you."

Lyting rose and presented the instrument to Skallagrim, just as Hakon returned from his watch.

"Your watch, 'monk.'" Hakon tossed his helmet to the ground before his tent and jerked open the lacings on his platelet-sewn tunic.

Lyting ignored the barb and went to gather his apparel. Donning his mail shirt and helmet, he next girt his sword and secured his great gray mantle in place. Casting one brief, last glance to Ailinn, he departed.

Ailinn watched after Lyting as he made his way to the camp's perimeter. Drawing up the hood of his cloak, he covered his bright hair and melted into the night.

Hours later, his vigil complete, Lyting picked a path around low-burning fires, sleeping bodies, and scattered tents.

Arriving at the site he shared with Skallagrim and Hakon, he discovered that Ailinn and her stepcousins were not in sight.

He bit back the vow that sat on his tongue. For Ailinn he did not fear. Skallagrim stated earlier that he would keep her in his tent this night for added protection. But as to Deira and Rhiannon, he suspected that Hakon had either shared them with others or had kept them both for himself to sate his own appetites.

Lyting's lips sealed to a line. How he longed to reach the Imperial city and set everything aright.

Fatigue lapped at him like an endless tide that stole a little part of him each time it hurried back out to sea. Depleted, and with only a few hours remaining before dawn, he divested himself of his helmet and mail, retrieved his pallet where it waited by the chieftain's tent, and spread it before the fire. Freeing his sword from its scabbard, he placed the length of steel alongside his mean bed.

Wrapping himself in his mantle, Lyting lay down and quickly fell to a light slumber. There, he drifted upon the topmost layer of sleep—a nether region that lay between repose and wakefulness.

His inner ear pricked, a movement detected.

The rustle of cloth. A footfall.

He surfaced.

Lyting's breath stilled, his ears straining. Again it came. The soft padding of footsteps, approaching . . .

Lyting rolled. Catching up his sword, he came to his knees and leveled the blade straight for the heart of his assailant.

Rhiannon froze in place. She clutched a sheet to her breast, her eyes shifting from the point of the steel to Lyting.

Spying the partially open curtain on Hakon's tent, Lyting realized that she had slipped from inside. Evidentally Hakon had fallen asleep after spending himself on her.

Rhiannon raised her chin. A smile spread slowly over her lips. She shook out her wealth of ebony hair, sending it cascading down her back, leaving her creamy neck and shoulders bare to his view.

In the semidarkness Rhiannon's eyes appeared as black as her tresses—two smoldering pools, huge and inviting. She released the cloth, allowing it to whisper from her fingers and puddle at her feet.

Rhiannon stood unblushingly naked before Lyting, presenting her lush contours for him to savor fully. A fire kindled in her eyes, and her ripe body seemed filled with waiting.

Lyting tightened his grip about the swordhilt, his arm remaining staunch as a rock, his blade aimed between her naked breasts.

Undeterred, Rhiannon lifted her hands and traced them over her breasts, encircling the nipples. She trailed them downward, drawing his eyes to the tautness of her stomach and abdomen, the curve of her hips, the beginning of her thighs, and, finally, the promise that lay between.

Rhiannon then opened her arms and raised them to Lyting, proffering herself unreservedly to him. She disregarded the blade he leveled at her and took a step forward, clearly expecting him to lower the weapon.

He did not.

Rhiannon barely caught herself, the swordpoint pricking her skin and drawing a drop of blood. She wrenched her eyes to his.

Revolted by Rhiannon's wiles, Lyting rose to his feet. He dipped his sword only long enough to snare her linen on the blade point and tender it back to her so she might cover herself. Even in so doing, he continued to center his blade directly at her heart.

Anger slashed an ugly path across Rhiannon's features, but Lyting maintained his silence. Hakon suddenly appeared at the opening of the tent, having risen naked from his bed. Regarding the two, he barked a laugh.

"Come, my high-bred slut. This one will not appease your appetites. But as you can see, I'm ready for you."

Hakon crossed the distance and hauled her against him, his firm shaft pressing against her belly. He seized a kiss from her lips, despite her infuriated protest and pummeling hands.

Hakon only laughed. Sparing a single glance to Lyting, he hoisted Rhiannon in his arms and carried her back inside his tent.

The rude jarring of the ship awakened Ailinn from her rest. She pushed upward and peered from beneath her lashes.

The waters ran swift and urgent about them, foaming and breaking as they rushed toward the third rapid—Gelandri, "Yeller," as Lyting called it.

Ailinn opened her eyes fully, hearing Gelandri's clamor echo off the steep granite wall of the west bank. A fine mist hovered in the distance where the currents convulsed over and about huge boulders, roiling and roaring, following the river's treacherous descent.

Never had she seen the like. Eire possessed nothing to compare to the cataracts of the Dnieper. Earlier, Lyting warned that the rapids grew ever fiercer ahead, where gorges constricted the great river and, farther on, where the torrents took a significant bend.

She glanced ahead to where the chieftain and Lyting strained at the oars, their backs facing her. To the rear of the ship sat Hakon.

Deira's movements drew her eye. The girl rocked back and forth, highly distracted, gripping the folded girdle to her chest and dragging her fingers fitfully through her hair.

Rhiannon bent to Deira's ear, the din of Gelandri rivaling her voice. Whatever she spoke clearly disturbed Deira. The girl's face looked pinched, her expression almost pained. Her eyes strayed constantly about.

Deira's unrest became Ailinn's unease. Rhiannon had become exceptionally dark-tempered and vexatious these last days, her tongue cutting to the point of cruelty. But whatever fueled her morose mood, she must cease her destructive remarks and leave Deira be.

Ailinn leaned across and plucked Rhiannon's sleeve. Gratefully iron chains no longer hampered her arm, for Skallagrim continued to allow the three of them to remain unfettered while upon the river.

"Rhiannon," Ailinn called out, but her stepcousin did not hear—or simply paid her no heed. "Rhiannon," she repeated, raising her voice. "Deira looks unwell. Leave her rest atime."

"Indeed. She does need her rest, as most of us do, but not for the portage alone." Rhiannon breezed a glance to Hakon and back. "See how the gleam postures in his eye? He thinks forward to tonight. To Deira and—"

"Be silent, Rhiannon," Ailinn snapped, abhoring her waspishness.

"I speak but the truth. Look at him," she sneered. "Look at them all. Adventurers. 'Tis why they hazard this voyage—for the prospect of battle, wealth beyond avarice, and for *us*—a horde of women they can ravish at will and then dispose of to bring yet more riches."

"Cease this, Rhiannon." Ailinn's anger erupted.

"You would like that." A fire burned in Rhiannon's eyes. "Of course, 'tis different for you, the 'virgin' of Clonmel. And even for Deira, too, whom you be ever so anxious to coddle. Hakon reserves her solely to himself of late. He'll not sell her or release her in Constantinople. Why do you give her false expectations? 'Tis a low, mean thing to hold forth hope where there be none."

"Shut up, Rhiannon! You have a serpent's tongue. I can understand your wishing to strike at me, but not Deira. She does you no harm, yet you torment her. Leave her be, or be warned. I am at an end with words."

"Stop! Stop!" Deira hunched forward, covering her ears, and rocked forcefully.

"But you *must* hear me in this, Cousin." Rhiannon forced Deira's hands away from her head, her fingers tangling in the cincture that Deira still gripped. "I speak you no falsehoods, but plain truth, so that you might prepare and strengthen yourself for what is to come."

Deira pulled from Rhiannon's hold and hugged herself tight, tears streaming over her cheeks as she continued to rock.

"You're destroying her, can't you see?" Ailinn seized Rhainnon's arm, but she wrenched free.

Skallagrim looked back, and Hakon grumbled several words that might have been a charge for them to cease. Rhiannon disregarded them both, drawing energy from the clash with Ailinn and from her control of the moment. She turned again to Deira.

"Each of us bears her own cross, Cousin. You must find a way to suffer yours and endure the course of time, for you will never be rid of Hakon until the day he tires of you. Then he will either keep you to pleasure his friends, or he will sell you in the marketplace as he did Lia."

"Deira, do not listen," Ailinn called above the increasing roar of the waters.

"*Do* listen, and listen *well*." Rhiannon's eyes flashed her malevolence. "You are Hakon's slave, and you best think more of pleasing him than displeasing him, lest he reject you and condemn you to a worse fate."

Deira shook her head in fierce denial. Choked with tears, she pressed the girdle to her mouth, her shoulders shaking.

Rhiannon's eye fell to the girdle, her temper flaring. "I told you before to stop clutching that! Murieann is dead. She cannot help you any more than anyone else can. Leave the girdle be!"

Rhiannon tore the cincture from Deira's hands, but Deira grappled for it and snared its end. Again, Rhiannon yanked it stoutly. Ripping the cording from her cousin's fingers, she pitched it into the river.

"*Ní he . . . a . . . . a!*" Deira thrust upward and lunged for the girdle. With arms outstretched she toppled overboard and into the churning waters.

"Deira-a-a!" Ailinn shrieked and began to rise, the boat tipping dangerously back and forth beneath her feet. Skallagrim rounded, then forced her back down.

Lyting twisted and looked back. Following Ailinn's gaze, he spotted Deira as her head appeared above the surface. She gasped for air, gulping great mouthfuls of water, and fought the currents as they bore her away.

Without pause Lyting let go the oars and shoved the boots from his feet. Keeping his eyes fixed on Deira, he rose and took a forward leap into the river, feet first, his body angled slightly forward, and his arms raised sideward to slow his entry and prevent his totally submerging.

Frigid waters sheathed Lyting. At once he pressed his arms downward and brought his legs together, fighting the sinking motion, striving to keep his face above water and his sight upon Deira. Not too far distant she thrashed against the coursing river and inadvertently slowed her furtherance.

Lyting allowed the force of the current to carry him forward. Its vigor increased steadily, sweeping him along. As he gained on Deira, he waited for the suitable moment, then began taking powerful strokes to cut across the currents, striving to reach her.

Deira continued to flail, panic-ridden. Lyting knew he need approach her with care lest she drown them both. He battled the water until he came within several arm's lengths of her. Making a quick vertical dive beneath the surface, he approached her from underneath. Coming up, he grasped her about the knees, one hand in front, one in back, and turned her away from him. He then began to work his way up the sides of her legs, hips, waist, and back. Just as he prepared to surface, bringing one hand up to cup her chin in his palm and secure her, the brawling river surged, hurtling them forward into a cragged boulder and jolting them apart.

Stunned momentarily, Lyting drifted with the current, then sighted Deira nearby. The rapids carried them together, the turbulence growing worse as they moved toward the heart of the rapids.

Again, he fought the currents, straining to reach her. He readied to attempt the maneuver again, determined this time to grip her beneath the arms rather than the chin. Before he could initiate his dive, the waters heaved him forward, into Deira's reach.

Frantic, she lunged for Lyting's head, smiting him with her iron wrist cuff and cutting him above the brow. Lyting took a quick breath of air and tucked his chin to protect his throat from her crushing embrace. Her hold proved inordinately strong. He would need submerge the both of them and force her to release her grip.

Before Lyting could draw her under, Deira scrambled upward, trying to climb onto his shoulders and reach the highest point. Frenzied, she shoved him beneath the waves, kicking his jaw and cheek. With no recourse, Lyting swam out from beneath her and surfaced beyond her reach.

They continued to move with the raging currents together, but she appeared to be tiring. Her head slipped under the water, then she struggled upward, coughing and sputtering what she drank. Lyting fought his way back and straight toward her, deciding on a different, more direct approach.

This time he allowed the currents to drive him close in to her. Extending his arm, he spread his fingers.

"Grab on to me!" he shouted above the uproar of the river.

At once Deira flung herself toward him and gripped hold of his arm. At the same time he blocked her from coming nearer, bracing his outspread hand against her upper chest and preventing her from seizing him about his neck or head.

"Hang on," he called again.

Lyting began to turn onto his side so he could work his way toward shore. He saw Deira's eyes widen, then felt the sudden acceleration of the currents as they were sucked into a whirlpool.

Deira's fingers began to slip down his arm as the vortex spun them round and ever downward with incredible force. Lyting strove to draw forth his free arm and grab her, but he felt as though a great anchor weighted him in place. He vied against the unseen force that held him, and with every last reserve of strength, reached to grip hold of Deira. Just as his fingers brushed hers, she let go.

Ailinn went white as she saw Lyting and Deira disappear from sight. She clung to the side of the ship, her hands bloodless. Skallagrim and Hakon rowed furiously for shore, having progressed far deeper than normal into hazardous currents. The ship tossed and plunged upon the tempestuous river. Ailinn noticed not at all. Her eyes remained fixed to the distance, searching the empty waters where last she saw Lyting and Deira.

Lyting spun downward, deep beneath the whirling waters, then felt the undertow grip him, as though two giant hands clamped about his legs. It dragged him a rapid distance and released him abruptly. Lyting labored toward the surface, growing short on breath. Breaking through, he gasped for air, his chest aching.

Pushing the wet hair from his eyes, he glanced hastily about for Deira. Not finding her, he scanned the area once more. He spied her dark head just as the rapids convulsed and dashed her against a huge boulder. She appeared already limp when she struck the rock, mayhaps unconscious. But now he saw that her eyes were closed and her head lolling as she slipped beneath the waters.

Lyting's heart slammed against his ribs. With a fresh burst of energy he battled the river to reach the boulder. He hoped against hope that the rock trapped and held her there, and that she hadn't already been dragged farther downriver by the undercurrents.

Gaining on his mark, Lyting made a quick surface dive and searched desperately for Deira. Minutes later he exploded to the surface and gulped the air. Again he dived and hunted the area. And again he erupted from the waters, his lungs screaming for air. The currents fought his efforts mightily, dragging him downriver against his desire.

Lyting began to bear the penalties for his exertions, finding it difficult to breathe and his muscles turning to lead with exhaustion.

Reluctantly Lyting relinquished his search and allowed the current to carry him as he made his way obliquely toward shore. Pain centered in his chest with each inhalation, yet he scarely took note, lost to thought. He had failed. Deira was gone.

After grounding the ship, Skallagrim leapt ashore and hastened downriver along the banks. Others quickly joined him in search of Lyting.

Ailinn started to follow, but Hakon restrained her, trammeling her arm. Ailinn wrested free, then planted her feet firmly on the shore and waited. And waited more.

An eternity passed, along with a thousand agonies migrating through her soul. At long last the men returned. Skallagrim and Arnór bore Lyting between them, each upholding him beneath an arm. His head dropped forward, but she saw that his legs moved and he attempted to keep pace with the others. Her heart swelled. He was alive.

Desperate for sign of Deira, Ailinn cast her gaze amongst the others but did not find her there.

A cold dread sliced through her.

She silenced her thoughts and held firm rein of them, wishing yet not wishing to ask the question she knew she must. She looked once more to Lyting. As though he felt the pull of her gaze, he lifted his face and raised solemn eyes to hers.

"Ailinn . . . I am sorry. . . ."

Ailinn wavered, stumbling back a pace. Stunned, she looked out upon the river, then back again. Her eyes pleaded with Lyting to tell her that Deira lived. That she waited for them somewhere downriver. That they hadn't lost her. But as their gazes held, she knew the truth. Deira was dead.

Tears clogged Ailinn's throat and stung the back of her eyes. Turning, her gaze drew to Rhiannon. Rhiannon. Even now her look gave challenge. Anger collided with anguish, welling up to erupt, full-force, from the pit of Ailinn's being.

" 'Twas your doing that wrought this sorrow. Deira's death hangs on your soul, Rhiannon. If you have one!"

Rhiannon bristled, her nostrils flaring. "Deira was a little fool. Had she listened to my—"

Ailinn shrieked her fury and sprang for Rhiannon, felling her to the ground. Over and over they rolled, scratching and kicking, yanking fistfuls of hair.

Lyting loosed himself from those who supported him as Ailinn and Rhiannon pitched on the bank in a swirl of gowns, clawing and tearing at each other, contesting even Gelandri with their shrilling.

Hakon joined him, and together they hauled the two warring females apart. Ailinn twisted beneath Lyting's iron grip, striving to get at Rhiannon. But he held her solidly against his chest and, despite her struggles, would not let her go.

Ailinn vied, then suddenly the high pitch of her fury plummeted to the raw chasm of unspeakable sorrow. Her anger flowed out of her. Awash with grief, her knees gave way, and she became as fluid as water. Lyting sank to the ground with her. As they knelt together, she bent to the earth and braced herself, her dark red hair spilling forward and shrouding her face. Without word, Lyting eased his grip of her.

Tears burned Ailinn's eyes. Seizing up fistfuls of dirt, she raised clenched hands to Heaven, then released the soil in a fine stream and began to keen for Deira. Again, she caught up the soil, and released it, lamenting her stepcousin, lamenting all the days that had gone before, lamenting all that was lost.

Then the torrent of tears came.

And came.

"Deira . . . Deira . . . Deira . . ." she choked out in misery.

An effusion of emotion overwhelmed Ailinn, carrying her back to that distant morning in Clonmel when the dragonships blackened the River Suir. Her heart could no longer contain the anguish, and now it rushed forth and racked her through and through.

Time slipped into a void as Ailinn spent her grief. At long last she fell silent, tears yet coursing over her cheeks, and 'came aware that Lyting still knelt beside her.

Ailinn lifted her face toward the heavens, her eyes glistening, her voice strained.

" 'Twas a fine spring morn when last I arose to greet an Irish dawn. Then all didst blossom so beautifully to life—the dew clung upon the rose and the birds sang in the hedgerow." Ailinn's voice roughened. "But that day didst die before the sun could reach its height. Now the petals have all fallen, and my heart is filled with thorns."

Ailinn closed her hand over her heart, and, bowing her head, she spoke no more.

Chapter 12

Lyting gazed solemnly ahead, plying his might to the oars, a welcome exertion, for the sheer physicality of the labor purchased him a calm that escaped him otherwise.

Ailinn. His concern welled. He first feared, after Deira's death, that Ailinn might descend into an abyss of despair, similar to the one that had entrapped her stepcousin. But Ailinn's emotions ran high for a full day passing, scaling from anger to outrage, then descending to the depths of sorrow and soul-wringing grief, and finally mounting again to a burning defiance for all who had robbed her of those she had most cherished in life. Then late yestereve Ailinn withdrew into a shell of silence.

Since then her features possessed a new sharpness, and Lyting noted that whenever she regarded the Norsemen of the convoy, 'twas with looks of icy disdain. Yet, her eyes smoldered with obvious detestation whenever they alighted upon Rhiannon.

Skallagrim, heedful of Ailinn's moods, kept the two women separated, as now—Ailinn to the fore, Rhiannon to the rear, the chieftain sitting midship, his bulk dividing them. Lyting could feel Ailinn's presence directly behind him, though she never effected a sound.

Mayhaps Ailinn's ire served her to the best advantage, Lyting reasoned, for as long as she directed her choler outwardly, 'twould likely stay her from slipping into a downward spiral of melancholy. Lyting fixed his attention to the distance and his thoughts to Byzantium. They could not arrive at the gates of Miklagárd soon enough.

Lyting heard Aïfor before he saw it, and when the rapids came into view, 'twas not the boiling, frothing waters and boulder-choked course that drew his eyes, but the narrow granite gorge compressing the great Dnieper between its high walls.

" 'Ferocious,' " his kinsmen called it. How many memorial stones had he counted along the journey since Gotland, raised to those who had perished here? An ill portent?

Lyting spurned the thought lest he court a fate most dire into reality. His trust rested in God. Yet, though he embraced the cross fully, as he looked to the mist rising cloudlike between the scabrous ravine, 'twas the image of Fenrir Wolf that sprang to mind, the beast's jaws ready to devour any so bold as to venture there.

The convoy would not. But the passage overland held its own perils. 'Twould require the entire day to make the portage around Aïfor—the morning alone to walk the captives and goods to the new departure point downriver. For that reason they had camped nearby last night, so that they might embark early, just after the break of dawn. Lyting spied the rugged shoreline, disliking the potential coverage offered by the many boulders and clusterings of trees there. The tall grasses on the plain would also afford opportunity to any of a mean set of mind this day.

As they rowed toward shore, Lyting briefly glimpsed Ailinn. He would not burden her by look or word with the foreboding he felt deep in his bone. Training his eyes ahead, he gird himself for the trial of Aïfor.

Ailinn waited while those of the guard vaulted from the ships and dispersed to compass the surrounding area.

She knew from the procedure at past portages that these men belonged to an initial force that would remain behind with the ships. A second guard would escort the slaves and goods downriver. Thankfully, at this portage, Lyting was to be among the latter.

The detachment reappeared moments later, signaling for the

fleet to proceed. The guardsmen then took up positions at regular intervals, forming a partition, their shields and axes at the ready, while the ships were off-loaded.

Ailinn rose, expecting Skallagrim to aid her ashore. Instead, 'twas Lyting who waited to assist her.

His hands spanned her waist before she could gather a thought, and he lifted her weightless from the craft. As her body shifted against him, her hands instinctively went to his shoulders, and in so doing, brushed his bright hair with her fingertips.

Ailinn gazed upon the wound healing over his left brow, and the bruise marking his cheek, wrought in his struggle to save Deira. Her heart caught. For Lyting.

As he set her to the ground, she felt an urgency to speak to him, to express her gratitude for his selfless efforts to save her stepcousin, but he moved apart to help Rhiannon, and, instead, she found herself turning away.

"Ailinn. 'Tis time." Lyting's voice fell soft behind her a moment later.

She knew he need shackle her. Enduring Rhiannon's presence, Ailinn lifted her cuffed arm for him. Rhiannon returned her gaze no less stonily.

Lyting vented a breath as he brought forth the familiar linkage. "I am loathe to chain you, Ailinn. Believe that. Yet, it remains your best protection, as I have told you in the past. Should we come under attack, prostrate yourself on the ground at once and press close to the other women. Likely we will come under a hail of spears and arrows at the first. As long as the men of the convoy hold the victory, no harm from the tribesmen should befall you."

Lyting affixed the chain to hers and Rhiannon's wrist irons, then led them to the rear of one of the files of women. With a second, longer chain he attached it, first to Rhiannon's cuff, and then to the ankle iron of the last woman in the line. Ailinn suspected he might have done so to spare her, herself, from having to bear the chain's encumbrance.

"Remember what I have told you." Lyting's blue eyes grazed hers.

Again, Ailinn wished to speak to him, but he turned on his heel and returned to the ship to arm himself.

A small wave of panic broke through Ailinn as his features

disappeared beneath his helmet and he took up his shield. At first she could not identify the source of her alarm. Then she realized, for all she had lost, she yet feared to lose more. She feared for Lyting.

"Dia dhuit," she whispered. "God be with you."

The hours passed slowly, uneventfully, each man taut with readiness, keen to every sound, every bird's cry, every breeze that sighed through the grasses.

Early along the passage, Lyting regretted not bringing his bow and a quiver full of arrows, wishing to meet the tribesmen on their own terms. 'Twas their tactic to keep to a distance, shying their arrows and javelins before moving in for close combat. Then 'twould be mainly a contest between their curving, single-edged sabers and the Norsemen's axes and double-edged broadswords.

But the Steppe nomads wielded two other novelties, deadly metal-headed clubs and ropes with their ends tied into what the Franks called "laces"—nooses to snare prey.

The sea of shimmering grasses swayed before the breeze. Unseen birds called out in trills and "wheets" and many a "ki-ki-ki." Their notes were lost for a time to the thunderous roar of Aïfor as the convoy progressed on foot around it. Just past the rapids two black-necked cranes burst into flight from coverage, startling everyone as they bolted upward and winged away. But nothing more dramatic transpired, and at length they reached their destination.

Mayhaps God afforded them a respite this day, Lyting thought as he removed his helmet and wiped his brow. Still, in the hours to come, the convoy would be at its most vulnerable. The guard must divide itself again, leaving a watch to protect the captives and goods, while the rest returned to rejoin the others and transport the boats. His own lot fell with those making the return, as did Hakon's. Skallagrim, however, would stay here.

Lyting refreshed himself with a cool draught of water, then sought Ailinn where she settled herself among the other women. He despised leaving her. She looked up at him of a sudden, as she so often did, as though she could tangibly feel the pull of his gaze.

Tracing her features to heart's memory—unsure of what he

read in her eyes—he rehelmeted himself and departed with the others.

Dire portents bristled down Lyting's spine the entire journey back to the ships. But the force arrived without incident and found all aright. The men of the first guard were fairly bored for their idleness, having met with no greater excitement than the appearance of a stocky little water vole from its burrow on the bank.

After a brief respite they set themselves to the task of portaging the boats. Agreeing upon a rotation of turns for carrying the craft and keeping the watch, they commenced their rigors.

The sun shone brilliant overhead against a sweep of blue sky as endless as the plain. The men shouldering the boats quickly grew hot beneath their toils, while those among the guard were tested anew as the sun's glare began to play tricks of light over the rippling grasses.

Dark spots moved over the golden plain. Cloud shadows, Lyting told himself. Surely, horsemen could not conceal themselves there.

His apprehensions lingered as the spots continued to appear and disappear through the wavering grasses. Still, the birds sang heartily and even the insects buzzed noisily, as if to proclaim all was well.

The hours passed slowly, unremarkably. As Lyting shouldered the boat with Hakon and two others, he estimated they should soon reach the embarkment point.

Ailinn's lovely face flowed to mind, and he felt a renewing rush of energy. He prayed she fared well and grew anxious to see her with his own eyes.

Likewise, he was eager to be rid of the boat and don his mail shirt once more. It had been necessary to remove the ringed corselet, lest the weight of the boat drive the metal links straight into his flesh. It lay at hand, just inside the craft, along with his bow, arrows, and shield. Though he wore a padded, leather tunic, he felt nude without the mail. 'Twas only a brief distance now, he told himself, and centered his thoughts on Ailinn.

He would speak with her this eve, comfort her however

needed. She might reject his efforts, he realized. But he could not change the blood that flowed in his veins. By birth he was and ever would be Norse.

Lyting's thoughts snapped back to the present. Unsure what had netted him there, he admonished himself for having allowed his attention to drift.

His ear strained. For sound. All had frozen in unnatural silence.

Lyting steeled. He began to look to the guard when his vision blurred, a javelin thudding into the side of the boat, directly before his eyes. The shaft shivered with the impact as a clamor arose off to his left—a wail of horn followed by fierce outcries and howlings akin to those of wolves.

"Petchenegs!" someone shouted.

Lyting and Hakon dropped to their knees with the boat, arrows hissing about their heads, several finding their home in the wood. Lyting flattened himself to the ground and quickly shifted around the end of the ship to the opposite side. Hakon joined him a split second later.

Coming up into a low crouch, Lyting waited for the rain of arrows and spears to lessen, then snatched for his shield inside the ship. Covering himself, he retrieved his bow and quiver.

Notching an arrow, he eased back to the end of the ship. The assault overhead abated, and a horn wailed a second time. With that a trilling went up among the Petchenegs, and they advanced on the Norsemen.

Hakon leaned against the boat and freed his ax from his belt. "This is how we deal with Petchenegs, 'monk.'" He flashed the ax's smiling blade. Hakon then flung himself from the protection of the craft and joined the fight.

Lyting's eye drew to a Petcheneg arrow that had fallen fallow of its mark nearby.

"Mete for mete," he reaffirmed his intent to reciprocate in kind, using their own techniques to advantage and then some of his own.

Grabbing a fistful of arrows, Lyting bolted from coverage and stabbed them into the ground next to where he knelt. Renocking his arrow, he drew on the string, marked an approaching horseman, and released. The shaft burred the distance and found its home. Before the man hit the ground, Lyting let fly another arrow and another, continuing in rapid succession until he had exhausted his supply and felled numerous horsemen among their onrushing front.

A shout of elation went up among the Norse. Invigorated, they surged forward to engage the foe, their axes whirring and hewing.

Lyting cast his bow into the boat and grabbed for his shield. Turning back, he caught sight of two Petchenegs as they spurred their horses forward, targeting him, anger chiseled in their faces.

Lyting loosed his sword from its scabbard as the first descended, snatching up a lace and whirling it overhead. Lyting dodged, but the horseman proved agile. Like a raven, he swooped down—black-haired and swarthy, his hard eyes gleaming like pebbles of jet.

The lace caught Lyting high about the shoulders as he sought to duck it. Immediately he gripped hold of the outstretched rope and yanked the tribesman from his horse. The man rolled, reaching for his club, but Lyting gave him no quarter and ran him straight through.

The second horseman closed in, his sword raised and his teeth bared, his eyes filled with fury. Lyting pivoted to confront him, sweeping up his broadsword to block the downward stroke of the tribesman's saber. Steel bit steel, refracting the sun with a blinding flash of light.

Their eyes clashed, and Lyting found himself staring into two obsidian pools—bottomless wells of death.

A coolness prickled over Ailinn's skin, setting the fine hairs on end. A faint breeze? Strange, she had not noticed one, and the day itself had grown unusually warm.

Lyting and the others should be returning soon, she calmed herself, feeling a knot of tension tighten in her stomach. The many hours had crawled past snail-like, fraying her nerves and racking her soul. Was he all right? Didst he fare well?

She listened to the rushing of the river. All seemed so quiet, as though the sun's heat had lulled nature into somnolence.

Ailinn cast her gaze over the captives with whom she sat, about twenty in all, she herself the last of the line. Rhiannon rested beside her, brows drawn together, but whether to shield her eyes against the intensity of the sun or to brood upon some new scheme, Ailinn could not say.

Skallagrim stood guard next to them, sweat trickling in little rivers from beneath his iron helmet, coursing down over his flushed cheeks and into his beard. Uttering something she thought to be a curse, he gestured for Ailinn to assist him with his shield.

Rising, Ailinn relieved him of the round wooden buckler as she had done many times already. Skallagrim removed his helmet, uncovering matted, dripping hair. He then caught up the skin of water at his side, poured it over his head, dribbled it over his face, then into his mouth. Revived, he ran an eye over the landscape and, detecting nothing amiss, returned the skin to his belt and donned his helmet.

Ailinn held forth his shield. As Skallagrim's hands closed on its thickness, he suddenly jerked his head back around to the right, something drawing his attention. Ailinn felt him pull on the shield, but before she could release her grip, three arrows rooted in his chest.

Ailinn screamed as Skallagrim purpled and pitched forward, dragging her with him to the ground, both still clutching the shield. The chieftain fell partially atop her, but Ailinn shoved and pushed free, dragging herself from beneath him. She collided with Rhiannon at the same moment an arrow whizzed overhead. In unison they threw themselves to the earth.

A deafening cry went up as barbarous tribesmen flooded the area, seemingly from nowhere. Ailinn twisted to see, then looked with horror upon the warrior-horsemen of the Steppe.

They came riding, their long ebony locks flowing, and their dusky features obscured beneath heavy beards. From belts of silver hung bow cases, sword scabbards, and metal-crowned clubs. Ropes looped the pommels of their saddles, and they bore small circular shields and javelins in their hands. Spurs glinted on their heels.

Petrified, the women shrieked wildly, clutching their heads between their arms and hands. Ailinn observed Jorunn taking up an ax, but did not see her daughters.

Rhiannon shoved her urgently. "Get the keys!"

"Ní hea," Ailinn protested as Rhiannon crawled forward and grabbed for the ring of keys at Skallagrim's belt.

Ailinn pulled at her arm, trying to stop her, but Rhiannon wrenched away and turned to hunch over the locks that secured her wrist cuff. Rapidly she fitted one key, then another into the mechanisms. One lock sprang free, releasing her from the chain that bound her to the other captive's ankle iron.

Spying the keys, several women snatched for them, but Rhiannon snarled and hauled Ailinn apart with her, a chain yet joining their wrist cuffs.

"Rhiannon! We *must* remain with the others." Ailinn struggled against her hold. "Lyting said—"

"Forget what he said," Rhiannon snapped, pulling Ailinn along with her, behind another nearby boulder. "He's no help to us now, is he?"

Rhiannon peered around the rock, marking the center of the conflict where the men raged and then the immense plain that awaited with its cloaking grasses. She leaned back and worked quickly, thrusting the last of the slotted keys into the lock and disengaging the piece.

Wresting the cuff from her wrist, Rhiannon tossed down the keys and left the manacle and chain to dangle from Ailinn's arm. Shouts drew their attention. When they looked up, they saw a horseman whipping his horse toward them.

"Come!" Rhiannon seized Ailinn and dragged her up with her, forcing her into a run.

The man closed in fast upon them, a fierce gleam in his eyes. As he broached the final distance, Rhiannon shoved Ailinn into his path, then veered and ran apace, away from the heart of the battle, and headed toward the grasses.

Pain grated Ailinn's arms and palms as she jolted against the ground. The horseman swerved his mount and came alongside, but Ailinn gained her feet and broke into a run.

The horses' hooves pounded in her ears as the barbarian bore down upon her. As he pressed his advantage, Ailinn grabbed up the chain that dangled from her wrist and struck out at his leg and thigh. The horse skewed, but the man reined him back in an instant. With a growl he bent from his saddle and snared her about the waist.

Ailinn screamed in terror, twisting in his grip and scratching at his hands as her feet left the ground. His arm suddenly stiffened as he jerked upward, arching his back. A moan escaped his lips and his arm slackened.

Ailinn toppled back to the earth and stumbled to her knees. A heartbeat later the man dropped from his saddle and landed with a "whoof" right before her, an arrow projecting from his back.

Ailinn scrambled backward, her heart in her throat. As the horse moved away, she saw additional Norsemen pouring into the clearing. Amongst them came Lyting, running toward her, his bow in hand!

"Get down, Ailinn! Down!" he shouted, knocking another arrow in place and targeting an onrushing tribesmen.

He felled three more scarcely before she could draw a breath. Exhausting his supply of arrows, he slung his bow to his back, drew on his sword, and fought his way toward her.

Prostrate, Ailinn dragged herself back behind the boulder. Squeezing her eyes shut, she gasped for air and began to shake. Bootsteps rushed forth, and she started. Flinging herself back against the rock, she scrabbled upward and prepared to flee. Just then, Lyting came into view, and sweet joy sang in her breast.

"God's mercy, stay down, Ailinn!" he shouted again, his sword singing out as he met the blade of a Petcheneg. He moved apart, raining blow after blow on the enemy's shield and saber.

Fear cleaved Ailinn anew as she thrust herself to the ground once more. She lay there invoking the heavens in a rush of prayer. Most desperately did she implore God's protection for Lyting.

The roar continued in her hearing—the clash of metal, furied shouts, shrieks of pain, and screams of death, and the hysterical wails of the shackled women.

Ailinn swallowed deeply and looked out from the rock. All appeared chaos at first, then she realized that the Norse closed steadily in like a wall upon the outnumbered fore, choking off pockets of tribesmen and brutally devouring them. Others, seeing themselves outmatched, retreated, yipping in parting, which proved a signal for the others to withdraw.

Heaving for breath, Lyting stabbed his mottled blade into the ground and dropped to his knees beside Ailinn.

"Elskan mín." He drew her against him and buried his face in her auburn hair.

Remembering himself, he loosened his hold, though he did not fully release her. Brushing back the tumble of fiery locks from her face, he touched her cheek briefly, then helped her to her feet.

No sooner did they step free of the boulder than a bellow went up in the distance, drawing both their gazes. They looked as one to see a fleeing horsemen lean out from his mount and swoop down, reaching into the grasses. He came up with a struggling figure. A woman. Rhiannon.

Ailinn started, but Lyting held her firmly against him. Rhiannon's shrieks reached them as she kicked and thrashed and clawed at her abductor. Unfazed, the Petcheneg threw her across his saddle and spurred his horse across the plain.

"There is naught we can do, Ailinn," Lyting stressed, his tone solemn.

Stunned, benumbed, Ailinn leaned against his chest. Together they watched as the tribesmen bore Rhiannon across the shimmering expanse. Dwindling to a speck, the warrior-horsemen vanished into the immensity of the Steppe.

Ailinn squeezed her lashes tight against the image and turned to Lyting, her head sinking forward against his chest.

Lyting's arm encircled her at once. He returned his gaze to those of the convoy in time to see Hakon stride across the clearing and stand over Skallagrim's lifeless body.

Withdrawing his helmet, Hakon wiped the sweat and blood from his face and knelt beside his uncle. A scant moment passed before he directed his interest to Lyting.

Their eyes met and held, then Hakon's gaze slid to Ailinn.

Lyting felt as though a cold, steel blade passed straight through him. With Skallagrim's death, everything had changed.

By the Law Code, Ailinn now belonged to Hakon.

Chapter 13

Hakon intended to kill him.

'Twas in his eyes.

But counter to his nature and with little subtlety, Hakon bridled his impulses and bided his time.

Lyting could hear the chafing in Hakon's soul.

He would not long restrain his hand, Lyting knew. Hakon wanted Ailinn. Badly. Thus far, he withheld himself from her, evidently anticipating that the moment he sought to deal her a harm, Lyting's steel would be there to stay him. Permanently.

Hakon was right.

Much had changed since Aïfor and Gelandri. Even if it had not, he'd see Hakon in the fiery realms below before he would allow him to violate Ailinn.

Lyting plied his strength to the oars as the convoy made its way downriver. He ill-liked his position in the fore of the boat, Ailinn situated behind and Hakon astern, plotting at his back.

In truth, he had expected Hakon to make his move at the previous, fifth rapid, Baruforos—"Wave-force"—but then, everyone in the convoy, including the captives, were preoccupied with the possibility of another attack.

But the attack never came, and now they gained on the sixth rapid, Leanti—"Seether." Again, they were to pole the vessels through as at Baruforos.

Lyting felt deep in his bones that Hakon intended Leanti to be his grave.

And so he waited, keen to every sound, every movement within the boat, his concern for Ailinn weighing heavily upon him.

Ailinn's gaze touched Lyting's back, then drifted out over the waters, seeing yet not seeing, her thoughts thick with memories of the last days and bound with fresh cares.

The boat jarred and pitched as the waters roughened about them, and they approached yet another rapid. Hakon shouted past her ear, motioning Lyting to row toward the bank at a point slightly downriver.

Lyting turned to attend Hakon's words, affording Ailinn a view of his clean profile. His brow flickered downward briefly, as though Hakon's charge gave him pause, but he then fixed his gaze to the place ashore and dipped his oars.

The craft rocked and plunged through the choppy waters, the din of the rapids increasing as they pressed on. Glancing past her shoulder, Ailinn saw the other vessels of the convoy begin to angle toward land, one by one, none continuing so deep into the currents as they.

Ailinn started to reach to Lyting and alert him, but the boat suddenly heeled to the right, a weight shifting inside. Before she could utter a sound, Hakon swept her hard aside and into the hull, coming forward with an ax upheld in his hand, aimed for Lyting's back.

A scream scaled Ailinn's throat, but even as it did, Lyting wrenched aside, twisting back in the same motion and coming up with a length of chain from the bow. In a rapid blur he entrapped Hakon's wrist and ax and yanked him forward, pulling him through on his own momentum and propelling him to the bottom of the ship. The ax blade lodged solidly in the wood.

Without pause Lyting seized Hakon by the back of the neck and hair and slammed his head into one of the sea trunks stored in the bow.

Hakon grunted as though dazed but quickly snaked back his free hand and slipped a knife from the top of his boot. Driving upward, he stabbed for Lyting, but in an instant Lyting snared his wrist.

"Get back!" Lyting called out to Ailinn as he vied with Hakon, the menacing blade wavering directly above her.

Ailinn gasped, staring up at the knife's sharp tip as it danced over her breast. She dragged herself backward, grasping hold of the lashings that secured the goods aboard.

The boat continued to toss and heave, swamping as the waters buffeted it from without and the men's struggle caused it to cant from within. Ailinn felt a damp chill spread along her spine and legs as the flooding soaked through the back of her gown.

Lyting and Hakon strove on against each other, their strengths pitted, Lyting still hampering Hakon's right hand with the chain while staying his left with the force of his own grasp, the knife flashing betwixt them.

Seeing Hakon's side open beneath his raised arm, Ailinn lay hold to the abandoned oar beside her, hauled it forward through the back oarlock, and struck for his ribs.

Hakon snarled and jerked to the right, taking Lyting slightly off balance. Kicking back, he caught Ailinn in the waist and chest and thrust her into the stern. Swiftly he recoiled, pulling apart from Lyting enough to draw up his leg and boot him in the hip and stomach, breaking the hold and hurtling Lyting over the trunk in the bow.

Hakon freed himself of the chain as Lyting clambered upward. Together they launched themselves at each other, the boat tipping madly, Hakon's knife slashing through the air. Lyting impeded his assault once again. Grappling for the advantage, they fought to their feet.

The boat lurched, then smacked against a boulder and bounced off, hurtling the two onto the rail with Lyting pinned beneath.

The craft listed dangerously, taking on water, their weight and Ailinn's loading the port side of boat. Hastily Ailinn scrambled to throw herself to starboard for ballast, but found herself tethered by her own arm, her iron wrist cuff caught on the goods and lashings.

Hakon's hand moved to Lyting's throat, half-choking, half-pushing him out over the edge of the ship. Lyting countered, shoving his open palm up beneath Hakon's jaw and pressing his fingers into his face while he straight-armed him and pushed back his head.

Meanwhile, the dagger hovered above Lyting's shoulder, clenched in Hakon's iron fist. Their arms trembled, muscle locked against muscle. Hakon bore down with both force and weight against Lyting's resistance. The blade descended slowly, turning toward Lyting's neck.

Ailinn cried out from the stern, terrified for Lyting.

The sound of her voice renewed Lyting's vigor. He held her before his mind's eye as he began to compel Hakon's arm out and away, over the boat's side. At the same time he slipped his thumb down and around to the underside of Hakon's wrist, then drove it into the flesh and bones there. Hakon growled above him, his fingers flowering open like so many petals and dropping the knife into the churning waters below.

Inflamed, Hakon ripped himself free of Lyting's grasp, then lunged again, seizing Lyting about the neck with both hands and shoving him farther out over the side.

The boat rolled and dropped again as it moved deep into the heart of the rapids, the currents dragging it swiftly toward Leanti's treacherous, boiling descent.

Alert to the approaching hazards, Lyting reached over the side and felt for the foreward oarlock and oar to his left. Finding it, he grabbed hold. With his other hand he clutched the front of Hakon's tunic, brought his knee up between Hakon's legs and groin, and crossing himself mentally, flipped up, back, and over, taking Hakon with him overboard in a duel somersault.

Ailinn shrieked in horror as she saw Lyting disappear over the side, his hand slipping from the lock and skimming down the dangling oar as he dropped from sight.

She flung herself toward the rail, heart pounding. Straining against her trapped arm cuff, she fiercely scanned the fermenting waters.

Hakon surfaced at a distance, his eyes open and boring into her as the currents carried him toward Leanti's rising mists and thundering decline. His look froze her, as if to say even the rapids could not defeat him. He would have her still.

Lyting's bright head suddenly appeared toward the fore of the ship where he clung to the oar, holding it forced to an angle against the lock so it couldn't slip through as he worked his way up. Grasping for the rail, he hoisted himself up enough to get one arm over it, but his weight caused the boat to heel and take on more water.

"Ailinn. Pass me a line," he gasped, lowering himself again, clinging to the oar and oarlock. "Anchor one end to something solid. We are going through the rapids, and I cannot get back on board."

Frantic, Ailinn scoured the stern of the hull, and finding a heavy coil of line, she dragged it up.

"My hand is caught!" she shouted above the roar of the waters, unwinding the coil with her free hand, desperate because she did not know how she could possibly tie it with any security.

"Wait!" she called again, hope quickening as she looked to the oarlock at the stern.

Ailinn forced the oar through the lock, letting it fall into the coursing river. She then threaded the line through the eye of the lock, a generous length, dragged it up again and threaded it through a second time.

Briefly she debated whether Lyting would need both ends of the line, but, deeming the remaining coil to be weighty enough and herself unable to heave it, she tossed him the unfurled length.

The line fell short.

Feverishly Ailinn pulled it back. Leaning forward as far as she could manage, she hurled it again.

Lyting stretched out, nearly losing his grip on the oar, but trapped the line. Immediately he pulled it toward him and secured it about his arm and wrist, then began to work his way along the side of the boat toward Ailinn.

Still, she leaned forward, her knuckles white on the rail. He began to call to her to draw back, but the boat jarred abruptly as the hull hit another boulder. His warning died in his throat as the vessel tipped precariously, losing much of the free board and toppling Ailinn over the side, into the water.

For a heart-stopping moment he thought to have lost her. But as the boat buoyed up and the surging waters retreated, he saw that she hung by her arm, the iron manacle still caught on something within the craft—something that thankfully had been tied fast to the hull itself. Fearing the cuff would come free any moment, he labored toward her. As he looked to Ailinn, his heart stopped for a second time. Her head lolled and she appeared unconscious, a bright red patch spread along the side of her forehead, above the temple.

He redoubled his efforts, battling against the roiling waters and heaving craft. The moment became an eternity, but he fought on, single of mind, refusing to let the great river Dnieper have her. Seconds later he reached her.

Wrapping his arm about her, Lyting caught Ailinn up, keeping her head above water as best he could while anchoring her in his grasp. He endeavored to shield her with his body, taking the jars and jolts against the vessel himself, fearing that at any second they could be smashed against the rocks.

Ahead the mists loomed. Lyting thought to spy Hakon there, just as the racing currents bore him into the vaporous veil. Lyting braced himself, clenching Ailinn tight, as they and the boat followed moments later and were swallowed by the mist.

At once they plummeted as though the earth had been thieved from beneath them. Yet, still they rode the rapids, having never left the watery courseway, sweeping downward now along a steep, frothing incline, through a series of tortuous steps. Lyting tucked his head, gasping for air at intervals, holding on to Ailinn and the lashings with all his might as the ship dragged them on.

Many minutes later Leanti spewed them out at the bottom of the run, and the currents slackened.

Amazed to have survived the rapids, Lyting thanked the heavens above, then used his legs to propel the vessel, crosscutting the brisk waters and guiding it toward shore.

The instant his feet touched the floor of the river, Lyting hefted Ailinn up into the ship and drove the craft aground. She looked deathly pale, her skin mottled and her lips and fingertips blue.

Tense and silent, Lyting worked apace, raw emotion devouring his insides. In a trice he unsheathed the knife from his belt, sliced through the lashing that entangled Ailinn's wrist cuff, and freed her. Scooping her up in his arms, he carried her onto shore and laid her on the bank.

At once he opened the neck of her gown and pressed his ear against her chest. To his relief, he heard a faint but rapid heartbeat.

Ailinn moaned, then took a shivery breath. Her lids parted over dark eyes and touched Lyting, but a fit of coughing suddenly seized her.

Lyting braced her up, aiding her as she choked the congestion from her lungs and throat. A spasm of shaking overtook her, and he quickly pulled her across his lap and enwrapped her in his arms.

Shouts reached Lyting from farther up the bank as members of the convoy appeared—Ragnar, Orm, and a dozen more.

"Hurry!" Lyting called. "I need blankets, furs, anything to warm her."

Continuing to hold her against his body, he began rubbing her arms. Surely something dry could be found within the ship, for the goods had been carefully protected in waterproof ox-hide for the voyage.

He ignored the cold that seeped into his own bones and examined the wound on Ailinn's forehead. Fortunately, 'twas no more than a graze, and the bleeding had stopped. She would have a bruise, but nothing more. Feeling her quake against him, he dropped a kiss to the top of her head and held her close.

"Easy, *elskan mín*. Rest easy."

Orm reached them first, quickly doffing his mantle and spreading it over Ailinn before he went to search the boat.

Ragnar draped Lyting's shoulders with his own cloak. "How many lives do you have, Lyting Atlison?" He grinned down and moved off.

Shortly others brought blankets and pelts, then gathered kindling and started a small fire. The majority of the men continued on, down the riverbank, in search of Hakon. Those who remained behind labored to drain the boat and salvage the goods.

Ragnar returned, his smile still in place. "You are welcome to join Orm and myself. Vifil and Leidolf can take your boat on for you. Doubt if you're up to more rowing today." His smile widened. "Be there aught you need before I rejoin the others and begin the portage?"

"*Já.*" Lyting nodded. "See if you can find a key or a tool to rid Ailinn of this manacle."

Ragnar looked from Lyting to Ailinn, gave a stout nod, and went in search of the key.

Lyting eased Ailinn onto a blanket. "You cannot remain in these sodden clothes, *elskan mìn*."

Ailinn stirred as he brought forth his knife. Their eyes met and held. Realizing his intent, but too weak to protest, she closed her lashes and turned her head aside.

Without wasting another moment he cut through the fabric. Lyting's heart thudded in his ears as he peeled away the gown, exposing creamy breasts pebbled with cold, a slender waist and shapely hips that joined long sleek legs and trimly turned ankles. He swallowed against the knot that blocked his throat.

Quickly he worked to wrap Ailinn in several layers of blankets and lay her atop a thickness of fur, buffering her from the chill of the earth. Finishing, his gaze lingered over Ailinn's fragile beauty and found her color much improved, though still pale, and a faint blush stroking her cheeks.

Ragnar returned with the key. Relieving him of the piece, Lyting fit the key to the lock on Ailinn's wrist cuff, opened and removed it. Pushing to his feet, he hurled the iron into the river. Never would she be shackled again. He swore it on his life's blood.

Even should Hakon be found, Lyting would demand his due by the Law Code. Murder had its fines, even an attempted one gone awry. He would demand Ailinn herself as recompense for Hakon's cold-blooded treachery. Should Hakon resist, he would demand settling the matter through a combat of arms—to the death.

The hours slipped past. A small guard remained with Lyting and Ailinn while the vessels were transported and readied for departure. The search party returned after a prolonged quest. Hakon could not be found.

" 'Tis time." Ragnar indicated they should board.

"*þakk*," Lyting acknowledged, then looked to where Ailinn slept peacefully by the fire, her glorious auburn hair spread out around her. His heart warmed, momentarily dispelling the great weariness he carried in his bones. And yet, despite his fatigue, he felt much renewed, clothed now in fresh, dry garments and having rested atime.

He rose, lifting Ailinn in his arms. She snuggled against his chest as he carried her to Ragnar's boat, and he could not help but smile tenderly upon her.

A great millstone had been removed from about his neck and shoulders. But Lyting harbored no grievance for having to bear it. The ordeal of the passage to Byzantium, especially that of Leanti, had won him Ailinn.

With Hakon's removal there existed no further need for trials or combat. He could claim her forthright and twice over—as expiation for Hakon's offense, and again as the sole surviving member of the boat's crew.

According to the Law Code, Ailinn now belonged rightfully to him.

Chapter 14

The air grew drier as the convoy journeyed farther down the Dnieper, making portages around the last of the cataracts before traversing the great ford of Krarion and coming to Saint Gregory's Island.

Disembarking, the company went straight away to offer prayer and sacrifice before a gigantic oak tree that dominated the site.

Lyting and Ailinn stood side by side, looking on but not participating, respecting the observances made by the others while silently lifting their own thanks heavenward.

A short time later they rejoined Arnór and his family at their ship. Since Leanti, Lyting had chosen to sail with them—for her protection, he had explained. Ailinn knew Lyting worried on those times he would need leave her alone, such as when he kept watch. He could not, *would* not, leave her with the women slaves. Of that he was adamant.

Arnór's family, especially Jorunn, herself, provided an agreeable solution. Most men treaded with caution about Jorunn, especially where her daughters, Ingered and Ashild, were concerned, recalling her adeptness with an ax at Aïfor.

At Ailinn's own suggestion, Lyting had presented Jorunn with the magnificent bridal mantle that was once Rhiannon's. Jorunn was more than willing to tolerate her presence and keep watch over her for the prize of the cloak. In addition 'twas solely because of Ailinn that Lyting joined the family. Despite

Lyting's intention to enter the monastic life, 'twas obvious Jorunn viewed him as a prospect for one of her daughters.

The daughters expressed their annoyance with Ailinn's presence more openly, sometimes with looks and gestures, sometimes tittering amongst themselves in such a way that 'twas clear they belittled her. Most often they directed her to perform the meanest of tasks in camp. But all this they carried out most cunningly, as though a game, and only when Lyting was not about.

"*Nei*, Ailinn." Lyting's voice broke through her thoughts as she bent to catch hold of one of the sealskin bags filled with iron cooking implements and drag it. "The *hudfat* is far too heavy for you. Here. . . ."

He snared a yew bucket filled with onions and a bread trough from among the other supplies that had been set ashore beside the ship. After handing them to her, he then took up the *hudfat* himself and companioned her to the chosen campsite which they were to share with Arnór's family.

All in the convoy worked long and hard, off-loading provisions from the vessels and busying themselves with the details of establishing the camp. Soon a small village of tents dotted Saint Gregory's Island.

As Lyting returned from the ship, bearing a small soapstone caldron that Jorunn had requested, he saw Ailinn pause in her task and look toward the ancient oak. Before it, men marked out a large campfire ring with stones.

"Tonight there shall be a gathering of all and feasting aplenty," he said as he joined her and set down the caldron. " 'Tis the first time we have been able to relax our guard even a little, but we are beyond the usual range of the Petchenegs now and nearing our destination."

Ailinn's brows pulled together, and her gaze strayed to the slaves. "Then, there will be much drinking?"

Lyting paused, realizing how difficult this was for Ailinn. "*Já*," he conceded, unable to deny it or the obvious implications.

She caught her lip between her teeth and gave her attention back to the dough trough, where she continued to measure out flour.

Lyting returned to where he had earlier erected the frame of the women's tent. He began to spread the tent cloth over the structure and to secure the bottom edges underneath the sides, all the while thinking on the slaves.

Would that he could help them all, but he knew he could not. There *would* be much drinking and wenching this eve. 'Twas inescapable. The journey had been hard and perilous. Now the men would have what they deemed to be their due.

Another concern crowded in on Lyting. Ailinn's fiery beauty drew the others as moths to the flame.

Yestereve—and not for the first time since Leanti—he had been offered a considerable sum for Ailinn. Declining, Lyting reaffirmed that he had released Ailinn from her bondage and considered her free. On hearing this, the man pressed him to take the sum and more, as a bride-price, even though he had three wives already.

Again, Lyting worried over the course this evening might take with the men in their cups.

He ducked inside the tent to finish securing the cloth along the sides, beneath the bottom rods, and to hang the curtains over the triangular openings at either end of the structure.

As he began to emerge from the tent, he observed Arnór's older daughter, Ingered, step to where Ailinn bent at the trough. Ingered dropped two buckets beside Ailinn and motioned for her to fetch water from the river. When Ailinn upheld her hands to show they were sticky with dough and pleaded for a moment, Ingered assumed a superior stance, pointing to the river, and scolded sharply in Norse, fully aware that Ailinn could not understand her.

Lyting's eyes hardened. Although he had not made a formal declaration, Arnór's family knew beyond question that he had granted Ailinn her freedom and that she now held the rank of a freewoman.

Lyting started to depart the tent, but just then Ashild moved to join her sister. He waited. Ashild's tones echoed Ingered's, as did her gestures.

Ailinn said nothing. Regarding them each with a measured look and a patient eye, she washed the dough from her hands and rose. Taking up the buckets, she headed toward the river. As she went, Ingered and Ashild stood, side by side, laughing at her back.

Lyting boiled.

Only the sight of two men on the bank, abandoning their work to assist Ailinn, stopped him from chastising the sisters forthwith. Instead, he quit the tent and headed for the river. By

the time he arrived, three men hovered about Ailinn. Lyting's
black look alone dispersed the group.

"Moths," he uttered with disgust.

Without another word he relieved Ailinn of the buckets,
filled them, indicated she should follow him, and with his jaw
rock hard, tread back to the campsite where Ingered and Ashild
watched.

Ailinn hurried to keep pace with him, his stride long, his
face set. Never had she seen Lyting angry before. And
certainly, by the look of him, he was that. She worried as to the
reasons, forgetting her own cares of the foregoing moments.

Lyting halted before Ingered and Ashild and half set, half
dropped the buckets to the ground, sloshing the water over the
sides. He addressed them in the Nordic tongue—short, crisp
words that caused them to pale.

He left then, a brooding look layered upon his brow as he
went to complete the construction of the second tent.

Throughout the next hour Lyting continued to work, keeping an eye to where Ailinn prepared the meal with Jorunn and
her daughters. He mulled the matters concerning her. One
thing stood clear. He need proclaim her a freewoman before
all. Publicly. 'Twas something he should have done before
now. Tonight there would be a most fitting and "lawful"
opportunity—before the full assemblage, convened at the great
oak. He would need make his declaration before his kinsmen
drank too deeply of their cups, he added the mental note ruefully.

'Twas a mammoth task to travel with a virgin, especially one
of such beauty. Therein lay the problem. Not only did the men
hunger for her, but likely they wished to be the first to breach
those fair portals. Lyting felt his blood rise from a simmer to
a boil all over again.

A surprising thought birthed itself into his mind. So forceful
was the notion that he sat back on his heels. It thoroughly
intrigued him. Yet, 'twas directly opposed to the path he
purposed to follow and a veritable cross of temptation that he
would inflict upon himself. If the other "moths" fluttered
about the "flame," then he in essence would be throwing
himself straight into the fire.

He rejected the thought outright, thinking it surely to be the
Devil's temptation. And yet . . .

The thought lay discarded on the floor of his conscience. He
stared at it. Pondered it. Picked it up with mental fingers,

weighed it and turned it, then viewed it from every conceivable angle.

On the surface the idea seemed completely counter to the avowals he had made. But beneath, 'twas a perfect answer, one that could, in a single stroke, grant Ailinn a superior status amongst his kinsmen, equal to that of his own, and at the same time place her completely under his protection.

They would need pledge themselves before the others, true, but the beauty of the design lay in that, while his kindred would recognize and uphold the legality of that plight, Holy Mother Church would not recognize it at all, thus Ailinn's honor, virtue, and future would not be compromised in any wise. Truly, the plan was God's own inspiration.

His decision made, Lyting finished his chore and went directly to the boats. Brimming with energy and purpose, he retrieved additional equipment from among his own stores, carried them to the campsite, and set about erecting a third tent. All the while he continued to turn the plan in his mind, assuring he had considered every aspect and did not embrace this course for any selfish, misguided purpose.

At last, with everything settled and arranged to his satisfaction, he came forth from the tent and approached Ailinn where she knelt before the fire, removing the last of the bread rounds from the cooking iron.

Her eyes drew upward to his, then to the yellow-gold fabric, folded and draped neatly over his arm.

"Come, Ailinn." He took her by the hand and raised her to her feet, ignoring the looks this brought from Jorunn and her daughters. " 'Tis near time to gather with the others. Mayhaps you would like to freshen yourself and exchange your gown for one more cheerful." He reached for the cloth on his arm. "Skallagrim's trunks yielded a number of garments. This one will become you, I think, and looks to be of a proper size. I hope you will find it to your liking."

Lyting opened out the yellow-gold dress for Ailinn's approval, aware that Ingered and Ashild bumped each other, straining to see.

"Oh, Lyting . . ." Ailinn's voice fell softly, her eyes moistening. " 'Tis very much to my liking. 'Tis my own gown, seized from my coffer in Clonmel."

Lyting's brows lifted in surprise. He had chosen it solely for its color, thinking how it would flatter the dark fires of Ailinn's hair.

"Then it pleasures me doubly to restore it to you," he said with heartfelt sincerity and gave it over to her.

Ailinn's gaze lingered over the gown, a mixture of joy, wonderment, and distant memories mingling in her expression. She smiled her appreciation, the words catching with emotion in her throat. Receiving the gown from Lyting's hands, she hastened inside the women's tent.

Swiftly Ailinn discarded her worn clothes. Locating the small pitcher of water kept in the corner, she splashed her face, neck, and arms, then took up a clean linen and washed more thoroughly. Her ablutions complete, she slipped the bright gown over her head, savoring the feel of its fine-woven texture. She next loosened her hair and fingered it through. With a final straightening of her gown, she stepped from the tent.

Ailinn halted, her heart colliding with her ribs. Lyting awaited, splendidly arrayed in clothes of pearl gray, a scarlet cloak swept about his broad shoulders, fastened over the left with a costly brooch of silver and gemstones.

On seeing her, he smiled—a generous slash of white that lay siege to her heart. Ailinn felt her bone melt to liquid as he came forward to claim her. In that single moment it seemed the world contained but the two of them, suspended in a droplet in time. Lyting's eyes never left hers as he placed her hand on his arm and lead her toward the massive oak.

Heat climbed into Ailinn's cheeks as they joined the others. Sly smiles and nudges gave her to realize that they were busily pairing Lyting and herself in their minds and in a thoroughly carnal way.

Did these Norsemen think of naught else when they weren't warring? Did they not realize or accept Lyting's intention to join the Christian brothers in cloister? Of course, such a calling might be unthinkable to a pagan Norseman, and Lyting was one of their own. Likely, they would gladly see him abandon that course and give into fleshly temptations.

For his part Lyting appeared undisturbed by their misperceptions. Indeed, 'twould seem he encouraged it, which baffled her further. Ragnar and Orm beckoned them over just then and opened a space on the ground for them to sit. Lyting accepted but made a point of bidding Arnór and his family to join them as well.

Mildly disappointed, Ailinn assumed he did so out of courtesy, maintaining good relations with Arnór. And yet, as he settled down beside her, so close that their arms brushed, it beseemed he intended that the daughters should endure his attentions to herself. Jorunn looked none too happy, either.

Lyting continued in good cheer, attending to her needs and seeing that she enjoyed her choice and fill of food and drink, despite their limited selection. If his attentiveness perplexed her, then 'twas like to drive the daughters wild. Ailinn thought she might see their hair burst into flames any instant, so heated were their looks. But even they could not fault Lyting, for he remained congenial to all, including themselves—he, the very soul of courtesy.

As the men sated their bellies and slaked their thirst, they fell to recounting tales of their journey, the most popular being the adventures at Riga, retold and expanded upon by the men who had originally sailed from Gotland. As they hailed Lyting now and again, he accepted their praise but refused to belabor the stories further.

Instead, he rose to his feet and upheld his hand to hush everyone. He then settled his gaze on Ailinn, his smile spreading, and drew her upward to stand beside him. Keeping her hands within his, he again called for silence, then in a clear voice, addressed all those gathered there in the Norse tongue.

A chill rippled through Ailinn as their eyes shifted to her. She could not read their looks, but many nodded as if in approval, or at least in acknowledgment, of what Lyting spoke. A low murmur rumbled through the crowd when he finished. Again, Lyting upheld his hand for quiet.

His next words brought looks of surprise. But 'twas his following pronouncement that caused their gazes to leap back to her and nearly in unison. Ragnar's mouth actually sagged open. Ashild gasped, and Ingered looked about to unsheathe her claws.

Ailinn moved closer to Lyting. Feeling his thumb stroke the back of her hand, she glanced up, only to encounter his beautifully melting smile.

"Ailinn before all, I have formally released you from your bonds of slavery and declared you a freewoman."

Ailinn assumed this to have been the cause of the first looks she received.

"I have also pledged my intentions toward you as your . . .

protector." Lyting chose the word with care, not wishing to mislead her, yet reluctant to reveal everything, lest it cause her undue concern.

"As a freewoman, you must agree to this of your own will, for you now possess status and rights. I ask you to do so and accept me now, so that all here will understand that you consent and wish it so."

Lyting gazed with all earnestness into Ailinn's eyes.

"I do this so no one will bedevil you or even think to cause you the least of grievances. Understand that there are few women on this voyage, and your beauty tempts them sorely. Our customs differ somewhat from yours, but by accepting me, you will be regarded with respect and considered as sharing the same status as I. Indeed, your worth will be considered greater than most if not all here."

Ailinn felt a tenseness move subtly through Lyting as he awaited her answer and continued to hold her gaze.

"What say you, *elskan mín*? Wilt you have me?"

Something moved deep in Ailinn's heart. She smiled, wide and unsparingly, so all might understand by her manner alone.

"*Já*." She nodded. "Is that not your Norse word for it? *Já*," she pronounced distinctly, for everyone to hear. "I accept you, Lyting Atlison."

Slipping her hand from his grasp, Ailinn placed it on his chest, over his heart.

An agreeable murmur rose, broken by cheerful outcries and many a hailing with full cups. It surprised Ailinn that Lyting's declarations concerning her and her acceptance of him should foster such a mood of celebration.

She did not question it but warmed in the knowledge that Lyting had done great things for her. Not only had he restored her freedom, but now he gave her dignity and a place under his protective wing.

Lyting smiled upon her. "Let us retire from here, *elskan mín*, before the feasting becomes too boisterous."

Ailinn accepted his proffered arm, aware of the cheerful calls that followed them as he led her back to their campsite. But instead of conducting her to the women's tent, he directed her to the one that stood alone, the one she had assumed he raised for himself. Before she could remark on it, he reached for the curtains that covered the entrance and drew them aside.

Her gaze fell to the bed. There lay the gleaming harp of Eire.

" 'Tis yours, Ailinn, as are all the items among Skallagrim's belongings that were seized from your uncle's hall. I restore them to your possession."

Tears stung her eyes. She stood speechless before Lyting's boundless generosity. Then, seized by impulse, she threw herself against him, her arms wrapping about his neck as she pressed a kiss to his softly bearded cheek.

"Go raibh maith agat," she whispered in Gaelic. "Thank you."

As she continued to embrace him, she became aware of how her breasts pressed against his hard chest, and how his hand had moved to her back. Their eyes locked and held for an endless moment—golden brown melding with crystal blue.

Lyting's hand moved up her spine, sinking into the richness of her hair and cradling the back of her head. His lips hovered above hers, a hundred emotions scudding through his eyes like clouds on a wind-driven day.

He took a hard swallow. "If I kiss you, Ailinn, I fear I will never stop, then you will have no protection at all."

Ailinn made no reply, her heart racing within her breast. She felt him shudder against her and saw a hunger deep in his eyes. For a moment she thought he would lay siege to her lips despite his words, but then his features hardened with resolve, and he slowly pulled away. She did not miss the look of pain creasing his eyes.

"The night grows late, and you must rest for the morrow." He held aside the curtain so that she might enter.

" 'Tis your tent, is it not?" Ailinn found her voice.

"Henceforth, *elskan mín*, 'tis ours."

Lyting raised his hand to forestall her next words. "Ailinn, trust me in this, I ask of you. All is perfectly proper and acceptable according to the customs of my people. Upon my word, I will return you to Eire and will do so with your honor and virtue unblemished."

It struck Ailinn like a thunderbolt that their "pledge" was of a different nature than she assumed, one by which he could claim her with some measure of legality and set his mark upon her as his alone. Had he declared her his concubine before all? Such practices were not unknown to her. How she wished now that she knew more of Norse ways.

But ever Lyting proved himself to be a man of honor. 'Twould be foolish, she decided, to fret about the details and circumstances he might use to protect her from his kinsmen.

"Sleep now," Lyting urged once more, gesturing for Ailinn to enter the tent. "If the men grow loud in their merriment, do not fear. I shall be near. And should you wake in the night and find me resting on a pallet within, again, have no worries. I shall be keeping watch of you, even then."

A mixture of gratitude and confusion reigned in Ailinn's thoughts. Quietly she nodded and entered in.

Lyting stepped several paces apart.

Steeling himself against the force of his desire, he looked up to the scattering of stars overhead, then closed his eyes and breathed deeply.

The vision of stars continued to glitter in his mind's eye—a spangling of light that suddenly transformed itself into the shimmering silver lime of Hedeby.

Lyting tried to shake the haunting image, but it remained, and Brienne's words floated back to him:

"... like a beautiful woman ... not without her trials. ... Each ordeal ... a testing of a man's true mettle. ... A testing of his very heart and soul."

Had he done right by Ailinn this night? He felt certain he had. And yet because of it, he had crucified his flesh anew. For while she would continue to play upon his heart, he must faithfully preserve her, knowing that, according to the Law Code, Ailinn was now rightfully his in every meaning of the word.

God give him strength.

For nearly two weeks the convoy progressed down the Dnieper, coming at last to the headwaters of the great river and to the island of Berezany, Birch Island.

Stopping briefly, they reequipped their ships with rudders, masts, tackle, and sails. Then, sheeting their sails to the wind, they proceeded, descending a series of terraces to where the river opened up and emptied into a great body of water.

Lyting leaned forward and touched Ailinn's shoulder. "At last, *elskan mín*, we are here."

Ailinn turned to him, a jubilance rising in her breast.

As Ailinn's and Lyting's gazes embraced, the convoy departed the mighty Dnieper and entered the Black Sea.

PART III

"Sometimes the darkness holds the light."

Chapter 15

Sunlight danced over a profusion of copper roofs and domes, firing them with molten brilliance—crowned heads rising above high towered walls—bedazzling all who approached the "Great City."

Constantinople. Jewel of Byzantium. Heart of men's desires.

The vessels of the convoy slipped beneath an expansive, multiarched bridge and entered the magnificent, winding harbor known as the Golden Horn.

Here, the waters funneled between two peninsulas, one commanded by the Imperial City and the other quartering the fortified towns of Galata and Pera. Here, crafts of every land and description crammed the watery thoroughfare, trafficking goods between the Black Sea and the Aegean.

Ailinn stared in openmouthed wonder as they progressed along the imposing seawall with its multitude of gates, bastions and soaring towers. As she drank in the matchless sights, her mother's words flowed back to her. Perhaps this was the "light" of which Fianna spoke.

Lyting smiled warmly, no less transfixed by the marvels than Ailinn, and yet he found himself more captivated by the maid herself. As he leaned into the oars, he caught Ailinn's gaze.

" 'Twas the Blachernae Palace we first saw as we passed beneath the bridge, one of the royal residences."

"I thought this to be your first visit to Constantinople," Ailinn called back, then sucked her breath at the sight of a small, bright craft darting in and about the larger ones, swift as a water bug.

"*Satt*. True. But my brother once served here with the Varangians. He detailed a map of the city so that I might move about with greater ease."

Lyting refrained from adding that Rurik insisted he memorize the map as a precautionary measure, in the event he find himself in need of the knowledge.

"We will dock at the Gate of the Drungarii. It still lies at a distance. The Golden Horn is remarkably long, as you can see."

"Where does the harbor lead? Is there an outlet?"

Ailinn turned her honey-brown gaze fully on him. Again his blood stirred.

"It joins the Bosporus at the tip of the peninsula. There the waters open out into the Sea of Marmara which surrounds the south and west sides of the city. In turn, Marmara empties into the Aegean."

"Such magical names." Ailinn smiled, although a fine line appeared between her brows. "Have we come then to the edge of the world?"

Lyting chuckled. "*Nei*. There be realms beyond, and the Empire trades vigorously with them for every manner of luxury, I assure you." He fell to silence as, together with Arnór, he maneuvered their boat through the harbor.

As he plied the oars, Lyting studied the varied ships and barks of other lands, trying to discern the Persian from the Indian, and the Arabic from the Italian. Likewise, he scrutinized the Byzantine merchant ships with their triangular "lateen" sails and blunt-ended crafts.

Shortly after they closed on the Plateia Gate, the Gate of the Drungarii came into view. Lyting's pulse livened as he pressed firm, even strokes to the oars. But even as he did, an astonishing sight claimed his interest—that of two immense galleys moving ahead, each equipped with three square sails and two banks of oars.

"Do you know what manner of ships they be?" Lyting called to Arnór, who was arrested by the sight as well.

"*Dromons* of the Imperial fleet. 'Runners.'" Arnór turned

back. "'Tis said they be fitted with the deadliest weapon known to man—tubes that hurl a volatile mixture. 'Greek fire.' It ignites on contact and can consume entire ships and their crews and set the water itself aflame."

A shiver ran through Lyting as he imagined the horror such a weapon must wreak on its victims. Just then, Arnór whistled and swiveled back again, grinning broadly.

"Look to the *dromon* on the right, to the pennant on its main mast. 'Tis the flagship of the Drungarius." At Lyting's questioning look Arnór added, "The High Admiral of the Byzantine fleet, lad. Likely he is making his way down to the 'Harbor of Phospherion' where he can enter the city nearer to the Sacred Palace."

"Do you know of the man?"

"Only rumors a summer old. There exists a rivalry of sorts between the Drungarius and the Domesticus of the Scholae— the Supreme Commander of the Empire's land forces. If one believes the tattle of the crowds, both men vie for the empress's support and more."

Arnór turned to face forward but spoke over his shoulder. "Obviously, he who holds sway with the regent-mother can hope to rule the Empire. Not so repulsive a task, either, I should think. The widowed empress is said to be a woman of striking beauty."

"Then, they wish to gain her hand in marriage and power over young Constantine's throne?"

"*Nei*. Both men have wives, though 'twould not surprise me if their aspirations—and loins—are intent on the empress's bed. But, she is strong-willed and not easily beguiled. I understand the Empress Zoë remains above reproach and acts with naught but her son's interest at heart. As regent, she has shown herself capable enough, and when I departed last summer, she held the favor and confidence of the people."

Arnór and Lyting navigated the boat alongside the wharf. After pulling up his oars, Arnór turned back, a gleam in his eyes.

"If both the Domesticus and the Drungarius are in residence this season, I should very much like to be a bug on the palace walls. Think of the wagers to be made in the streets!"

As Arnór climbed out of the boat and lashed it to a piling, Lyting contemplated him with heightened interest.

"And how would you place your wager?"

Arnór grinned again, aiding Jorunn from the craft. "I say both men are to be watched. The Domesticus is an aristocrat, and aristocrats are no novices to duplicity and palace machinations. But the Drungarius is an artful one. He was born of Armenian peasants and rose steadily in rank and power for years. 'Twas the late emperor, Alexander, who elevated him to the position of Drungarius."

Lyting halted in his movements, Rurik's suspicions flooding to mind. Suspicions of a shadowy man behind the throne, in collusion with the degenerate, pleasure-seeking Alexander, who usurped his nephew's crown.

Heedless of the brooding look on Lyting's face, Arnór continued, now helping his daughters gain footage on the wharf. "A man's station, however low, does not keep him from rising to the highest levels of power in Byzantium. Nor, for that matter, does murder."

Lyting's gaze leapt to Arnór, but, unmindful, Arnór chattered on. "Oftimes, 'tis all that lies between a man and a crown. The emperor's grandsire did as much—Basil, another peasant who ascended the ranks and mur—"

"Enough, husband." Jorunn reached out and plucked his beard. "You gossip like the Byzantines in their forums. We must gather quickly before the gate. Have you forgotten? They will allow only fifty of us to pass through at a time when we arrive in such numbers."

"*Komið*. Jorunn is right," Arnór said. "Leave your sword, Lyting. Except for the Varangians, we Norse are not permitted to bear arms within the city."

Lyting began to protest, but Arnór held up placating hands. "By the terms of our trade treaty—"

"What treaty?" Lyting returned a bit too strongly, but he was not of a mind to leave behind his trusted blade.

"Our kinsmen attacked the city in recent memory—a great host under the Kievian Prince Oleg. He did not breach the walls, but he did wrest a favorable trade agreement, which we have honored since. Still, the Byzantines remain wary of us. While they accommodate us with many concessions and privileges, they deny us our weapons and dog our movements within the city with their guards." He lifted his palms skyward. "Byzantines! Such a double-sided people. But the riches to be had are worth the aggravation. Come, now. I see that our men who drew lots for the watch are arriving, and we mustn't tarry."

Lyting dropped his gaze to his sword and scabbard, his displeasure at having to leave them behind gnawing in his bones. If the spider spun his threads in the palace of the Caesars, Lyting held no wish to walk into a web without a blade at hand.

He would need seek the Varangian Koll straight away and arrange to deliver his missive to the Imperials. Mayhaps then he could regain the privilege of wearing his sword and enjoy what time was left to himself and Ailinn before they joined another convoy and returned homeward.

Storing the sword and scabbard out of sight in the bow of the boat, Lyting made a last assurance that the goods were secure, then climbed to the wharf and extended a hand to Ailinn. Moments later they joined the convoy members assembling at the gate.

Ailinn's excitement swelled, playing brightly over her features. When at last the great bronze doors drew open, she laughed and, with lighthearted abandon, grasped Lyting about the upper arm and urged him forward.

A trickle of apprehension slipped down Lyting's spine as he covered Ailinn's hand with his own and, together, they passed through the Gate of the Drungarii.

Ailinn pressed close to Lyting as they threaded their way through the swarming, colorful crowd, past fishmarkets, stalls, and warehouses, a hundred tongues buzzing in the street.

Ahead, a Byzantine official accompanied them. Tall, dark, and sufficiently handsome, he wore a knee-length tunic of bright blue silk, embroidered lavishly over the shoulders and about the hem with threads of pure gold, all winking with gems. In his right hand he carried a spear and in his left, a great circular shield.

Arnór hastened to keep pace with the official, advising him through gestures and a spattering of Greek of the group's destination—the grand boulevard, the Mesê.

Ingered and Ashild crowded the man's other side, obviously impressed with his station and finery and wishing to capture his regard. The man strode on, impassive to their presence and

outwardly unfazed when, time and again, they brushed against
him, feigning to have been jostled by the crush of people.

Ailinn found their artifices repugnant. But when, at last, the
official broke his silence and made a reply to Arnór, his
high-pitched voice carried back, taking her by surprise. Beside
her, Lyting gave a snort, while ahead, the smiles drained from
Ingered's and Ashild's faces. They quickly shrank back to walk
with their mother.

"Our watchdog is a eunuch." A grim smile etched Lyting's
lips. "I should have realized the man's ailment from the first.
Not only are his cheeks as smooth as a baby's behind, but he
scarce took note of you, *elskan mín*. Yet, see how the interest
of nearly every other man in the street trails after you."

Ailinn's eyes widened. She whisked her glance about and
immediately met with several bold stares. She stepped toward
Lyting, unintentionally jarring him. Lyting chuckled and brought
his hand around her back to steady her.

"At least I need not worry on our escort, or on a fair portion
of the male population. Byzantine, that is. My brother tells me
there are many eunuchs in Constantinople. Still, the city is
filled with men of every land. Mayhaps I should shroud you in
dull colors and put a veil over your fiery tresses to forestall
them."

He flashed her a heart-skipping smile, giving Ailinn a
squeeze to bring forth one of her own.

Ailinn felt her legs would melt beneath her under the
potency of Lyting's smile. Glancing ahead, she saw the official
divert their numbers into a side street off to the right. Jorunn
waited there, displeasure in her face. Her daughters tarried
there as well, their scowls more distinct.

As Lyting and Ailinn drew near, the three turned into the
side street and followed the others. Ailinn wondered if Lyting
had noticed the women's manner as well, but reserved her
comments as they left the main road, paralleling the seawall,
and entered the narrow, cobbled offshoot.

As Ailinn's vision adjusted to the abrupt darkness, she
realized that the passage was no more than twelve paces wide,
flanked by tall buildings on either side, rising as many as nine
floors high. Balconies hung from their fronts, further narrow-
ing and darkening the street below.

The street rose steadily upward, growing especially steep

toward its upper end. Slightly out of breath, Ailinn leaned forward, into the last of the climb, the back of her legs burning.

"Here, lean on me." Lyting caught her beneath the elbow and aided her. "Our journey on the waters did not prepare us for the hills of Constantinople."

As they gained the top of the hill, the street opened onto a tiny, sun-drenched courtyard, shrubbed in greenery and bedecked with bright flowers. At the center, water flowed in tiers into a marble fountain.

Ingered and Ashild lingered there. What was it about the sisters that reminded her of two vipers, lying in wait in the day's full sun? Ailinn wondered.

As she crossed the courtyard with Lyting, Ingered and Ashild slid to his opposite side and engaged him in conversation. Ailinn rolled her eyes when the sisters continued in their company, monopolizing Lyting's attention.

As they entered another shaded street, fresh concerns intruded on Ailinn's thoughts. In the last days, Arnór's daughters had found new ways to annoy and beset her. At the same time they had renewed their fawnings over Lyting. What emboldened them remained unclear.

Since Saint Gregory's Island, 'twas obvious Lyting wished for his kinsmen to think he and she shared their bed each night, intimately—that she was his consort. She assumed he had dispelled, for his kinsmen's sake, any impression he would enter the monastery. Could it be, she wondered, that the clever sisters suspected the truth—that Lyting kept himself from her, and that she remained an untried virgin?

If they, themselves, were familiar with fleshly intimacies, then mayhaps her innocence was plain to them. She wouldn't possess the glow of a woman who had known a man in the carnal sense. Doubtless, such things would be reflected in a woman's eyes and countenance, in the very way she looked upon her lover.

Mayhaps the women believed Lyting found her lacking or displeasing in some wise and hoped he would set her aside. On the other hand, it might not matter. The Norse were accustomed to their men keeping more than one woman to warm their bed, be they slaves, concubines, or wives.

The burning in Ailinn's legs reminded her that they were

climbing again. Just as they emerged from the street onto another small, sun-filled square, the incline leveled off. Here, a red-marble fountain stood at the center, surrounded by matching benches and waxy-green shrubs. Statuary marked each of the courtyard's four corners, backed by stately spires of black cypresses, reaching to immense heights.

Leaving the square, they entered a pleasant avenue, wider and brighter than the first two, bustling with carts and people. Fine homes, only two and three stories high, verged on the street, their fronts faced with either brick, stucco, or sometimes marble. On the upper level, many had windows set with colored glass.

Another square followed, grander than the last, with flowers and bronze statuary and plump golden pigeons pecking about the fountain. An imposing church occupied the corner of the next street, its heavy stonework interrupted by shallow niches, patterned brickwork, and a multitude of windows.

Continuing on, they passed more magnificent dwellings, ofttimes interspersed with lesser ones and having no particular order—some no more than hovels, others the multistoried tenements.

"That must be the Aqueduct of Valens." Lyting pointed off to the right. "The Mesê should lay just to the other side of it."

Ailinn followed Lyting's arm to discover what appeared to be two arched bridges, standing one atop the other and towering above the city. She tilted her head, perplexed.

"Why do the Byzantines build a road so high over the land? Do their armies use it?"

Lyting's brow dipped, but he quickly replaced his quizzical look with a gentle smile. " 'Tis not a roadway. The aqueduct supplies fresh water to the city, a Roman device. Have you no aqueducts in Ireland? I thought the Romans raised them throughout all the reaches of their empire."

She shook her head. "Their aggressions did not extend so far. They confined their plunderings to England and did not cross the Irish Sea. Thanks to the Almighty for that. At least, we were spared *their* offenses."

Too late, she realized the double inference of her words and the bitterness that had crept into the last of them. She dropped her gaze away, unable to meet his eyes.

"The sorrows of Munster bide ever in my heart—the attack of the Danes, all those lost, enslaved, and lost again." Emotion scoured her voice. "I shall never forget the miseries the Norsemen visited upon my people. Never."

Lyting held his silence. When she dared looked to him, she found his beautiful blue eyes contemplating her, their depths grayed with thought and concern.

"You have every right to despise my kinsmen, especially those of Danmark. Would that I could roll back time itself and set that day aright. Unhappily, yesterday is no longer ours."

He glanced to the distance, once more silent, turning his thoughts. Ailinn felt his frustration as he slowly expelled a breath and folded his feelings deep within.

"Come," he said quietly. "Let us partake of the day that has been given us. 'Tis all that is truly ours."

Lyting brought up his hand to usher her forward, then dropped it away as though believing she would not wish him to touch her, for he, himself, was a Dane.

Ailinn regretted the shroud she had thrown over the light mood they had shared until then. Unhappily, Ingered and Ashild, who now moved ahead, had noted the exchange.

Side by side, Ailinn and Lyting proceeded along the street without touching, without speaking, coming at last to the grand boulevard, the Mesê.

Wonderment flooded Ailinn as she and Lyting stepped onto the wide, stone-paved avenue with what seemed the rest of humanity.

Marble colonnades stretched in either direction, lining the boulevard and sheltering the stalls of artisans, tradesmen, and moneyers whose tables were heaped with goods and spread with coin.

Following Arnór's lead, she and Lyting moved along the edges of the crowd, diverting when necessary around street magicians and acrobats, who performed their feats and bedazzled spectators for what favors they might gain. Vendors barked their wares, proffering everything from sandals, soaps, and mare's milk, to costly enamel brooches and embroideries worked with silver and gold.

Arnór bid them on, crossing the avenue at an angle and heading toward a great canopy erected on the opposite side. The Byzantine official tracked after him, as did Jorunn, their daughters, and a half-dozen members of the Norse convoy.

"What has become of the others?" Ailinn called to Lyting as

they worked their way through the congestion of the street, realizing of a sudden how greatly their numbers had diminished.

"They separated into smaller groups during our walk from the harbor." Lyting caught her by the arm and drew her back as a litter passed. " 'Tis my guess their interests led them elsewhere along the Mesê. This is but a small portion of the boulevard. It stretches nearly the entire length of the peninsula, from the Sacred Palace to the land walls, branching at one point into two avenues."

They paused for the passage of several nobles on white horses and a cart filled with furniture.

"Did you notice our armed escort—Byzantine soldiers—on the fringes of the crowd who were following us?"

Ailinn's eyes widened and whisked her glance about.

" 'Tis all right. They have withdrawn now, no doubt to trail after our men, wherever they wander, and we will see naught of any of them until when we reassemble at the Gate of the Drungarii."

As Lyting finished speaking, Ailinn glanced toward the side of the street. Her eyes widened at the sight of an ungainly creature there. It stood chest high to its master and was ponderous in size with a wrinkly gray hide, large ears, and an overlong snout. For all its oddity, it possessed a sweetness about its face, and Ailinn believed it to be a babe amongst its kind.

"Oh, Lyting, look!" She started forward, pointing.

The clacking of hooves and racket of metal wheels on stone assaulted her ears. Lyting's arms swept around her, hauling her back and catching her up, off her feet as a carriage clattered past.

Startled by the vehicle and its nearness, Ailinn seized hold of Lyting, wrapping her arms tightly about his neck. The pounding of her heart in her ears replaced the din of the carriage as she realized how close she had come to being trampled.

"Saints' breath, Ailinn!" Lyting gripped her no less fiercely than she did him. "We did not survive the perils of the voyage to lose you beneath a carriage wheel."

The words poured from him with passion, yet they carried neither anger nor reproach. Ailinn heard in them naught but his staggering concern. Her eyes drew to Lyting's. She gasped for the intensity she discovered there, and for the alarm that lay naked in their depths.

The shadows that had lingered betwixt them since the aqueduct vanished. Once more, the special closeness and oneness of spirit they had earlier shared, returned, flowing back and enveloping them as a warm tide does the shore. Joy stole through Ailinn, sweet and silent.

"Have a care, *elskan mín*. You nearly stopped my heart." Lyting relaxed his grasp of her, breathing more easily, but made no effort to set her down. He smiled in earnest. "I can hardly return you to your people with a wheel mark down your front."

Ailinn laughed at his jest, her eyes shining upon him.

The roadway thinned before them, clearing of carts and horsemen. Standing to the other side, the Byzantine official waited with spear and shield in hand. Impatience lined his features. Jorunn stood beside him, bearing a similar look which darkened at the sight of Ailinn in Lyting's arms.

"I see we have been missed," Lyting commented dryly as he started forward, carrying Ailinn.

Joining Jorunn and the official, Lyting set her to her feet. As he began to conduct her forward, to the canopied area where the others waited, Ailinn glanced along the street, wondering what had become of the curious creature she had seen there. To her amazement and delight, she found the owner leading it directly toward them.

"Oh, Lyting, look!" she exclaimed, gesturing to the incredible animal as it approached with a swaying, ambling sort of walk.

Surprise broke over Lyting's features. "Is *that* what claimed your attention?" He smiled at the wrinkled, gray beast utterly fascinated.

Arnór came behind, bearing cups of wine. Seeing the animal, he waited and advised Lyting cheerfully in Norse.

"Arnór says 'tis a young elephant, and that there be many such wonders in Constantinople."

"I cannot imagine anything more wondrous, or strange, than this little fellow," Ailinn avowed, wholly enthralled.

Seeing their interest, the owner indicated they could touch the animal. Ailinn gingerly patted the animal's head, which proved dry and possessed a sprinkling of coarse hairs. Lyting stroked the little elephant's jaw and the top of its amazing nose, which seemed to please the animal.

Several long minutes later the owner prodded the animal forward, and they moved off at an unhurried gait.

Arnór cleared his throat, then seized the moment to give over his offering of wine and speak with Lyting. Even as he did, he motioned them to step beneath the great canopy. Ailinn saw now that it overspread an enormous market.

"A moment, *elskan mín*." Lyting touched her arm, gaining her attention. "I must speak with our 'escort.'" He indicated the Byzantine official with a meaningful glance, then withdrew. Arnór accompanied Lyting to assist him in communicating with the man.

While Lyting and Arnór occupied the eunuch, Ailinn moved along the rows of tables where Jorunn, Ingered, Ashild, and those Norsemen remaining in their group were already inspecting the wares.

Never had Ailinn seen such a diversity of goods gathered in one place. One side appeared devoted to basic provisions and foodstuffs—everything from flour, butter, oil, fruits, and cheeses, to lamps, string nets, collections of baskets, stacks of fine quality pottery, and more. The other side contained row upon row of luxury items—exotic spices, scented woods, carved ivories, perfumed candles, brilliant enamels, gems, and myriad religious articles that included beads, vials of holy water, and painted icons, gilded with gold.

Stepping to the edge of the tent, Ailinn gazed out over the boulevard and absorbed its colorful sights and sounds. There, Byzantines clothed in fine silks, glinting with gems, mingled with foreigners in fanciful attire. Litters and carriages passed, lavishly painted and gilded with gold. 'Twas a most glorious place, Ailinn bethought. A portion of Heaven on earth.

Her mother's words reverberated through her. *"Sometimes the darkness holds the light."*

Had she not been delivered from the darkness of captivity? Surely, this *was* the light. If she truly be free, as Lyting said, mayhaps she would choose to stay here, in Constantinople, and begin her life anew.

But even as Ailinn considered the possibility, she felt a twinge deep inside. Lyting would not stay in Byzantium. He would return West. To Francia. To Corbie. Whenever, wherever they parted—whether upon the Golden Horn or the shores of Eire—he would take his own warmth and light and leave a hollowness within her heart.

Her fingers slipped upward and touched her breast.

"I must leave for atime," Lyting announced as he came to stand beside her.

"So soon?" Ailinn spun around, cutting short his words. Warmth rose to her cheeks as he inclined his head.

"I need attend to some business on my brother's behalf. 'Tis best you stay with Arnór and his family. Arnór has dealings to conduct with this merchant and a number of others along the Mesê. 'Twill afford you the pleasure of shopping the boulevard."

Ailinn glanced to where the three Norsewomen picked through a mound of figs. Twin threads of caution and unease twisted through her as Jorunn's gaze lifted to hers.

"I would much prefer to accompany you," Ailinn pressed Lyting.

"As I would also prefer, but I go to the barracks of the Varangian Guard. 'Tis no place for a woman. My mind will rest more at ease, knowing you are with Arnór."

Ailinn skimmed the thick congestion in the street.

"But what if I should become separated?"

Lyting's brows drew lightly together, as though he detected in her voice the anxiousness she felt within. He studied the street in both directions, then directed her attention to the other side.

"Keep the aqueduct in view. By it, you can always find the point at which we entered the Mesê and the street that leads down to the harbor and the Gate of the Drungarii. I shall rejoin you there, later.

"For now, I go south to the Sacred Palace and will return the same way. The Forum of Constantine interrupts the boulevard between here and the palace. You will know it by a great column of porphy—a purple marble—surmounted by a gold cross. By that, too, you can find your bearings to return here."

Arnór joined them, signaling to Lyting with a nod that he would look over Ailinn. The Byzantine official waited several paces behind.

Lyting embraced Ailinn with his gaze. "I must leave now, *elskan mín.* The official informs me that the gates to the palace grounds close midafternoon. He will escort me, though I see a new guard is already in place to watch over you all."

Ailinn glimpsed the Byzantine solider, spear and shield in hand, observing them from a short distance apart.

Slipping a small pouch from his belt, Lyting placed it in her hands. "Enjoy the day. Should anything take your eye, pleasure yourself and buy it."

He dropped back a pace and touched her chin lightly, in parting. "But if you see any more elephants, be mindful of carriages." He winked a smile and started away, following the official.

Though she did not move, Ailinn's heart followed after him. She watched as the distance increased between them, his bright head shining above most other men's.

As Lyting disappeared into the throng of the Mesê, Ailinn felt suddenly very much alone.

Turning, she found Jorunn waiting at her side.

Ailinn matched her pace with Arnór's and Jorunn's as they proceeded north along the boulevard. Ingered, Ashild, and the remaining convoy members followed directly behind, while at a small distance the armed guard dogged them.

As they progressed, Ailinn gave her attention to the people crowding the Mesê. The Byzantines she could differentiate—or so she believed—but there were many from lands unknown to her, especially those of the East.

The diversity was as unendless as it was exciting: dark-skinned men in flowing striped robes, with extraordinary headdresses that reminded her of plump cushions, bound with wrappings of cloth; others in long, fitted coats that tied across the chest and slippers that curled at the toes. To one side she saw a trio of coarse-looking men with shaven pates, ritual scars on their cheeks, and chains for belts. In contrast, to the other side strolled a man whose hair and beard were meticulously curled and dressed with oil so that it glistened in the sun.

Reaching the stalls of the leatherworkers, Arnór led them beneath the covered arches, past displays of boots, belts, pouches, gloves, and other apparel. Ailinn saw now that the passage beneath the colonnade opened onto workrooms, where artisans toiled and additional tables were spread with goods.

Arnór conducted them on, halting at last before the shops of the saddlers. One of the men there recognized Arnór and rose from his work, greeting him by name. Minutes passed as Arnór introduced the other men in their company, who, Ailinn realized now, had also come for the purpose of trade.

Jorunn chafed visibly while the men continued to posture and exchange formalities. Imposing herself at her husband's side, she engaged him in a brief dialogue, then withdrew and indicated for her daughters and Ailinn to follow.

Ailinn much preferred to stay with Arnór but had no way to communicate this to him. She would also be sorely out of place while he and the others conducted their business.

Resigned, Ailinn hastened to follow the three women, who were advancing briskly along the portico and now veered to depart from its shelter. Moments later Ailinn emerged from beneath the arches and found Jorunn poised to cross the street. Jorunn looked to Ailinn. Before she could fully catch up, Jorunn moved on.

Ailinn fumed as she trailed after Jorunn and her daughters, hard pressed to keep pace with them as she worked her way across the boulevard, dodging carts and litters. Gaining the opposite side of the street, Ailinn found Jorunn waiting once more, her look sharp, unreadable, and yet expectant somehow. Jorunn pivoted and directed them southward until they came to a stretch of the colonnade that housed the cloth merchants.

As before, stalls lined the portico, these offering a mind-boggling array of silks, linens, woolens, and brocades. Ailinn drank in the sight, utterly amazed, and understood Jorunn's eagerness to be here.

Thankfully, Jorunn slowed to examine the tables of goods. Ailinn couldn't believe the sheer quantities of silk available—so rare and costly in Ireland. Not only did she find the abundance staggering, but the variety. They ranged in weights and textures from those light, smooth, and airy, to those more closely woven, firmer and heavier. The vibrancy of the colors fairly assaulted her eyes—strong, vivid colors to which she was unaccustomed but instantly loved.

As Ailinn glanced up, she saw Jorunn bid Ingered and Ashild to the entrance of one of the shops, then lead them inside. Reluctantly Ailinn abandoned the lustrous red silk she had been admiring and followed.

The workroom proved a noisy, congested place, where women vied with one another over rolls of sumptuous cloth stacked on long trestles. Jorunn stood toward the end of one of the tables, holding up a length of shimmering brocade for her daughters' inspection. Ailinn picked her way toward them, stopping a moment to linger over a display of embroidered goods—smaller items including elegant handkerchiefs and headcoverings.

Ailinn's spirits brightened as she lifted one of the beautiful veils there. 'Twas the lightest material she had ever held—a sheer whisper of silk, embellished with silver about the edges. She wondered of its cost—whether she could afford it, whether she should.

Ailinn smoothed her hand over the exquisite veil, yearning to have it, yet not wishing to squander Lyting's coin. Taking the pouch he had given her, she checked inside, more to affirm that she should *not* spend the few coins she expected to find there. Ailinn gasped aloud at the little hoard of gold, silver, and gemstones that winked back at her.

"Blessed Saint Pádraig! May he smile upon your generosity, Lyting!" she muttered half to herself and smiled greatly, confident she could make the purchase without seriously depleting his supply. At the very least she could ask the merchant's price and attempt to strike a reasonable bargain.

Ailinn pursed her lips, scanning the room, wondering whom she might approach. Surprisingly, Jorunn came to her aid, catching her eye and directing her attention to a man several tables away, toward the back of the room. He appeared to be accepting monies and weighing coins.

Ailinn nodded her thanks to Jorunn and began working her way over to the man. She waited as he finished a transaction with the two women before her. Happily, she looked over the veil and its precious embroidery once again, thrilled to have found it. Glancing back to the front of the shop where she had left Jorunn, her heart leapt.

The Norsewomen were gone.

Ailinn scanned the workroom. Dropping the veil on a nearby table, she hastened outside.

Ailinn scanned the crush of people along the portico, rising on tiptoe to look right and left, as far as she could see. Without success, she stepped beyond the arches and stared out over the sea of confusion in the street. If they were there, she could not sight them. Ailinn retraced her steps, checking once more inside the workroom, then scouted along the portico until she determined beyond question that they were gone.

Ailinn's ire mounted, bubbling in her veins. The three had purposely abandoned her.

Suppressing her anger, she looked to the aqueduct and felt comforted to see its upper portion looming in the distance above the Mesê. What did Jorunn and her daughters hope their mischief would accomplish, when she could so easily find her way back to the saddlers and rejoin Arnór?

Ailinn plucked up her determination and stepped out onto the boulevard once more, crossing to the other side and continuing northward to the section of the leather workers. Locating the shop of the saddler, she proceeded directly inside, but found that Arnór and those in his company had already moved on.

Ailinn reemerged, feeling the bite of frustration.

Arnór and the others could be anywhere along the Mesê, which, according to Lyting, extended far. She assumed that Jorunn, when she took her leave of Arnór, arranged to meet him elsewhere later. But where?

Ailinn took her bearings on the boulevard, once more using the aqueduct as her landmark. She thought of making her way down to the ships, but she wasn't ready to return there. In truth, she wished to continue her exploration of the Mesê.

She took a fortifying breath. If Constantinople were to be her new home, she refused to be afraid. She had a purse of money to cover her needs and felt confident that she could find her way back to the Gate of the Drungarii whenever she wished.

Ailinn looked southward in the direction of the palace. Lyting said he would return that way along the Mesê. Certainly, the possibilities of their finding one another between here and there far exceeded those of her venturing out to find Arnór in the other sections of the boulevard.

Her mind decided, Ailinn headed southward, toward the palace, eager to discover more of the marvels of the city and hopeful she would chance on Lyting. Her cheer returned as she temporarily left the Mesê and entered the Forum of Constantine, a great public square that divided it.

Graceful double-tiered colonnades embraced a large open area, enclosing it with curving arms—the "square" being not square at all, but oval in shape. A multitude of statuary ornamented the colonnade, flanking it with heroes and mythological beasts. At the center of the forum rose a tremendous column of purple marble, topped with a gleaming cross of gold. At its base a sizable crowd collected.

As Ailinn began to cross the expanse, she became aware of the increasing number of people passing her at clipped gaits, headed toward the gathering. Clusters of finely robed men broke from their conversations to reassemble at the column where the crowd steadily swelled.

Excitement filled the air, infecting Ailinn as well. 'Twas as though a bell had been rung, or a horn sounded, announcing an event about to take place. The Mesê appeared to be emptying from both sides into the forum, everyone hastening so as not to miss the distraction.

The stream of people thickened about Ailinn, carrying her forward. She thought of the delightful little elephant and did not resist, anticipating the diversion to come. Had not Arnór said there were many wonders in Byzantium? She made a silent vow to not miss one of them.

The press of people quickly became so dense that, even should she wish to turn out of it, she could not. It carried her to the great porphy column. Several of the more aggressive souls surrounding her bore her on in their company, taking her with them through the jam of people to the forefront of the crowd.

With so much jostling and pushing, Ailinn took little notice of the increasing vocalness of the crowd. 'Twas only when she verged on the front did she realize that the utterances about her were not ones of buoyant good cheer but were wrathful and jeering.

Before she could take heed, someone muscled from behind, pushing at her back as they tried to gain better vantage. Ailinn found herself propelled roughly forward and thrust into the open, beyond the front of the crowd.

Catching herself, she began to straighten, then halted. A man knelt a short distance before her, his hands bound and outstretched in front of him upon a wooden block. Officials waited to the side, one presently signaling to someone who stood beyond her edge of vision.

Color drained from Ailinn's face as a hooded axman stepped forward, spit to the side, then marking the man's wrists, drew the blade up and sliced through the air, sweeping it down.

Ailinn screamed, the crowd roared, and the blade whirred home.

Ailinn swung around and battled with all her might through the wall of people. Driving and shoving and pushing her way through, she gained the outer perimeter of the crowd many long minutes later.

Nauseated, she broke into a run and headed toward the exit on the south side of the forum, where it rejoined the Mesê. Escaping the forum, she spun around and threw her back up against its outer wall, bracing herself for support and heaving for breath. She could not extinguish the sight of the man from her mind.

Ailinn remained panting several minutes longer. She became aware of a supplicating voice nearby. Dragging open her eyes, she found a beggar without eyes. Ailinn pressed away from the wall. More Byzantine justice? she wondered, distraught.

Composing her ragged nerves, Ailinn set out again on the Mesê. As the poundings of her heart began to slow, she realized, by the stalls and displays along the arcade, that she had entered the section of the goldsmiths and silversmiths, the gem crafters and jewelers. But 'twas not the finery they offered that captured her attention, but the men bent over the workbenches—ironbands around their neck, some with chains on their ankles. Slaves.

Ailinn's heart sank, the days of her own enslavement ever haunting her soul.

Progressing on, she came to another gathering, blocking a portion of the street directly ahead of her. Ailinn possessed no desire to see what fascinated the crowd, her curiosity slain. She began to skirt the body, but the spectators parted before she could draw her gaze away. At the center of their interest was a shaggy brown bear.

Ailinn viewed the animal from its back. At first the sight amazed her, for the bear stood upraised, shuffling on its hind legs for the crowd's amusement. But as it turned, she saw the chain attached to a ring in its nose. The sight saddened Ailinn for the poor creature. Her thoughts went to Lyting, and she knew he would be saddened, also.

Lyting. She must find him.

She glanced briefly back along the boulevard and discovered

that the aqueduct was no longer visible, the forum obstructing it from view. But she refused to enter it again without Lyting, and certainly not while public punishments were being meted out. Looking south again, to the far distance, she thought to see the end of the Mesê, marked by a gigantic bronze statue of a man on horseback. The Sacred Palace must lie beyond it, she reasoned.

With her new goal in sight, Ailinn set forth, ever searching the crowd for Lyting. Halfway down the avenue, she began to notice women, heavily made up with lip tints and eye darkener, and carrying stools. When she saw how they approached the men in the street, she realized they were prostitutes.

The clatter of wheels alerted Ailinn of a carriage. Tearing her gaze from the women, she stepped without looking from the street, directly into the sizable stomach of a man, standing just outside the arches. His hands caught her instantly and held her as he helped her regain her balance. Ailinn voiced her thanks, suddenly enveloped by an exotic, woody scent.

Lifting her gaze, she found the man to be like another she had seen earlier, his ebony beard and hair carefully curled and glistening with perfumed oil. He wore a black robe which parted over his protruding belly, showing a bright red sash.

He continued to hold her in his grasp, his dark eyes moving over her as he addressed her in his native tongue. Questions, she thought. Perhaps he only asked whether she was all right, or the whereabouts of her escort.

Ailinn relaxed somewhat when he released her. He remained courteous, smiling, evidently offering his aid. She sought to assure him she was all right and began to back away, but he caught her by the arm once more, then upheld a jeweled finger as though asking her to wait a moment.

Turning, he beckoned to another man, a servant, who stood before one of the stalls, collecting a parcel. The servant hastened to his master's side and held forth the bundle.

Ailinn watched as the man opened the cloth wrappings and drew out a stunning necklace of emeralds set in gold. He faced her and held the piece outstretched, against her hair, then nodded with great satisfaction. Lowering the necklace, he laid it across the base of her throat and left it there.

Astonished, Ailinn caught the piece before the precious

jewels dropped to the ground. The man's hand moved to touch her hair, captivated by its color, then came to rest on her shoulder. He spoke again, his voice honey-smooth, the beam burning in his eyes all too familiar.

Ailinn's throat turned to dust. Frantic, she twisted to scan the crowds for Lyting. The man's grip tightened on her shoulder, and he snapped his fingers to a litter waiting nearby. Without delay the driver brought it forth, and the servant scuttled to bring out a cushioned stool and set it on the ground to aid his master's climb.

Realizing the man's intent, Ailinn thrust the precious necklace back into his hands and shoved his hand from her shoulder.

Surprise, then anger, scored the man's features as she rejected his generosity. Gripping her by the upper arm, he dragged her toward the litter. Ailinn fought his hold, striking out at his chest and demanding he release her. Her actions only angered him more.

Seizing her by the wrist, he twisted it painfully and forced her onto the stool. Ailinn cried out and tried to jerk free, managing only to step off the stool again. The man then barked orders to his servant, who promptly came to assist him.

Desperate, Ailinn screamed and kicked as they lifted her from her feet. Did no one hear? she raged. The people in the street merely looked on, but no one attempted to aid her. Did they think her to be one of the prostitutes and, therefore, unworthy of protection or without rights?

Ailinn felt suddenly weightless as the two men tossed her into the litter. She sprawled gracelessly onto the cushion-lined bench there. Shoving upward, she scrambled for the side, but the man climbed in after her and flung her back down onto the cushions.

In a pitch of emotion he snapped out orders. The driver cracked his small whip at the mules while the servant hastened ahead, clearing a path before them with a gilded stick.

As the litter lurched forward, the man turned to Ailinn and spread the necklace of emeralds across her neck. His lips spread with a smile, his teeth gleaming. 'Twas as though he envisioned her in naught but the jewels.

Growling his approval, his hand moved to her thigh.

Chapter 16

Koll was dead. The fifth of the "Dragons" had been removed from around the throne.

Lyting hardened his jaw as he left the palace grounds in the company of Thord, an officer of the Guard, and a troop of a half dozen Varangians.

Rurik had been right. The missive from Dyrrachium was a trick to lure him back. Now, only he remained of the original six. 'Twas Rurik who had been the central figure, the key person, in foiling the plot against the emperor, Leo Sophos— the one the "spider" would want to entrap above all.

Lyting knew he must gain the Imperial ear and quickly. He need couple the information Rurik had shared with him with what Koll might have imparted to the empress.

Following the enclosure wall that surrounded the palace, they entered the Augustaeum, the large public square that lay before the Sacred Palace. The Hagia Sophia rose off to his right, annihilating in size. To his left, stood the famed Hippodrome. Lyting and the Varangians traversed the square, then proceeded past an enormous equestrian statue of the emperor, Justinian, and moved onto the Mesê.

Lyting began to ask Thord of Koll when a commotion down the street caught his eye—two men struggling with a woman, her dark red hair swirling about her.

Lyting's heart slammed against his ribs as his focus sharpened upon a thickset Syrian and his scrawny servant forcing Ailinn into a waiting litter.

Lyting grabbed for his sword but found naught but an empty scabbard. Breaking into a run, he shouted back for Thord and the others to follow and raced down the Mesê.

Panic seized Ailinn as her abductor's fleshy hand slid farther up her thigh, desire shimmering in his eyes.

Snatching the emerald necklace from her throat, she hurled it at him, then spat on him fully so he could not misinterpret her rejection of him.

The man crimsoned, rage flaming his features. With a snarl and a curse, he cast up his hand to strike. Ailinn braced herself for the coming blow.

As he began to swipe downward, his fierce mien flooded with surprise. His eyes enlarged as he strained against an unseen force and his hand remained rigidly locked in place. In the same moment the litter jarred to a halt.

Ailinn's gaze flew past the man. She gasped a quick breath, her pulse leaping wildly, for there stood Lyting, trammeling the man's wrist and slicing him straight through with eyes of ice.

"You are in possession of something that is mine," Lyting ground out in imperfect Greek, anger scalding through him.

"Be away with you, the woman is mine for this night and quite possibly many more," the Syrian barked back, not about to surrender his prize. But his eyes widened further as they lodged on the seven hulking Varangians that surrounded his litter, their fearsome, double-headed axes rising above their heads.

Thord lowered his blade, the sun's light kissing its edge with a smile as he set it against the Syrian's neck.

"Do as he says," Thord warned.

Infuriated but outflanked, the Syrian could do naught but sit powerless while the white-haired Norseman claimed the beauty beside him.

As Lyting leaned into the litter for Ailinn, she grasped for his hand, rising and hastening over the Syrian's silk-robed legs, much relieved. Her arms wound about Lyting's neck as he lifted her to the ground, then slipped lower to hug his waist as he anchored her to his side.

"I will not soon forget this incident, Norseman," the Syrian snarled. "Nor will I forget *you*."

With that, the Syrian bellowed to his driver and servant. The litter lurched forward and rumbled down the stone paved avenue of the Mesê.

Lyting's blood simmered as Ailinn recounted all that had befallen her since he left her in the company of Arnór and his family.

He had miscalculated where the women were concerned, and that made him doubly mad with himself. Their jealousies had been plain. He should have foreseen the deceit. Lyting determined not to spend another night in their company. He would not subject Ailinn to any more of the women's connivances.

"What is it, my friend?" Thord asked of a sudden, seeing Lyting's scowl.

"We will need lodging for the night. The convoy is to be housed outside the city, but I have no desire to stay there." Lyting related an abbreviated version of what had happened.

Thord appeared sympathetic. "Can't say that I blame the Syrian, though," he jested. "The woman is a rare beauty. Is she your mistress or your *kona*?"

Lyting marked how the interest of the other Varangians drifted continuously to Ailinn.

"She is my *kona*," he declared flatly, so there would be no doubt in any of their minds.

"You are a fortunate man," Thord said buoyantly. "I insist you come with me and stay the night at the house of Melane. She is a special friend of mine and will be honored to have you both. She is also one of the wealthiest women in the city. I think that you will find the accommodations she can provide are more than comfortable."

From the warmth and tone of Thord's voice, Lyting suspected Melane to be his mistress.

"On the morrow," Thord continued, "I will accompany you to the palace and help you make the contact you seek. I, too, will stay at Melane's, and we can talk into the night of Koll, Askel, and the others, if you desire. I knew them well, and much has happened since your brother's departure."

Finding Thord's offer agreeable, Lyting apprised Ailinn that they would remain within the city. The Varangian would serve as their "official" guard should the Byzantines require it.

She walked quietly at his side. Too quietly.

"Are you all right, *elskan mín*?"

"I am now that you are here," she returned, smiling up at him and placing her hand on his arm.

They walked southward, back toward the statue of Justinian, following Thord. He directed Lyting and Ailinn to one of the side streets, pausing to speak with his comrades. Minutes later Thord rejoined them while the others headed for the Augustaeum and the Sacred Palace.

The afternoon grew late as they passed along the streets and through shrubbed courtyards with fountains and statuary. Dark-haired children laughed as they ran past, rolling wheel-like hoops with sticks, and vendors cried their wares.

The house of Melane, like many they had seen before, was two-storied, its exterior almost stark, except faced with marble so highly polished it reflected the street and the sky. A row of jewel-like windows smiled from above.

Thord rapped at the door with his knuckles—a distinctive tune. Brief moments later the door drew open to reveal a small but lovely woman, Melane.

Swathed in vivid reds and gold, she stood no taller than Ailinn's chin. Her honey-blond hair was swept up and fashioned into an elaborate coil studded with gems. Her frothy veil, affixed to the back of her head, spilled to the floor, where silk slippers peeked from beneath her gown.

As Thord presented Lyting and Ailinn and explained their needs, Melane's striking green eyes encompassed them.

She smiled warmly. *"Ipodhohi. Embros."*

"She says 'welcome' and 'come in.'" Thord grinned and motioned for them to enter.

Lyting and Ailinn followed Melane into the central hall, a spacious area filled with light. Marble columns rose to an airy height, supporting the upper level, while at the back the entire wall opened onto a courtyard.

Ailinn marveled at the murals that covered the walls, realistic paintings of idyllic landscapes. On second glance she realized they contained small figures—a creature half-man, half-horse playing a lyre; a bearded man crowned with grapevines sipping wine; partially robed couples reclining, many a man fondling a woman's breast. Ailinn's brows flickered upward. She cast a glance about the hall.

Melane clapped her hands, sending several servants scurrying from their presence on a string of instructions. The women returned scant moments later bearing an embossed silver ewer and matching goblets.

"Melane tells me the other women who occupy the house are out this evening, attending a private banquet. Except for the servants, we shall be alone." Thord grinned roguishly, his hand moving to Melane's hip, confirming Lyting's earlier suspicions of their relationship.

As Ailinn accepted a goblet brimming with wine, one of the servants relieved her of her mantle.

"She will see it is cleaned," Thord explained as the servant disappeared down a corridor.

Lyting paused his cup midway to his lips and took a long, appreciative look at Ailinn. He found himself swallowing. In the weeks since he had freed her, she had begun to regain some of the roundness she had lost on the journey, filling out in all the right places. Now the folds of her dress clung to all those right places.

Melane also drew an eye over Ailinn's hair and clothes. She then gave the men a sharp assessment, her gaze drawing down to their dusty boots and sandals. She spoke to Thord, bringing forth a good-natured laugh. He turned to Lyting.

"Melane says we should take ourselves to the men's baths. She insists, none too delicately, that we are sorely in need of the visit!"

Lyting rubbed his beard and then looked down at his garments and boots. He grinned. "I think she is right, and I would certainly enjoy the luxury."

"Come, my friend." Thord stepped toward the door. "Melane will see to Ailinn's needs and prepare your room. You should enjoy the experience of a 'Roman'-style bath. There is nothing to compare—cool and heated pools, saunas. Even the floors are warmed from beneath. If you like, you can even have a massage." Thord's smile widened.

Lyting turned and explained his departure to Ailinn. "I will be gone only a short time. Melane will see that you are freshened and comfortable. We will stay here tonight."

He traced the side of her face with his forefinger, hating to leave her, then turned and departed with Thord.

* * *

Ailinn stepped from the scented bathwaters, feeling wondrously restored. The servants attending her quickly toweled her dry, directed her to a marble bench, and rubbed precious oils into her skin. Enveloping her in linens, they led her to a room at the back of the first floor.

The room proved tiny but stunningly beautiful. Sumptuous fabrics draped the walls and covered the bed, which consumed most of the room. An elegant table and cushioned chair sat to one side, both of ivory and encrusted with mother-of-pearl. Silver lamps glowed softly about the room.

Such decadent luxury, Ailinn sighed, to have such a room all to herself. A realization tripped on the heels of that thought and struck her solidly. Undoubtedly, the room was meant for both her *and* Lyting to share.

Before her eyes, the room began to shrink.

Melane appeared, smiling and gesturing for Ailinn to sit on the chair. Two servants followed, one laying clothing on the bed, and the other bringing a mirror, comb, and fine silk cording twined with strands of little pearls.

Melane chattered to Ailinn in Greek as she began to work with her hair, sweeping the sides from her face and catching it atop her head. Ailinn listened without comprehension, enjoying the ministrations as Melane wove her tresses with silk and pearls.

Drawing up the remainder of Ailinn's long locks, Melane encircled the base of their thickness with the garnished braid, creating a small crown to secure it in place, but allowing the wealth of Ailinn's hair to cascade back down her neck and shoulders.

Melane held up the hand mirror for Ailinn's approval, then motioned to the servants, who quickly dispossessed Ailinn of her linen toweling. They returned, each holding matching panels of fabric—diaphanous clouds of silk.

As they moved to stand, one before Ailinn and the other behind, Melane joined them and fastened the cloth at each shoulder with identical jeweled pins. She left the neck opening wide enough so that it bared Ailinn's shoulders. Melane next girdled the fabric at Ailinn's waist with a thin belt of gold, arranging misty folds so that they covered Ailinn's hips but separated partway down her thigh, allowing a glimpse of bare leg.

Melane and the servants stepped back nodding and smiling over their handiwork. Ailinn's concerns, however, grew as she viewed herself through the transparency. 'Twas a gown for seduction. Obviously, Melane believed she was Lyting's lover and prepared her for his pleasure.

Ailinn desperately hoped the women would provide her with a more concealing robe. Instead, Melane set out a pair of embroidered slippers and began to leave. Another servant appeared momentarily with the cleaned mantle and lay it on the end of the bed.

As the women withdrew, Ailinn's thoughts skipped ahead to Lyting's return and back to the dimensions of the room. She moved to take up her cloak. 'Twas going to be a long night.

Lyting greeted Melane as she emerged from the back room, closing the door softly behind her.

"*Kalispera sas*. Good evening, Melane," he spoke haltingly in Greek. "Your servant, Dita, said I would find Ailinn here."

"She is waiting for you. Enjoy your leisure. I hope you will find everything to your satisfaction." A secretive smile sparkled in Melane's eyes. "Now I must see to Thord. He, too, will be waiting." With that, Melane floated down the hall in search of her lover.

Distracted by Melane's words, Lyting reached for the door and, without knocking, entered in, eager to see Ailinn. His footsteps solidified as his gaze fell on her. She, too, went perfectly still where she stood beside the wide, inviting bed, reaching for her mantle.

Heat coiled through Lyting. Ailinn looked like one of the classical goddesses whose sculptures graced the city—Venus come to life, her beauty stirring the most primal passions known to man. Known to him, but long denied.

His heart began a strong, heavy beat as his gaze traveled downward. The misty gown covered all but concealed nothing. He drank in the sight of her high, lovely breasts, full and round and tipped with rose. His gaze lowered to her incredibly small waist and flat stomach, then lingered over the indentation of her navel which beckoned to be filled with sweet wine and relished there. The curve of her hips he imagined hot beneath his hands, and her sleek legs wrapped around his waist. Heat suffused his loins. Ailinn haunted his dreams looking just so—the nymph of his most erotic desires and untamed passions.

Ailinn stood unable to move, stunned at Lyting's sudden entrance, then again by the sight of him. His beard was gone, his face clean shaven. Once more she gazed clearly on his features. She felt a tightening in her breasts, a tingly ache that spread downward and settled between her thighs. Inordinately handsome with the beard, Lyting was devastatingly so without one. 'Twas painful to look on him.

Desire swamped Lyting's senses. Why did Ailinn remain unmoving before him, not even attempting to cover herself?

Ignoring the distant voice of wisdom, his gaze went to her silken shoulders, where the jeweled fasteners invited him to remove them and let the fabric whisper away, fully exposing her creamy breasts. His gaze descended to the juncture of her legs and dark triangle there. He swallowed hard, feeling each drub of his heart.

Raw desire battled with will. His eyes pulled slowly to hers. She remained still as a doe, waiting. He clenched his hands as will began to bend and a molten fire raged forth. A groan rose from his depths. In a single stride he closed the distance and swept Ailinn into his arms, hard against his chest.

"God's holy might, Ailinn! Wouldst you torture me apurpose? There be many eunuchs in Byzantium, but I assure you, I am not one of them."

His mouth descended over hers, covering her lips and ravishing them thoroughly. Startled, Ailinn's mouth parted under the assault, and he invaded at once. His tongue mated hers in a frenzied dance—commanding, possessing, plundering all at once, claiming her as his alone.

A bolt of liquid heat shot through Ailinn, melting her against him. His tongue continued to stroke and seduce and steal her breath straight away.

He molded her against him, sliding his hand down the curve of her spine and pressing her hips against his. She felt the hard proof of his desire. Felt an answering throb between her own legs. Her senses whirled and her body ached with startling need before Lyting's unleashed passion.

A white heat of emotion possessed Lyting as his hand moved

to the side of Ailinn's waist and met with bare flesh where the gown parted above the belt. Ailinn arched against him as though inviting his touch of fire. His hand slowly continued upward seeking the warm mound of her breast.

Deep within, he knew if he began the intimacy, he must have more. He must have all of her. There would be no stopping, his passions too long strained, the blood of the North flowing hot and thick in his veins. In the frenzy of unshackled desire, he would take her, bury himself in her, be she willing or not. Then he would be no better than those who had attacked and violated her kinswomen. Where then would be his sworn word to her? Where would be his honor? Ailinn would find herself ravished by a Dane after all.

Reason warred within the dense haze of passion. With fierce concentration, Lyting mastered himself enough to break the kiss. They both gasped against each other for breath. Dropping her softly to the bed, he staggered back a pace.

"A man has his limitations, Ailinn. I am at the end of mine. Remember it, if you wouldst preserve your virtue."

With that, Lyting pivoted and flung himself through the door and out of the room. He dared not look back, knowing how she would look, spread upon the bed and so easily his.

Breathless, Ailinn stared after Lyting, her lips burning from his fiery possession, her heart pounding beneath her breast. She pressed upward as he disappeared from sight and remained staring out the empty doorway, utterly astounded, empty and aching within.

Hours later, in the dark of the night, the moon a fingernail in the sky, Lyting still walked the streets of Constantinople.

He returned earlier from the tenements in the Magnaura district outside the city, after visiting Arnór and dealing with Jorunn, Ingered, and Ashild. Arnór had been shocked by Lyting's revelations, having received a different version of Ailinn's disappearance from his wife and daughters. Arnór proved wholly understanding of Lyting's decision to take separate lodgings and agreed to send his goods on to Melane's the following day.

On reentering the city, Lyting had then spent considerable time cooling his ardor with a long walk in the evening air. He moved along the streets with his hood drawn up, for his white hair ever brought him notice and marked his passage. Tonight he longed for privacy as he dealt with the concerns that plagued his heart and soul.

Surprisingly, the streets were fairly well illumined with torchlight. But, while walking along the seawall on the Golden Horn, he encountered a little scab of a man, loitering there, who became highly insistent that he carry a brand for him. The man looked to belong to Constantinople's poor. Believing 'twould be charitable to allow him to do so, Lyting employed the man. He now walked slightly ahead, lighting the way back to the house of Melane.

As Lyting arrived in front of the house, he paused outside a moment and contemplated the entrance. He would request another room. Near Ailinn's. He should warn her to block her door.

God give him strength. He was not wholly sure he could make it through the night without climbing into her bed.

Lyting retrieved a small coin from his pouch and paid the man, then went and rapped on the door. Almost immediately a servant whisked it open.

Steeling himself, Lyting entered in.

The man waited until the Norseman disappeared into the house, and the door closed behind him.

He turned and hurried off, rushing at a hobbling gait along darkened streets and alley ways, until he came at last to a palatial mansion that sat upon one of the city's many hills and overlooked the lights of the Golden Horn.

Hastening to the back of the building, he stopped before a thick, planked door of knotted oak and knocked rapidly, heaving to catch his breath. When no one answered, he pounded harder, insistent, urgent.

A small inset panel in the door slid open, revealing a pair of eyes.

The man from the wharf yanked open the neck of his tunic, pulling it down to expose the mark on his left shoulder.

"What is it you wish?" a voice rumbled behind the door.

"Pass the word. Atlison is back!"

Chapter 17

Ailinn awakened slowly, feeling wonderfully rested and deliciously lethargic. She stretched out in the soft, comfortable bed. She hadn't slept so well in ages.

Opening her eyes, she found the room quite dark, the only light coming from without, seeping in the cracks around and beneath the door.

Lyting. He had not returned to their room last night. Was he still in the house?

She flung her legs over the side of the bed and began to rise, groping for her mantle.

Just then the door eased open and a shaft of light penetrated the room. A servant, seeing Ailinn awake, spoke a soft greeting and entered with a tray of food. She gibbered in Greek, which was lost on Ailinn, but she realized the woman wished for her to sit back. When she did, the woman set the tray of sliced melons, figs, and bread upon her lap, then turned to light the elegant silver lamp on the table.

Ailinn saw now that clothes had been brought during the night and left, folded on the chair. She wished to ask of Lyting, but having no way to communicate, she waited for the servant to leave.

Setting aside the tray, she rose to dress, deciding to go in search of Lyting. Gratefully, the new gown proved a solid, nontransparent weave—a sapphire blue patterned all over with small golden stars and circles. A *stola* of currant-red silk, bordered with gold, accompanied it.

Ailinn thought to hear feminine voices from without. Easing the door open, she slipped into the corridor.

Light spilled through narrow windows that opened onto the courtyard, washing the interior spaces with bright sunlight and revealing 'twas much later in the day than Ailinn first guessed.

Voices and stringed music drifted from the courtyard. Ailinn pressed on, glimpsing rooms in passing, furnished with costly hangings, couches, carpets, piles of cushions, and small figurines on marble pedestals.

Entering the main hallway, Ailinn encountered a couple descending the staircase. The man looked to be a soldier and adjusted his uniform, his hair tousled. The woman's face was becomingly flushed and her lips pinkened. 'Twas obvious, even to herself, that the two had just finished their tryst.

Ailinn quickly turned and headed toward the courtyard. She emerged beneath the cool shade of the portico, overlooking carefully tended gardens and a marble fountain at its center. There she observed two women entertaining a man where he lounged on a long, open-sided couch.

One woman played a lyre while the other amused him, feeding him from a tray of fruits. Both women were comely, elegantly dressed, their hair carefully arranged. Ailinn saw that their eyes were enhanced with darkener and their cheeks lightly rouged. Their clothes were much like the one Melane had created for her—draped rather than sewn, but theirs were pinned over only one shoulder, leaving the other shoulder and arm bared.

The oddest of feelings spiraled through Ailinn that they dressed to simulate the ancient Romans, such as in the statuary she had seen along the Mesê. And the couples in the wall mural.

Ailinn watched, unnoticed, as the one woman fed the man from a cluster of grapes. He smiled as he ate from her hand, his own idly tracing over the ample swell of her breasts, then dragging her gown from her shoulder to expose them to his view.

The woman laughed throatily as he pulled her to him and suckled her nipple. Enjoying the play, she tossed back her head, then froze as her gaze fell on Ailinn.

The man paused, feeling the woman stiffen beneath his attentions. Turning, he spied Ailinn. He stared openly, then raked her with heated eyes as though considering her for his next course.

Ailinn blanched. Turning on her heel, she fled back to her room, her cheeks flaming as she realized that this was a house of courtesans.

Lyting made his way back to Melane's alongside Thord, thoroughly disgusted.

Since the palace gates opened at dawn, he had endeavored to gain audience with the Empress Zoë. But he was, himself, unprepared for the labyrinthine bureaucracy of the Byzantines, which proved supremely frustrating and rested in the hands of as many eunuchs as not.

One wished to relieve him of the golden *solidus* and purple silk; another wished to arrest him for possessing it. Gratefully, Thord had intervened.

Midafternoon, having made no headway, he was forced to give up his efforts, for 'twas time for the palace gates to be closed. They would not be opened again until the morrow's dawn.

Thord then took him to the Baths of Zeuxippus where the Varangian Leidolf and, lately, Koll had been slain. Evidently, Koll's assailants had abandoned him, thinking him to be dead. But Koll lived enough to scratch a clue into the marble floor, using the brooch pin from his mantle—a single letter, the Cyrillic *omega*.

Lyting thought on the inscription in Askel's armband and wondered, if Koll had lived longer, if he might have added a Cyrillic *I*.

Lyting readjusted the hood of his mantle, pulling it forward once more to shade his sensitive eyes from the brilliance of the sun, then glanced right and left. He could not shake the feeling that had persisted since leaving the Sacred Palace that someone watched him. Yet, he never saw anyone overtly staring or following him. As now.

Nearing Melane's, Lyting and Thord came upon a singular sight, that of a man standing naked on a pillar, his matted beard reaching long enough to grant him a measure of modesty. Men gathered around the base of the column as he proclaimed his impassioned message.

"The man is one of their religious ascetics, a *stylite*," Thord explained with a smile. "They be hermits who stand on their pillars the year round, never sitting or kneeling, never coming down. They pray their devotions and offer their counsel to those who seek it. This one is more fiery than most." Thord gave a short laugh. "Twice a day he preaches a peppery message of salvation and repentance to Constantinople's wayward populace."

"A modern day John the Baptist?" Lyting smiled, taking interest, though the words were lost on Thord.

Thord started to interpret for Lyting, but Lyting stayed him. "I can understand the language better than I can speak it."

Lyting concentrated, pleased as he captured most of the holy man's pronouncements. As Lyting looked up, his hood slipped back, exposing his snow-pale hair.

"You young men think you know the will of God. But you do not!" the holy man snapped. "You see, and yet you are blind. You hear, and yet you are deaf. Repent! Repent!"

Spotting Lyting, he stretched a long, bony finger toward him. "Take the block from your eye and hearken the way of the Lord. 'Walk in the paths *He* has chosen,' not those you have set your foot to."

A chill rippled down Lyting's spine, for the holy man quoted, in part, the same scripture once given to his sister-by-marriage, Brienne, when she left her convent walls. Ones which had proven prophetic. Ones she had gently quoted to him when he had sought her advice. Advice about entering the Abbey of Corbie.

Thord's laugh broke his thoughts. "Must be that white mane of yours that singled you out."

"*Já*," Lyting concurred, distracted as he adjusted his hood and they moved off. "It marks me all too well."

Arriving before the house of Melane's, Lyting paused a moment, seeing a young boy playing hoops in the street, and bid him over. With Thord's help he hired the lad to deliver a message he had written out earlier, addressed to the father of Rurik's deceased love, Helena.

"Do you know aught of Alexius Dalassena?" Lyting asked Thord as the boy scampered off down the street and they started for the door.

Thord shrugged. "The name brings no face to mind, but there be nearly a million people in Constantinople."

"He would be a court official, I presume."

Thord shook his head. "Sorry, my friend. You have seen the 'heart of the empire' for yourself today in the great complex of buildings at the Sacred Palace. 'Tis a hive of activity. There be officials by the thousands."

Lyting nodded his understanding. "I hope the boy will find him at the address Rurik provided."

As the two Northmen disappeared inside the house, the young boy trotted happily on, a small bronze coin in one hand, the folded piece of paper in the other.

Turning at the end of the street, he bumped into a figure waiting in the shadows of the building. Hands clamped down on the boy's shoulders, startling him further.

Looking up, the child began to tremble, recognizing the man. The man released his hold of one of the boy's shoulders and, snapping his fingers, opened out his palm and waited expectantly.

Shaking, the boy gave over the note the pale-haired Norseman had entrusted to him.

"Ailinn?" Lyting rapped soundly on the door to the room. Melane had assured him she was in the room, but when he attempted to open the door, it knocked against something solid, obstructing the other side.

"Ailinn, are you all right? Open the door."

"Lyting?"

There was a slight desperateness to her voice. Lyting tensed. He next heard movement on the other side—the sound of furniture being dragged aside. A bed? he wondered.

The door opened a crack, and Ailinn's eye appeared. In the next instance she flung it open fully and cast herself against him, her arms wrapping around his waist.

God help him, he appealed heavenward as he felt her breasts flatten against him. He could not survive another encounter like yestereve without losing his sanity.

"What is it, *elskan mín*? Didst you think I would not return? You need not have stayed in the room all the day."

"Oh, but I did!" she exclaimed drawing back, then her voice fell to an urgent whisper. "Lyting, we must talk." She caught him by the hand and pulled him inside the room with her. In a rush she related all she had seen earlier when she ventured from her room.

"Melane runs a house of courtesans!"

Lyting's face registered his surprise. As Ailinn chattered on, he massaged his temples, wearied by the long day and sleepless night, with another meeting yet to face.

"Ailinn, I am grateful to Melane for her hospitality. We will have to make the best of it until we can find other lodging. At the moment, Melane wishes us to join her and Thord in her private dining room."

Ailinn nodded, folding away her concerns. As she and Lyting moved through the corridors, they encountered a number of couples lingering in the halls and side rooms. Lyting received considerable interest from the women of the house, and Ailinn an equal share from the male visitors. Lyting began to better appreciate Ailinn's guarded seclusion in her room. His hand moved possessively to her back as he ushered her into the dining room where Thord and Melane awaited them.

The room was airy with a high ceiling and one wall open to the courtyard. Soft murals covered the other walls, similar to those in the hall—bucolic scenes of which Lyting took a closer look, then raised a brow at the frolicksome couples who were engaged there in more than mere fondling. Clearing his throat, he joined the others at the table.

The four passed the time in pleasant conversation over a light meal of fish in a white sauce, asparagus, and boiled eggs. Despite Melane's profession, Ailinn found that she very much liked her, and Melane's and Thord's affection for each other was both obvious and warming.

As they relaxed to the music of a lyre floating from the courtyard, Lyting drummed his fingers noiselessly on the table, impatient to receive a reply from Alexius Dalassena. Many songs later a servant appeared bearing a sealed parchment and presented it to Lyting.

Lyting's spirits rose. He quickly broke the glob of red wax, the seal's impression unreadable as though it had been made by an unsteady hand. Lyting thought little of it. According to Rurik, Alexius was quite elderly.

Lyting opened and scanned the missive. His brows drew together in thought as he considered the words.

Thord eyed the parchment. "What is it, my friend?"

"Alexius asks that I meet him at Helena's crypt, in the cemetery outside of the Gate of Charisius—a somewhat unusual request."

"Not if the father commonly visits his daughter's crypt," Thord offered. "Too, there may be things of which he wishes to speak but cannot in his own home with the overlarge ears of servants about."

Lyting's eyes went to Thord, the truth of the statement striking him. He hoped Alexius did know something of the conspiracy or of the more recent murders that might prove helpful. Helena had secreted the child out of the palace during the attempt on Leo Sophos. 'Twas likely Alexius had also been involved as well and aided her. Lyting was anxious to speak with the man.

"The Gate of Charisius lies at the northern land wall, at the end of the Mesê," Thord advised. "I would take you there myself, but I must report for duty in the next hour. I could draw you a map, if you like."

"No need. I have one committed here." Lyting smiled, tapping his forehead. "My brother insisted. He did not tell me the location of Helena's grave, however. Alexius is rather old, silver-haired and distinguished-looking. He should not be too difficult to identify."

Thord nodded in agreement. "Be sure to be back inside the city before the gates are locked, or you will be spending your night among the dead."

Thord's jestful words settled ill in Lyting's tones.

As he explained matters to Ailinn, she pressed that he take her with him. Lyting preferred to leave her with Melane, but reconsidered, seeing the house's patrons were already arriving. Of those couples who strolled in the gardens, many a man's eye strayed from his consort to where Ailinn sat beside him. Thord would not be present either to watch over her.

Finding no other choice, Lying agreed to take Ailinn with him.

Lyting and Ailinn passed through the Gate of Charisius and arrived at the cemetery early evening. The light was beginning to descend, dusk spreading its gray veil over the graveyard, casting the legions of tombs and markers into long shadows.

As they started down the wide central path, Lyting wrestled

with his conscience in silent turmoil. He could not simply leave the city after delivering Rurik's message at court and forsake a ten-year-old boy—emperor or not—to the hands of his enemies. He knew he must remain long enough to solve the mystery of the "spider's" identity, or Constantine Porphyrogentius and Zoë would surely die.

Lyting wondered whether the man waited to make his move on the Imperials because he plotted to catch Rurik in his web as well. He would be disappointed to learn that Rurik had not taken his bait and returned to Constantinople. But Lyting knew that the one behind the palace intrigues and murders would not wait forever to ensnare the young emperor and his mother. He must move quickly to reveal this man.

Lyting tugged the hood of his mantle forward as he and Ailinn continued along the path.

She leaned forward to better glimpse his face, smiling. "'Twas my guess you wished to pass through the city unobserved, but none will mark your passage here, if you wish to rid yourself of your hood."

Before he could respond, Lyting caught sight of a silver-haired man standing down one of the side paths, in front of a row of tall, marble sarcophagi. Ailinn started to speak again, but Lyting touched her arm, staying her, then gestured toward the man.

"There," he said in a hushed tone. "That must be Alexius Dalassena."

Leaving the central walk, they passed more of the numerous common grave stones that filled the cemetery—some leaning with age—huddled in and about more elaborately carved tombs and monuments, those crowded with biblical figures and motifs. Minutes later they approached the silver-haired man. He stood with his head bowed before a marble sarcophagus as though praying.

Lyting and Ailinn did not disturb the man as they joined him. For the moment they stood solemnly and respectfully beside him while he finished his prayers.

Lyting scanned the sarcophagus. 'Twas a masterpiece of sculpture, covered with a double row of carved reliefs, illustrating Old and New Testament themes. At the very top of the sarcophagus—above the carvings, but just beneath the

lid—ran a smooth band, carrying an inscription and the name
"Helena Dalassena."

After a prolonged moment the silver-haired man raised his
head and looked to Lyting. His face remained partially hidden
in the shadows of evening.

"Rurik." The man drew the name out in a low, hoarse
whisper. "You have returned, my son. Good." He fell silent
and turned again to contemplate Helena's tomb.

Lyting began to correct the man's misperception. Understandably, he had expected Rurik, not himself, and that was his
own fault. Lyting could not say what had prompted him
earlier, but when composing his letter to Alexius, he had
signed it simply "Atlison." Mayhaps Byzantine duplicity was
catching, Lyting thought grimly.

On the other hand, 'twas common enough for him to be
mistaken for his brother, for their facial resemblance was
exceedingly strong. 'Twas their hair that set them most apart
and, at the moment his was concealed beneath his hood. Too,
it had also been many years since Alexius had seen Rurik.
Lyting started to respond when the older man sighed and gazed
upward to the band of writing that carried his daughter's name.

"They murdered her—my beautiful flower, my Helena." He
shook his head sadly and lowered it again, yet his shoulders did
not sag as one might expect of a man weighted with sorrow or
defeat. Tension stiffened his shoulders and spine.

"Be you certain?" Lyting digested the pronouncement,
keeping his own questions to simple Greek sentences.

The older man nodded darkly. "Poison."

"A potion?" Lyting struggled for the precise words, finding
his grasp of the tongue strained and his understanding spotty.

The man shook his head. "They be more clever than that.
'Twas in the scented oils she used—part of her daily ritual, to
perfume and soften her skin, to make herself more beautiful . . . for you, Rurik. Ever for you."

Lyting felt the stab of those words and wondered if Alexius
used them apurpose to torment Rurik. He was glad he could
take the prick in his brother's stead. Was the man embittered?

"Even as she lay sick and dying, she asked to be anointed
daily, wishing to smell of jasmine, her favorite scent . . . for
you. Even as you kept vigil over her, the poisons in the oils
reached deep inside and killed her."

Lyting realized at once, if the substance had been used so extensively—over torso and limbs—then Helena must have absorbed the poison into nearly ever pore of her body. No wonder she had succumbed so quickly. Someone hated Rurik greatly to murder Helena as he watched helplessly at her side.

The Varangians, Thengil and Vegeir, had died on separate occasions but in similar manner to Helena's death, Lyting recalled. Officially they died shortly after trysting with a woman, presumably a prostitute. Though poison was suspected, Thord confided that both their bodies had been fragrant with oils when discovered. The prostitute was never found, but 'twas certain at least one woman was in the employ of the "spider." Lyting sorely wished he could speak with Rurik and find who had tended Helena and were present at her sickbed.

"Didst Askel the Red speak with you?" Lyting asked at last.

The man did not answer. Lyting thought mayhaps his Greek was incorrect or his accent too thick. Lyting's thoughts went to Askel's armband and he quoted it.

" 'The spider yet spins in the halls of the Caesars.' Didst the 'spider' kill Helena?"

"Not the 'spider.' " The older man rounded on Lyting. His eyes gleamed in the shadows shrouding his face. "Beware," he rasped. "Beware the 'scorpion' who sits beneath the throne. The spider does naught but his bidding. But the 'scorpion' poises to strike."

Lyting puzzled his words. The man began to move apart. Did a smile etch his lips? Lyting turned toward Ailinn, who waited silently by his side. But as he looked to her, his gaze alighted on the sarcophagus next to that of Helena's and on the inscription carved on the band beneath its lid.

There, he read: *Alexius Dalassena*.

Lyting reeled and bolted for the man. Catching him by the tunic, he dragged him around. The man tried to jerk free, but the fabric rent, splitting open to reveal a stylized symbol on his left shoulder—a small scorpion created by two letters of the Cyrillic alphabet—an *I* for the stem of the lower body, surmounted by an *omega*, which took on the look of two claws curving above a brief head.

Lyting tightened his grip on the man and began to demand answers, but the rush of footsteps filled his ears, followed by Ailinn's startled scream.

Whirling around, he caught sight of two men dressed in black coming, knives glinting in their hands. Lyting twisted, hurling the older man into them and crashing the trio to the ground. Lyting seized Ailinn and began to run, heading back down the pathway for the main passage. She gave no resistance but ran for all her worth, striving to keep pace with him.

A figure suddenly sprang from behind an aged monument, catching Lyting in the ribs, breaking his clasp of Ailinn and driving him to the ground. Lyting and the man collided with the earth, the impact jolting them apart. Instantly Lyting rolled and came up, clenching his fists and slogging the man's jaw to the heavens, then clouting him hard in the stomach. The man groaned and crumpled to the ground.

Again, Lyting seized hold of Ailinn, and they raced to reach the main path and free the cemetery. Just as they neared it, three men closed off their escape, blocking their way, while a fourth leapt down from the top of a sarcophagus directly behind, cutting off their retreat.

With instant reflex Lyting shoved Ailinn from the path and kicked out to the side, striking the man behind him in the chest and sending him sprawling into the dirt. The others rushed forward, their daggers drawn.

"Come on, Ailinn!"

Lyting grabbed her and pulled her with him as they entered the jungle of graves, darting in and around the them, dodging markers and monuments and slipping around crypts, rushing hurriedly in the direction of the gates. They heard the pounding of feet from behind then the scraping of swords off to the left. Lyting rued his own scabbard was empty.

"The gate!" Ailinn gasped. "I see it ahead. There, between the stones."

Just then another assassin lunged into view, swiping his blade before him horizontally in a wide arch. Lyting pitched to the side, taking Ailinn with him to the ground and covering her at once. The steel rang out overhead, striking the sarcophagus next to them and gashing the hand of a prophet. The man dropped his blade and grabbed his wrist, wincing in pain. Lyting gave him no quarter and rolled, knocking him from his feet. Coming up, he struck the assassin solidly across the jaw and felled him.

Voices called out. Ailinn scrambled to her feet and grasped

Lyting's hand. Together they raced for the iron cemetery gates. Flying through them, the Gate of Charisius came immediately into view, but it appeared the guard was closing it. Lyting called out and madly waved his arm, and Ailinn followed his lead. The guard recognized them from before and blessedly did not try to detain them as they rushed past and reentered the city.

On they rushed, hastening along the Mesê without slowing, but when they heard their assailants' shouts from behind, they abandoned the boulevard and fled down one narrow street after another.

Still, the assassins pursued them like a pack of hounds on the scent. Lyting quickly sprinted through his knowledge of the streets. An inspiration struck.

"Come, Ailinn. This way." He pulled her along. "Just a little farther."

The street ended, opening onto a square. There, Lyting snatched a torch from its iron grip on one of the buildings and quickly swept the brand before him, searching feverishly.

"What are we looking for?" Ailinn panted, breathless.

"Stairs."

Ailinn looked up, but then saw that Lyting was looking down. She searched with him but saw nothing.

"There!" He proclaimed triumphantly and dragged her along with him.

Ailinn saw it, then—a short, steep flight of stone stairs leading into the ground and ending at a door. She followed Lyting. He gave over the torch, forced the door open, then retrieved the torch once more. As he thrust it into the darkness, Ailinn saw that the stairs disappeared into a black abyss below.

"This is it. Hurry." He started downward.

Ailinn swallowed her newborn fears and followed after him, knowing the others would be upon them any instant. Quickly Lyting reclosed the door. They continued a half-dozen steps farther and waited, pressed against the wall. Footsteps tramped above, then faded from hearing.

The place was chill and damp, and Ailinn huddled into her mantle. They continued to wait lest the men return, retracing their steps. When all remained quiet, Ailinn prepared to climb from their sullen prison. Instead, Lyting held out the torch so its light could spill down the stairs. He reached back for her hand.

"Come, Ailinn. This way."

Her eyes grew huge. "This way?" she gasped, none too certain she wished to descend into the inky depths which looked all too fitting a place for beasts to lurk. "What is this, this . . . ?"

"A cistern," he replied easily as he began to descend, obviously undisturbed by thoughts of hidden beasts. "Remember the Aqueduct of Valens? It brings the water here. 'Tis one of the underground reservoirs for holding the city's water supply."

"I hope 'tis all that it holds," Ailinn commented dryly, following Lyting and ignoring his chuckle.

Picking her way down, she counted thirty-nine steps before reaching the bottom one. There, she joined Lyting and looked over the cistern as he held up the torch. They could make out a vast body of water—as though a lake—and rising from it a forest of magnificent marble columns, upholding a vaulted ceiling. Even the capitals of the columns were carved with delicate stonework—a lacy foliage. The cistern looked as though it were a beautiful palace—its water, a shiny floor.

"We can reemerge many streets from here, in another section of the city. Rurik told me that small boats are kept in the cisterns at the various entrances."

He held the torch out and moved it before them. There were none by the steps. A moment later he spied one moored to a nearby column. After giving over the torch to Ailinn, he doffed his mantle and tunic. Their eyes locked when his hands went to his trousers.

Ailinn looked aside, her heart tripping anew. She heard the cloth drop to the step, then the soft splash of water as he entered the cistern. Saints forgive her, but she could not repress the image that rose to mind of Lyting standing naked at the rapids of Essupi.

After he returned with the boat and dressed, they set out on the waters. Lyting rowed in thoughtful silence until he felt Ailinn's eyes upon him and found a curious smile playing on her lips.

"Have you found humor in this night after all we have endured?"

"I was thinking of how quiet, even dull, 'twill be for you behind your monastery walls if we survive this journey and you yet intend to go there."

"I will have memories aplenty to liven my days," he returned lightly, but his look gave Ailinn to realize those memories would be filled with her.

"I, too, shall remember these days. For all time."

Their eyes held, their souls touching at a much deeper level.

Lyting broke the gaze and, relying on his sense of direction, rowed southward while Ailinn held the torch and they glided among the legion of columns.

Lyting forced his mind to the events of the night. 'Twas clear he had been mistaken for Rurik, and that Rurik—and now *he*—was marked for death. Neither of them had anticipated that he might be mistaken for Rurik, himself. Yet, they should have.

At the same time Lyting reminded himself that Ailinn had been seen with him and was possibly in danger as well. He castigated himself for placing her at added risk.

He would need keep her close to him and deliver his message to the Imperials without delay. The "spider's" waiting was at an end, and the "scorpion" was poised to strike.

Much later they emerged from the cistern in another part of the city and made their way cautiously along the darkened streets to Melane's.

Chapter 18

As the first glimmerings of light brightened the skies, Ailinn accompanied Lyting to the Sacred Palace.

Along their walk, Lyting explained his purpose in coming to Constantinople—his mission for his brother, Rurik, and his need to deliver his message and warning to the Augusta, the Empress Zoë. Yet for all he confided, Ailinn suspected he kept much more locked inside himself.

And then there was the matter of the attack in the cemetery last night. Lyting owned that his brother had enemies in the city and assured her the attack was the result of his being mistaken for Rurik.

Still, Lyting had not disclosed what passed between him and the silver-haired man at the crypt, and she guessed his mission held more dangers than he cared to speak of. Not for the first time she looked forward to leaving the golden city. On the day of her arrival she realized Constantinople was not the "light" of which her mother had spoken.

Ailinn shifted her harp from one hip to the other as they entered the Mesê. Lyting's and her goods had arrived late the day before at Melane's. She brought the precious harp with her, for the women of the house showed it such interest, she feared they might abuse it in her absence.

Reaching the boulevard's end, they entered the Augustaeum. To the right, a pair of bronze horses adorned the entrance to the Hippodrome. There, Lyting informed her, the games were held, the chariot races being the first love of the male populace and life of the city. There, too, the factions gathered. The fate of the Caesars had been made and remade when the fires of dissent flamed into riots.

To the left stood the immense Hagia Sophia—"Holy Wisdom"—a ponderous building that rose in stages with buttresses and half-domes supporting a huge central dome overhead. And yet, for all the building's massiveness, a multitude of windows pierced its exterior, including a row just beneath the mammoth dome. In the early morning duskiness she could see that lights burned brilliantly within, God's holy light a beacon to the harbor.

Lyting and Ailinn continued on, along with a multitude of others, streaming toward the palace grounds—people of every station: workers, couriers, diplomats, and senators. It amazed Ailinn still that Lyting's affairs should be so high-placed—with the emperor, Constantine, and the Augusta, Zoë.

"We will enter at the Chalkê Gate." Lyting gestured ahead as they followed the enclosure wall. " 'Tis also called the 'Brazen Entrance' and provides access to the grounds."

Ailinn viewed an exquisite building with magnificent gilded doors and gilded roof—bronze, Lyting informed her. Perfumers' stalls crowded the gate, their sweet scents layering the air and wafting pleasantly through the doors of the vestibule as Lyting and Ailinn entered.

Inside, Ailinn found herself standing in the most dazzling room she had ever seen. A blaze of mosaics covered the walls and ceiling, and multicolored marbles dressed the floor—greens, reds, blues, and white.

"Thord tells me that is Justinian's great general, Belisarius." Lyting pointed to one of the brilliant mosaic scenes. " 'Tis made of *tesserae*—colored glass. The colors are more varied and intense than marble, and many contain gold." He smiled at her astonished look. She obviously had never seen such beauty.

Emerging onto the grounds, Ailinn beheld a rambling complex of buildings in a setting of matchless beauty. Here were shaded walks, gardens, ponds, fountains, and arbors. Here also was a multitude of buildings, each a lovely gem of architecture—some made entirely of a single colored marble:

yellow, verde, or red. Ailinn believed them each to be a palace unto themselves.

Lyting informed her, however, that while some were pavilions of the Imperial Family, others were workshops, storehouses, stables, and government offices such as the Hall of Tribunals with its numerous statues and the Senate building which he pointed out.

Looking to the distance, she saw how the land sloped toward the harbor and looked out to the placid blue waters of the Marmara. For its many thousands of workers and attendants, the grounds possessed a sense of tranquillity.

As they progressed, Ailinn noticed with some surprise that the fashion within the palace grounds was to wear red slippers sewn with pearls. Somehow, she could not imagine Lyting wearing them and secretly smiled at the thought.

For the better part of the morning, Lyting and Ailinn dealt with the cumbrous Byzantine bureaucracy, moving from one official to another, chamber to chamber, building to building.

For all his forbearance, Lyting's patience wore thin. He suspected these men played him a game, using their authority to wield their petty powers and thwart others at will. Some of the eunuchs were obnoxiously imperious. Other officials, more completely endowed, eyed Ailinn openly—one no so subtly suggesting that Lyting and he come to an "arrangement," the object of that arrangement being Ailinn.

Refraining from striking the man and flattening him straight out, Lyting quit the building and escorted Ailinn outside. There he strove to cool his ire and collect himself.

"Ailinn, I regret this has taken so long. Would you prefer to wait on the grounds? There seem to be guards aplenty. You can enjoy the airs and the view of the harbor. There remains one more office Thord suggested I approach. Judging by the last ones, I shouldn't be long."

"Do not hurry yourself." Ailinn smiled, touched by his concern. "I have my harp to entertain me and will wander down the path here and seek a place to rest."

Lyting touched her cheek in parting, sending a shiver through her. Ailinn watched as he strode back toward one of the fine buildings and disappeared inside. Glancing about, she deemed that naught in all of Eire could compare to this. Her homeland seemed an impoverished country by comparison.

Even Hedeby, which once struck her as so advanced, seemed piteously rustic measured to the Imperial City.

Turning, Ailinn strolled down along the path, noticing peacocks, ibis, and pheasants wandering about the grounds. She happened on one fountain and found wine springing from a golden pineapple into a marble basin filled with almonds and pistachios.

She soon came to a small but lovely pavilion, its colonnade lined with alternating columns of green and red onyx. It seemed a quiet place, tucked away, adorned with shrubbery, and overlooking its own private garden, which in turn stretched toward the Marmara.

Ailinn discovered a marble bench sitting before the seaward side of the pavilion and settled herself there. Looking out over the waters, her senses filled with the mingled fragrances of the sea and its incredible beauty.

Utterly content, she slipped the wrapping from her harp. Assured she would neither disturb nor be disturbed by anyone, she plucked out a run of notes, then began a simple but enchanting melody, one she had loved as a child. She sang it softly, closing her eyes as she gave herself to its lilting tune.

Ailinn's lashes parted. She thought to hear a rustling amongst the shrubbery. She suspected an errant bird to be caught there and continued to sing. Again, came a rustle of leaves. Glancing to her left, she found a young boy standing amid the greens where he had been hiding.

She continued to play and sing, for his eyes were intent upon her hands. Though he did not smile, he appeared mesmerized as her fingers stroked the strings and brought them joyously to life.

He eased from the bushes and quietly came to sit beside her. As she sang, she slipped a glance to him. He was a fine-looking lad—slim and broad-shouldered. His face was somewhat long, his nose slightly aquiline, and his eyes a pale but brilliant blue. The child possessed little color and appeared of frail constitution. Yet, as he studied her fingers, light brightening his eyes, she suspected a sharp and curious mind.

On she played, with a flourish of runs and trills, thinking in the back of her mind how the boy's garments alone—a stiff brocade shot through with gold and lavishly adorned with gems—would make her a wealthy woman for a lifetime at home. How opulent were the ways of the Byzantine nobility, that even their children should be dressed thusly.

Ailinn's curiosity grew of the child. She brought her song to a close, hoping to find a way to communicate with him. But as her fingers stilled, such disappointment flooded his features that, once more, she took up another song.

He smiled in earnest, transforming his features entirely, a liveliness coming into his eyes. Thinking he might like to play the harp, Ailinn continued to sing while she took her hand and patted the space beside her, indicating he should move there. When he did, she transferred the harp over to his lap and demonstrated how he could pick out a little run of notes.

A jubilant smile spread over the child's face as he set the strings aquiver and the harp began to sing.

Lyting grumbled in his thoughts, disgusted anew with Byzantine bureaucracy. He wished Thord were here to help him through the maze of officials and paperwork. His introduction—the cloth of purple and gold *solidus* of Leo VI—had thus far closed more doors than it had opened, and had raised considerable suspicion.

Again he thought of Thord. Though an officer, Thord was not a member of the inner circle of the Guard. They would need engage the help of the Akolouthos, or Acolyte—the head of the Varangian Guard—in order to seek an audience with the Imperials. Even then he could expect a period of waiting—a week or more—before he would be called to the throne room.

But he didn't have a week, Lyting thought with frustration. And perhaps neither did Zoë and her son.

Making his way down the path and toward the water, where he had left Ailinn, Lyting caught sight of her fiery tresses where she sat before a small pavilion, partially hidden by the shrubbery there. He headed toward her.

As he approached, he saw in the shelter of the green a lad of about ten years sitting next to her—dressed in shimmering robes of gold and on his feet, slippers of Imperial purple.

Lyting threw himself prostrate to the ground at once, realizing this to be none other than the child emperor, Constantine Porphyrogentius, Emperor of the Byzantine Empire.

"Ailinn. Get down!" Lyting called through his teeth.

"What?" Hearing Lyting's voice, Ailinn looked up and to her astonishment found him lying prone on the ground.

"Prostrate yourself, if you do not wish to loose a limb or be run straight through," he called urgently again.

Ailinn blanched, but before she could move, shouts sounded all around. There was a sudden rumble of feet and scraping of swords leaving their scabbards as soldiers rushed in from three directions and surrounded them.

Looking up, Lyting saw a retinue of officials, guards, and noblewomen sweep into view, hurriedly traversing the colonnade—and leading them all, a woman of striking beauty, dressed in resplendent robes of deep royal purple, a heavy diadem crowning her head—emblazoned with jewels and having strands of pearls cascading from the crown to her shoulders.

Lyting looked in awe upon the Augusta, the Empress Zoë.

Zoë whisked her gaze about, taking in the scene before her with her large dark eyes—eyes as black as coals. Her gaze touched her son, then Ailinn, then moved to Lyting.

Lyting prostrated himself twice more, all the while praying most earnestly that Ailinn would follow his example. The guards closed in about him and hauled him to his feet so the empress might better view him.

Looking on his features fully, the empress's hand flew to the great jeweled collar where it covered her heart.

"Rurik!" she gasped, astounded.

Her elegant brows pulled slowly together as her eyes shifted to Lyting's snow-pale hair. Her head tilted ever so slightly. "Rurik?"

"Majesty." Lyting bowed.

Straightening, he reached for the enameled box in his tunic. The soldiers stopped him abruptly, aiming their spears at his heart. One searched his tunic and, locating the box, presented it to the empress as she came forward.

Zoë smoothed her fingers over the box, a look of recognition flickering across her eyes. She opened it, then paused as she gazed on the cloth of purple. Fingering it aside, she lifted the golden *solidus* of Leo VI. Taking the coin, she pressed the image of her husband to her lips and closed her lashes.

"Majesty," Lyting began again. "I am *Lyting* Atlison, brother of Rurik the Varangian, who once served Leo Sophos and yourself and son so faithfully. I have traveled a great distance from the West to bear you his greetings and a missive most urgent."

Zoë opened her eyes and searched Lyting's face. She smiled and nodded, comprehension in her dark eyes.

"These be troubled times," she said in a voice rich and clear. " 'Tis good that an Atlison returns to Constantinople and the house of the Macedonians."

Lyting released a long-held breath as the guards withdrew their weapons. Slipping a glance to Ailinn, he saw that she sat speechless beside the young emperor.

A smiling warmth spread through his chest. Thanks to Ailinn, the critical contact had been made with the Imperials. He hoped the conspiracy could quickly be unraveled and put to a rest, and they could sail homeward, at last.

Ailinn relaxed in the warm, soothing waters, resting her head back upon a small pillow at the edge of the sunken pool and allowing her legs to float upward.

The pool was circular, lined with rich and pristine white marbles in a sunburst pattern—the undulating strips of blue radiating outward from the center and outlined with gold. She hoped Lyting enjoyed such luxury. After meeting the Imperials, they had been immediately separated, she taken to women's quarters by the empress's ladies-in-waiting, and he . . .

Ailinn's brows winged downward. She knew not where he had been taken, only that he left with the empress, her officials, and an armed guard.

Ailinn released a soft breath as she thought back on the encounter in the garden. Lyting had neglected to tell her that the emperor was a child of ten, or warn her of the strict formalities of court. She could not fault him, however. He had expected to gain a private audience.

The sound of feminine voices filled her ears and beckoned her back to her present surroundings. She trailed her gaze about the room, to the elegant court ladies who inhabited the quarters and the servants who attended them, to the silken draperies, brocaded pillows, silver tables, and ivory chairs.

Such splendor, Ailinn thought languidly and closed her eyes. Who could have thought such a place existed?

* * *

Lyting reclined in a sunken pool of veined jasper, as its steamy waters slowly extracted the day's tensions from deep in his muscles. His inmost core felt more liquid than bone. Shuttering his eyes, he lay back his head and reflected on his audience with the empress.

The first thing he had learned was that Zoë was never unattended. That he should have foreseen. A "private" audience included the central members of her Council of Eunuchs, and her personal guard.

Thord had been summoned to help interpret for him as needed and verify what he knew of Lyting's encounters since entering the city.

Thord allayed Lyting's fears as to the loyalty of the council members and whether they might be part to the conspiracy. Eunuchs, he informed, however one might regard their personal deficiencies, were highly respected members of society, holding some of the most distinguished ranks in the Imperial service. Only the throne and the chair of the Patriarch were barred from them. Without families to support and sons to inherit or intrigue for, they dedicated themselves to their offices, holding them on merit alone.

Still, Lyting worried about a dalliance for a relative, and Zoë agreed to dismiss all but two of her most trusted members of the council. They remained, as did two of the Varangian Guards, whose loyalty was also undisputed.

"Eunuchs," Lyting muttered, outstretching his legs.

All in all, the audience with Zoë went well. The empress, as expected, knew of the Varangians' deaths. She was also aware, during the reign of her husband Leo, that the person behind the plot was close to the throne. But the shadowy figure had disappeared without a trace after the plot was foiled, as Rurik had said.

Zoë suspected the man served Alexander. When Leo died and Alexander seized the throne, she feared greatly for her son. During that time, she had been imprisoned in a nunnery. Those were grave days. Days she dreaded that the one behind the plot would reemerge and see her son dead.

But if the man still lived, Alexander, once crowned, harkened to no one—profligate, waste of a man that he was. Alexander even plotted to make Constantine a eunuch so he could never inherit. Blessedly, Alexander died, but many more plots were afoot.

The empress reminded Lyting with severe, unsmiling eyes that she and her son had many enemies. There were numerous factions within the city. And of course, there remained her implacable enemy, the Patriarch, Nicholas Mysticus who still sniffed the road to find a way back to power.

Lyting sank deeper into the waters.

Over the years the man behind the palace plots had remained so quiet Zoë, herself, thought him to be dead. Until the last year. Then, one by one, the Varangians began to die. None of the deaths had occurred on palace grounds, and the man's proximity to the throne remained unclear. Obviously, the deaths were not the work of one person.

As the audience with Zoë continued, Lyting informed her of the parchment from Dyrrachium. This he presented to her. She and her officials examined the missive and its contents carefully. Lyting offered Rurik's suspicions as to why Askel the Red had ventured out of Constantinople and joined the army. He then brought forth the armband and read them the inscription.

Zoë paled, realizing that truly the "spider" must be within the palace itself. She had hoped against hope that she need not concern herself with the elusive conspirator. This year there had been a war to oversee against the Persians, and the threat of the Bulgarians to quell after their seizure of Adrianople and their attack on Dyrrachium.

Zoë had paused at that, her black eyes sharpening with thought. The *strategos*, or general, who led the troops to Dyrrachium had recently returned and was present within the palace complex. The council would question him.

Lyting warned Zoë that perhaps the man had been waiting for Rurik's return, wishing to eliminate the last Dragon, before he turned on herself and Constantine. He also spoke of Helena, the attack on himself and Ailinn in the cemetery, and his revelation that Helena had been poisoned. Zoë's eyes had narrowed at that, as though culling through distant memories as to who had been at Helena's bedside when she died.

Though Askel's arm cuff alluded to a "spider," the assassin Lyting encountered in the cemetery spoke of a "scorpion" sitting beneath the throne. According to him, the spider served the scorpion.

Then there was the gravings on the band, the mark on the man's shoulder. This was the first time a definite symbol could be associated with that man and it could be established that a circle of conspirators existed, its members bearing this personal emblem.

Lyting concluded that the person they sought must be very near, indeed, and ready to strike. Once he knew that he was not Rurik, and that Rurik was still beyond his reach, 'twas likely the "scorpion" would make his strike.

Fortunately, Rurik had narrowed his personal suspicions, and though the list was by no means conclusive, Lyting voiced those names for the empress.

Zoë recognized the names of men who had risen in rank over the past years—all advanced under the reign of Alexander. She hoped the list contained not only the "scorpion," but the "spider" as well.

At that, the empress, he, Thord, and the council members discussed how they might flush out the conspirators. At their parting, Zoë announced that they would all dine together this evening, officially, in honor of Atlison's return. Those who fell under Rurik's suspicions would be invited, as would several others where her own suspicions fell.

Lyting drew a wet hand over his face, bringing himself back to the present. Tonight he would dine with a murderer. Or two. He hoped Ailinn was well protected within the women's quarters.

A smile spread over his lips. 'Twas probably the safest place for her, with the eunuch guards protecting her from palace enemies and enamoured men like himself.

He thought on how she looked in the thin veil of a gown at Melane's and felt a familiar warmth in his loins.

Ailinn lay naked on a linen-draped bench, while one of the capable servants worked precious scented oils into her skin and massaged her from head to toe.

Another servant came forth, wrapping her in soft toweling and leading her to a pillowed chair. Ailinn waited as they fetched clothing, feeling wondrously alive yet deeply relaxed, tingly from head to toe.

One noblewomen, she noted, appeared to be overseeing her. She was a handsome woman with distinct features, ebony hair and kohl-lined eyes, which lent them a hardness. She had been present on the colonnade with the empress, in search of the young emperor. Ailinn had not missed her interest in Lyting, either. As the woman's eyes shifted to her, Ailinn felt a coolness in their depths. A little chill skipped along her spine.

Ailinn stood for the servants to dress her. Again she wondered idly of the woman as she received the undergown over her head, a soft teal color and having close-fitting sleeves. Over this, they draped a stole of patterned silk—a golden yellow flecked with red. To this they added the familiar red slippers embroidered with pearls.

Sitting her before a table covered with little glass jars of pomades and cosmetics, the servants dressed her hair, catching it up and twining ropes of creamy pearls in its dark fires. They then affixed a veil of palest gold to the back of her head. Ailinn knew that when she stood, it would reach to the floor behind her. When they sought to darken her eyes and tint her lips she declined.

As they handed her a mirror, Ailinn caught sight of a young girl standing silently behind her, to the right side. She was a lovely child—of Constantine's age—elegantly dressed and holding an ivory rod inlaid with mother-of-pearl. Her eyes, though directed to Ailinn, seemed vacant. Ailinn had seen the look before. The child was blind.

As Ailinn turned to her, the child gave a slight bow.

"My lady, I am Ariana Comnena. I am to be your interpreter," she said in precise Frankish, surprising Ailinn.

Ailinn smiled, utterly delighted. "And I am Ailinn. You speak the tongue of Francia quite well."

"I speak many tongues. I serve as a court interpreter. 'Tis a most important position," Ariana informed, quite serious and adultlike. "People of every land fill our city, and interpreters are in great need at court."

"And Frankish is one of your languages?"

"*Oui,*" the girl continued without a trace of accent. A small smile followed. " 'Twas one of my first tongues to master. My mother's sister is wed to a Frankish noble, who once served as an ambassador and later chose to remain."

"I am pleased you will help ease my stay here, Ariana,"

Ailinn confessed truthfully. "I know nothing of court formalities and have no friends in the women's quarters."

Ariana smiled, an elfish smile, the child appearing.

"Then we shall be friends." She stepped forward and held forth her hand, seeking Ailinn's. Ailinn took hold of her slim hand and gave a gentle squeeze.

"I would like that very much, Ariana."

The dark-haired noblewoman moved to join them, but before she could speak, Ariana presented her to Ailinn.

"This is Xenia Calaphates, lady-in-waiting to the Augusta Zoë."

Ailinn wondered if the child recognized the woman by her scent—a sharp, clear mixture of spices and aromatic oils. Xenia bent slightly and spoke with the child.

"We have been summoned to dine in the Daphne Palace. 'Tis one of the seven royal residences and has a most luxurious dining chamber. But do not worry, we needn't go outside. Many passages connect the palaces."

Ailinn realized by the child's words that the women here preferred to remain indoors, shunning the fresh airs. Such a thought was unfathomable to herself. She glanced about the room for her discarded clothing, which were in fact Melane's. Neither they nor her harp were in sight.

"Ariana, do you know what has become of my belongings?"

The child spoke to Xenia, who, in turn, indicated the servants who had taken the items. Ariana stiffened at the mention of one name, then crossed the room, using her ivory wand to assure no furniture stood in her path. She spoke firmly to one of the servants. When the servant brought forth only the clothes, Ariana promptly redressed her, surprising Ailinn. A moment later the servant retrieved the harp.

Ariana returned and gave over the items to Ailinn.

"You must watch out for that one. She is a thief," Ariana counseled solemnly. "If you wish, I can have your possessions locked into my own coffer."

Ailinn agreed to this, and Ariana called over another servant, giving her explicit instructions. With that accomplished, the young girl led Ailinn from the suite of rooms, down one of the passages of the complex that linked the palaces and contained some of the workrooms and factories of the noblewomen. Xenia accompanied them, as did several other ladies. Ariana followed the wall and used the ivory rod to tap along it and give her her bearings.

" 'Tis a wondrously fragrant wing," Ailinn marveled, breaking the silence.

"We near Xenia's workrooms. She is brilliant at combining scents and has her own perfumery. The scented soaps and oils used in your bath were provided by her factory. Most all the women of the *gynaekeion* busy themselves in some such enterprise."

The child spoke to Xenia, appraising her of Ailinn's comment.

"Xenia would be pleased for you to visit her workrooms and make a selection from her collection for yourself."

"That is very generous of her." Ailinn's gaze slipped to Xenia, whose eyes still seemed especially cool and hard. Ailinn's curiosity nipped at her, wondering what lay behind the look Xenia had given Lyting earlier. Ailinn bit the inside of her cheek, then, against better judgment, decided to question her.

"Ariana, would you ask Xenia if she knows Lyting Atlison." 'Twas impossible she could. Lyting had never been in the city before, but she posed the question nonetheless.

At the noblewoman's reply, Ariana interpreted. "Xenia knew his brother, Rurik, when he served amongst the Varangians."

This mildly surprised Ailinn. She culled through what Lyting had told her of his brother's time here. Aside from Rurik's station amongst the Guard and his foiling a palace plot, Lyting had revealed only that his brother once loved the beauty Helena, whose grave they had visited last evening. He had departed the city after her death.

Ailinn slipped a glance to Xenia. She had an icy aloofness about her. Ailinn's instincts told her that Rurik's acquaintance with the woman was not of an amorous nature.

"Then, mayhaps Xenia also knew Helena Dalassena." Ailinn ventured and noted how, when the child interpreted her words, the pupils of Xenia's eyes constricted to dots and her mouth thinned. Still, she answered in even, controlled tones.

"Xenia knew her well. Not only were they friends and both lived here in the women's quarters, but Xenia cared for Helena on her deathbed."

Ailinn looked to Xenia, somehow finding it difficult to think of this woman, who seemed marble beneath the exterior, befriending anyone so dearly.

"How very kind. And how devastating to have a friend die beneath your hands."

In truth, Ailinn was unsure how Helena did die. Lyting had indicated only that a sickness took her swiftly. Nothing more.

Strangely, Xenia made no response as they continued along the halls. She walked straight-spined, her chin lifted, the faintest of curves touching her lips.

Entering the Daphne Palace, Lyting and Thord traversed the resplendent hall. They strode past glittering mosaics depicting emperors and empresses of long ago. The marble beneath their feet was inlaid with designs of eagles, their wings outstretched. Chinese scent burners fragranced the halls, and tables encrusted with mother-of-pearl lined the walls.

Lyting gave the luxuries a cursory glance, his thoughts quickening ahead to the prospect of seeing Ailinn.

Emerging from the passageway and entering the main hall of the palace, Ailinn passed in awe of the silver columns and great lengths of purple dye-stuffs draped from ceiling to floor and tied back with gilded cords. The lower portions of the walls gleamed of a marble so pure, they appeared to be made of crystal.

Ailinn's step slowed, a thrill racing through her as her gaze fixed on Lyting, approaching from ahead. He moved with strength and fluidity, resplendent in Byzantine garments—the fabric midnight blue shot with silver. About his shoulders he wore a scarlet mantle which contrasted with his bright, shining hair and set it off to advantage.

Lyting, too, slowed his step on seeing Ailinn. She was a vision of breathtaking beauty.

As their steps closed together and the fires stirred in his veins, he knew without doubt, 'twas good they were lodged separately, she with a guard barring her door. Saints' breath, he could give no assurance that his ironclad restraint would not dissolve altogether if he were enclosed in a room with Ailinn one more night.

As Lyting and Thord joined the women in the hallway, Lyting proffered his arm to Ailinn. She accepted, her touch pure fire. Ailinn smiled on Lyting, scarce able to breath, heat darting up her arm from where her hand lay atop his. Together, they walked side by side, the splendor of the hall fading to nothingness.

Thord led the party to the Imperial dining chamber. On entering the room, Lyting was keenly disappointed to see that the women were to dine at a table separate from the men's. Reluctantly he escorted Ailinn to her place.

Not until that moment did he realize that the young girl who accompanied them was blind, so well did she handle herself in the hall. He aided her, also, and the other women as well, one of whom Ailinn introduced as Xenia, lady-in-waiting to Zoë. The child, she explained, was Ariana her interpreter.

Xenia held Lyting's gaze as she sank to her cushioned chair. He paused for a moment, unsure of what he saw glimmering in the depths of her eyes, if indeed he had seen anything. He then excused himself and went to take his place beside Thord at the banqueting table.

As he settled into his chair, he saw how the other men's interest lingered over Ailinn. Their wolfish looks touched a raw nerve, not that his was any less so.

At that moment the young emperor and his mother, Zoë, arrived. Immediately everyone moved to prostrate themselves. Once the empress had joined the women's table and the emperor the men's and everyone resettled themselves, the servants brought forth platters of roasted meats—pork stuffed with garlic, game, and poultry—varied sauces, asparagus, salad greens, little round biscuits, and stewed fruits.

As Ailinn began to address the sumptuous fare, she could not help but stop and look twice. Like the doors to the room, the table was made of ivory, inlaid with gold and mother-of-pearl. Each place was set with spoons, knives, and small two-pronged forks, all of gleaming silver, as were the plates.

The tiny fork baffled her. She was only familiar with large ones, used in cooking to tend and skewer sizable portions of meat. She glanced about the table to see how the others handled their utensils, especially the little fork, and thought it safest to follow the example of the empress.

Lyting brought his eyes from Ailinn as Thord began to make his introduction and those who collected at the emperor's table. Young Constantine sat directly across from him, and to his left, the High Admiral of the Imperial Fleet, the Drungarius, Romanus Lecapenus.

Lyting recalled Arnór's words when they first entered the Golden Horn and saw his flagship. This, then, would be the Armenian peasant, who had worked his way up through the ranks and secured the exalted position of Drungarius by appointment of Alexander. Lyting studied him closely. Thord had forewarned him that the Drungarius was a hard man, though not cruel. At the moment, Thord was retelling a story of Romanus's youth, that of his killing a lion single-handedly.

Next, Thord presented the Domesticus of the Scholae, Leo Phocas, Supreme Commander of the Empire's land forces. Leo, Thord informed, was the son of the great general Nicephorus. Thord also praised Leo as a great military leader in his own right.

Leo was a favorable-looking man, with golden brown hair, obviously aristocratic by his appearance and bearing. Lyting remembered the wager Arnór wished to make and wondered himself whether the aristocratic general or the peasant admiral would win over the other in time to come.

Thord continued, presenting the Logothete, Leonites Byrennius, Counselor to the Emperor and Director of Imperial Policy.

Next came the Eparch, Sergius Bardanes, Governor of Byzantium and overseer of trade.

And finally, and perhaps most interestingly, Andronicus Styliane, famed and heroic general, one of the *strategos* of the land forces, freshly returned from Dyrrachium. 'Twas under his man that Askel the Red had served. And died.

Many questions crouched in Lyting's mind, but he held his peace. Zoë had delivered the suspected men with those of her own choice as she said she would. Possibly, one of the men at table was the one they sought. Mayhaps, two.

As the courses were taken away and bowls of dates, figs, and almonds brought, Zoë came to sit between her son and Leo Phocas. An indication of the empress's favor? Lyting couldn't help but wonder. Though the men continued to eat, she did not partake of anything.

Lyting's gaze strayed to Ailinn, inhaling her beauty, then he reined in his wayward lust as he knew he must. He saw that the men present were no less immune to Ailinn.

When the Eparch's thin, nasal voice rose above the others, questioning Lyting of his presence in Constantinople, Lyting briefly appraised those gathered of his mission in Rurik's stead—that a conspiracy existed close to the throne. One which he hoped to expose for he brought new information to the throne.

Lyting drew on his wine, waiting for a reaction. After a measured moment, he settled his interest on Andronicus Styliane.

"Mayhaps you can help me. I understand that you have just returned from Dyrrachium." Lyting confronted the issue that so taxed him. "Would you know of the death of a Varangian named Askel the Red, or of a man named Stephanites Cerularius, head of one of the units of spearmen?"

Andronicus shook his head. "I remember the incident of the Varangian's death. He was found in the desert, dead, the morning after his watch. But I have no one serving under me by the name of Cerularius. I can have the roles checked, if you like, but I can assure you that I know each of my men who lead the infantry units, the *skutatos*. There is no Stephanites Cerularius serving me. The man does not exist."

Lyting sat back in his chair, trying to keep the surprise from his face. More Byzantine duplicity? he wondered. Who then sent the parchment from Dyrrachium?

"Do you remember anything of significance concerning Askel?" Lyting pressed.

Andronicus pondered the question. Again he shook his head.

"A symbol perhaps? One he might have scratched out on the desert floor or had marked upon his person?"

"What kind of symbol?"

"A small scorpion, made with two letters of the Cyrillic alphabet—the *omega* and the *I*."

The Strategos's eyes narrowed fractionally. Did anyone else's? Lyting wondered, his still fixed on Andronicus.

"Best take care, Atlison," the Strategos warned, easing back in his chair. "If those behind the plot believe you to be your brother, or that you have the full knowledge that he does about the matter, your hours could be numbered. They could be plotting your demise even as we sup."

Andronicus's gaze moved to Ailinn, and he skimmed her

closely, sending a burr up Lyting's back. "They might have their eyes on the spoils as well. Best move with care, Atlison."

"I intend to." Lyting's gaze did not waver.

Disliking the new bent to the conversation that encompassed Ailinn, Lyting decided to seize it straight forth and pull it back.

"Be assured, my brother kept nothing from me. And since my arrival, I've gained further information to refine his suspicions."

He stretched forth his arm on the table, revealing the wide, silver band of Askel the Red.

"Those names are graven on the underside of this arm cuff. Now I only await the answers to several questions, which I have already put forth," he fabricated. "Then will we know the name of the 'scorpion' *and* the 'spider' who serves him in the 'palace of the Caesars.'"

Lyting's gaze moved around the table, from man to man. He knew he had baited the trap and now felt very much like the prey waiting for the lion to strike.

The Norseman moved along the darkening Mesê, stopping at one of the open air establishments that offered ale and wine and skewers of braised meat.

The streetside, immediately before it, was jammed with tables where customers drank, relaxed in good humor, and exchanged the day's gossip. The owner stood behind a waist-high marble counter, serving from huge jars sunken into its surface.

The Norseman thrust his fingers through his dark gold hair, shoving it back, as he stepped to the counter. Slapping down a small coin, he ordered a goblet of ale, speaking in heavily accented Greek.

Relieving the vendor of the vessel, he took a quenching draft, wiped his mouth with the back of hand, then eyed the people crowding the counter and those sitting at the small tables on the walk. He turned once more to the merchant, speaking loud enough for all to hear.

"I seek a kinsman of mine, tall and pale-haired, with a scar on his left cheek."

One of the Byzantines twisted halfway round, supporting himself on the counter. A smile quirked the side of his mouth as he looked at the Norseman with a bleary eye.

"There be many of your pale-haired kinsmen in the city, *all* with scars of some description." He cackled and gulped down a mouthful of drink.

The Norseman hardened his gaze over the man. "This one you would remember. His hair is white as snow, and he travels with a beautiful woman."

"I know of such a man."

The Norseman pivoted toward the voice and found a thickset man, sitting at a small table with two women draped over him, one on either side, obviously street whores. The man wore a black coat and wide red sash about his expansive middle. His jet-black hair and beard were carefully curled and oiled. A Syrian.

The Norseman moved to stand before him.

"And the woman?"

"If the beauty be crowned with dark-red tresses."

The Norseman nodded darkly.

"You have business with your pale-haired kinsman?" the Syrian probed, though his tone sounded naught but of idle curiosity.

"Business at the end of my blade," the Norseman stated tersely.

Satisfaction suffused the Syrian's eyes. "The man you seek is with the Varangians. Not those who serve with the armies, mind you, but with the Palace Guard."

The Norseman downed the contents of his cup. His eyes glittered as he directed them down the Mesê in the direction of the palace.

"What is his crime?" the Syrian asked with intense curiosity.

"He erred," the Norseman replied. "He left me alive. Now he shall pay most dearly and return all that is mine."

Chapter 19

Lyting emerged from the Varangian barracks with Thord, into the freshening airs of early morn, and headed toward the *gynaekeion*, engaged in light conversation. His thoughts ran ahead, heartening at the prospect of seeing Ailinn.

As they verged on the central grounds of the complex, they found them to be in an uproar, with guards and ladies-in-waiting rushing about. Several called out in their direction.

Thord chuckled, cracking a smile. "They wish us to join them. 'Twould seem our little emperor has disappeared once more. This time he has vanished with Ailinn and the girl, Ariana."

Lyting shot him a look. "Vanished? By will or abduction?"

Thord's gaze locked with Lyting's, the dread possibility dawning in his eyes. Together, they hastened to join the others, forestalling and questioning those they encountered.

The three had been sighted earlier at the menagerie. Someone else glimpsed them a short time later at the Imperial stables. Word next flew that they had been spotted entering the Magnaura Palace, which overlooked the harbor.

Lyting and Thord hastened down the wooded slope, Thord in the lead. As they verged on the building, they glimpsed the empress as she disappeared inside, followed by the Domesticus, the Drungarius, and a bevy of guards and noblewomen, including the lady Xenia.

Moments later Lyting and Thord bolted through the grand

entrance doors and into the palace, trailing them. A great racket of noise drew their attention to where a pair of silver doors stood ajar, the growly roar of lions and twitterings of birdsong issuing forth.

"This way," Thord urged, calling behind. "Should have guessed it, myself. He has taken her to see the 'Throne of Solomon.'"

Before Lyting could respond, Thord quickened his pace and passed through the silver doors. Lyting heeled after him, catching up in the next instance.

Entering the throne room, the roars and chirpings assailed Lyting's ears, much increased in volume. With the exception of Zoë, all those within lay prostrate upon the floor before six gleaming white marble steps that led to a bare platform. To either side stood trees of gilded bronze, aglitter with jewels. Mechanical birds filled their branches, each bird singing a melody specific to its type.

Beside the trees, guarding the vacant space, were two gilded lions. Their tails flogged the ground as they roared with open mouths and exposed their shivering tongues.

Lyting followed the gaze of those who lay prone, for they all looked upward toward the ceiling. Then he, too, gasped and fell prostrate upon the floor. Making his obeisance, he raised upward and again looked to the ceiling. Hovering there, far above, was a gilded throne—the "Throne of Solomon." On its wide seat, with legs dangling down, sat the Emperor Constantine, fingering the Irish harp in his arms, and beside him, Ailinn and Ariana.

Lyting's breath caught in his chest at the incredulous sight. Slowly he regained his feet, praying the three wouldn't plummet to the ground in the next instant.

The Drungarius called up to the emperor, urging him in a forceful voice to return the throne to its proper place on the marbled platform. Instead, Constantine gave his attention to the harp and plucked its strings.

A moment later the boy emperor leaned forward, giving everyone below a start. He fixed his gaze on the Drungarius. Lyting strained to understand as he began to speak.

"'Tis my thought to ask the fair Ailinn to be my consort," he announced in a youthful but imperious voice. "When I come of age, of course."

Romanus's color darkened and his jaw hardened. Lyting's

heart did a little flip-over as he compassed the younger emperor's words. Before Lyting could respond himself, the Domesticus stepped forward to cajole the emperor into lowering the throne. Still, Constantine hovered above the room with Ailinn and Ariana and picked out a run of notes.

Zoë stepped forth, her spine stiffening as she moved apart from the others and called to her son. Her voice carried clearly, stern and unyielding, instructing him to bring the throne down to its proper place and at once.

Constantine pressed his lips to a thin pout but complied, touching something unseen on the arm of the throne. Slowly the immense chair began to descend. The lions and birds quieted as the throne poised above the steps.

Constantine's smile returned. "*Mitera*, Mother, we visited the cheetahs. Ailinn was greatly surprised that we use them to hunt bears. But she was most surprised of all by our giraffes from Affrike. I think they frightened her."

"Very well, Constantine. Mayhaps you will wish to escort Ailinn further about the palace grounds, but later. And *with* a guard," Zoë added gently but firmly. "Now, 'tis time to take our meal in the Pearl Palace, as you requested earlier."

Constantine brightened and turned to Ailinn. "You will enjoy the Pearl Palace. 'Tis one of the most beauti—"

He broke off his words at the sight of the Eparch, Sergius Bardanes, hastening into the throne room.

After prostrating himself the required times, the Eparch rose and turned to the empress, Zoë, and to the Domesticus and the Drungarius who flanked her.

"Majesty, I bear news of the greatest urgency." He turned and leveled a finger directly at Lyting. "There be evidence that this Atlison is a thief and a liar and not to be trusted. He speaks of scorpions and spiders, yet 'tis he, himself, who is a threat to the crown. I challenge whether he is even the man whom he claims to be."

Zoë's gaze leapt to Lyting while the guards immediately surrounded him, training the points of their spears at his chest.

Ailinn gave forth a small cry, trusting them not at all and fearing they would run Lyting through.

Lyting lifted his crystal-blue eyes to hers and with a slight shake of his head indicated for her not to move. At the same time Ariana interpreted for Ailinn the exchange that had taken place below.

Zoë's coal-black eyes returned to the Eparch. "What evidence do you hold?" she asked, her voice cool and even.

"Majesty, outside awaits Nikas Aristakes, our newly appointed Minister of Trade. He has long overseen the city's silk production and dealt with the Norse traders who sought its export. One such trader has come forth this season to press a complaint. 'Twould seem he sailed from the West in the company of a certain man, a man who robbed him of his goods and slave and left him to die."

The Eparch turned and targeted his game.

"The man he names is Lyting Atlison."

Hushed gasps and utterances sounded among the ladies-in-waiting and guardsmen, while the Eparch signaled the guard at the door. He, in turn, gestured to someone without. Two men entered immediately, one following the other. First came a corpulent man, dressed in jewels and fine silks, bald but full-bearded and having a nervous tick at the corner of one eye. Behind him strode Hakon.

Ailinn gasped audibly from her perch, drawing the attention of both men to herself. She shrank back against the throne as their eyes fastened on her.

Just as quickly their gazes dropped away, and they sank to the floor in accordance with court formalities. Hakon followed the minister's lead as they prostrated themselves. After the third time they rose once more.

Nikas's gaze returned to Ailinn, swiftly measuring her, while Hakon's eyes slashed boldly over Lyting, his look triumphant. Hakon's gaze then shifted toward the great Throne of Solomon which still hovered a man's height above its marble platform.

Studying Nikas, Lyting guessed him to be the man with whom Skallagrim had conducted his dealings in the silk trade—the man with the collection of concubines and for whom Ailinn had been originally destined. Lyting's blood began to boil at the thought of this man's hands—or any man's hands—moving over Ailinn.

Nikas assessed Ailinn with hungry, greedy eyes as though he expected to have her still. Obviously, Hakon had revealed Ailinn to be the maid Skallagrim intended for him and promised her still for Nikas's intervention.

But Hakon would never release Ailinn, Lyting knew. 'Twas assuredly a ruse, baiting the minister to gain the necessary audience and make his accusations. To that end, Hakon's intent would be to see Lyting arrested and to reclaim Ailinn. Lyting wondered what plans Hakon harbored for Nikas once the deed was done.

Nikas turned on Lyting then, his animosity manifest.

"Is it not true that you encountered the chieftain, Skallagrim, in Hedeby and also first saw there his beautiful slave and sought her purchase?"

"Já," Lyting responded, his inner defenses rising.

"And is it not also true that you subsequently arranged passage with the chieftain and his nephew, to sail in their company and that of the girl, eastward to Constantinople?"

"Satt. True. But his was the only vessel departing—"

"Is it not the custom of those merchants who sail together in convoy, in the same ship, to also share equally in the profit of the goods they transport and protect?"

"Já . . ."

"Yet, you brought no goods. Indeed, you paid for the privilege of transport, traveling as an emissary, and did not rightfully have claim to any of their goods."

Lyting did not respond, a muscle leaping along his jaw.

"Mayhaps you would recount for us the perils your convoy endured in the land of the Rus," Nikas said with overweening confidence. "Tell us of the attack of the tribesmen—those lost in battle, and those purposely left behind to perish."

Romanus vented an impatient breath. "What is your point, Nikas?"

The minister impaled Lyting with his dark, gleaming eyes. "When the chieftain, Skallagrim, was killed in the clash of arms, Hakon rightfully inherited all that was his uncle's. But Atlison preyed upon him, desiring the wealth of furs and coveting the girl for himself. He would have us believe he is to be entrusted, yet Atlison left this man, Hakon, to die in the Steppes and proceeded to steal his goods, including Hakon's sole remaining slave."

Nikas gestured to Ailinn where she sat, her ear bent to Ariana as the girl interpreted the minister's accusations. Fear clutched at Ailinn with each new pronouncement. Desperately her gaze sought Lyting's.

Hakon stepped forth then, and with Nikas's aid in translation, corroborated all that had been said, imparting the tale of the attack of the tribesmen which left his uncle dead and

himself to claim right to all that was the chieftain's. He then
twisted the facts surrounding the encounter in the rapids. Now
he asked retribution—Lyting's imprisonment and the restora-
tion of all that was his, most especially the slavewoman Ailinn.

"As you can see for yourself, she is a great beauty and
would bring a considerable price," Nikas concluded.

"From men like you?" Leo Phocas challenged, arching a
brow in obvious distaste for the minister of trade, apparently
knowing something of him.

"And you, Domesticus," Nikas returned smoothly, bringing
a narrow look from Zoë. "But it remains, the maid is a slave
and rightfully belongs to Hakon."

All eyes turned to Ailinn, where she sat with Constantine
and Ariana. The young emperor, not liking any of what he
heard and fearing they would try to take Ailinn from him,
pressed on the arm of the chair. Immediately it rose, ascending
toward the ceiling. The lions began to roar and the birds issued
a cacophony of sounds. Constantine looked down on them,
presenting his most imperious mien.

Nikas gazed anxiously after them, seeing his prize lift out of
reach. Hakon's eyes grew hard, calculating, as he studied the
throne, as though he would find the source of its magic and
disassemble its secrets to reach Ailinn.

Hastily the minister of trade appealed to the empress and her
advisers once more, pressing Hakon's claim and muddying
Lyting's name.

"What do we know of him?" Nikas gestured openhanded to
Lyting. "If he would abandon a kinsmen and steal his goods
for greed and lust, then how can we trust his word or anything
he tells us? Certainly, we cannot in matters that concern the
safety of our emperor."

Zoë turned to Lyting, her great black eyes searching the
depths of his.

"Do you respond to these charges?" she asked without a hint
of bias in her voice.

Lyting cast a long, sharp glance at both his accusers, then
returned his gaze to Zoë.

"I am who I claim to be, brother to Rurik Atlison. I bore you
his token—the cloth of purple and coin of gold."

"Mayhaps he stole that, too!" Nikas interjected bringing
scowls from Zoë's general and admiral.

Lyting held Zoë's eyes. "If the token is not proof enough,

Rurik's image is stamped upon my face. You know this to be true, Majesty. Also, do not forget the parchment from Dyrrachium, or the armband of Askel the Red. Five of your Dragons are dead, while I have already endured one attack, mistaken for the sixth, my brother. Helena, like Thengil and Vegeir, lies poisoned in her grave. The 'scorpion' is real, as is the 'spider,' and they will destroy the throne of the Macedonians provided the chance."

His words brought reactions from those gathered, but he could not read their looks all at once.

"And is the maid, Ailinn, rightfully this man's slave?" asked the Domesticus.

Hakon broke in before Lyting could answer, utilizing his own limited knowledge of Greek. " 'Twas I who first seized her on raid."

A half-truth, Lyting knew.

"And where did this raid occur?" Zoë asked calmly, her eyes lifting to Ailinn's dark red hair.

When Hakon and the minister remained silent, she pulled her gaze to them.

"Where?" she demanded.

"Ireland, Majesty," Hakon replied.

The minister suddenly looked pinched and withdrew a pace.

A storm gathered about the empress and fire kindled in the depths of her coal black eyes. Zoë fixed her gaze on Hakon, searing him with her look.

"Ireland is a *Christian* land," she said tightly.

"*Já . . .*" Hakon replied, his words light and dispassionate, but his confidence visibly waned.

Anger sharpened in Zoë eyes.

" 'Tis illegal to transport Christian slaves through Christian lands. As a trader, you know this well. 'Tis why the Rus bring us Slavs. Yet, you dare come before me and make this bold admittance before the crown itself?" Her indignation resonated through the room.

Hakon groped for words while Nikas shot him infuriated looks for revealing this information, his embarrassment acute and his anxiety over the girl plain.

Zoë turned once more to Lyting. "I do not doubt that you are who you say. Your brother, Rurik, ever served us fearlessly, honestly, and nobly. Now I wouldst hear of the journey from the West and its events from your own lips."

Lyting recognized he must put an end to the matter in its
entirety, not only Hakon's charges. He had seen others in the
court hunger after Ailinn. Their appetites were as great and
recognizable as those of his kinsman on the voyage. Since
meeting the Imperials and court, he had yet to establish his
relationship to Ailinn. He would do so now and place her
safely beyond their hope-filled fantasies.

"Majesty, I didst not steal but freed Ailinn from the chains
of her bondage—those of the chieftain, Skallagrim, who first
enslaved her in Clonmel, then Hakon's after he attacked me
aboard our boat and sought to kill me in the rapids of Leanti.
We fought in the waters, and they carried him off into the mists
while, by God's might, I clung to the vessel as Ailinn and I
rode the rapids. The members of the convoy searched for
Hakon, but none found a trace of him. We thought him to be
dead and finally sailed on."

Lyting took a breath, then forestalled the Drungarius who
was about to speak. "There is more."

A ripple of warmth purled through Ailinn as Lyting lifted his
crystal-blue gaze to her.

"Ailinn and I pledged ourselves to each other on Saint
Gregory's Island before all and espoused ourselves according
to the traditions of the Norse. She is my *kona*. My wife. Hakon
may verify this for himself by asking any member of the
convoy. Ailinn and I are wed."

As Ariana made the translation, Ailinn's mouth dropped
open, her eyes widening. For a moment she feared she would
slip right off the throne, so stunned was she.

"Why did you not mention this when we separated you and
Ailinn into different pavilions?" Zoë asked.

Lyting's thoughts skipped rapidly. "Majesty, ours was a
Norse ceremony. Both Ailinn and I embrace the Lord Christ.
We have agreed not to consummate our vows until we can
repeat them in a Christian ceremony, thus gaining the blessings
of the Lord and enjoying a true marriage."

The light softened in Zoë's eyes, and she, too, smiled,
greatly pleased by his answer.

Ailinn's mouth remained open as Ariana continued to
translate. The young emperor, who had been listening atten-
tively, came suddenly to life and grinned widely.

"We can see you wed! Can't we, Mother?" His bright blue

eyes sparkled with excitement, and he looked from his mother to Lyting and then to Ailinn.

"I regret I cannot ask you to wait for me, Ailinn. But 'twould be wrong to take you from Lyting, and I like him very much. He will make a fine husband for you."

Zoë looked up at her son in great surprise, but next to her Romanus voiced his support.

"An excellent idea, Majesty. And having waited so long, they would wish to wed at once. We can afford them a resplendent ceremony in any one of the churches of Constantinople. As you wish, of course, my emperor."

Ailinn's mouth dropped even further as she looked to Lyting. He, too, appeared speechless at the suggestion.

Hakon and the minister looked utterly astonished and about to object when Constantine made another imperious proclamation.

"Rurik Atlison preserved the throne of my father and, in doing so, mine as well. Now Lyting has returned to preserve it once more."

Constantine directed his brilliant blue gaze at Lyting.

"We could not fully reward your brother, as my father had wished. But we can reward you, Lyting Atlison. And 'tis well deserved. Not only do you serve the house of the Macedonians, but you have saved Ailinn from her dark fate."

Constantine's gaze fell harshly upon Hakon. "Guards! Take this man from my presence and expel him from the gates of the city. Take the minister, Nikas, also from my sight."

The guards began to roughly remove the two men from the throne room. Nikas affected shallow, hasty bows, backstepping out the door. Venom sliced Hakon's features. He darted a poisonous glare at Lyting as the guards forced him from the room.

Like the cat that ever found its way back, Hakon would seek his way, too, Lyting held certain. 'Twould be foolish to think otherwise, and fatal to underestimate him.

As Constantine pressed on the throne's arm and it began to descend, he addressed the Eparch, Sergius. "I wouldst know more of our Minister of Trade. I do not like him. I believe he knew Ailinn was a Christian slave and would not have urged Hakon to free her."

"As you wish, Majesty." Sergius bowed, not meeting the emperor's eyes, covering his own embarrassment.

"You might also visit Nikas's home," Lyting suggested. "I

believe you will find his residence filled with exotic concubines—beautiful slavewomen he accepts as gifts for minis-
terial favors. Skallagrim intended Ailinn as such a gift. 'Tis
likely why Hakon knew to approach him for aid and why Nikas
supported him."

This brought many a raised brow. Sergius flushed red.

As the throne settled on the marble platform, Constantine
rose and aided Ariana down the steps.

Ailinn pressed slowly to her feet, suddenly feeling shivery
and self-conscious as Lyting approached. Their eyes met, and
she suddenly found herself short of breath.

"Ailinn, I will aright this," he promised softly as he took her
hand and drew her down the steps.

She wondered what he wished to aright, still dazed by the
shock of Hakon's return, the horrid accusations and her fears
for Lyting, followed by his startling revelation. She tipped her
face upward.

"You married me at Saint Gregory's Island?"

"Ailinn, I realize it must displease you to find yourself
espoused to a Norseman. Bear with these things for now.
'Twas never my wish to mislead you, only to place you
indisputably under my protection from those who would harm
you. Now, 'twould seem necessary to do so and in like manner
once more, to place you beyond the reach of such men as
Hakon and Nikas and whomever else." A smile tugged at the
side of his mouth. "Besides, the emperor is intent on seeing us
wed, and we cannot easily say him nay."

His smile faded. "Have no fear, though. I will not press my
'husbandly rights.' The marriage will be in name only, and
once performed, I will request passage home from the emperor."

A muscle flexed along Lyting's jaw, and he looked away.
"When I return you to your people, you can initiate an
annulment. It should not prevent you from making a good and
desirous marriage someday."

Ailinn started to speak, her emotions knotting. But as she
opened her mouth, Xenia moved apart from the other ladies-
in-waiting and came to greet them.

Xenia's eyes pierced Ailinn's, a dark, indefinable look that
she shifted to Lyting as she addressed him in Greek.

"Congratulations," she breathed, her tone acrid. "You are

so like your brother." Her gaze trailed over his features, then to Ailinn, her lips forming a thin curve. "The Atlisons ever have an eye for a beautiful woman."

A chill prickled up Ailinn's spine as Xenia's gaze touched her. She watched Xenia glide off, wondering if Lyting sensed something disturbing about the woman as well.

Constantine's voice drew her back.

"The emperor is enumerating for the servants the many arrangements that need be made for your wedding," Ariana said happily as she joined Lyting and Ailinn. "He loves court ceremonials and will see that you have a magnificient wedding."

Ailinn looked to Constantine. Though the details would be in a child's hands, she was certain the wedding would be grander than even those celebrated by the kings of Tara.

Lyting moved off and stood speaking with the empress for several moments, then returned to Ailinn's side.

"Zoë wishes to convene her Council, and I must attend. Ariana and the empress's ladies-in-waiting appear eager to attend to you, my bride." He could not help but smile at that thought. "Go with them now. I will come for you later."

He traced her face with his finger, then tipped her chin, his blue eyes brushing hers, warm and golden brown.

"We shall yet see this through, *elskan mín*."

Reluctantly Ailinn withdrew from Lyting and crossed the room surrounded amidst great excitement—Constantine, Ariana, and the noble ladies-in-waiting all accompanying her. Lyting watched, a host of concern swarming through him.

A "spider" spun in the hall of the Caesars, a "scorpion" poised beneath the throne. Now, Hakon had returned. And if that wasn't enough, the Byzantines wished to place him squarely in the marital bed with Ailinn. If they did so with as much passion as was done in Francia, he just might not survive this last ordeal.

As Lyting left with Zoë and her officials, he wondered what more could possibly befall him this day.

Hours later Lyting emerged from the hastily called meeting with Zoë and her Council.

He smiled grimly. Things had become so twisted, so "Byzantine," as his brother would say. But mayhaps they had found a way to bring everything to culmination, at least concerning the conspirators lurking about the throne.

He was not overly happy with their solution, for it placed Ailinn in the midst of possible danger. Yet, 'twould likely flush the "scorpion" and his "spider" out.

Lyting reviewed the strategy in his mind. The wedding would serve as a trap. If the "scorpion" and "spider" were truly so near the throne—possibly among these with whom he supped last night—then they already knew his identity. No longer waiting to ensnare Rurik, doubtless they readied to strike at the throne itself—at Zoë and Constantine.

The wedding procession provided that opportunity. The empress and her council wished to ensure they take it, with the Imperial net waiting to trap them.

On the day of the wedding word would be circulated that several men had been seized, whom Lyting recognized from the incident in the cemetery. 'Twould be rumored that they were in the course of being questioned and had begun to supply names of others involved. A little later 'twould be spread that when the wedding procession commenced at dusk, all those named would be quietly apprehended.

The Council expected—given the announcement of imminent arrest—that they would force the conspirators' hands and that those guilty would either flee or attempt an open attack on the procession itself in which the emperor and the Augusta would be in attendance.

Zoë insisted that Constantine remain behind, safeguarded in the palace. A distant cousin who favored Constantine in appearance would take her son's place. In full regalia and the shadows of evening, the deception might go unnoticed, and she would strive to center attention upon herself.

The Imperial spies would be watching for those who sought to flee, while reinforced guards—both Varangian and Byzantine—would protect those in the procession. Aside from their leader, they would seek all those who wore the "sign of the scorpion."

For a second time the trap had been baited, Lyting reflected. But now it contained not only himself but Ailinn, the child emperor, and his mother. He liked it not at all. Now they must wait for the scorpion to strike, and the spider to spin out its entrapping threads.

Chapter 20

High excitement filled the *gynaekeion* as the women prepared the bride for her groom.

To Ailinn, it beseemed she was being carried on the swift currents of a great river, moving fleetly toward the appointed hour when she would become Lyting's wife.

She reminded herself for an uncountable time 'twould not be a real marriage. But that did little to quiet the fluttery entities that had taken residence in her stomach.

Two evenings past, after the tumult in the throne room, Lyting visited her at the *gynaekeion*. He explained they would need be separated while rapid preparations were made for the wedding. 'Twas forbidden for the bridal couple to see each other during that time.

Ailinn's spirits had plummeted at the thought, but she didn't miss the tension that visibly ran through him, nor the lines that appeared periodically between his brows. He withheld something, she knew. But what?

Before leaving the women's quarters, Lyting had assured her once more that all would be set aright. By direction of the empress, a ship was being readied for their voyage home, to leave eight days hence after the week of celebrations following their wedding.

Ailinn had not seen Lyting since. Now her hours were filled with waiting and haunted by a hollowness that only his presence could satisfy. She looked eagerly to being rejoined with him this day. Though they would share a chamber for the coming week, ostensibly as man and wife, and though it might pose a far greater trial than now, she far preferred that to this time of separation.

She whisked her glance about, bringing herself back to the sumptuousness and fervor that surrounded her. Precious stuffs draped the walls of the bridal chamber—rich satins and brocades, trimmed with gilded cordings. The ladies flickered about in various states of dress as they were bathed, massaged, and adorned for the evening.

While servants groomed Ailinn's hands and feet, Ariana detailed to her the myriad aspects of the ceremonies to come and recounted the marvelous things Constantine had arranged for herself and Lyting. The emperor intended this to be the most glorious of ceremonies for his new friends.

"Archbishop Theodore will marry you," Ariana informed, then lowered her voice. "The empress refused to consider the Patriarch, Nicholas Mysticus. They are adversaries, you know. Euphemius, the ex-Patriarch whom she does favor, is in seclusion at his monastery. Therefore, Archbishop Theodore will need perform the rites."

Ailinn blinked at the apologetic tone in the girl's explanation. "Ariana, I assure you I am quite honored the archbishop will preside."

Ariana smiled. "The matter of the church was much debated. The Hagia Sophia was deemed too immense for what the emperor purposes, and the Hagia Eirene too stark. 'Tis an iconoclast church," she added without clarification as though the word *iconoclast* was explanation enough.

"Constantine next suggested the Church of Sergius and Bacchus, for 'tis lavish in its decorations and is easily accessible, here on the palace grounds." Perplexion stole over her features. "Oddly, 'tis the very reason 'twas rejected. The Council—even the empress—insisted the procession pass out of the palace enclosure for a short distance—'for the enjoyment of the populace'—they said."

The fine hairs lifted on Ailinn's arms. She thought again of Lyting's visit and the gnawing feeling that he withheld something.

"Where will the wedding take place, Ariana?"

"Saint Euphemia's. It stands on the side opposite the

Hippodrome and contains some of the most beautiful mosaics in the city."

Ariana crimped a brow, winnowing her thoughts for what she might have forgotten, then brightened.

"A choir, comprising members of the Blue and Green factions, will accompany the procession in song as they escort you to the church. Such is usually provided for emperors on their wedding day, but Constantine has brought it about especially for you and Lyting."

"Truly, I am grateful," Ailinn rejoined, secretly glad Ariana could not read her eyes. Lyting's mission concerned the safety of the Imperial family. Why then would the procession leave the security of the palace enclosure? And could not an escort of these factions conceal enemies to the crown? Urgently she wished to speak with Lyting.

"Now we must see you prepared," Ariana voiced happily. "At sunset Lyting will come to claim you for his bride."

The thought sent shivers of warmth darting through Ailinn. But as she arose, Xenia appeared, cooling the sensation.

Xenia's eyes held a hard glint, and though she smiled, a brittleness played about her lips. From the folds of her gown, she withdrew a crystal vial fitted with a bright silver closure. Ailinn's gaze moved to Xenia's tapered fingers while Ariana interpreted her words.

"Xenia brings a wedding gift—precious jasmine oil. 'Tis her own blend. She says, 'Men love the scent. Rurik did.'"

Ailinn's gaze skipped to Xenia's. The woman's look was serene, yet unsettling.

"Jasmine stirs a man's ardor." Ariana continued to render Xenia's words. "You will wish to stir Lyting's this night. When you have finished your bath, the servants will massage the oils into your skin, softening you beautifully while wrapping you in its fragrance. The perfume will linger through the hours and still perfume your skin when you lay in your husband's arms."

The light altered in Xenia's eyes, causing a tremor to slide down Ailinn's spine.

"Rurik liked the scent of jasmine?" Ailinn asked more placidly than she felt while straightening her back.

Xenia's eyes glowed.

"'Twas once Helena's favorite scent," Ariana translated

literally. "Ever she wore it for him. Even as she lay dying, she insisted on our applying the fine oils so she might be pleasing to him. The scent of jasmine lingered about her even as we laid her to rest in her sepulcher. Some say it lingers there still."

Xenia's words sent a chill through Ailinn.

"I noticed no fragrance whilst there the other night."

Xenia's brows uptilted fractionally as she received the words through the child. The light changed in her eyes once again, and her lips curved with a smile.

" 'Tis only a story that bides," Ariana repeated for Xenia. "Since you know the brothers Atlison, I thought 'twould interest you. But enjoy the jasmine. 'Tis a beautiful scent. Lyting will long remember its potency."

As the girl finished, Xenia gave over the crystal, turned, and glided away.

"I am truly sorry, Ailinn." Ariana reached out and placed a concerned hand on Ailinn's arm. "Xenia should not speak of death on your wedding day."

"I'm sure she did not think of it that way." Ailinn did not betray her unease as she fingered the vial. She could not be with Lyting soon enough.

Just then the ladies-in-waiting came forward in two columns and surrounded Ailinn, smiles wreathing their faces. Each wore spotless white gowns, and their hair was caught up identically—parted at the center and wound into plump rolls encased in jeweled silk nets. Golden circlets sat above their straight brows, each affixed with a star-shaped diadem.

" 'Tis time to prepare you for your husband," Ariana said brightly.

Ailinn lay the vial on the small table beside her, then allowed the women to conduct her to the sunken pool. There she gave over her towel and entered the heated waters. A lute sounded in the background, and the women began to sing as they lined the pool and strewed petals over the water.

Ailinn realized that this, too, like most aspects of Byzantine life in the palace, was to be ensconced in ritual. She sank deeper into the water, relishing the extravagance as her thoughts went to Lyting.

Sometime later Ailinn emerged from the waters, feeling marvelously relaxed and tranquil. The women wrapped her in towels and led her to a cushioned bench for her massage.

Ariana returned to the table to retrieve the jasmine oil. As her fingers moved over the top, she found naught but the squat jars of cosmetics. The vial was gone. She bid over a servant who quickly scanned the room for her and answered her questions.

"Comita," Ariana fumed. When the servant apprised that Xenia was also absent, Ariana instructed for her personal tray of oils to be brought. Rejoining Ailinn, she explained the vial's disappearance with great regret and offered her own preparations.

" 'Tis not precious jasmine but a delicate floral blend that you will hopefully find pleasing. Comita has slipped away and is hiding somewhere, but she shall be punished, I promise you."

Recalling her horrid experience in the forum, Ailinn feared the servant might be dealt with harshly.

"Mayhaps we should forgive this one transgression. After all, 'tis my wedding day." Ailinn stretched out so the servants could begin applying the perfumed oils. "Let us not spoil the day with such matters."

Subsequently, when the servants finished their ministrations, the ladies-in-waiting led Ailinn to an elegant silver table. There, one had been selected to enhance the bride's face with cosmetics with the others gathered to advise.

Ailinn allowed only a light touch—just enough kohl to bring out her eyes and a trace of color on her lips. She refused the proffered drops of belladonna. 'Twas meant to contract the pupils of her eyes to small dots, like theirs. She did not find it so becoming and held firm against it.

Next they dressed her hair. Ailinn's dark auburn tresses were allowed to flow freely as a symbol of her virginity. Only the sides were swept back from her face and entwined with ropes of pearls.

The women then bid her rise and stand upon a small stool. The ladies-in-waiting brought forth the extravagant wedding garments, presenting each piece to the bride and then dressing her in it.

First came the *stola*, an undergown made of lustrous emerald-green silk with long, close-fitting sleeves. Deep borders of costly embroideries embellished the sleeves and hem. Over this they added a sumptuous tunic, constructed of a richly patterned brocade, stiffer than most fabrics, for 'twas woven with threads of pure gold and garnished with a profusion of gemstones—rubies, sapphires, and emeralds, adorning it with lavish abandon so that the garment was one of dazzling splendor, shining like a field of brilliant flowers. On her feet they placed jeweled sandals.

No sooner had the women finished dressing Ailinn than the empress Zoë entered unexpectedly into the bridal chamber, joining her women there.

Ailinn forgot the lavishness of her own dress, for to see Zoë was to see sheer majesty in splendor. She moved regally beneath her heavy gown—a deep, magnificent purple silk, emblazoned with gold, silver, and jewels. The edge of her mantle bore the *tablion*, a large square encrusted with a profusion of gems and marking her Imperial rank as the Augusta. About her shoulders and neck she wore the *manikas*, the great jeweled collar, and on her head a priceless crown with cascades of pearls flowing downward over her shoulders.

All the women began to sink to the floor, but the empress stayed them, especially the bride, who still stood on the stool.

When the servants aided Ailinn down, Zoë kissed her on both cheeks. She then gifted Ailinn with a pair of fine gold filigree earrings. Ailinn thanked her, setting the earrings to her ears.

From outside came a medley of male voices, lifted in song.

"They approach!" Ariana exclaimed. "The wedding procession brings your groom, Ailinn."

The women moved to where the doors opened onto the balcony but remained slightly back so as not to be seen. Below, scores of torches capered above the men's heads, licking back the shadows of evening and illuminating those of the procession. All, save the groom, dressed in snowy-white garments.

Ailinn's heart began to beat solidly, her pulse accelerating, as her eyes alighted on the tall, handsome figure striding in their midst. He towered above the rest, his bright head shining, a sapphire-blue mantle swathing his broad shoulders.

Joy welled, rich and warm, deep in Ailinn's soul. It rose to overflowing and engulfed the chambers of her heart.

"Lyting," she whispered on a soft breath. However briefly, he was destined to be her husband and she his wife, the fullness of that thought astounded her. The promise it contained, were circumstances otherwise, sent heat shimmering through her veins.

As though hearing her voice, Lyting lifted his face to the women crowded at the balcony, his eyes questing for her. Quickly the women drew Ailinn back and covered her with a filmy white veil that reached well past her knees in front and drifted to the floor behind.

"Come," Ariana said excitedly. " 'Tis time to receive your groom."

The choir of Blues and Greens took up a new song as the doors of the *gynaekeion* swept smoothly open and the bride appeared with her retinue.

Lyting's blood stirred as he left the center of the procession and proceeded forward to claim Ailinn. Coming to stand before her, the ladies in attendance raised her veil so he might gaze upon his bride.

Ailinn's beauty stole his breath away. Their eyes touched—a brief kiss that set his heart to pounding. Even as the women lowered her veil, Lyting could scarce pull his gaze from her. Moving to Ailinn's side, he offered his arm and felt a slight tremor there. He admonished himself for responding like a green, smitten lad. Green, no. *Smitten*, the word didn't even approach his feelings for Ailinn.

Lyting led Ailinn aside while the ladies-in-waiting parted into the double columns. Zoë appeared at the far end. Emerging from the *gynaekeion*, she progressed with Imperial grandeur, commanding the attention of all.

As planned, she drew interest upon herself, hoping to divert the assassins' regard from the child who would impersonate her son, as well as from the other innocents in the procession, such as her ladies.

For that, Lyting was especially grateful, for the procession included Ailinn. Yet, as the bride, Ailinn was already at the center of interest. She glittered with every movement she made and was equally as entrancing as the empress. Because of her association with him, Lyting worried that she, too, might be a target for revenge.

Zoë did not meet Lyting's gaze as she passed, but he saw her eyes held no fear, only undaunted determination to see this night through. All had been set to motion, the varying rumors circulated throughout the day. Now must they wait for the "scorpion" to attempt his sting and the "spider" to bite.

A contingent of Varangians met Zoë. Dressed in their ceremonial best, they bore lances and great scarlet shields. Each wore the famed *rhomphaia*, one-edged swords of heavy iron, suspended on a leather strap from their right shoulders. From their left shoulders hung battle-axes.

Lyting took reassurance in the Guard's well-armed presence, particularly since he was yet denied his own sword. 'Twas prohibited for the groom to bear weaponry into the church.

Lyting and Ailinn followed seven paces behind Zoë as the Varangians escorted them to the head of the procession, then conducted the bridal party toward the Sigma Palace.

Ailinn's hand warmed atop Lyting's. She had felt the tenseness enter his arm when the empress appeared. It bided there still.

She cast her glance sideways. Due to Lyting's height, she could see no higher than his chin. She would need tilt her head conspicuously to read his eyes. Instead, she lowered her gaze to the crimson brocade that covered his chest, its silver threads and scattered gemstones gleaming in the torchlight. Her gaze then shifted to their hands. Unexpectedly he turned his hand and caught the tips of her fingers with his, giving them a gentle squeeze.

Ailinn's eyes flew to his face and found his smile. Yet, 'twas a smile shadowed with concern. She took a small swallow, but against what she didst not know.

As the procession converged on the Sigma Palace, a second gathering greeted them, composed of high court officials and officers, prelates, musicians, and additional guards—both Byzantine and Varangian.

The emperor waited upon a small throne, beneath a canopy of purple silk. Arrayed in full regalia, he wore the *paludamentum*, a lavish purple robe bearing the jeweled encrusted *tablion*, much like his mother's but marking his rank as emperor. Upon his head, he bore a heavy diadem comprising eight enameled gold plaques. In his hand he held an orb, surmounted by a cross, and upon his feet he wore slippers of purple, embroidered with pearls.

Lyting studied the child imposter, amazed at the resemblance. He consoled his misgivings with the knowledge that the real emperor was safe within the palace, protected by senior officers of the Guard, headed by the Acolyte, and including, at his own request, Thord. Still, he hoped this child would come to no harm.

As they drew near, Zoë stiffened. In the same moment Lyting spied Thord among the guard that flanked the child. Lyting's gaze sprang back to the false emperor and fixed on his features. Lyting's jaw hardened. No imposter sat upon the throne. 'Twas Constantine, himself.

Ahead, he saw Zoë's hands clench into knots. But she did naught. Said naught. Evidently she intended to carry through their plans, knowing, as he, 'twas likely they were already watched by those they hoped to entrap.

Four distinguished-looking men crouched down beside the throne, and Lyting saw now that they meant to take up the litter positioned beneath it and the emperor. This, too, was another change of plan, for the child would offer an easy target carried high. As the men elevated Constantine, Lyting prayed these men were carefully chosen, for he recognized none of them.

He *did*, however, recognize the four officials who now took up the canopy, upholding its four poles and carrying the silk trapping aloft, over the emperor's head. It gave him no comfort to see the very men he most suspected capable of treachery: the Drugarius, Romanus Lecapenus; the Domesticus, Leo Phocas; the Logothete, Leonites Byrennius; and the Strategos, Andronicus Styliane.

Lyting noted that the Eparch, Sergius Bardanes, was absent from the gathering. Mayhaps, in investigating the Minister of Trade and his court of concubines, the Byzantines found something they disliked about the Eparch as well. Hakon also dragged on his thoughts. Though expelled from the city, he was a determined and cunning man. He'd find his way back in before long.

The bridal procession, now double in its length, slowly crossed the palace grounds, moving toward the Chalkê Gate accompanied by the choir's song.

Dignitaries walked to the fore of the cortege, carrying lighted candles which flickered like a sea of stars. Units of the Imperial regiments followed, then prelates carrying icons and richly embellished holy books before the emperor—"God's representative on earth."

Next came the Varangian Guards, flanking the Imperials and the bridal couple. Constantine reigned over the moment from his litter, and the Augusta Zoë walked slightly behind, succeeded by Lyting and Ailinn. Finally came the ladies-in-waiting and choir, again bearing lighted tapers.

Thord dropped back to walk alongside Lyting and Ailinn. "The boy refused to be excluded from the ceremonies," he gruffed. "Threw an Imperial tantrum. Being emperor, we could not disobey his direct charge, and his mother was not present to countermand him."

"And the litter? Whose idea was that, and why do guards not carry it?"

"Again, 'twas Constantine's doing. Only the highest peers of the realm may carry the Imperial personage. To have guards bear him would be an insult. Such a breach of etiquette would also signal our trap."

Lyting nodded his understanding, but wholly distrusted the turn of things. "Mayhaps someone should have checked their shoulders for scorpions," he muttered. "But I imagine that, too, would be an unforgivable insult."

"Take heart," Thord rejoined. "If the empress truly doubted those bearing her son, she would not allow us to take another step."

Lyting fell to a reflective silence. A muscle leapt in his jaw. "If aught should befall me, protect Ailinn. See she returns safely to Ireland and give her all that is mine."

Hearing her name, Ailinn's eyes drew to Lyting. He looked straight ahead but his expression caused her breath to catch. Foreboding seeped into her heart. Unconsciously her hand tightened on his.

The procession passed through the "Brazen Entrance," then advanced along the outside of the enclosure wall and entered the Augustaeum. Startlingly, an enormous crowd jammed the forum, awaiting the bridal cortege. Ailinn pressed closer to Lyting as they progressed across the square. Lights burned bright in the Hagia Sophia, and for a moment Ailinn wished their steps were directed there. 'Twas so near.

Passing onto the Mesê, the procession turned left to follow the street along the Hippodrome. Despite her unease, Ailinn could not help but be caught up with the gaiety and excitement surrounding them. The street and balconies overlooking the route were festively decorated with carpets and silk hangings. Onlookers hailed them with enthusiasm, raining petals of violets and roses upon them.

Lyting's gaze continuously roamed the crowd. 'Twas obvious the people loved their young emperor and equally so their empress. Zoë was at the height of her popularity, he had been informed, having affected a great victory this year over the Persians. The mood of the populace confirmed her high favor, but Lyting knew not everyone loved the Macedonians.

It concerned him anew that beneath the purple canopy, Constantine provided an easy mark for an assassin. The "scorpion" was clever in using others, and, as in Rurik's day, 'twas likely he and his men posed close to the emperor. Lyting withdrew his searching gaze from the crowd, leaving that matter to the guards and the Imperial spies. Instead he concentrated on those nearest the boy and his mother.

Continuing along the crowded street, the choir sung hymns, and the prelates swung their censers. St. Euphemia's stood halfway down the side of the Hippodrome. Just before it a street opened off to the right, running along the opposite side of the church and extending behind the Mesê.

As they verged on it, something flashed brilliantly from one of the balconies, and a clamor went up there. A ball of fire engulfed it. In the next moment several more balconies burst into flames, then a racket sounded from the direction of the Hippodrome. People began to run, screaming hysterically. Someone had loosed two of the lions kept there for the games.

Panic seized the crowds, and they began to disperse. Meanwhile, Lyting saw the shadows come to life in the side street as wraithlike figures, dressed in black, poured from their concealment and pressed hurriedly in the direction of the procession.

The Varangians closed ranks around the Imperials and the bridal couple, creating a wall with their overlapping shields and drawing on their axes. The Byzantine units dealt with the furor surrounding them as did the Imperial forces hidden in the masses.

Lyting shuttered his mind to the chaos, certain 'twas but a diversion from the real deed intended. If the "scorpion" wished to put an end to the house of the Macedonians, then 'twas Constantine he need kill.

Lyting drew Ailinn rapidly forward with him. Tossing court formalities to the wind, he caught the empress by the arm and propelled her to the ground and Ailinn with her.

"Thord, watch over them!" he shouted back, at the same time sharpening his eyes over those holding the canopy and litter. Another distraction escalated off to the right, but he ignored it and held his gaze firm.

The dignitaries quickly lowered Constantine to the ground and, much shaken, crouched there. Constantine twisted around and sought his mother, his eyes huge and filling with tears. The child's look tore at Lyting. He hastened forward, intent on plucking him from the throne that yet marked him and delivering him to Zoë.

The four officers still upheld the canopy, though the Drungarius and the Domesticus began to free a hand and reach for their swords. Lyting's pulse quickened, fearing their next move, but Romanus and Leo turned toward the crowd. Lyting's eyes skimmed to Leonites, Andronicus. His glance shot back to Leonites Byrrenius, the Logothete, just as a knife dropped from his sleeve into his palm and he cast himself toward the boy, releasing the pole that upheld the canopy.

Lyting vaulted, hurtling himself through the air and crashing down atop Leonites. They skidded beneath the canopy, disappearing beneath the silk trappings.

Ailinn gasped as she watched the canopy billow and heave as the men roiled beneath, the emperor and dignitaries trapped there, also. Andronicus grappled with the shifting length of fabric, then thrust beneath to join the fray.

The silk shot upward, looking momentarily like a small mountain with a peak. But in the next instant a gleaming blade ruptured the peak and split the fabric. Two arms appeared, straining over the knife. Ailinn recognized Lyting's at once. Fear rioted through her.

The mountain disassembled as the men plummeted to the ground and rolled in the cloth. Romanus and Leo scrambled to pull the canopy free, managing to fell Andronicus in the effort, who swore blackly beneath the cloth.

Lyting and Leonites strained over the knife. Suddenly there were hands—Romanus's and Andronicus's intervening, dragging them upward to their feet. Lyting gripped tight the neck of Leonites's tunic, but as the Logothete struggled, it tore, exposing a scorpion branded on his shoulder.

Lyting heaved for breath, still holding Leonites in his grip. Leonites sought to jerk free, looking fiercely about as though he expected aid. No one came forth except Leo Phocas, who bent to the ground, then rose with a small velvet pouch. Opening it, he drew out two brass rings, each with raised symbols on their surfaces—one bearing a Cyrillic *omega*, the other with an *I*.

Leonites's expression changed to that of a trapped animal. A furor suddenly seized him. He fought Lyting with an outburst of energy. Wrenching within Lyting's grasp, he lunged for Andronicus, taking Lyting with him. A blade flashed in Andronicus's hand and as the three toppled to the ground, Andronicus drove it into Leonites's heart. Lyting's weight, as he fell atop him, forced the knife deeper.

Leonites's hand clawed for Andronicus's face, then dropped as death overtook him. Lyting dragged himself off Leonites and pulled the body from Andronicus. As they stood, Romanus collared Andronicus.

"Why did you kill him?" he shouted angrily. "He could have provided the names of those who serve him."

Leo Phocas imposed himself between the two men, gesturing to the commotion in the street and on the balcony. "We have more work to finish for now. The cats have been caught, but the conspirators flee." He moved off, commanding his soldiers to cull the crowd. Romanus and Andronicus followed.

The Varangians continued to maintain their shield-wall, protecting those within. Seeing Constantine shivering upon his throne, Lyting moved to the throne and caught the boy up in his arms. Carrying him to the empress, he restored the child to his mother. The two sat clasping each other on the ground.

Ailinn rose to her feet, her shakiness overcome by her utter awe of Lyting. Once more was she witness to his incredible prowess—her magnificent silver warrior.

"Are you all right, *elskan mín*?" His hands came to her shoulders, for she looked as though a breeze could carry her away.

"So long as you are near," she whispered truthfully, bringing a smile to his face.

Those of the procession slowly regained themselves. The populace returned as the streets were quieted, bringing wine to refresh the wedding party. When at last the procession began to reassemble, Zoë and Constantine came before Lyting, smiling their gratitude.

"Once more an Atlison has saved the throne of the Macedonians," Zoë commended in her rich smooth voice. "We are eternally indebted, Lyting."

Pale but composed, Constantine looked to his mother. "*Mitera*, we need honor and reward those faithful to the crown. Let us begin by seeing Lyting and Ailinn properly wed. They have waited long enough. Besides, if we do not hurry, all the candles in the church will be burned down," he added in a childlike manner.

Those around smiled and softly chuckled. Constantine ordered the damaged canopy raised, then took his place once more on the litter and throne.

Lyting turned to face Ailinn and held forth his hand.

"Come, *elskan mín*. 'Twould seem our presence is needed." A teasing light sparkled in his eyes. "We are already late for our wedding, but the emperor is determined we not miss it altogether."

Ailinn laid her hand in Lyting's, a wondrous joy stealing through her as he drew her to his side.

Lyting's pulse raced at her touch. The fight was done. 'Twas time to claim the prize and return homeward. Gazing on Ailinn, he regretted he could not claim that prize fully. His soul knew a most painful yearning.

Still, he intended to enjoy their wedding celebration to the full. 'Twas the only one he would ever know, and Ailinn was the only women he ever wished to marry, even if in name only.

This moment in time was theirs. He would savor it for eternity.

Chapter 21

In magnificent ritual and splendor the wedding procession escorted Lyting and Ailinn to the Church of Saint Euphemia.

Ailinn gazed on Lyting in wonderment and awe, her heart racing madly. Who was this man? she asked herself anew, even as she had that distant day on the waters of Riga. Who was this shining lord, this star-bright warrior? And how was it possible she should find herself here, about to exchange vows with him and become his wife, even if in name alone?

The semicircular portico that fronted the church greeted them with welcoming arms. The procession passed beneath its arches and entered the church proper—a solid-built structure, octagonal in shape with a massive dome and buttressing vaults. Yet, as they stepped through the portal, all heaviness departed, and they entered a luminous realm of shimmering mosaics which floated over the surface and rendered the walls naught but weightless shells.

The archbishop awaited the bridal couple in the narthex. Once the procession gathered inside, he opened his richly covered gospel and began the Rites of Betrothal.

Ariana stood behind Lyting and Ailinn, translating the many prayers so they might fully comprehend the ceremony, which was considered the actual contract of marriage.

The choir sang the responses, and the deacon instructed Lyting and Ailinn to bow their heads for additional prayers.

The archbishop next took up the rings and blessed the

couple, making the sign of the cross with the ring of the bride over the groom. "The servant of God, Lyting, is betrothed to the handmaiden of God, Ailinn, in the name of the Father, and of the Son, and of the Holy Spirit."

He next turned to Ailinn and made the sign of the cross with the groom's ring over her and prayed similarly. Repeating the blessing and vows three times over each of them, he placed the rings on their right hands, then indicated for them to exchange the rings.

As Lyting lifted Ailinn's hand and slipped the ring in place, a fire traveled through his heart and scorched through the bonds that had long immured his passions. This ring belonged upon her finger. If only it could remain.

Intensely aware of the warmth radiating from Lyting's hands, Ailinn guided the wedding ring onto his third finger. She began to withdraw her hands, but he caught them and held them firmly in his as the archbishop's voice rose in prayer.

The heat of Lyting's hands entered her own and spread up her arms. It flowed over her shoulders and downward again, warming her breasts and stomach before centering low in her abdomen.

Swallowing, she dropped her gaze to their joined hands and concentrated on their wedding rings. Identical save for size, they possessed wide octagonal hoops, decorated about the faces with tiny biblical scenes. The coin-like bezels surmounting the bands depicted the bridal couple with Christ standing between, joining their hands. Ailinn looked again at the artistry, amazed, for the miniature couple on each resembled herself and Lyting.

The archbishop concluded the prayer, and the bride's attendants hastened to draw back Ailinn's veil. Her cheeks flushed as Lyting's smile fell on her, for 'twas a smile that reached up and filled his eyes and wrapped her intimately in its embrace.

As the archbishop led the procession into the nave of the church, Lyting offered Ailinn his arm. Breathless, she placed her hand on his and accompanied him through the doors and into the main body of the church.

'Twas as though they stepped from one realm into another. Leaving the brightly illumined narthex, they passed into the darkened nave where candles burned sparingly. Yet, the unevenness of the mosaics caught their flickering lights, casting and reflecting them over a million cubes of gold *tesserae*, setting the entire nave aglitter. As Lyting and Ailinn moved through the church, it seemed they floated through a firmament of stars, a radiant heaven in otherworldly splendor.

Ailinn gazed up at Lyting, the lights glittering about them. Truly, they walked in a mystical realm, somewhere between a dream and reality, she and her silver warrior.

Lyting looked on Ailinn, his breath catching. Against the scintillating field, Ailinn looked precisely as he once envisioned her against the shimmering lime tree of Hedeby. From that moment he could scarce take his eyes from her. Surely, they no longer moved on earth.

Coming beneath the great dome, the procession divided, veering off to assume their places and leaving Lyting and Ailinn before the altar with their attendants, Constantine and Ariana.

Magnificent cloths draped the altar, and icons adorned the spaces before the sanctuary. Images of prophets, saints, martyrs, and the Virgin, looked on from over the altar and the aspe behind, witnessing their joining. Directly above, in the center of the dome itself, staring down was the immense, awe-striking mosaic of Christ the Pantocrator, the Ruler of the Universe. He gazed down in majesty from his golden Heaven, his hand raised in blessing.

The archbishop commenced the opening prayers of the Mass and, within the context of the liturgy, celebrated the crowning of the bride and groom. As the prayers were read, Constantine and Ariana stepped up on cushioned stools and imposed golden crowns on Lyting's and Ailinn's heads.

The Great Litany followed, and at the conclusion the archbishop raised his hand in blessing: "Grant these, Thy servants, Lyting and Ailinn, the fruit of their bodies, fair children, concord of soul and body. May they abound in every work that is good and acceptable unto Thee, so that finding favor in Thy Sight, they may shine like the stars of Heaven. Unite them in one mind; wed them into one flesh, granting to them the fruit of the body and the procreation of fair children . . . unto ages of ages."

Lyting gazed warmly on Ailinn as he assimilated those words, imagining their begetting children, and through their children's children, their joining reaching into eternity.

The choir sang the *koinonikon*, while Lyting and Ailinn received Communion and partook of the cup. Joining their hands, the archbishop led them around the altar three times in a circle, the symbol of eternity, emphasizing the permanence of their marriage. The choir then sang the *troparia*, and the bridal couple came before the altar once more for the final blessing. The archbishop raised his hand and made the sign of the cross over them.

"May the joy of this day last your lives through."

Lyting and Ailinn broke into wide smiles, their eyes shining as they turned and departed the altar. Once more they passed through the glittering field and into the narthex. Emerging from the church, they pressed through the waiting crowd, who showered them with violet and rose petals and tossed small apples at their feet.

An elegant carriage awaited, drawn by matching white horses. Lyting aided Ailinn up and into its cushioned-lined seat, then joined her. At once the driver urged the steeds forward, and the carriage began rolling back toward the palace.

Guards fell into stride beside them, while the crowds waved enthusiastically to the heroic bright-haired Norseman who had saved their beloved emperor and empress this day, and to his ravishing bride, whom rumor held he had also delivered from the hands of fate.

As the carriage progressed, Lyting and Ailinn waved to the cheering populace. Lyting's gaze stole over Ailinn. Her beauty filled his senses, and a hot rush of love spilled over the rim of his heart.

She turned to him, as though drawn by the power of his gaze. Their eyes met. And held. Unable to stay himself, Lyting reached for Ailinn and gathered her into his arms. As his mouth descended over hers, the crowd broke into ecstatic cheers, casting their petals high so that they returned to earth in a snowy blizzard. In the same moment Ailinn went to liquid beneath his strong but gentle kiss.

The procession returned to the grounds of the Sacred Palace and continued to the Boùcelon Palace overlooking the harbor. The choir accompanied them with song to the bridal chamber, where Lyting and Ailinn removed their crowns and placed them on the bridal bed. For a time they received guests, and Lyting gifted Ailinn with a golden bridal belt, decorated much like their rings. Everyone then made their way through the corridors linking the palaces, to the Dining Hall of the Nineteen Couches, where they were to partake of the wedding breakfast with their guests.

Here, everyone reclined on couches in the Roman manner around a table shaped like a Latin *D*. The young emperor sat at the center of the arced side, with the Augusta on his left and the officials on his right. On this occasion the women were included in the party and reclined along the left. Lyting and Ailinn reclined side by side next to the emperor.

To the accompaniment of lyre and zither, a lavish wedding banquet was served. Servants bore in platters of suckling pig, roasted game, and grilled birds with sauces. An array of soups, salads, artichokes, asparagus, dwarf olives, and mushrooms followed.

Lyting and Ailinn exchanged glances, astonished to be served on plates of pure gold. Again, they were provided silver spoons, knives, and small two-pronged forks. Ailinn gasped when three immense bowls descended from the ceiling. These, also, proved of gold and contained a bounty of fruits. Too heavy to lift, the bowls remained suspended, and by means of a mechanical device, servants moved them from guest to guest.

While acrobats entertained, Lyting's gaze wandered time and again to Ailinn. He restrained his increasingly unruly passions, hoping most sincerely that the Byzantines did not embrace the custom of stripping the groom and tossing him naked in bed with his equally naked bride. Despite his word and honor, he would be lost. Lyting drained his cup and held it forth for the servant to replenish.

The miming and dancing continued, until at last the festivities came to an end. The guests surrounded Lyting and Ailinn and with much merriment and song escorted them from the dining hall, back along the passages to the wedding chamber.

Lyting's heart drubbed in his chest as he and Ailinn arrived before the doors and, facing each other, waited while the others finished their song.

Ailinn's heart beat high in her throat, unsure what to expect. The doors opened to the chamber, and she saw that servants waited within. For a moment she feared all present would accompany them to the bridal bed itself and see them into it. She had not considered that till now and swallowed to her toes

as she thought on the many forms the bedding could take.
Slowly she entered the chamber.

She and Lyting stopped inside the door and sought each
other's gaze with breathless uncertainty. As the guests finished
their song, tension knotted through Ailinn. Surprisingly, everyone remained outside the chamber and did not breach the
portal. Instead, the servants came forward and swept the great
doors closed, sealing Lyting and Ailinn into the privacy of the
bridal chamber.

Together, Lyting and Ailinn released a long-held breath,
then laughed softly, realizing they had both been holding it for
the same reason.

The servants ushered Ailinn toward the bed, where they
removed her long veil and the stiff, shimmering overgown.
When they began to draw off the emerald-green *stola*, Lyting
stayed them, saying he'd prefer to undress his bride himself.
They bowed at his dismissal, laying out soft, silken robes in
parting and seeing that a pitcher of cool wine and fruits waited
on a small table to the side.

Lyting and Ailinn gazed at each other across the room for a
long moment.

A smile lifted the corners of Lyting's mouth. "Mayhaps I
should not have dismissed the servants so quickly. Are you
able to free yourself from your dress or will you require my
assistance?"

"I believe I can manage," she returned softly, suddenly
mindful of their seclusion together.

Lyting cleared his throat. "I will turn away and see to myself
so you can have some privacy."

Ailinn nodded, but did not move as he crossed to a chair,
removed his mantle, and began to draw off his brocaded tunic.
Seeing that he did so with difficulty, she went to his side to aid
him.

"Here, bend forward more." She took hold of the ends of his
tunic and pulled stoutly, stripping it away and baring his back.

Unable to stop herself, she gasped as her eyes alighted on
the many forgotten scars that covered Lyting's back and the
one particularly vicious-looking gash. Lyting straightened,
locking eyes with her but not before Ailinn's gaze went to the
scar on his cheek. 'Twas a painfully awkward moment, and
Ailinn's stomach twisted at what he must think.

"You have a scarred husband, Ailinn," Lyting said soberly, the lightness leaving his mood.

The scars ever reminded him of his failure one grim night in Normandy. At the same time Ailinn's words at the aqueduct returned to him. She would ever despise Norsemen. Surely, his many scars served as a painful reminder of his own heritage and the turn of fate that rendered her married to a member of her sworn enemies.

"On the morrow I will see what progress has been made with the arrangements for our return West," he said abruptly. "As I promised, I shall return you to Ireland. Then can you initiate an annulment to this marriage."

Lyting's eyes held her somberly. He would never initiate an annulment himself. Every day he drew a breath of life, no matter where he bided in this world, he would hold Ailinn in his heart as his one true wife.

Lyting's words wrung Ailinn's heart. She could not think on them. Inadvertently her gaze went to the scar lining his cheek. He visibly flinched and moved to take up his robe from the bed. Lyting's reaction stabbed at Ailinn. Gazing on his back, she found she could not let it pass.

"I have often wondered how you might have gained such wounds," she braved as he began to turn, then met his piercing gaze more boldly than she felt.

Emotion gripped Lyting. "Wielding my sword, Ailinn." He hesitated a moment, then added, "Do not forget, I am a man of Danmark."

Ailinn stiffened and he regretted the need to make the remark. But 'twas best to place a wedge betwixt them and for her to think on the Norse blood that flowed in his veins. The high spirits of the day, the flowing drink, and more important, her melting look right now was fast eroding his grip on himself. Better she look on him with a measure of hardness in her heart, before he became her undoing.

"Look on my scars, Ailinn, and remember I have long been a man of the sword, my fighting skills honed amongst the Danes."

Ailinn shrank back a little before his words. Not until this moment did she think on Lyting as a Dane. Only as a man. Why did he wish to dispel the blissfulness of the last hours?

'Twas torture to her heart. A torture she could not bide.
Bracing herself, she met his words headlong.

"What warring then wrought such scars?"

He stared at Ailinn. Why didst she question him on the
matter? 'Twould be best for her to look on him as she did any
other of his kindred.

" 'Twas not warring that marred me, but one encounter, the
night I fought my own blood kinsman—my half brother."

"Your half brother did this?"

"He and his two henchmen. My only regret is that I did not
kill him myself."

His words visibly took Ailinn aback, and he rued startling
her. Yet, he held it as necessary.

Ailinn pondered Lyting's many scars and the one particularly deep wound—all on his back. He was excellently skilled.
Yet, he had been outnumbered. The beasts must have taken
him down. His back would have only been opened to them if
he had no longer been able to wield his sword or stand his
ground. Such venom. Why would his half brother have wished
to kill him?

"Your reasons for fighting must have been very strong."

Lyting's gaze held her. She would not let it go.

"We fought over my brother's wife."

Ailinn recalled the dark-haired beauty at Hedeby, standing
next to the golden lord who would have been Rurik. Despite
Lyting's words, she knew the truth at once.

"You defended her," she stated, not understanding why he
might wish to lead her into thinking less of him.

A wave of exhaustion rolled over Lyting. Physically spent,
the evening's drink taking its effect, Lyting moved to sit on the
bed. Ailinn saw through his words, and he could not deal with
the tender look of concern in her eyes.

" 'Tis a long story," he said tiredly. "One that haunts me still
and fills me with anger and regret. Because I failed that night
and did not kill my half brother, Brienne nearly died."

"But—"

"Ailinn, this is no talk for our wedding night, though
thankfully it has diverted my mind for the moment. I will be
plain with you. You have come all this way undefiled—
miraculously so. But if you do not wish to yet be ravished by
a Norseman, then look on me with no softness nor tempt me

further from my vow. The passions of the North flow strong in my veins. I fear if I must continue to look on you thusly, I shall have you in an instant, and even you will not realize the deed done until after it is wrought, so strained am I."

He dragged a hand over his face. "Tomorrow, I will see about the arrangements for our voyage home. The court expects us to celebrate our marriage for eight days. Now, *elskan mín*, prepare yourself for bed. I shall not watch or violate your privacy."

Lyting crossed to the bed and, lying down, threw an arm over his eyes. His holy call in Francia seemed a dim and distant thing at the moment, but the pledge he had made to Ailinn was not. He must honor that vow, even though it continued to crucify his flesh anew. Releasing a long breath, exhaustion overtook him.

Ailinn fumbled with the lacings of her gown, which were fast becoming as knotted as her insides. Moving off toward one of the reclining couches, she quickly drew off her *stola* and wrapped herself in the brocaded robe. Her thoughts and emotions whirled with dizzying effect.

Lyting. Ever noble, ever righteous. She should have known how his scars were gained. Never had she seen him wield his sword or might otherwise than nobly, courageously, and to an honorable end.

Her thoughts leapt back in time. From the first he sought to free her from captivity. And though he sailed with the chieftain for reasons of his mission, she had ever felt beneath his protective eye. At Riga, Lyting triumphed over the pirate fleet, and at Gelandri, he nearly gave his life for Deira. He saw them through the dangerous lands of the Rus, fought tribesmen, defended her against Hakon, and saved her several times since their arrival in Constantinople. Today, he saved a child, his mother, and his throne.

Ailinn thought of Lyting defending his sister-by-marriage. Thought of the treacherous half brother and his henchmen raining blows on him. Imagined Lyting's pain as he took their steel into his body, then strove to comprehend his frustration and guilt for not having won that battle.

Noble Lyting. Her shining warrior. Her protector. Her husband. Her love.

The word blazed through her. As she faced and compassed

that love, a fiery ball centered in her chest, threatening to consume her.

She *did* love Lyting. Desperately.

Ailinn's thoughts scrambled to find the thread of that love and follow it to its beginning. It took her back through weeks, through months, to the first moment Lyting lifted her from the street of Hedeby and held her in his arms. Ailinn could not breathe for a moment as the fires of her love for Lyting flamed high in her heart.

She turned and looked toward the bed. He appeared to be sleeping, his arm dropped down alongside his head. Slowly, softly, she crossed the room. Ailinn drew shallow breaths as she gazed on him and traced his handsome features.

How proud she had been to walk by his side this day and exchange vows with him. She was Lyting's bride, she thought with awe, the fire increasing in her breast.

When was the last time she had thought on Lyting as a Norseman or a Dane? Whenever she had, she could no longer remember, so little did it matter. Where was her defiance now for the men of the North? a voice clamored at her from deep within. Truly, her revulsion remained for most of his race. But not for Lyting. Her great love.

Ailinn's gaze lingered over the scar on his left cheek. Again she felt his pain. Recognized his nobility. Recognized her enormous, all-consuming love for this man.

Easing upon the mattress's edge, she watched him in sleep, listened to his even breaths, skimmed his features once more—the bright hair, the fine, straight nose, the firm lips. Her gaze shifted to his cheek.

Ailinn's heart moved, touched by all he ever suffered. Overcome with emotion, her heart aflame, Ailinn leaned forward and pressed a kiss to the scar on Lyting's cheek, ever so lightly. Her gaze went to his mouth and lingered there. Unable to resist, she touched her lips to his.

Lyting stirred in the sweet depths of his dream, where an angel's kiss brushed his cheek. Light and shadow shifted. Someone poised above. He began to climb from the valley of sleep, then realized 'twas Ailinn who hovered above him. Incredibly, she bent and kissed him. Her lips soft, warm, and honey-sweet.

Through the drugged haze of sleep, Lyting sought to return

Ailinn's kiss. He dragged his heavy hand upward, a terrible weight. Clumsily his fingers caught in Ailinn's tresses, discovered their silk, stirred their fragrance to tease his senses.

What manner of dreams' illusion could conjure this? he wondered in a beclouded part of his brain. Questioning it no further, he responded to her kiss, seeking their nectar, struggling toward consciousness, yearning to claim her lips fully and wrap her in his arms.

Sleep lay over him like a huge body of water. He battled against it, fighting upward. Just as he began to slice through the slumberous depths and surface, he felt cool air rush between his and Ailinn's body.

He struggled furiously then, realizing she was withdrawing and trying to find her in the dark. The weight of his hands fell back to the pillow. On he vied, breaking the surface to wakefulness and finding himself breathless for the effort. He dragged open his lids, felt the cool of the sheets beside him. Ailinn was gone, the bed empty.

Bracing himself up on his elbow, Lyting peered into the room's darkness. Lamps softly illumined the chamber but did not reveal Ailinn. A flutter of fabric drew his gaze to where double doors opened onto the balcony.

There Ailinn stood with her back to him. A light evening breeze billowed the silken fabric of her robe and stirred her long tresses. She remained as still as the statues that graced the balcony, all frozen in time as they looked over the harbor.

Lyting clenched his fist and warred within his soul. Dear God, how he wanted Ailinn. More than life itself didst he want her. He wished to bound from the bed and snatch her up, then return and press her into the mattress, all the while telling her he had no intention of returning her to Ireland or seeking the cloistered walls of Corbie.

A beast raged within. His Norse blood fired his veins, urging he seize the prize and mate her at once—tonight and all nights left to him upon this earth. Lyting shuddered with repressed desire. Ailinn—the one woman he wanted most in this world, the woman honor and vows prevented him from having. But even if his call dimmed in the mists of time, his vow to Ailinn did not. Even if it could be laid aside, she would never accept a Dane.

Emotion ravaged him. Lyting cast himself to his other side.

Gripping the mattress itself, he anchored himself to the bed as flesh and spirit warred fiercely on the battlefield of his soul.

Tears spilled over Ailinn's cheeks as she stood upon the balcony, looking to the stars in the heavens. The fires of her love burned brightly in her heart, yet darkness enveloped her world once more.

'Twas her great misfortune to so desperately love a man God had already chosen and called to Himself. Lyting was to set his foot for Corbie, and he had indicated no change of heart otherwise. She could not, in good conscious, tempt him like a harlot from his holy call for the passions of the flesh.

Heavyhearted, she lifted her gaze to the stars, points of white light shining in the heavens.

"Sometimes the darkness holds the light."

Ailinn wavered as she beheld the night sky, illumined by a million stars.

"Her "star-bright" warrior. How often had she referred to Lyting precisely as that? Again her thoughts reached back in time—to her mother, Fianna, as she lay dying.

"Hold fast, my dearest Ailinn. Sometimes the darkness holds the light," Fianna had said, then raised loving eyes to Lorcan. Lorcan. A sharp jolt of realization plunged through Ailinn.

Fianna herself had been taken in a raid—by Lorcan—during an Irish *tain*, a cattle raid. Whether by mistake or apurpose, Lorcan fell instantly and irrevocably in love with Fianna and refused to return her to her clan. 'Twas only Fianna's insistence that she wished to stay and wed Lorcan that averted a clan war.

Now Ailinn understood. The "darkness" to which Fianna referred was her captivity, but the "light" was Lorcan himself—the light she found in the darkness, her love.

Ailinn's thoughts went to Lyting. Truly, he was the "light" who had turned her darkness into brilliant day. She would love him forever.

Lifting her damp lashes, she looked to the stars shining high above. One shone brighter among the rest. Like the stars, Lyting lay forever beyond her reach.

Early morn the choir arrived singing at the chamber door, waiting to accompany the bridal couple to a dining hall to break their fast.

The servants had already seen to their baths, which Lyting and Ailinn managed to partake of separately.

Lyting had used a small vial of goat's blood to sprinkle the sheets, suspecting they would be displayed, or at very least examined as in the West to prove the bride's virginity and the consummation of the wedding. He did not wish for any to think Ailinn had been previously defiled at the hands of his kinsmen. Now those men who had wandering eyes for her at court would truly accept their marriage as valid and direct their attentions elsewhere.

When the maid servant took the sheets away, she seemed well convinced their marriage had been consummated.

Once more Lyting and Ailinn joined the procession to dine in yet another of the many splendid halls and enjoy more lavish wedding entertainments arranged by Constantine. Lyting and Ailinn sat patiently through the ceremonies throughout the day.

Night came all too quickly, and again they were faced with the temptations of the night. The day's tension, wrought by Ailinn's nearness and too many beakers of wine, depleted Lyting. Still, he waited until Ailinn fell asleep before he stretched out beside her on the bed.

As the first glow of dawn illumined the skies, Ailinn awakened to Lyting's warmth and found him sleeping beside her. He lay atop the sheet, bare to the waist, his lower half swathed in a separate linen.

Ailinn watched him in repose, aware of the empty ache that pulsed through her body. Shifting onto her side, she raised herself carefully to her elbow and gazed on him.

Love spilled through her. As the night before, Ailinn eased forward and gently touched her lips to the scar on his cheek. Then gathering her courage, she kissed him fully upon the lips.

Lyting's eyes opened instantly. Ailinn froze, her heart jolting against her ribs.

Lyting stared at Ailinn, wondering if this be yet another dream. Ailinn's hair tumbled about her face and shoulders in entrancing disarray, and he felt the heat of her body pressed against his side. She leaned over him partially, her slim hand holding the sheet just beneath her heart. His gaze traced over the smooth column of her neck, her bare shoulders, and the beginning swell of her breasts.

Heat pervaded his loins. The warmth of her breath and the

tendril of her hair brushing his cheek told him this was no
dream. Ailinn continued to gaze on him, her lips poised above
his, looking for all the world as if she was about kiss him
again. God help him, he felt himself swelling beneath his
covering.

"Ailinn," he rasped, catching her arms. "I have warned
you. I am no eunuch."

She remained silent, her eyes fixed on him, huge and dark.
Her gaze drew to his lips, her own lips parting as if half in
yearning, half in invitation. At the same time she shifted
against him, unaware that her hand had dropped slightly,
taking with it the sheet.

Lyting sucked a breath as he looked on the ample curve of
her breasts, the cloth scarce covering their tips. A river of fire
surged through his veins. Groaning aloud, he rolled Ailinn
beneath him.

"God above, I am no eunuch," he vented raggedly. "Nor am
I a saint."

Lyting's mouth crushed down on hers, his ravenous desire
overtaking him. He kissed her hard and deep. Reaching for the
sheet, he yanked it free of her hand and bared her breasts.

Ailinn gasped as flesh seared flesh, and he pressed her into
the mattress. He invaded her mouth at once, hungrily ravaging
its depths and stroking her tongue with his in an erotic dance.
His hand moved to capture her breast, his thumb caressing her
nipple till it pebbled, hard and erect. Waves of passion broke
through Ailinn, and she clutched at him, glorying in his
possession of her.

His mouth left hers to trail a path of hot kisses over her
throat and collarbone. Ailinn arched against him as she felt the
warmth of his mouth close upon her breast. He swirled his
tongue over her nipple, tormenting her with a fine madness.
She sank her hands into his hair and held his head there as a
burst of sensations radiated from her nipple downward to
between her thighs, setting her afire.

Lyting abandoned her one breast to feast on the other,
bathing her nipple with his tongue before taking it in his mouth
and suckling it. Ailinn moaned at the exquisite torment and
thought she would melt beneath him. Sliding her hands over
the hard muscles of his back, she pulled at the cloth that
enveloped him, impatient to be rid of its barrier.

Lyting rolled slightly, dragging the cloth free. He then swept away the sheet that yet covered Ailinn's hips and legs. His eyes grazed her full, naked length. Heat, white hot, surged through him. Moving over her once more, he captured her mouth and plundered it thoroughly.

Ailinn met his urgency with her own, tension coiling through her. She pressed against him, instantly aware of his manhood, hard against her abdomen. Abruptly his lips left hers, and his mouth, tongue, and hands were everywhere and all at once. He lavished a blanket of kisses over her breasts and stomach, then covered her sensitive inner thighs with more and continued downward to her knees, calves, and ankles and back up again. Just when she thought he would devour her whole, he returned to possess her mouth.

Her lips parted, then widened further in shock as his hand slipped between her thighs and his fingers entered her intimately. Ailinn bolted against him as he began stroking the ultrasensitive core of her womanhood. The sensation spread wildfire through her, growing almost unbearable in its intensity. She hurtled toward some unknown precipice; still, he caressed her, unrelenting.

Lyting's mouth returned to Ailinn's breasts, and he savored their taut, waiting nipples. He found her wondrously responsive, already hot and wet inside, her womanhood swollen and ready for him.

He clung tenuously to his control. It had been so very long since he had known a woman. There be none he wanted more in the world than Ailinn, and though he wished this moment to be perfect for her, he knew he could not master himself much longer.

Lyting urged Ailinn's legs apart and settled between her thighs. As he continued to caress her, he slipped his fingers in deep and located her maidenhead. He hated to bring her pain, but there was no help for it.

Positioning himself, he entered her and began to push slowly in. He quickly met the obstruction and decided on a swift thrust to be done with the pain. Claiming her mouth in a deep, distracting kiss, he drove forward. Ailinn cried out as he breached the barrier and sheathed himself in her to the hilt.

Lyting quieted her with kisses and gentled her with words. She was incredibly hot and tight. His every instinct clamored that he begin thrusting, but he remained still, striving to maintain his control, hoping to last just a little longer so he might bring Ailinn to fulfillment.

He began kissing and caressing her anew. She responded as passion eclipsed pain and moaned beneath his touch. Perceiving her to be ready, he began thrusting slowly against her, guiding her hips with his hands. Abruptly he stilled, his control slipping.

Ailinn looked to Lyting, her senses in an upheaval. Why did he cease. Did he think he hurt her? But she ached with such urgent need, she began to move against him, rubbing her sensitive core against his smooth, hard shaft, maintaining the contact. Tension mounted sharply in Ailinn as her pleasure heightened.

Lyting gasped as Ailinn moved her hips against him, stealing the last of his restraint and hurtling him beyond the brink of control.

"Ailinn, forgive . . . can't wait," he grit out, then released a primitive groan as he exploded in an earth-shattering and sundering release. He surged against her, thrusting long and deep, triggering her own response and taking her with him to spiral ever upward.

Ailinn cried out, meeting his thrusts with her own, their bodies mating in an ancient rhythm. Ailinn thought she might die of the intensity of the feeling that suddenly erupted into a starburst of fire, so acute in its pleasure 'twas near indistinguishable from pain.

Driving against her, Lyting emptied himself into Ailinn, spending himself fully, then collapsed breathless atop her.

As Lyting's sanity returned, he plummeted from the soaring joy of ecstasy to a chasm of repentance.

"*Elskan mín*. Ailinn," he panted above her. "My God. What have I done?"

Seeing the look of astoundment on Ailinn's face, he rebuked himself thoroughly and dragged himself from the bed. He covered her with the sheets, then searched for his clothes, devastated that he had violated her.

Breathless, Ailinn watched Lyting, her heart pounding in her breast, her body trembling with exhilaration. She looked on his powerful, sleek body, his manhood still erect. She had no idea that lovemaking could be so cataclysmic.

Dressed, Lyting came to stand before her. "I am sorry, *elskan mín*. I protected you from everyone save myself."

She started to disclaim his guilt, for 'twas she who had initiated the passion, but again he spoke.

"Upon my vow, I shall return you to your people as I have promised. No one will hold the blame to you for being ravished by a Norseman."

With that, Lyting turned on his heel and quit the chamber.

Ailinn stared at the door, her heart compressing that he should talk of parting. She rose from the bed shakily, her body still alive and tingling with the memory of Lyting's touch and all they had shared. Slipping into her robe, she felt heartsick of a sudden for the pain and guilt she caused him. Yet, she treasured his total possession of her and regretted it not at all.

Her emotions in turmoil, Ailinn wandered out onto the balcony and stood looking over the Boucelon Harbor. Her heart burned with love for Lyting. Yet, 'twas a love she would ever be denied.

Behind, Ailinn heard servants enter the chamber. She turned and glimpsed the chamber maid stripping the sheets from the bed.

The woman stopped, seeing the virginal blood upon the cloth. She shook her head in dismay as she plodded from the room, obviously baffled that a maid could be twice a virgin.

Chapter 22

Lyting knelt before the column of the *stylite*, seeking the holy man's direction and thoroughly revolted with himself for having violated Ailinn. Yet, a part of him remained unrepentant. For at least once in his lifetime, he had known intimacy and ecstasy with Ailinn. The remembrance made him hot with desire to bury himself in her again.

He bowed his head.

"I have lost my direction, Father," he prayed aloud in Greek. "I thought I knew well the way the Lord set before me, and yet I find myself lost in the wood."

The holy man contemplated Lyting, his sharp eyes piercing him, as though seeing straight to his heart.

"Why do you torture yourself, my son? You will know peace in your soul only when you take up the true path God has chosen for you. Only then can you serve Him with your whole heart. Look for that path. Look where He leads you."

"But I have looked and there are paths aplenty to lead me amiss. I am hard-pressed to choose the right one."

"Look again, my son. The way is not so obscure as you believe."

"But how will I know which is the right way?" Lyting's voice held his bewilderment.

"Look for our Lord. Already He stands there in the midst, showing you the way," the holy man said cryptically and fell silent.

"In the 'midst'?" Lyting repeated, puzzled, tumbling the word in his mind.

He closed his eyes and bent his head once more. Pondering it, he balled one hand into the other, then raised them and pressed his lips against the back of his fingers. He felt the cool metal of his wedding ring.

Drawing away his hands, Lyting gazed on the coin-shaped bezel. It displayed a miniature of the bridal couple, so detailed it could be considered a likeness of himself and Ailinn. Standing in their midst, Christ joined their hands.

Lyting thought to feel the earth move beneath him. He rose unsteadily to his feet, his eyes locked upon his ring.

"God means me to be married? But   . . ."

His thoughts vaulted back in time to when he lay at the brink of death, decimated by Hastein's perfidy. Day by day he had crawled a little further back to life, until he was whole again. 'Twas later, while helping rebuild Saint Wandrille's abbey, that he had been inspired by sermons of the sagacious Wilibrod of Corbie and deemed he had been spared for a greater purpose— serving God within His cloistered walls.

But *he* had chosen that path, he realized now. He had assumed 'twas God's will he take the cowl of the Benedictines. Though he believed it to be a blessed calling, he also believed 'twas the Divine hand that diverted him to a much different path, sending him on the journey to Byzantium to rescue Ailinn and aid the Imperials.

A partial smile lifted one corner of Lyting's lips. 'Twould appear, when he was too thickheaded to yield to God's intentions, the Almighty had directed circumstances that saw him twice wed to Ailinn. He thought of the Pantocrator looking down on their marriage, His hand raised in blessing. The holy man once told him to remove the block from his eyes. How could he have been so blind?

The call to priesthood was sacred, certainly. But so also was the call to marriage. And the vows that bound them united them in "one mind" and wed them into "one flesh"—"unto the ages."

Lyting felt as though the last shards fell from his eyes and he could see clearly. 'Twas not for Corbie he had been saved, but for Ailinn—to save her, to free her, and to take her to wife.

Ailinn was indeed his wife in every meaning of the

word—their vows sealed, their union consummated. Concern welled in his chest. Though she responded to him in passion, she may never be able to accept marriage to him, a Norseman. There was also his promise of annulment and of returning her to her people. They need talk. At once.

Overcome with a fierce joy of being free to claim Ailinn as his wife, and a naked fear of her rejection, he raced back toward the Sacred Palace, his energy unbounded.

As Lyting approached the Mesê, he caught sight of a figure moving through the crowd. Recognition jarred through him and stopped him midpace. 'Twas the silver-haired man from the cemetery.

Lyting's jaw hardened. He hated to delay his steps to Ailinn's side, but he could not let this man slip away.

Lyting followed at a discreet distance, turning along varied streets and heeling after him up one of the city's steeper hills to a mansion overlooking the Golden Horn.

The man slowed as they approached the dwelling. People stood clustered in the street, gaping toward the edifice, listening to the commotion that thundered within. Voices clamored and steel rang out. Soldiers suddenly spilled out the doors dragging their iron-bound prisoners.

The silver-haired man reeled at the sight and started to flee. Lyting bolted for him. Seizing him by the shoulder, he spun the man around and gripped him by the neck of his tunic.

"In a rush?" Lyting smiled grimly, lifting the man off his toes. The man's eyes widened with shock, and he struggled to tear away.

Meanwhile, more troops emerged from the mansion. Lyting saw now they were a mixture of Imperial troops and Varangian Guards. Among them came the Domesticus, Leo Phocas, dragging the Strategos, Andronicus Styliane. Thord appeared behind the two, further surprising Lyting.

Seeing Lyting, Thord hastened forward.

" 'Twas no time to find you, my friend." He panted for breath. "We found the link you sought since your coming—the identity, or rather the significance, of the name 'Stephanites Cerularius.' 'Tis that of the distant maternal grandsire of none other than the Strategos, Andronicus Styliane. We also loosed the tongues of several followers, seized during the wedding attack. One of the wharf rats we caught decided to talk and confirmed what we suspected. The Strategos is our 'scorpion.' He almost slipped away again."

"What of Leonites?" Lyting asked, still gripping the man but having returned his feet to the ground.

"Leonites was an underling. When he discovered Andronicus had deceived him—that there wasn't any support or help to flee after the assassination, as promised—he went for Andronicus. Andronicus killed him so he couldn't talk."

"Andronicus must have also dropped the pouch containing the rings whilst beneath the canopy," Lyting observed.

"*Satt*. True. But there be two other matters you need know." Thord's face darkened. " 'Tis known Andronicus recently took a new man into his employ. Hakon. We are searching for him and suspect he was charged to murder those apprehended during the attack. We know not how."

"And the second?"

"The woman Xenia. She has long been known to be Andronicus's lover. We've been looking for a woman connected to the 'scorpion.' Though 'tis only a suspicion that she might have been involved in the deaths of the Varangians, she does operate a perfumery in the women's quarters. 'Tis likely she is the 'spider' we seek. Xenia was observed with Hakon this morning but has also disappeared."

"Ailinn," Lyting breathed, his gut clenching.

Lyting thrust the silver-haired man into Thord's hands. "Here is another of the 'scorpion's' scum."

With that, Lyting sprinted back down the hill.

Ailinn paced the chamber restlessly, having sent Ariana to locate Lyting. The slave Comita had been found a short time ago, dead, the stolen vial of perfume lying empty on the floor beside her. Its oil, Ariana revealed when she came with the news, contained a deadly poison.

Ailinn realized Xenia meant the poison for her. The thought sent a chill rippling through her bones. Had Helena also died beneath Xenia's hands? Ailinn did not compass all the implications but suspected Xenia was part to the conspiracy Lyting sought to uncover.

Ailinn turned, wringing her hands, and crossed the room to where the doors stood open to the balcony. She needed fresh air to clear her mind. As she verged on the portal, a figure loomed, stepping from concealment at the door's edge and blocking her path.

Ailinn sucked a startled breath. 'Twas a Varangian, dressed in the distinctive palace uniform—a scarlet tunic with a sword suspended on a strap that hung from his shoulder and lay across his chest. In his hand he gripped a long-shafted ax. Loosing his helmet with its obscuring noseguard, he dragged it from his head.

"Hakon!" she hissed.

Gliding silently into view behind him was a veiled woman. Xenia.

Ailinn backed slowly into the room, fear stalking her. Hakon matched her, step for step, uttering something in his Nordic tongue. She understood naught of it but realized his purpose in coming was to steal her away. Every nerve in her being screamed out, the nightmare of her first seizure in Clonmel replaying itself. He would not have her again!

Ailinn whirled, a scream tearing from her throat as she ran for the door. But Hakon covered the distance between them in several easy strides. Dropping his helmet and ax, he seized her about the waist and clamped a hand over her mouth.

"Did you think I would not return?" Hakon hauled the Irish beauty against his chest. "You are mine. And no man or child emperor will say me otherwise. Certainly, no monk," he hurled derisively, caring not at all that she didn't understand him. "Has he mated you, my sweet?" His hand slid over her breast, then downward over her abdomen. "Has he claimed your maidenhead? No matter. He'll not have an opportunity to pleasure himself on you again."

"Nor will you!" Lyting's voice boomed across the room from where he stood, just inside the door. He reached for his sword, and this time it waited in its scabbard. The hilt filled Lyting's hand, and he arced the blade free. "Let us see this to an end, Hakon, once and for all."

Hakon's grip slackened on Ailinn. He then shoved her toward Xenia. "To the end," Hakon growled and reached to his back. Seizing on the short-hafted ax tucked in his belt, he brought it forth and hurled it at Lyting.

Lyting pitched aside as the ax burred past his head and gashed the marble wall before clattering to the floor.

Hakon snatched up the longer-shafted ax and bolted forward, slicing low for Lyting's legs. Lyting leapt back. With both hands he brought his broadsword down with a powerful stroke and smote the ax's shaft in two.

Hakon threw down the severed wood and drew on his sword. Lyting met him, stroke for stroke. Steel sang out, blade biting blade. On they strove, neither yielding. The swords clanged and flashed, some strokes sweeping high and wide, others slicing down, fracturing tables and rending precious silk hangings.

Hakon swiped for Lyting's head, but Lyting ducked and the sword struck a marble column instead. Before he could recover, Lyting slogged him in the ribs with both fists, still gripping his sword. Hakon stumbled a pace but regained himself and came up, slashing for Lyting's stomach. Lyting canted and blocked the stroke. Their blades locked, and for a moment they strained, muscle to muscle. Hakon kicked high, of a sudden, catching Lyting in both hip and side and sending him backward to the floor.

Lyting scrambled to his feet, but as he did, Hakon raised his sword and struck downward, opening himself a fraction too long. Lyting thrust forward with his sword, stabbing into Hakon's midsection. Hakon doubled over the blade and crumpled to the floor.

Lyting heaved for breath. Retrieving his sword, he pressed his forehead against the flat side of the blade, near the hilt, and mentally uttered his thanks heavenward. 'Twas done. Hakon lay motionless before him.

Slowly Lyting turned to Ailinn. She started toward him, reaching out her arms. But then she halted, and all color left her face.

Ailinn's eyes rounded, and she screamed as she saw Hakon come to life, slipping a knife from his boot and rising behind Lyting.

At Ailinn's outcry, Lyting began to turn, bringing up his sword. He caught a blur of movement in the edge of his vision, and next felt fire piercing his shoulder blade as steel lodged in his flesh. Ailinn's screams resounded in his ears.

Before losing his hold on his sword, Lyting covered his right hand with his left and gripped tight. Reversing the blade, he arced it down and around, sweeping beneath his arm and driving back. The sword caught Hakon straight on, running him through to the spine.

Hakon shouted out in pain and dropped facedown to the floor. Expelling a long breath, he succumbed.

Lyting sank forward onto the floor, a knife protruding from his back as he braced himself up with his left arm. Ailinn rushed to his side, and he next heard footsteps, then voices—that of Thord and other Varangians.

"Where is Xenia?" Lyting meant the words for Ailinn, but they came out Norse. "I saw her standing on the balcony."

Thord scanned the room and, not seeing Xenia, signaled his men to go in search for her. "She'll not get far on the palace grounds," he promised, dropping down beside Lyting.

Pain riveted Lyting as Thord withdrew the knife from his back. He felt a hot rush of blood, then Thord's fingers stanching the flow.

The world began to recede, swirling about him. Ailinn cried out his name as he pitched forward, then plunged headlong into darkness.

Chapter 23

Lyting drifted in a shadowy nether region, between semiaware-
ness and total unconsciousness.

Voices spoke rapidly over and about him, one more urgent
than the rest. Ailinn's. Her anguished voice rose, thin and
unnatural, constricted with tears as she bid the others to lift him
gently and pleaded for him not to die. Then, he heard Ariana's
voice comforting her, and Ailinn as she broke into sobs.

Lyting ached to reach out and solace her but could neither
move nor speak in the darkness that entrapped him.

Footsteps rushed about. He heard the soft swish of silk and
the murmur of voices as people hovered about him. Hands
lifted and carried him. Fresh pain tore through his shoulder
blade. He next felt himself lowered onto the softness of the bed
and eased onto his stomach. The sound of fabric being sliced
away filled his hearing, then he felt a rush of cool air over his
back.

Hands continued to work on him. Cleansing waters soothed
the throb in his back, followed by tiny stabs of pain. Dimly
Lyting thought of the physician plying his needle. 'Twas an old
wound, he objected vaguely as though the man could hear him.
Why should he need stitching again?

Darkness pulled him downward into the mists of time.

A nebulous fog swirled about Lyting. As he gazed into
the brume, specters materialized and began to emerge, three
horsemen bearing down on him. He heard their shouts and the

sound of swords scraping from their scabbards. One whirled hook-ended chains above his head.

A woman's scream pierced the gloom, a soul-wrenching cry. Then Lyting saw clearly. 'Twas Hastein mounted before him, his colorless eyes gleaming and as cold as death. Hastein kicked forward, his sword flashing.

Lyting found himself mounted and armed as well. He spurred his horse, driving toward Hastein. The shock of steel reverberated through his arm, their blades clanging together and grating apart. Hastein hammered down on him, but Lyting pitched and parried, meeting the blows and turning them aside. Lyting flinched as the hot sting of Hastein's blade lay open his cheek.

Again a woman screamed, sobbing his name. Brienne? *Nei*, not she. His heart caught as he recognized that anguished voice. 'Twas Ailinn.

Gaining strength he fought on, holding Ailinn's image before his mind's eye. Steel on steel, he battled back, raining blow after blow on Hastein. The other horsemen faded from sight, and now he faced his half brother alone.

Hastein's features suddenly began to transform. In his face Lyting saw Hakon's features appear, overlaying those of Hastein. A rage took hold of Lyting, that these two men should seek to despoil those he held most dear. In an explosion of soul-blinding fury, Lyting plunged his sword through the twin images, planting it deep in their obsidian hearts.

The sword's bright steel absorbed their evil, turning pitch black. As he continued to look on them, the specters of Hastein and Hakon dissolved to ash. A light breeze arose, diffusing the dark cinders and carrying them away.

All dimmed and Lyting floated peacefully for atime as though moving in the currents of a great river that carried him toward a light.

He sensed someone beside him, then felt an angel's kiss upon his cheek. And again upon his lips. He struggled to gain consciousness, but only once did he manage to peer through the groggy veil that enshrouded him. No one held near, but then he glimpsed Ailinn standing on the balcony. She turned toward him, looking to the bed. Tears washed her cheeks. Stifling a sob, she buried her face in her hands.

Lyting strained to console her, his heart wringing with hers.

He would set all aright, he promised her silently, but then slipped beneath the surface again and drifted in partial consciousness.

He must tell her. Of the holy man. The *stylite*, on his pillar. He need not leave her, ever.

"The sorrows of Munster bide ever in my heart," he heard her voice echo through a tunnel in time. "The attack of the Danes . . . I shall never forget . . . never . . ."

Dread gripped him. Would she refuse him? Could she find love in her heart and leave her homeland for a man of the North? A Dane?

He fought the darkness that surrounded him, desperate to break through to Ailinn. He called her name, but no sound left his throat.

The inkiness began to pale to a pearly gray, and he surged toward the brightest spot. As he approached consciousness, he heard Ailinn's soft sniffles and whispered prayers. Heard his name upon her lips.

The mattress sank beside him, and he sensed her leaning over him. A hot tear fell upon his cheek, followed by the warmth of her lips as she gently kissed him there. Several more tears wet his skin, then she pressed the side of her face against his and buried her face in his hair.

Lyting dragged his lids open and swallowed against the dryness in his throat. He felt Ailinn's shoulders shake against him and knew she was crying. Slowly he pulled his hand upward and lay it to the small of her back.

"*Elskan mín.* My love," he whispered hoarsely.

Ailinn started, lifting herself upright. "Lyting?" her voice rose in astonishment. Her pulse skittered to find his crystal-blue eyes shining upon her. Then she broke into an enormous smile. And a fresh flood of tears.

Ailinn covered Lyting's cheeks, eyes, forehead, nose, chin, and throat with kisses, her fingers following as though to assure he were truly alive and awake to her.

Lyting wondered at Ailinn's response. Dare he believe she bore him love? Or was it the fright of losing him that prompted this outrush of emotion? Or both?

Speechless, he caught her hand in his. He need tell her he would not be taking the cowl of the Benedictines and that 'twas his heartfelt desire to honor their marriage vows and return with her at his side to Francia.

Collecting his thoughts, he brushed back the damp tendrils of hair from her face. But before he could speak, she captured his hand and pressed her lips to its back. Tears slid from beneath her lashes and bathed his skin.

Lyting's chest constricted. Gently, he wiped the wetness from her cheek.

"Why do you cry so, *elskan mín*?"

Ailinn raised dark eyes to his. "Because I feared you might die," she said miserably. "The physic assured 'twas the loss of blood alone that caused you to faint and that there be no vital damage. Still, I prayed and prayed."

Ailinn's eyes were open pools of pain, and Lyting knew she did not tell him all.

"Why?" he asked again, urgent to know her true feelings.

She swallowed a breath. "Because I love you most desperately." Her chin quivered. "I have lost so much, but the thought of losing you slays my very soul. Yet, even now, I know you will leave me. For Corbie."

Her gaze dropped to their joined hands, her throat aching raw. "Saints forgive me, but I never believed God intended you to be a monk, Lyting. I will not attempt to seduce you from your course, but know I have no intention of seeking an annulment, ever. I will honor you all the days of my life as my husband and will seek none other. Should a child come of our brief union, I shall count myself blessed. Know I shall keep and cherish our child always, for 'twill be a most precious part of you."

Thunderstruck by Ailinn's profession of love, Lyting lay momentarily speechless. Waves of emotions pounded through him, followed by a profound and cleansing relief. He raised his hand and stroked Ailinn's cheek, his love for her palpable.

"Ailinn, my heart. I was returning to tell you, I shall not be joining the brothers of Corbie. I have no desire to leave you. Only a desire to keep you ever at my side."

Ailinn looked on him with astonishment. As he told her of his words with the holy man, her gaze dropped to her wedding ring, then to his. A radiant joy flooded her whole being. Her eyes misted.

"*Elskan mín*, do my words bring you tears?"

"Oui, oui," she said, nodding. "A heartful of the sweetest tears I have ever known, for it suddenly comes to me that no force awaits to separate us—no chains to bind, no perils to thwart, no shadows to threaten. There be naught to keep us apart, and the enormity of that thought doth overwhelm, as well as disburden me of all that has weighed my soul."

Lyting, too, felt the vast reach of her words and knew a boundless yearning to be one with her again. He eased upward with some discomfort but counted the pain as naught.

"Come then, love, and let us be apart no more. We have consummated our vows with our first coupling. Now I would consummate it with our hearts as well."

Heat stole through Ailinn, igniting small fires beneath her skin. "As would I," she whispered.

Seeing the love and desire that shimmered in his beautiful blue eyes, her breath grew shallow and her heart picked up a light, rapid beat. She rose from the bed, her hands trembling slightly as they moved to the sash of her robe and freed it. Drawing open the robe, she let it slide from her shoulders and pool at her feet.

Lyting's passion flamed sharp and bright, heat building in his loins. He drank in Ailinn's beauty, savoring the sight of her breasts, full and round with rose-hued tips. His gaze roamed lower to her taut stomach and abdomen, her creamy thighs, the dark auburn curls that concealed her femininity and the promise of ineffable joy that awaited within.

Lyting drew aside his coverings in invitation, and Ailinn's eyes strayed to the undeniable proof of his arousal. Her eyes widened, and her heart skipped madly. She had felt . . . but not seen . . . well, not like that. A flush spread over her skin.

"Come, wife," he bid her softly.

Moistening her lips, Ailinn pressed him gently back down to the mattress and began to stretch out beside him. But he caught her hips and shifted her over him so that she straddled his pelvis. She gasped as he guided her down atop him and began to fill her—gasped, half in surprise at the action, half in wonder that she could fully receive him. Yet, she did so with ease, and reminded that she had done so before and would do so again, for this was the physical bonding of marriage.

Ailinn took another swift breath as Lyting smoothed his

hands over the soft pliant mounds of her breasts and caressed their taut peaks. An ache spread through her, her senses blossoming beneath his touch. 'Twas as though he knew which course they followed, for his hand trailed after them, from the sensitive tips of her breasts to the core of her womanhood, where he began to stroke her rhythmically, his touch pure fire.

Pulling her forward, he captured her nipple with his mouth. She arched, passion spiraling through her as he lavished it with the warmth and moist silk of his tongue, all the while continuing his sweet torture between her legs.

Ailinn moaned and Lyting felt her femininity clamp tight about him, suddenly searingly hot and wet inside. His hunger sharpened. Moving to her other breast, he made love to it with his tongue, at the same time drawing her over, onto the mattress. He left her pouting crest and began a downward path toward her navel. When Ailinn objected to his withdrawal from her, he moved her hand to envelop his manhood.

They both sucked their breath—he at his flaring desire and need for release, she with surprise at the heat and length and feel of his blade of passion, so wondrously smooth and hard.

They cherished each other then, losing themselves in the fires of passion. With mouths and tongues and hands, they explored each other thoroughly and intimately—she moving down over his throat and chest to trace the tight nubs of his nipples and flick them with her tongue as he had hers; he causing her to quiver as he pressed kisses behind her knees, then upward over the sensitive silk of her inner thighs, moving higher and higher.

When she squirmed at the direction of his path, he smiled and moved over her, claiming her mouth in a deep and ravishing kiss, trusting there would be many nights to teach his bride the numerous ways of love.

Their bodies blended, Lyting's merging with Ailinn's as he pushed deep inside her and began to move with fluid power. Ailinn wrapped her legs about his, joining him in that ardent pace, her excitement mounting with his, her pulse thudding in her veins.

On they surged, their rhythm increasing as they tasted and touched and whispered words of love with feverish haste. Their whispers quickly became groans, their pleasure gaining a fierce intensity, setting them aflame and lifting them upward, out of time and place.

Lyting and Ailinn gloried in each other as they rode their passions higher. Ailinn cried out Lyting's name as her nerves convulsed, then took Lyting with her, roaring to his completion. Together, they cleaved and strained in a joining of bodies, a melding of hearts, a fusing of souls.

Later, as they lay together in the afterglow of their lovemaking, comfortably entwined, Lyting's hand leisurely stroked the curve of Ailinn's waist and hip. He dropped a kiss to the top of her head, a final concern wearing at the edge of his soul.

"My heart, I am sworn to my brother. I am his liege man. We will need live in Francia, yet, I have promised to return you to your home in Ireland."

Ailinn tilted her head back to look up at him, feeling wondrously languid in his arms. "You may."

Her eyes sparkled, and she laughed softly as surprise glanced through his blue eyes. She smiled, shifting so she lay atop him, and brushed her lips over his.

"*Some day,*" she added. "Mayhaps to visit. But my home is now in you, my love. Wherever you go, there shall I follow, for my heart is in your keeping."

"*Elskan mín.* My love." Lyting cupped her face in his hands. "I loved you from the moment I first saw you, and every moment my heart has beat since. It seems I have waited a lifetime to find you and another to claim you. I pray God grants us an eternity of days together, so I can go on loving you."

Ailinn thought her heart would burst, her love for this man overflowing and bringing tears to her eyes.

As Lyting's mouth descended over hers, Ailinn met him fully. Their breaths mingled and became one, their desire quickly mounting.

Together, they scaled the heights of passions until the earth could no longer bind them. Then, their love burst forth in a brilliant shower of light as they attained a heavenly rapture and joined the stars.

Epilogue

On a crisp, clear day in early autumn, Lyting and Ailinn traversed the waters between Francia and Saxon England, skimming the Frankish coast. At Lyting's charge, the crew turned the vessel into the headwaters of the River Toques and set course for Valsemé.

A blaze of color fired the woods lining their passage—scarlets, golds, russets, and cinnamons. Overhead winged a flock of swallows, swift and elegant, their long, twittering song heralding the ship's approach.

Lyting's anticipation mounted, as did Ailinn's.

In time a familiar sight came into view. Lyting lifted his arm and pointed ahead. "There. The keep of Valsemé." He squeezed Ailinn's shoulder, the sweetest of joys pouring through him. "We are home, *elskan mín*. 'Tis my hope you will come to love Valsemé as much as I."

Ailinn covered his hand, then a smile stole over her lips. "Lyting, listen. Do you hear it?"

Lyting glanced landward, his ear catching the distinct and joyous ringing of a bell.

"Valsemé's church possesses no bell," he declared, then hesitated. Lyting swallowed around the knot that rose to block his throat. In his heart he knew 'twas the bell of Saint Anskar.

The wharf came into view, and now they could see people, filling the banks, waving their handkerchiefs deliriously and cheering their return.

Ailinn turned to Lyting in wonder. "How didst . . . ?"

"I sent ahead a message when we changed vessels at Dives," Lyting replied as he spied Rurik's golden mane and Brienne standing beside him, waiting on the quay.

The twins scampered about their mother's skirts. Ketil towered above all with his flaming ruff of hair, and diminutive Aleth stood before him. Little Elsie clutched a fistful of flowers, and Waite scooped up the mongrel, Patch, and waved his paw. There was the Seneschal, Bolsgar, and Brother Bernard and many of the men-at-arms with whom he had long worked and trained, and a multitude of others.

"Now, my lady wife, we are truly home." He pressed a kiss to her temple. "It pleasures me beyond words to present you as my bride."

As their boat glided alongside the pier, Rurik and Brienne came forth to meet them.

Lyting climbed onto the planking, then aided Ailinn from the ship. Turning to greet his brother, he clasped forearms with Rurik and shared a manly hug. Smiles split their faces, and as they parted, a trace of moistness glazed their eyes.

Ailinn felt the invisible bond that joined the two men.

"I am glad you have returned to us whole and hail," Rurik declared. "I have sent many a message seeking word of you both but heard naught till your missive from Dives."

Brienne raised on tiptoe and kissed Lyting on each cheek, then welcomed Ailinn with a warm embrace. "We have all been so worried about you two, heartsick for want of news."

Rurik dragged a hand along his jaw, a fresh smile breaking over his face as his steel-blue eyes moved from Lyting to Ailinn and back again. He inclined his head toward Brienne.

"I believe I have never seen Lyting look better, *astin mín*. Or more rested. He doesn't possess that keen edge of one ever looking over his shoulder. Instead, he looks to be a man who is supremely content," Rurik baited with a grin.

"That I am." Lyting encircled Ailinn with his arm and gathered her to his side. Her mantle slipped back, exposing her rounded stomach.

Rurik elevated a brow. "I see you have been busy these past months, *broðir*. I assume you have reconsidered your call to Corbie. Or, at least, I *hope* you have."

Ketil, who had come to join them with Aleth—and seeing

the swell of Ailinn's stomach—grinned broadly from ear to ear and rocked back on his heels.

Lyting pinned Ketil with a look. "In truth, we have been married twice over. We must speak of it anon, for there is much to tell, and our adventures are many. Suffice it to say, we have returned to make our wedded life here and to enlarge the population of Valsemé."

"Welcome once more, dear sister." Brienne kissed Ailinn's cheeks. "You, indeed, are most special for Lyting to have chosen you. He, himself, is a very special man."

Ailinn warmed at Brienne's open acceptance of her. She knew 'twas Brienne who had first spurred Lyting to take pity on the maids of Clonmel in the streets of Hedeby and, because of it, brought his attention upon herself.

Rurik also welcomed Ailinn into the family with a brotherly kiss and hug. The twins took that moment to dash onto the pier and throw themselves at Lyting. As he caught them up, one in each arm, they laughed gleefully.

"Uncle! Your bell is ringing!" Richard cried in delight, pointing back in the direction of the church.

"Bell ringing," Kylan echoed.

The others broke into laughter, and Ketil roared with jovial mirth. "I'd say it has done a might more than ring!"

"Lyting! Are you blushing?" Brienne teased with great mischievousness. "In truth, the bell has hung silent until this very day. Rurik purchased the bell of Saint Anskar, knowing how you wished it for Valsemé's church, but once installed, he forbade it to be rung until your return."

Lyting looked in amazement at Rurik. "And if I had not?"

Rurik's smile sobered, the laughter draining from his eyes as he held Lyting's gaze. "Then the bell would have hung silent for all time."

Moved beyond words, Lyting stood silent and felt a stinging at the back of his eyes.

"We have much of which to speak." Rurik cleared his suddenly roughened voice. "But not this day. 'Tis a day of thanksgiving and celebration, for God has brought you both safely home to Valsemé."

Brienne looked to Ailinn. "Come, you have not met Ketil and his wife, Aleth."

Now the pieces fell into place as Ailinn looked at the fiery giant and the diminutive Frankish lady with honey-brown hair.

"But I do remember you both, from Hedeby," Ailinn said as she received their greetings.

"There is someone else here from Hedeby." Ketil grinned, looking for all the world hard-pressed to contain himself.

Ketil and Aleth stepped aside, revealing a petite young girl with dark brown hair, waiting on the wharf at the end of the pier.

Ailinn's hands flew to her mouth. "Lia!"

Tears bleared her vision as she started into a run and hastened along the pier, as did Lia. They met midway and gripped each other fiercely.

"Dear God, Lia. I thought you to be gone forever."

Hot tears cascaded over Ailinn's cheeks, wetting Lia's hair, as Lia's did hers. The others waited, allowing them the moment until they could compose themselves. When they did, not a dry eye remained amongst any of those assembled.

"I was told you were sold to a fierce-looking Norseman."

"She was!" Ketil's beard parted with a grin as he and the others joined them. "I found Lia being sold in the market. She reminded me so much of my sweet Aleth, well . . ." He shrugged. "I couldn't bear to leave her there. I thought for sure Aleth would think I'd gone mad, but she understood, and we took Lia under our wing."

"Lia was sickly for a time," Aleth added, brushing back the girl's hair in a motherly gesture. "Lady Brienne and I nursed her to health. But she had a fitful spell the day you sailed. Lyting, you remember. 'Twas why we couldn't see you off at the harbor."

Ketil picked up Aleth's story. " 'Twas later that same day that we discovered Lia spoke Frankish and learned you were stepcousins. We told her Lyting went with you and assured her he would bring you home."

Lyting arched a brow. "Confident, weren't you?"

Ketil's eyes sparkled. "My faith has never wavered in you, lad."

Ailinn looked up to Lyting. "You never mentioned Lia."

"Upon my word, I didst not know of your relation until this moment and saw her only briefly whilst in Hedeby. As I recall, most of my time was spent in alleyways watching over you, *elskan mín*, if not cooling my considerable ardor in the river."

This admittance brought laughter all around.

Lia touched Ailinn's arm. "Do you know aught of Deira and Rhiannon?" she asked hesitantly. "When Lord Rurik and Ketil went in search of them, they were told they had sailed with the chieftain Skallagrim."

Ailinn's head sank forward as she searched her heart for the words she must speak. She took Lia's hands in hers.

"Deira sleeps in a more heavenly place now. I like to think she has found her peace, where no pain can touch her, and knows a greater joy in God's presence than we here on earth can possibly conceive. Surely, she smiles down on us even now."

Lia received this news quietly, her eyes filling as she looked apart. "And Rhiannon?"

Ailinn's voice grew slightly sharp. "For her treachery, Rhiannon was carried off by tribesmen and is amongst them now, somewhere on the great plains of the Steppes. Skallagrim and Hakon are both dead."

Lia pressed her lashes shut against the images, gained strength from the last, then turned and hugged Ailinn once more. "Praise God, for you have been restored to me this day."

"As have you." Ailinn held her tightly.

Brother Bernard moved beside Lyting and rested a hand on his shoulder as they watched the scene.

"I see you have found your calling, my son. God needs his warriors afield, even as He needs those such as I, to pray for those such as you, and most earnestly, too." He grinned wide, enjoying his verbal play.

As Lyting escorted Ailinn from the pier, they were enveloped in a sea of well-wishers. After many long and cheerful exchanges, the gathering assembled at Valsemé's church to celebrate Lyting's and Ailinn's return with a Mass. They then entered into the bailey and went to the manor house, where a great feast awaited. Many a tale was shared, and many more promised for future nights.

Much later, Ketil and Aleth sat at a gaming board. Lia sat at another with a man named Alain, one of the Franks in Rurik's service. Lyting and Ailinn shared a look, wondering if perchance Lia had found happiness at Valsemé.

Rurik and Brienne shared a knowing smile and moved from

the dais. As they departed the hall, Rurik looked to Lyting. "My lady and I will be walking by the lake this eve."

Lyting did not miss Rurik's unspoken message, which gave him to know what places would be unoccupied this eve.

"Come, *elskan mín.*" Lyting took Ailinn by the hand. "There is something I wish you to see."

Leaving the manor house, he led her toward the keep. Ailinn looked up at the daunting tower and the wooden stairway that rose ever upward. Lyting rubbed his jaw. With a grin—light and laughter filling his eyes—he swept her from her feet and climbed the stairs.

When they gained the top and entered in, Ailinn insisted he set her down. They continued upward, resting at intervals for Ailinn's sake, until at last they came to a low-ceilinged room in the uppermost part of the tower. There, a small ladder led up to a door in the ceiling. Opening it, Lyting aided Ailinn up the rungs.

As they emerged on top of the keep, the sight stole Ailinn's breath away. The sun's fiery ball hovered over waters of the Toques, setting the waters aflame with crimson and gold, and burnishing the gently rolling hills all around for as far as they could see.

Lyting drew Ailinn in his arms. "This day shall we take up our lives anew, my heart. Here shall we live and love and birth our children into life. Here shall I cherish you unto the ages."

Ailinn's heart overflowed, her eyes misting. "As I shall you," she whispered, her voice thick with emotion.

She tilted her lips to his, softly parted and inviting. Lyting accepted that beloved offering and covered her mouth with his.

As he drew her into a deep, soul-reaching kiss, their love flamed brightly, fused and spun out, lighting the fires of eternity and turning the nights to day.

Author's Postscript

THE VARANGIAN GUARD: Although it was not until later in the tenth century, during the reign of Basil II, that members of the Varangian Guard were "officially" installed in the palace as the emperor's personal bodyguard, the Varangians had been in service to the Imperial crown dating well back to the ninth century. An elite corps, the Varangian Guard was reputed for its exceptional fighting skills and its fierce loyalty to one another and to the emperor. Constantine Porphyrogentius, as an adult, wrote of the Varangians in his work *De Administrando*, placing them in the palace at Christmas as they performed their "yul" dance. With some liberty, I have depicted the emperor's Varangian bodyguard to be in place in the early tenth century, but have otherwise been faithful to their portrayal.

BYZANTINE WEDDING CEREMONY: My source for the ancient ceremonials and rites was *Marriage: An Orthodox Perspective* by John Meyendorff, St. Vladimir's Seminary Press: Crestwood, NY 10707 (1984).

THE FATE OF THE HOUSE OF THE MACEDONIANS: In 918 A.D., Zoë's popularity plummeted after the Byzantine army endured two annihilating defeats at the hands of Symeon the Bulgarian. In her struggle to retain her throne, she relied heavily on Leo Phocas, now a widower and with whom she may have considered marriage. However, the Patriarch Nicholas Mysticus moved swiftly to remove Zoë from power only to be countered by Romanus Lecapenus who successfully usurped the throne and within a month married his daughter Helena to thirteen-year-old Constantine. Through his efforts, Romanus undermined the loyalty of the army to Leo Phocas. Leo was seized in flight and his eyes put out. Zoë, who had been allowed at first to remain in the palace at the desperate pleadings of her son, was caught in another palace intrigue and dispensed once and for all to the convent of Saint Euphemia. Meanwhile, Romanus solidified his power. Within two years he had Constantine elevate him to the status of *Caesar* and subsequently crowned himself as co-emperor. In time, he further displaced Constantine, taking the mantle of senior emperor and raising his three sons to the throne. In 944 A.D., Romanus's sons seized power and dispatched him to the monastery on the island of Proti. Constantine in turn, discovering the brothers' intention to kill him, supplanted them and sent the brothers into exile with their father. In January of 945 A.D., Constantine Porphyrogentius came at last into his own rule at the age of thirty-nine.

Winner of the Golden Heart Award

ANITA GORDON

__THE VALIANT HEART 0-515-10642-9/$4.95

By birthright, Brienne was Baronne de Valseme–but the black-haired maiden was robbed of her legacy by plundering Norsemen. Offered against her will as a bride to Rurik, the enemy, their people are joined in a delicate and uneasy peace–but destiny decreed that Brienne and Rurik would join an everlasing, enthralling life...

"Anita Gordon gives the ring of authenticity to her first Medieval Romance."–LaVyrle Spencer, *New York Times* bestselling author of *Bitter Sweet*

"An exciting confection; I read it with avid enjoyment!" –Roberta Gellis, bestselling author of *Fires of Winter*

__THE DEFIANT HEART 0-425-13825-9/$4.99

A fiercely handsome Norman lord stole the ravishing Irish beauty from a life of slavery, angered to see the lovely maiden treated as a possession. But soon there stirred within him a powerful desire to possess her himself–as only a lover could...

National Bestselling Author
PAMELA MORSI

"I've read all her books and loved every word."
—Jude Deveraux

WILD OATS

The last person Cora Briggs expects to see at her door is a
fine gentleman like Jedwin Sparrow. After all, her more
"respectable" neighbors in Dead Dog, Oklahoma, won't
have much to do with a divorcee. She's even more
surprised when Jed tells her he's just looking to sow a few
wild oats! But instead of getting angry, Cora decides to get
even, and makes Jed a little proposition of her own...one
that's sure to cause a stir in town—and starts an unexpected
commotion in her heart as well.

___0-515-11185-6/$4.99 (On sale September 1993)

GARTERS

Miss Esme Crabb knows sweet talk won't put food on the
table—so she's bent on finding a sensible man to marry.
Cleavis Rhy seems like a smart choice...so amidst the
cracker barrels and jam jars in his general store, Esme
makes her move. She doesn't realize that daring to set her
sights on someone like Cleavis Rhy will turn the town—and
her heart—upside down.

___0-515-10895-2/$4.99